GODKILLER

GODKILLER

HANNAH KANER

HARPER
Voyager

GODKILLER. Copyright © 2023 by Hannah Kaner. All rights reserved. Printed in the United States of America. No part of this book may be used or reproduced in any manner whatsoever without written permission except in the case of brief quotations embodied in critical articles and reviews. For information, address HarperCollins Publishers, 195 Broadway, New York, NY 10007.

HarperCollins books may be purchased for educational, business, or sales promotional use. For information, please email the Special Markets Department at SPsales@harpercollins.com.

Harper Voyager and design are trademarks of HarperCollins Publishers LLC.

Originally published in the United Kingdom in 2023 by Harper Voyager UK, an imprint of HarperCollins UK.

FIRST U.S. EDITION

Map and interior illustrations © Tom Roberts 2023

Library of Congress Cataloging-in-Publication Data has been applied for.

ISBN 978-0-06-334827-1

23 24 25 26 27 LBC 11 10 9 8 7

For my father, who reads every word

MIDDREN

FELLIC FARNE

ENNERTON

GEFYRTON

SAKRE

LESSCIA

WEILD

IRISIA

TRAADA

ALICIA

PINET

BLENRADEN

RESTISH

TRADE
SEA

BELHAVEN

WSIRIN

SICARA

PROLOGUE

Fifteen Years Ago

HER FATHER FELL IN LOVE WITH A GOD OF THE SEA.

The god's name was Osidisen, and her parents named Kissen and her brothers in honour of his attention: Tidean, "on the tide"; Lunsen, "moon on water"; Mellsenro, "the rolling rocks." And, finally, Kissenna, "born on the love of the sea." Osidisen filled their nets with fish, taught them when to ride a storm and when to hide, and brought them safe home with their catch each day. Kissen and her family grew up in the sea's favour.

But the sea god didn't bring fortune to the lands of Talicia. Eventually, the villages on the hills were enticed by a god of fire, Hseth, and her promises of riches.

Everyone wanted the wealth of the fire lovers. In Hseth's name the Talicians burned their boats and felled their forests to forge weapons, heat brass, and make great bells which rang from sea cliff to mountain border. Osidisen's waters emptied, and smoke rose over the land. Soon other, darker stories of violence spread from town to village: sacrifices, hunts, and purges in the fire god's name, enemies and old families burned for the fire god's pleasure.

One night, the night after Mellsenro's twelfth birthday, when his fingers were inked with his name, eleven-year-old Kissen woke to smoke, strangely thick and sweet smelling. It scratched at her throat.

She came to, and realised she was being carried by men with cloths tied over their mouths, their faces daubed with coal dust, and bells shining in their hair like little lamps. Kissen's limbs wouldn't move, and her chest was heavy as if dreams still lay on it. The sweet smoke, she recognised it: a sleeping drug made by burning sless seeds, along with other scents she didn't know. Below her house, the sea was lashing at the cliffs. Osidisen was angry.

She tried to speak, but her mouth wouldn't work, her tongue sticking against her cheek. Her head flopped to one side, and she saw Mell too, his fresh-inked hand dragging along the floor.

"Mmmelll," Kissen tried again, but her brother didn't stir. The drug smoke was seeping through the shutters, through the walls. It hung in the air.

"Quiet," said one of the men holding her, giving her a shake. She knew that voice, those smudge-green eyes.

"N-Naro?" Kissenna asked, her voice a little stronger now. The waves crashed outside, and the smoke stirred as some sea wind forced its way through the cracks in the wattled walls. She felt a fresh bite of salt air across her face, on her lips. Her head cleared a little. Naro glanced at her, panic in his eyes.

"They said they wouldn't wake yet," he said through his mask.

"Hurry." The other voice she recognised too. Mit, Naro's brother-in-law. The masks were protecting them from the drug. "Hurry!"

They were carrying her deeper into the house, to the hearth at its centre. "What are you doing?" Kissen asked, her voice thick but clear. Her body still wouldn't move.

They reached the hearth, a round stone beneath the thatch roof which opened to the sky so smoke could escape. Around the embers of their evening's fire, a tangled cage had been set, in the shape of a bell, forged out of driftwood and metal. Her parents were already bound to its outer edges. Her brothers were being tied: ankle, ankle, arms, neck. Offerings. Kissen was the last.

Naro and Mit flung her against the bars next to her father. The sea wind tore through the smoke hole in the roof, ripping around the beams. The shutters rattled and the house shook with the sounds of angry water.

"Naro, stop," said Kissen, stronger now; the sless smoke was almost gone from the air, though it bound her limbs still. "Why are you doing this?"

Naro was twisting her legs to tie them to the foot of the cage while Mit strapped her hands to the bars. Lunsen was crying, hiccupping with fear. She had lost sight of Mell. Kissen found the strength to struggle as they bound her against the metal, but they were bigger and stronger than she was. Outside, bells were ringing, their sound broken and battered by the rising wind. The sound could have been from thousands, though the village was barely a hundred souls. All of her neighbours must be out there. They had planned this together, to catch the sea god's favoured family. Kissen could smell hot pitch close at hand. Terror clawed down her throat.

"We're not sorry, *liln*," said Mit. How dare he call her "little one?" That was what uncles did, friends. He was not a friend. He was a traitor. "It is what must be."

Kissen drew up her strength and snapped at his hand with her sharp teeth. He leapt away, clutching his thumb pad where she had caught it.

"Leave her," he snapped. "It's time. They won't wait for us."

They ran. Kissen was shaking. She spat out Mit's blood and tried to breathe, turning against the ropes to find the closest family. "Papa." He was not far from her. "Papa!"

Bern, her father, was breathing badly. His mouth was torn and bloody, his face bruised. They must have beaten him in his drugged sleep. That ruined mouth had kissed the god of the sea, but now coal daubed his forehead in the bell-shaped symbol of Hseth.

The air thickened with smoke again, not sweet this time but bitter and sticky, hot and black, rising up through the floor. Their village had lit the pitch beneath their stilt foundations.

Kissen yanked at her wrists, her legs. "Papa!" she cried. They had left her neck unbound when she had tried to bite. She writhed, tugging her arm into strange contortions, the bones popping as she craned her neck towards her closer hand. There. She could reach. She set her teeth to the rope, gnawing and tugging at the knot. It was sea-rope, not meant for fraying, but she didn't want to die.

Tidean was awake too. "You filthy castoffs," he was shouting, struggling against his bindings, choking as they tightened on his throat. He coughed on the smoke. "You saltless traitors!" His voice was raw.

The heat was rising. Kissen could feel it on the soles of her feet.

"Be calm," their mother said, her voice drug-thick. "Be calm, my loves. Osidisen will save us. I promise."

They couldn't see the flames yet, but the air swam. Osidisen's sea wind was still forcing its way inside, and the smoke and air were dancing together like oil and water. Kissen's mouth, her eyes, her nose dried out. She set her teeth to the rope with renewed force.

"I'll make you all pay for this!" Tidean yelled his promise over his mother's, but he was bound too tight, tighter than Kissenna. His wild thrashing did no good. The floor cracked in places. Bright light peeked through from the foundations. The walls blackened. Then, an ember, a spark, a lick of flame, and the wooden doorway caught alight, sending sparks into Tidean's eyes. He screamed, and thrashed.

"Breathe deep, my son," said his mother. "It's all right, Osidisen will come." She was lying, lying to ease their deaths, lying to herself. Osidisen was a water god; he would not come far past the shoreline, not even for them, just as no fire god would dare swim in the sea. Gods couldn't save them now.

The rope sliced the delicate flesh between Kissen's teeth, and blood poured thick and hot across her tongue. She growled and bit down hard, wrenching at her restraint. A shot of pain, a grinding in her gums, then a snap. The rope! The rope was loose, her canine still buried in it, ripped clean from her mouth.

Kissen snatched her wrist free and went to work on the other, letting her salt blood drip down her chin onto the stone below, where it hissed and steamed.

Second hand, free! Her feet. She bloodied her nails on the ropes, snarling with desperation. She would save them. She had to. Her breath was hot, her eyes stinging, but she would not stop. Her mother was coughing now.

"Breathe deep, my children," she said. Kissen could hear the tears in her voice. Lunsen was whimpering now; Tidean's struggles were less and less intense. Mell had not even stirred. "Let the smoke take you to sleep, and Osidisen will come for you."

Kissen's ropes came away, and her feet were loose. The floor was now on fire, and the sea wind was doing nothing but thinning the smoke, losing them the chance their mother wished for: a painless death.

"Papa." They had tied her pa hard to the metal, which was getting hotter. Kissen climbed anyway, her hands burning.

"Kissenna," Papa mumbled through his swollen lips. His eyes were open. They shone with dazed relief. "My girl, run."

"I'm going to save you," she growled between coughs. "I'll save you all."

Kissen pressed her fingers into the hard sailor's knots; they were tight, but she could work them, releasing her papa a piece at a time. Her eyes were stinging. Mell woke at last and yelled as the flames reached the edges of the hearth, nipping at his heels. Good, all awake. If they were awake, they could run. She freed her father's left hand and moved to his foot while he unbound his right. They were losing time. The sound of the bells outside was rising, sonorous, merging into a single note, louder than the fire.

The flames changed. They twisted together, spinning up the walls, then plunging to the floor in a pillar of fire, sparks spinning out like snow. Laughter crackled in the smoke, harsh and delighted.

The fire span and blossomed into skirts of light and embers. Within them, a woman twirled, her arms wide. Hseth, the fire god. Her hair sparked with yellows and poisoned red, and heat rose from her, cracking and splitting the wood and beams.

"Sea god!" she cried, then she called him by his name. "Osidisen! Look how they turned from you and gave your loves to me. You cannot touch me, you gutted old water goat! This land is mine!"

Hseth did not look at Kissen or her family. She did not flinch at their screams. She burst through the ceiling in a scourge of flame and the roof came crashing down.

Kissen blinked. Black heat. Then light. Then pain. The cage was shattered under the heavy beams. Mell had stopped screaming. She blinked again. Her father was there, free from his ropes. Her head hurt. Her mouth was full of ash.

"Pa . . ." she choked out. He was wrenching the rubble from her, but he could not lift the warped metal that had buried itself into her right leg, shattering it below the knee. By flesh and bone she was trapped. She was going to die; she could see it in her father's eyes.

"It will be all right, Kissenna," he said, lying like her mother had, in the soft voice Osidisen admired. He stroked her hair as if putting her to sleep. "Be brave, my love, my daughter."

"Run away, Papa," she said, stifling a sob of fear. "Please."

"Don't cry, Kissenna," he said. "It is better this way."

Pain. Blinding, atrocious pain. It drove into Kissen's leg. She screamed, but the smoke stuffed the noise back into her throat. Her papa had orange-hot metal sizzling in his hands, fresh and hissing with both of their blood. He heaved it up high.

"Her leg for her safety, Osidisen!" he cried. "I beg you, save her from this place in return for this, her flesh, blood and bone, my own making."

He brought the metal down another time and *turned*.

Kissenna screamed again, the pain devouring her faster than the fire. But her father was not done. Her vision went black, white. When she came to, her papa was dragging her out of the wreckage, leaving the bottom of her leg behind. Charcoal ran down his face, cut through with tears, streaming into his beard.

Then she saw the seas below their shattered walls. Raging, impotent, beating at the base of the cliff. The salt air rose. It had stung Kissen awake for a moment. The waves were catching each piece of wood as it fell from the house and tearing it apart.

"My life, Osidisen!" her father cried. "My life for hers, the last thing I will ever ask."

"No!" Kissen croaked, barely conscious.

"This you owe to me! My lover, my friend. You owe it to her now. My life for Kissenna's!"

The sea rose, tearing up the cliff as if to reach him. Osidisen's face rose from the waves, his eyes as dark as the depths. For a moment, Kissen hoped he would deny it, save her father instead.

But gods love martyrs.

He nodded.

Kissenna tried to struggle. She did not want a god's promise; she wanted her father, her mother, Tidean, Lunsen, and Mell. She wanted her family. Her papa clutched her a last time to his chest and scratched her face with his beard as he kissed her.

"I love you," he said, and threw her to the sea.

BY WRIT OF

KING ARREN
THE SECOND

HERO OF BLENRADEN, THE RISING SUN OF THE WEST,
NOW IN THE THIRD YEAR OF HIS REIGN

After Saving Our Country From the God War

WORSHIP OF GODS IS PROHIBITED WITHIN THE BORDERS OF THE NATION OF MIDDREN

This law carries from the NORTHEAST border with the DANGEROUS TALICIAN
LANDS to the WESTERN SEA PASSAGE and TRADE ISLANDS

HARBOURING SHRINES, TOTEMS, CHARMS, and SYMBOLS associated with any named GOD is PUNISHABLE BY LAW	PILGRIMAGES to HOLY SITES will result in FINE, GAOL, and PUBLIC WHIPPING of your DISLOYAL FEET

THE VEIGA, KILLERS OF GODS, NOW OPERATE IN THE NAME OF THE KING

If you SEE or SUSPECT a SHRINE, a GOD, or LAWBREAKERS,
REPORT THEM TO YOUR LOCAL SETTLE

CHAPTER ONE

Kissen

IT WAS HARD TO KILL A GOD IN ITS ELEMENT. KISSEN reminded herself of that with every cursed step she took up the steep hilled slopes of midwestern Middren, Talicia's once more powerful neighbour. That was until it lost its eastern trade city of Blenraden, and half the people in it, to bickering gods. Terrible for Middren, but good for the coin purses of godkillers like Kissen.

The air was close and chill with the morning; Middren had barely begun to shake off winter's grasp. Though her right leg was built for hiking, and she had double-bound her knee, she could already feel nubs of blisters forming where her prosthesis met her flesh that would cause her a world of pain later.

The narrow way through the forest was thick with mud and half-formed ice, but Kissen could trace the shape of a foot in the moss here, a turned rock there, even drops of blood in places that told her this was the right way; this was the kind of path people would pray on.

Despite her tracking skills the sun was half risen by the time she had found the marker: a line of white stones at the edge of the track where the ground levelled out to a nearby stream; a threshold. She rolled her shoulders and took a breath. She could perhaps have lured this god to a smaller shrine, but that would take time and patience. She had neither.

She crossed the line.

The sounds changed. Gone was the birdsong of the early morning and the scent of leaves and mulch. Instead, she could hear rushing water, sense depth and cold stone, and smell the faintest traces of incense in the air—and blood.

It was harder to unmake a god than to begin one. Even a recent-born god like this, barely a few years old. Harder still to tempt one with a coin or a bead when it had developed a taste for sacrifice.

The smell of incense grew as Kissen moved carefully down the bank. The god knew she was here. She stopped on the stones of the shore accepting the ache of her legs, the cold of the morning, and sharp nip of blisters. She did not bare her sword, not yet. The river was shallow, but the current was strong, white with foam from the nearest falls.

The air cooled.

You are not welcome here, godkiller. The mindspeak of gods was worse than a needle to the skull. It felt like a tearing of her mind, an invasion.

"You've been greedy, Ennerast," said Kissen. The air hissed. Names have power, and gods felt the tug of theirs like a hook in their gills, pulling them into the open. But Ennerast was not going to be enticed out by her name alone.

It was just a little blood, said Ennerast, *just a calf or two. None of the humans' own spawn.*

"Come now, you starved them till they gave it to you," said Kissen, casting her eyes about, assessing her surroundings. "You let their waters run rank with disease. You dragged their children, their elders up to your banks and threatened their lives." There were few advantages to be had where she stood. The river was lapping at her boots.

Really, the local settle should have called for a veiga sooner. No self-respecting leader of a town the size of Ennerton should have let a god live long enough to grow this powerful. Though shrines were banned, gods kept appearing. Beings of power, spirits, given life and will by people's love and fear until they became strong enough to exploit. Humans were foolish creatures, and gods were cruel.

"You hurt them," said Kissen. The waters at her feet had stopped flowing, and instead were swirling and twisting by the shore.

It is my due. I am a god.

"Ha." Kissen laughed without humour. "You prey on the frightened, Ennerast. You're a rat, and I'm your catcher."

Kissen reached inside her waxwool cloak, tracing her fingers over her pockets of relics and totems, tools and incense, the tricks of her trade. She found what she was looking for by the little ridged markings on the jar, and stuck her nail beneath the cork, easing it loose. Within was a curl of leather, inscribed.

The air around her tensed, nervous and excited. The water began to froth. *What is it?*

Kissen couldn't sense what gods could: fear, hope, desperation; emotions they enjoyed toying with but didn't care for. But she knew what would drive them, what they craved. "It's a prayer," she said, not releasing it entirely.

I want it.

"A young man's prayer, from a faraway village." Kissen thumbed the cork. "He wants to be saved from drought and the fires of his forests, to save his crops and animals. He is desperate for water."

Give it to me.

"He promises anything, Ennerast." Kissen smiled. "Anything."

Mine.

The waters surged upwards, twisting into a green torrent that manifested in a head as smooth as stone, arms thick with weeds. At her centre, in a torso of running water, was a dark mass: a heart of blood. She reached for Kissen, who firmed her stance and drew her blade in a single fluid movement, slicing through Ennerast's fingers. The god shrieked, pulling back, water re-forming where her river-flesh had been torn.

"It burns," she said out loud, more surprised than injured. Her eyes were flat and grey, like pebbles. The sword was light and harder than steel, durable, made of a mixture of iron and Bridhid ore, like Kissen's leg. It could cut a god's matter as surely as a person's, from the smallest god of lost things to the great god of war. A god like Ennerast, recently manifested in this mountain river, had never been hurt before by a briddite blade.

The god bared her fishbone teeth and struck at the bank beneath Kissen's feet. It gave way, and Kissen plunged into the river. She tried to rise, but weeds wrapped around her wrists and dragged her deeper. Water filled her mouth and nose, seeking her lungs.

Kissen dragged her sword forward against the weeds and plunged the blade into the riverbed. It struck a stone and held. Her right leg she rammed down hard, gaining some stability. With all her strength she ripped her blade out of the water, slicing through the current and the weeds with its edge. She rose up and slashed clean through Ennerast's arm as the god reached to push her under.

Ennerast's flesh fell in a cascade of water. She shrieked, the current weakening with her distraction, and Kissen saw what she was looking for. Behind the waterfall was a flash of bone, a drift of coloured ribbon, and a stone: the river god's shrine. Ennerast was no old god with so many shrines, so many prayers, they could travel the world at whim, she was a new god, even if she was born in the wild: she needed her shrine to live.

She gave Ennerast no time to re-form and leapt forward, lifting her blade to strike.

Ennerast fell for the trap. She dove to protect her shrine, and Kissen turned at the last moment, twisting on the join of her knee to drive the sword up, up.

It plunged through Ennerast's dark torso and straight into the blood mass at her heart. The god bellowed like the roar of a dam breaking. She snatched at Kissen's sword hand, grasping it hard enough to grind her bones.

"Please," said Ennerast. "Let me live, veiga; you may yet have need of me."

"I have no need of gods," said Kissen.

"So says one with Osidisen's promise still wrapped around her heart."

Water was a secret-spiller; stories were shared from drop to fall, from rivulet to sea. Nothing could stop a water god's gossip.

"I can rid you of it, you know," said Ennerast, leaning forward over the blade, pressing her face close to Kissen's. "This promise, the scars, the memory." She brushed Kissen's cheek.

"More powerful gods than you have made me offers, Ennerast," said Kissen, "and I killed them just the same."

Ennerast hissed. "I curse you then!" she cried. "I—"

Kissen ripped her sword out through the god's side in a stink of blood and dank water, and the shrine behind the waterfall shattered. Ennerast made no sound as her flesh turned back into the current and sank into the river Ennerun, releasing it for the town and villages it fed, to thrive or fail. But she managed a last barb to Kissen's mind.

When Middren falls to the gods, your kind will be the first to die.

The sounds of the river receded, and the sweet scent of incense faded into loam and damp once more. The birdsong returned.

Kissen shivered. She was soaked to the bone, yet her work was not done. The god was dead, but gods could come back. The shrine was her memories, her sacrifices, her anchor to the world.

Kissen approached the shrine. It was damaged, not broken completely. Two animal skulls had shattered. Most gods demanded animal sacrifices before human. Kissen scraped them together and tossed them into the forest to rot. The incense had crumbled, but the ashes remained. She poured some into a little glass vial, and the rest into the water. Many of Ennerast's other offerings were still intact. Enough, if left, to bring her back to life. Kissen kept a woven strip of silk, handmade, with a prayer in the weaving and blood mixed in with the threads. A love request, it looked like. Very tempting for a god. Few other prayers were worth keeping. Kissen piled up the remains of the shrine and set them alight, far from the water and in a ring of stones. She carefully watched the makeshift pyre burn down to ash.

She kept only one other thing: a limestone totem, carved with a head, high cheekbones, flat eyes. About the size of her own palm. It had cracked down the centre when Ennerast died; but it was from this that the god had taken her shape.

Kissen stank of steam, mud, and tar smoke by the time she finally retrieved her horse from the bottom of the mountain path and made it the long way back to the town of Ennerton and the settle that had called for her. Settles were pomped-up caretakers put in place in towns and areas to take care of business for whatever noble owned the lands. The House Craier, in this case. Kissen didn't care who owned what patch of mud; it didn't matter as long as the silver was good.

Kissen knocked on the door of the courthouse. The older woman who opened it greeted her with a scowl, rubbing inkstains from her dark olive skin.

"You veiga used to use the back door," she said.

Kissen smiled, showing her gold tooth. Before the war for Blenraden, godkillers were barely more than assassins or exterminators. Kissen and the veiga who trained her had been paid under the table. "These days we have the king's blessing," said Kissen. "Or do you want to take it up with the dead of Blenraden?"

The woman flushed and let her through the door and Kissen blew her a kiss. These days, she no longer had to pretend her vocation was a sin.

The settle was annotating ledgers in his office at a large oak desk sat proudly before a gaudy framed picture of King Arren. He looked up warily as she entered, the rattle of copper earrings in his left ear glinting in the lamplight. They had left blue marks on his pale lobe.

"It is done?" he asked.

"Hello to you too, Settle Tessys," said Kissen. "I thought the Craier lands were the welcoming sort."

Tessys had a sour kind of face, like it had been stepped on too many times. "I'll be needing proof." He looked a bit peaky about it. The proof was in the smoke still rising up the mountain on a wet day, just where Ennerast's shrine had been. The proof was in the scent of rage that clung to Kissen like the static of a dying storm. No matter; small men liked to hold big things.

Kissen placed Ennerast's broken limestone totem on his desk. Such a thing, he would know, could only have been plucked from a shrine. The settle stared at it, afraid.

"Destroy that," said Kissen, pulling her leather-wrapped veiga documents out of her cloak pocket and sliding them across the table. "And wash the worry from your heart, or she'll be back before winter."

He glanced at her, irritated, then the papers, and thumbed his quill. "You said you'd killed her."

"Gods are parasites. They'll come again if there's fear to feed on." A reborn Ennerast would go the same way eventually, even without the memories of her shrine. Gods all had the same cravings: for love, for sacrifice, for blood.

The settle sniffed. Could Kissen report him for failing to remove Ennerast's shrine earlier? He'd face a hefty fine, if not lose a finger. Perhaps she should, but it wouldn't change his nature. Gods were born out of human prayers, and no one wanted to be on the bad side of those. If she tattled to the nearest knight every time someone needed a veiga, her work would soon dry up.

The settle fetched a stamp out of his drawer, alongside a bag of silvers. His inkstone was already wet, so he pressed the stamp to it, then to her papers in the three-pointed symbol of the veiga. Kissen took the silver first and weighed it in her palm. She might not report him, but she had still charged him a premium.

"Now go on," he said, pushing her papers across the desk and waving her away, unable to look her fully in the eye.

"No other business you could send my way?" Kissen asked. Why not?

"No other god problems here," the settle said with a tight smile. "I'll send to your local settle at Lesscia if needed."

Kissen shrugged and pocketed the silver.

"You're not going to sort that, are you?" she said, pointing to Ennerast's totem. It wasn't a question. He was afraid, not just of the dead god but of her followers. They would be looking for someone to blame, and the settle was the one who had called for a godkiller. Perhaps he would preserve the relic; perhaps he would let them bribe him for it.

Ennerast's last words drifted back into Kissen's mind. *When Middren falls to the gods . . .*

Kissen drew her sword and, with a flick, shattered the totem with the flat of the blade. The man leapt back as the face of Ennerast crumbled into the desk, leaving a large dent and a scatter of white pieces.

"How dare you—" he began, but faltered when Kissen smiled a gold-toothed smile at him and cast her eyes to the portrait of the king hung behind his desk. His foot rested on a stag's head, the sun rising behind him over the burning city. It was his word that he must obey, whatever the townspeople thought. The settle swallowed his anger.

"Thank you," he said through gritted teeth.

Kissen showed herself out of the courthouse, trying to shake those words out of her mind. The great gods were scattered, their hunt dispersed, their war in Middren long over. Ennerast's words meant nothing, just the last, desperate breath of a dying god.

Kissen touched a hand to her chest, where in sea-script Osidisen's promise, her father's sacrifice, still weighed on her heart.

CHAPTER TWO

Inara

INARA CRAIER HELD HER BREATH AS THE WOODCART SHE was hiding in trundled to a halt. Today was always wood day for Ennerton, not that she had any idea where it was delivered to. She clutched her furry companion, Skedi, tightly to her chest beneath her waistcoat and peeked through the canvas that covered the cart. They had stopped outside a big gate on a busy cobbled street. Inside, people were sparring with swords and bucklers in the damp courtyard, all wearing the pale blue and grey of House Craier. Above the gate was a sign of three trees with a bird flying over them. Her mother's heraldry: Lessa Craier, the head of the House. This must be a barracks of some sort.

"Deep breaths," Inara told herself, pulling back from the awning, the whisper coming out of her mouth in fog. "Deep breaths."

She had never been to Ennerton. Actually, she had never been beyond the Craier manor lands, not once in her twelve years. It looked smelly and noisy out there. And bright. Too bright, with too many colours.

It's noisy enough that we won't be noticed, said her companion. *Do what I showed you, let the colours go.*

Inara swallowed and slid out the side of the cart. Her mother was brave, confident, strong. Inara had to be too, for her mother. For Skedi.

No one looked at her as she stepped away from the cart, instead wrapped up in their own businesses: carrying, working, shouting, laughing. The colours surrounded everyone in Ennerton like a cloud of light, falling from their hands, rippling around their shoulders, dancing over their heads. An inconstant, moving kaleidoscope that flashed and disappeared, flickered like lightning, then dimmed. Inara took a deep breath. Only she and Skedi could see the colours; she had to look through them at the street, at people's faces. The shimmering faded into the background.

Don't run, her little friend said to her, crawling into her sleeve to hide in the crook of her elbow. *Just walk, walk slow.*

Inara almost "walked slow" into a woman carrying a dead goat bound by its feet to the staff on her shoulders, backing out of the nearest door.

"Sorry!" she said.

"Save your sorries, little fool," the woman said, skirting around her. Her colours spiked out, orange and aggressive. Inara caught her breath.

Keep going. It's just their emotions, they can't hurt you.

Inara clutched her cloak about her. Skedi was right, she should be used to the colours by now, faint and blooming around the servants of the Craier household or the workers who tended the orchards, steadlands, and cattle. Since Skedi had come to her, or soon after, she could see them. Five years of colours and secrets.

It was a crisp spring night, the frosts of winter lingering still, so she had come out in a padded jacket and travelling cloak, with a kerchief over her hair. She was the only one dressed so thickly. Here in the town, a few hours" cart ride down from the house, the air was warmer. Inara tightened her kerchief and ducked her head so she wouldn't be recognised. Everyone here was under her mother's guardianship, but no one gave her so much as a second glance.

Inara moved away from the barracks and immediately stepped ankle deep in a puddle clogged with offal from the nearby butchery. She shook her foot out of it and managed to hop and avoid a shower of someone's stink being thrown from an upstairs window. Her heart thudded against her chest. This was stupid. This was mad. She was risking everything, and she didn't know where to go.

"—does the veiga have to stay here, Settle Tessys?" Inara heard a snippet of conversation as two men jostled past. The man speaking wore a collar held together with a crumpled strip of silk; the other had copper rings all up his ear. His robes were fine wool and buttoned with mother-of-pearl. Someone important. "You know Ennerast's hill followers will want trouble. It's better that she leave."

"She's a rude, proud woman and she wants us all to know it," said the man with the copper earrings. The town settle, it seemed. She sometimes overheard her mother talk about him. "I refuse to spend one more moment speaking to her. Besides, I've heard she's too busy flirting with Rosalie the barkeep." He gestured at a nearby tavern. It was surrounded by people sipping out of steaming mugs that smelled of hot wine. "Be wise, and take yourself elsewhere."

The first looked uncomfortable. "What if—"

"I paid her; my part is done."

Inara saw the tavern was called the King's Will, its sign a sun over a burning city. Blenraden. Of course. Inara remembered only moments of the war in the blur of her childhood, but no child could forget their mother returning home in the darkest days, injured, heartbroken, and quiet.

Clearer in her mind was the day it ended. She had been nine and they had cracked open the wine and brandy in the cellars and made fires explode in the sky for the servants. Lady Craier had held Inara so close and tight. But by that point Inara was keeping secrets.

Now the good times were gone, and the secrets remained. Lessa Craier spent most of her days away in Sakre, the capital, trying to regain King Arren's favour, so the servants said. Her visits home were brief.

She had appeared that very morning at breakfast, fresh from the road, her hair neatly braided down her back, and had showered Inara with attention, probing her about her lessons, her reading, her archery, not showing how tired she must be.

Then a runner had come. An anxious-looking woman from the settle's office flustered to find the lady at home, hoping to only leave a note saying that a godkiller had been sent for to deal with the local river god Ennerast. Inara wasn't supposed to listen. She was supposed to make herself hidden when anyone new came up to the house, and she had, but by now she knew where she could hide and still hear.

A godkiller.

They were rarely seen in these parts, or if they were, Inara hadn't heard of them. This was her chance. Their first chance at freedom. When would Skedi get another one? The runner had left, and Inara had plucked up her courage.

Her mother had been in her study, poring over a letter and writing one in return. The scent of lemons hung in the air, a bright citrus tang. These days, all the letters she wrote smelled like lemons.

"Ina," said Lady Craier, catching sight of her and stuffing the paper she was reading away. Not before Inara caught a glimpse of a symbol in brown ink, like a tree branch. Her mother looked harassed and worried, but unlike most people, her colours were hidden. A lit candle stood on her desk, though it was broad daylight.

Inara swallowed. Skedi had been hiding in her pocket, and she put her hand in so he would press his nose against it. "I want to talk to you about gods."

It was brief, the colour that burst out from her mother. A split of grey and white, like lightning. It disappeared, but not before Inara understood what it meant: panic.

"No," said Lady Craier. "You are not to speak of gods, Inara, it is dangerous."

"Mama, it's important." She wanted to tell her about Skedi, about the colours, to explain why she had kept the secret for so long. Maybe if she explained it, her mother would take her to see the godkiller in the town; maybe they would have answers.

"You will understand one day."

"But—"

"Enough." Anger flashed around her, but then she came over and softly tucked a stray curl behind Inara's ear, like she had when Inara was little. Lessa's hands were dark gold-brown, while Inara was fairer, Lessa's hair black and straight while Inara's was brown and curled. She looked like her father, Lessa had said, though had never explained in more detail. "I mean it. Wash it from your mind, dear heart. Please. For me. Yes?" She had stood up then, her shoulders blocking the light from the window. Lessa was barely home, and when she was, she wouldn't listen. Wouldn't even try. They were too different. Inara would have to do this alone.

Lie, Skedi had said to her then.

So, Inara had.

"Yes, Mama."

Now, Inara slipped inside the tavern. The air was thick with smoke and heat from the fires, and it stank of sweat, dogs, and vinegar. The people drinking here were mostly local folk. Inara could tell by the clothes, brushed and dyed wools or cottons in similar cuts to those the servants wore. Some, the richer, were trimmed with coloured thread sewn in fanciful patterns. There were others too in travel garb, wools and leathers and thick boots. This was a trading town, she knew from her tutor; lots of people passed through.

Despite her sheltered upbringing, she spotted the veiga immediately. The woman was sitting at a table wearing leather that looked hard enough to be used as armour and just low enough at the throat to show a tattoo at the top of her chest, a kind of loose spiral. No one was mistaking her for a trader or farmhand. Her looks were Talician—pale and freckled, and her auburn hair cropped by her ears and bound in place with some rough-tossed braids and a leather band.

The veiga was chatting to the barkeep, and as she smiled the light shone on the pale outline of a scar like a spiderweb, woven from her left eye to her chin. It sent a shiver up Inara's spine. She had seen such things only in parchments and books: a dead curse.

A curse meant she had hurt someone enough for them to make a deal with a god for a curse. That, or she had angered a god so much they had put the black mark of their power on her without another's prayer or sacrifice. A dead curse meant the veiga had killed the god or somehow shattered their will, turning the mark white as bleached bone.

Perhaps this is not a good idea, said Skedi.

"It was your idea," Inara whispered. He had helped her lie her way to bed early, though her mother barely noticed, and out of the manor under everyone's noses. He had been excited to escape the grounds, be out in the world, but now that he saw the godkiller, he was afraid. Should she be afraid too?

As Inara watched, the veiga took the hand of the barkeep and kissed her on the wrist. A gentle gesture, a human one. The barkeep smiled and leaned down to top up her beer, using the movement to whisper in her ear. The veiga's smile was broad as she laughed, her sea-grey Talician eyes alight with mischief. Inara couldn't see the colours of her emotions, just like she couldn't with her mother, so she had to read her face to guess what she was thinking.

A group further into the tavern called for the keep, aggressively waving their cups and beating them on the table. Their colours were easy enough to make out—prickly saffron and salty pink. They didn't like seeing the veiga flirting with their server. The keep took her hand away, lingering just long enough to touch the veiga on the chin, and went to fill their mugs.

Inara was here now, there was no going back, so she used the moment as her invitation.

Be careful, said Skedi.

She slid into the chair opposite the godkiller and waited.

The veiga peered at her over the edge of her cup as she took a deep gulp. Before her was a plate of crumbs and bones, picked clean. Inara's stomach rumbled. It was long past her bedtime, and she had been too nervous to eat as she'd planned her secret journey. Never mind, she would eat when she got home. If she wasn't in *too* much trouble.

She gritted her teeth. That was a problem for later. The problem now was the woman in front of her, whose broken curse looked deadlier up close. Her hands shone with scars as well, old burns that gnarled the skin.

"What do you want?" the godkiller asked.

Inara blinked, somehow surprised to be addressed first, and so rudely. Her mouth dried with nerves.

"You're a godkiller, aren't you?" Inara began. The veiga raised an eyebrow and said nothing. "A runner said you were come to get rid of Ennerast, the one who was starving the river for blood."

"And why does a little noble girl give a shit?"

Inara flushed. She had covered her hair and worn her simplest, warmest riding clothes. She thought she was dressed like the servants—how could the veiga know? "I'm not a noble."

"Right." The veiga shrugged, clearly not caring a bit either way. "Whatever you are, get lost, *liln.*"

Liln, a Talician term meaning "little one." The godkiller's accent was

Middrenite but had some of the round, deep lilt of Talic, like once-sharp rocks beneath the surface, stones worn down by the sea.

Don't tell her the truth.

"My name's Ina. I need your help."

"Then ask the garrison." The veiga thumped her chest and belched. "I'm not a hand for hire, or a babysitter."

"They can't help," said Inara, trying to hide her disgust, "not for this."

A roar burst up by the fire as two patrons commenced an arm-wrestling match and people started taking bets using chips of silver. The barkeep walked past again, unbothered by the noise. "Rosalie," Kissen called her.

"Veiga?" she said, smiling. Inara was almost relieved at their flirting; it made the godkiller seem more human.

"Please, a wine? Bring your own cup and let me lose this wastrel." Inara shrank as Kissen gestured at her. "Which noble does she belong to? Craier?"

Rosalie looked her over, and Inara's heart plummeted, but the keep's colours were cool and grey: no recognition, no surprise. "No noble kids around here," she said. "Lady Craier has no children now, and the family's estranged. Merchant's daughter, probably."

It took Inara a moment to bite down her proud protest. She was the heir to the Craier lands. People from Ennerton might not be directly employed by Lady Craier, but they should at least know Inara existed. What did "now" mean, anyway? Skedi butted her with his head.

Annoyed is better than caught.

So Inara stayed silent while Rosalie winked at the veiga. "I'll bring you wine when I'm good and ready," she said.

"If it's no trouble to you." The veiga nodded towards the group who had parted them last time.

"Oh, they're no harm," said Rosalie. "Just set in their ways. If I want to dally with a veiga they can keep their ways to themselves."

Kissen grinned. "Well then, I'm glad I decided to stay the night."

Rosalie departed, and Inara was tired of being flatly ignored. She put up with it enough from her mother. "You know about gods, yes?"

The godkiller sighed. "If you're looking for a priest or a scholar, I am neither." She was clearly hoping Inara would disappear.

"No, I . . ." Inara lowered her voice. She wanted to prove the godkiller wrong, that she was worth listening to. The last thing she and Skedi wanted was to get caught by the people of Ennerton—she needed to keep her mother's name out of this, but it was this woman's job to help her. "I have a god problem."

The veiga's gaze sharpened on her, disbelieving, and Inara caught a glimpse of her gold canine as she looked ready to laugh. Inara scowled.

"Come out, Skediceth," she said.

We didn't agree on this, he protested.

"Please. For me."

Skedi crept down her sleeve. *I don't like it at all.*

Whatever the godkiller was expecting, it was not the harelike face and antlers of the squirrel-sized god that poked its nose out of Inara's cuff, his feathered wings tucked tightly against his back. Skedi looked like a cross between a hare, a deer, and a bird.

In the barest moment, a knife was in the veiga's hand. Skedi shrank to the size of a mouse and fled back up Inara's sleeve as the blade sank into the wood of the table.

"Do not hurt him!" Inara said, ripping her hand back to her chest and cradling the shivering Skedi. The metal of the dagger was a duller grey than iron. Briddite. She had seen it before in her mother's rooms: the sword she had brought back from the war was briddite. It could kill Skedi in an instant.

"Where's its shrine?" said the veiga. One or two people glanced over, but the loud tavern barely stopped in its stride. Inara bit her lip. "Answer me, girl."

"You don't command me," said Inara in her mother's tone. The godkiller was not impressed. But they needed her. Both of them. "He has no shrine," she relented.

"All gods have shrines. Even wild gods have shrines." The veiga extracted the knife from the table.

"Why do you think I am here?" Inara hissed, looking around. She and Skedi had spent so long hiding, hoping, sneaking, searching. The godkiller chewed her cheek and sat back. "He just appeared. Five years ago. He's . . . bound to me somehow."

She had been barely big enough to draw a bow but woke one

morning with a small god in her cot who could not move much more than twenty paces from her. If they tried, it hurt them both.

"And we can't tell anyone because I'll be arrested," Inara added. "Or my mother will, and he'll be killed. It's not his fault; he doesn't remember what happened."

"And what makes you think I won't have you arrested and kill your little rodent for silver?"

Inara caught her breath. No, that was exactly what they didn't want, and she hadn't even told the veiga about the colours she saw. What would the godkiller make of her then? Would she kill her too? Was this all for nothing? Had she made it all worse?

Let's run, said Skedi in Inara's head. They couldn't run; they would just be caught or back exactly where they had started.

"Because, godkiller," said Inara, "I've read everything in our library and I can't find anything about gods without shrines, or why we're stuck together. Because it's not his fault for being alive, but I'm trying to do the right thing and let him go without getting my family in trouble. Because if we had any other options we wouldn't be sitting in front of a rude, smelly veiga asking for her help."

The godkiller's eyes narrowed, but before she could reply there was a shout from the door of the tavern.

"There she is!"

Inara turned to see a young boy wielding a crudely wrought crossbow that no weaponsmith would have sold for shame. And he was aiming it directly at the godkiller.

"For fuck's sake," the veiga said as Skedi darted further into Inara's skirts to hide. With one hand the godkiller picked up the stool beside her and flung it out in front of Inara. The chair shook with the thud of the bolt as it hit the seat, a hand's span from Inara's face.

"Oi!" yelled Rosalie. "Not in my—"

"Die, godkiller! For Ennerast!" Three more people burst in through the side door of the tavern, one with a common log-splitter in his hand.

The godkiller flipped the knife, catching it by the blade, and flung it like a skipping stone. The pommel caught him, hard, in the eye and he fell, the axe landing on his chest. Blade up. Lucky. Inara's collar was yanked, and she shrieked with surprise as the veiga dragged her out of her seat and flung her bodily into the corner by the window, away from the mayhem.

The veiga took two strides across the floor and swung the stool into the back of the crossbow boy's head. He hit the floor. The woman by him had a smaller axe and cried aloud as she raised it, but the godkiller cracked the stool straight into her lifted jaw and then rammed it into her stomach.

She hadn't noticed the fourth lad slip behind her.

"Look out!" cried Inara. He swung a scythe he had roughly short-ened and straightened into a weapon into the veiga's right leg with a sickening thunk.

The godkiller did not falter, and instead swung the stool into his knees. His legs collapsed, and she drew the sword at her waist, putting its point to his throat. The blade was dark: briddite again. His apple did a quick hop as he swallowed.

"Go on, then," he said. His voice, half-broken, squeaked like underoiled wheels. "You killed our god; you may as well kill me too."

Inara caught her breath. She wouldn't, would she? Skedi spoke into her mind.

She is too dangerous.

The godkiller scoffed. "I don't kill people," she said, and put the sword away. The youth fell back, his last bit of courage failing as he burst into tears. The rest of the tavern was still, waiting for something else to happen.

The veiga looked up at Rosalie, who gave her a pained expression. "It's all right," the veiga said with a sigh. "I'll get going."

She did not apologise. She hadn't caused this splintered mess.

The godkiller came back to the table, her gait changed, but not apparently in pain, and picked up her saddlebags before she locked eyes with Inara. Inara didn't know if she was glad or horrified to have been remembered.

"You," said the veiga, with a face that could cast a curse. "Come with me."

Inara didn't know what to do except follow her outside. The square was empty and dark, the sun set but the moon not yet risen.

"What kind of god is it?" said the veiga.

"A god of white lies," said Inara shakily, looking back at the chaos of the bar. Skedi was clinging to her wrist.

"Terrific," the godkiller replied, her tone dripping with sarcasm. "Fine. I'm taking you and that parasite back to your parents. You can call me Kissen."

CHAPTER THREE

Elogast

ELOGAST LOVED FOLDING DOUGH. ONCE AND OVER, TWICE and over. Simple, absorbing. It calmed him, eased his thoughts, soothed the beating of his troubled heart.

Bread was a living thing: pleasant and true to itself. The warmth of the oven, open to release some heat, breathed on his cheeks, stirring the yeast-dusted air to life. It was the end of a brisk spring day, and his bakery in the western lowlands of Middren had made good coin.

Now he was starting bread that would be proved overnight and baked in the morning, as well as preparing for the evening's workers, the mining crew who were changing shifts to pluck the silver out of the nearby seams. The top of his kitchen door he had ajar to cool the room, and to bring in the fragrance of his neighbour's lilac tree as he worked. Small pleasures, he told himself as his hands beat out their rhythm.

Gods, he was bored.

Once and over, twice and over, the dough rippling as he rolled it through the flour on the wooden countertop. That was the pride of his bakery, commissioned especially from Irisian smokewood, from the land of his mothers, the same beautiful dark, warm brown as his skin, and the pale ground wheat flour stood out on both like stars or snow. This bench was a better surface than the crowded kitchens of the Reach in Sakre, the palace of Middren's capital, where he had squired. Better still than the flat stones and mud of a battleground.

His fingers stopped, trembling slightly, and a tightening pain squeezed through his shoulder and chest. He breathed slowly and put his hands back into the dough, feeling its softness, its delicate nature. Precious. The pain faded, and then so did the tremor.

Elo covered the dough and put it in the cool room to prove. It was a slow kind of life. A strange one. He was barely thirty but had put down his sword and shrugged off the honours he had trained for since he was nine years old. After three years, he still didn't feel used to it. Like he was wearing someone else's armour.

He now started on the nameen, nut-, seed-, and herb-painted flatbreads. Cobnuts, oil, and thyme were easy enough to buy from local orchards, but Irisian spices were more expensive now in Middren: the savoury nip of zither plant, the crunch of toasted benne seeds. His mother still living sent him generous parcels when she could. The meal was originally north Irisian too, but a popular enough working supper across the Trade Sea. Elo had perfected the recipe over the campfires of the God War. It had been good to eat in the bright mornings outside Blenraden, when the sun rose over the city and its broken towers. He could still see them, if he closed his eyes: the towers, and his friends, and his heart ached, tugged between emotions: mourning, and . . . longing. King Arren too, still a prince then, the dawn light painting him even younger than he was. Back when Elo never thought anything could change their friendship.

A step at the door. Elo's first instinct, still, was to put a hand to the knife at his belt that was no longer there.

The step shifted, and Elo saw a flash of light on the opposite wall. A blade.

He picked up the rolling pin he used for pastries and turned, smacking the sword aside and driving it into the wooden worktop, then grabbed its wielder by the throat.

"I see you haven't lost your touch, Ser Elogast," said the intruder.

Elo let go. King Arren was grinning, his blade still buried in Elo's fine worktop. He wasn't in his state dress, but wearing sheepskin leggings, a lined twill cloak, and a rough shirt of brown hemp he must have stolen or bought from a labourer.

"I see you still haven't hired guards good enough to stop you sneaking off, Arren." That was a nasty trick; Elo's heart was still beating fast. Still, he couldn't help but smile.

"I remember you weren't so good at keeping me penned yourself, my friend. In fact, I always roped you into coming with me."

Although his visits were rare, Arren always showed up without warning, without letter, and most often for no reason at all. But there was something different about him this evening, as if Elo's thoughts of his friend had summoned him into being. A new intensity also burned in his eyes. It was most of a day's ride from the Reach to Elo's bakery in Estfjor village, and he looked half-wild, as if he himself had run the whole way.

"What's wrong?" asked Elo. Arren blinked, his mouth twitched, and he shook his head.

"Does something have to be wrong?" he said. He still grinned lopsidedly like the naughty squire he had once been. Elo's mothers, Ellac and Bahba, both women of good trades who owned several ships, had sent Elo to squire at the castle as a child at his insistence. The strings they pulled had found him a bed in the hall, close to the fire, only steps away from this fourth-born child of five, and least-loved prince of the queen. That's who Arren was back then, just a squire with the rest of them, skipping lessons and getting Elo into trouble.

"You're still a bad liar, Your Majesty," said Elo. He resisted the urge to touch his hair and make sure it was sitting well. It had grown out, its finely textured black coils needing more moisture and care than when he was a knight, his beard too; back then he had always been clean-shaven or wearing protective braids.

"Come now, stop with the titles, Elo, it's me," said Arren. He didn't care. He had seen Elo more dishevelled than this, hungover on a sparring morning, or pulling on armour as they ran towards an attack.

Elo shook his head. Since he had left the king's service, he had tried to think of him as his sovereign, not so much his friend. It didn't work. Arren would always be Arren to him, no matter their disagreements, or that Elo had left his side after almost two decades of friendship and barely surviving a war.

Arren picked up Elo's pot of oils and seeds as Elo hid his floury hands behind him to disguise the tremor that came with thoughts of Blenraden. "That is a familiar smell."

Elo knew something was wrong, Arren just hadn't figured out how to explain what plagued him. He had always been like that. His mother's fault; the queen had not cared if Arren was beaten, scolded, or bullied. In the end, it was Elo who'd protected him. Elo knew Arren as if he were his own brother, and he could see he was carrying anxiety around him like a cloak; he couldn't stay still. "Is this to sell tonight?" Arren asked, instead of saying whatever he was thinking. "Can I help?"

Elo sighed. Best to let him speak in his own time. Perhaps it was politics. They usually tried not to touch on the subject, sticking instead to their childhoods and the sweet idiosyncrasies of the people in the village. They didn't want to stray too close to why Elo was here, selling bread, rather than in Sakre, where they had been born and raised, Arren's knight commander as he once was.

"I can always do with some help," Elo lied. He picked up one of the soft doughs he had been resting and flattened it with his rolling pin, then held it out. Arren grinned and dipped his fingers in Elo's sack of flour, took the dough, then began to paint it thickly with the herb and nut paste without disturbing the surface. Elo smiled. Arren hadn't lost the knack he had taught him. It was good to see his friend handle his work so delicately. Arren had always had nimble hands, too frequently covered in blood. Sometimes his blood, sometimes others.

The flash of golden armour in the pitch dark. The splatter of red. Screaming.

Elo shook his head, then set to the rhythm of work, flattening the dough and passing it on to Arren.

"Are you still happy here?" Arren asked at last, on his eighth nameen.

"Yes," Elo lied again. "Why, are you going to try convincing me to run away with you again?" He meant it as a joke, but Arren went quiet.

"It's not running away if you're coming back."

Elo laughed, though his heart stirred. Oh, not a small piece of him wanted to run away from himself, from his night terrors, from his memories, from his pride and his past. "Arren, you are king."

"Elo," Arren picked up the same tone, smirking, "I have noticed." The smile didn't reach his eyes. "I don't know how the queen did it."

He rarely called his mother "mother." When Arren was a child, Queen Aletta's first- and last-born had been struck with red fever, the eldest, Elisiah, dying within days and the younger, Mosen, barely clinging to life. To save him, she had bargained with a god. Whatever she promised, the god had accepted. After that, the queen had spent more and more time in Blenraden rather than the capital, holding court with gods and nobles and most precious Mosen. Arren had been neither her surviving eldest, Cana, nor her only girl, Bethine. Least-loved Arren, cast aside.

Now king.

Cana and Mosen were dead, killed with the queen as war broke out at one of her grand parties in Blenraden. Bethine too, his elder sister, struck down while trying to save her people from the old, wild gods as they crushed the refugee ships in Blenraden's harbour. Arren had been left alone to finish a war he hadn't started.

Not alone. Elo crushed the dough in his hand, squeezing out some of its air. He loosened his grip. That time was gone. The war was over. They had survived, if only just. Arren was fine. Full of strange energy, but well. And, most importantly, alive when they'd all come so close to death. Elo wished seeing him didn't bring up so many bad memories.

"Let's speak on this later," he said. "Put the first batch in."

"Yes, boss," said Arren, and began using the paddle to shuffle in the breads, comfortable in a warm silence that had been years in the making.

Boots came tramping down the street as the first of the nameen crisped in the oven. Elo went to his door and folded down the tray he had fashioned on its lower leaf. There was a large basket for the bread and a smaller one for coin. He filled the large one with the warm nameen.

"Ho, Elo!" said Kelthit, the shift balist who gathered the others for their work. He put a tin coin in the basket and picked up a flatbread. Elo didn't charge much for the miners' supper. Most of them no longer had the gods that used to protect them in the dark beneath the hills, now that Arren had banned them. They were not well paid for risking their lives in the earth. "Your pal's back to help, is he?" He looked curiously at Arren, who was keeping his back turned and an eye on the breads. The many paintings of Arren that hung in settle offices, courthouses, taverns, and other places across Middren did not all look much like him, nor did the little figurines of brass on people's window-sills, but it took just one astute pair of eyes and a mid-range memory to associate Elo with Knight Commander Elogast and his friend with the king of Middren, the destroyer of gods.

"Just passing through," said Elo. Kelthit shrugged. He had enough on his mind that it didn't need crowding with kings and gods and knights.

"My daughter wants you to come for breakfast tomorrow, so you'll bring her honey treats. Say yes this time?"

"Honestly, Kelthit," said a woman, elbowing him out of the doorway so she could drop in a tin and pick up her supper. "She just wants to look at his pretty face." She winked at Elo. "And Kelthit wants you to marry her so he can retire."

Elo smiled. "Next time," he said. Kelthit would ask again tomorrow. One day, maybe Elo should. Should try. He was still young. But he didn't know how to settle into this place; the working folk of Estfjor felt worlds apart from court and gods, and death.

The line continued after Kelthit, exchanging bread for a clink of coin. One or two put a pebble in instead, with their initials on it. A promise to pay the next week, or when they could. They exchanged some small words, about the weather or the sudden bloom of the lilac, some blessings to the king, which Arren must have smirked through. It was a lonely life Elo had made for himself, but it was a good one. He should enjoy it, being alive. He didn't.

When they were gone, Elo closed the door to the fading evening, and the other shutters in the room as well, instead lighting candles amongst the embers and the scent of yeast. Arren was breaking the flatbread he had kept for himself and offered some to Elo. He took it.

"It's burned," Elo pointed out, taking a bite. It was good, the dough light enough, though he had put a drop too much salt in the herbs.

"Only a bit, fusser-fiend." Arren was licking the crumbs off his fingers as strange, conflicting emotions passed over his face.

"No one will be here till morning," said Elo. "Wine?" He suspected they would need it for whatever Arren was here to talk about. When Arren nodded, Elo pulled out one of his cool stone jugs, which he kept above the cellar. If he were pouring for himself, he would have watered it down, but for Arren he filled a generous cup, then went to pull his supper out of the oven. He had prepared it before the breads, and had put the covered pot in the back to slowly bake. When he lifted the lid, it billowed with steam: a river fish on a bed of cut green marrow, citrus, and herbs. He had covered it with rough-ground grain and crushed nuts which had crisped on the top.

It wasn't enough for both of them. Elo put the fish on the worktop as Arren thumbed his wine, and went to open some of his jars of preserved foods from the previous summer. Pickled onions and sheep's cheese, white and creamy, stuffed into a pot of oil and herbs to preserve them. He put them on the surface with the food, olives too, which were now full and fat after soaking in brine since the autumn harvest, and a paste of rose petals and peppers that would go nicely with some bread.

The nameen was gone, but Elo had half a loaf he had baked in the morning, a spongy slab, oiled and salted with rosemary on the top crust. A south-Middren bread, good enough for a quick meal. He was relieved he had pulled something together, and helped himself to some wine as well. His friend was staring into the oven, the light from the fire's embers dancing across his face.

Embers, the glint of them in Arren's eyes. Elo felt the familiar tension run across his shoulder, into his lungs. It was like fear had infected his body, seeped into his blood and bones and now, three years later, his every day was still stained by it. His hands still trembled with it. The war. Always the war came back to him, no matter how far he left it behind.

"I won't leave you."

"You must!"

The strike. Spatter. Screaming.

Elo raised a trembling hand to his mouth and took a shaky draught. Haunted, yes, he was haunted.

"We need to go back," said Arren, as if he could feel the echo of Elo's memories.

Elo almost choked. "What?"

"You knew why I was here, Elo," said Arren. "Let's do it. Let's go back."

Elo half laughed, but Arren's expression was set, and serious.

"Arren, you can't. *We* can't. By your own laws only the knights protecting Blenraden can set foot in it . . ."

Arren came to look at the spread of food. "Don't you want to go back? To put the past to rest? Despite our differences, how it ended . . . we were there for each other. We achieved the impossible."

Elo hesitated. He wasn't wrong. They had won a war that destroyed Arren's entire family, half the trained army, locked them out of their own city. But that was because they had gods on their side. Gods of fortune, smithing, fisherfolk, and others. They had recruited common people into the army to replace the knights that had run, and bent them on revenge for the royal family, stoked their fury against the wild gods and their destruction of the city.

Then Arren had taken the revenge further and turned on even the gods who had fought with them, broke their shrines, banned them from their lands. And Elo could not forgive him for it.

The "differences" had meant that Elo's mothers returned to Irisia rather than lose their freedom of faith in Middren, despite its prime trade ports from east to west. Their "differences" were so great that Elo had given up everything he'd worked for, his sworn brother, his friends, his titles, and his wealth, to live alone in Middren, unable to abandon the country he had been born in and fought for, because he couldn't bear to uphold Arren's laws.

Arren patted Elo's shoulder. "Come, sit, think on it. I'll fill your plate. You must be tired."

Arren went about piling up the food, and Elo did decide to sit down, pulling a stool towards the fire. He did want to return to Blenraden to put the past to rest, to move on from the constant tug of memory back to the war, to see that shattered ruin of the city and its broken shrines, and let it fade. Even better, with Arren, to talk through the distance Arren's choices had put between them. Be like they once were.

They couldn't. They mustn't.

Arren passed Elo a plate then leaned against the worktop with his own, grunting with approval as he dipped his bread in the rose paste and took a bite. Elo's appetite had faded; he picked at his food. This was too sudden. Arren wouldn't have come to him unless he was desperate.

"*I need you for one last fight, Elo. Just one. Please.*"

"What's happened to make you want to do this?" Elo said. "You banned people from being in Blenraden so its gods would be forgotten, so you could eventually rebuild it. What's changed?"

A flash of bitterness passed over Arren's face, but it faded quickly. He pressed his hand to his chest, and Elo frowned, a cold shiver passing over him. "People are quick to forget what the gods did to us. They want them back, their madness, their prayers. They want me gone."

"Gone? Why?"

"There are sixteen Houses, Elo, and not all of them love me." He put his plate down and folded his arms, and looked like he used to as a child when his brothers backed him into a corner: afraid yet still stubborn. "Some are stoking dissidence," he said. "Rebellion."

"They want to dethrone you?"

"That's a polite way of saying 'murder,'" said Arren with a wry, sad smile.

Elo put his plate down. "Who?" he said, angry now. He had kept his sword when he left the army. It was stashed now under the mantel: his knighting sword, a gift from Arren. His fingers, steady for once, itched for it. He might have left his titles behind, but Arren was still his friend. Elo had protected him against his childhood tormentors, and he would protect him from his enemies.

"I don't know yet, not exactly," said Arren. "I have my suspicions. They press against my laws, all squabbling for power while we're trying to rebuild a nation. They make us weak."

"Could they be appeased?"

Arren clicked his tongue and stood, pacing in the darkness between the worktop and the warm oven. "Appeased?" he said. His face was pale. "No, Elo. We are surrounded on all sides by Talicia, Restish, Irisia, and Usic, all who would see us fail. Impossible. We cannot return to the infighting of gods or Houses, bloated on their own pomp and power. You saw first-hand the damage that power can do, the devastation the gods caused my family, hundreds of families." He balled his hands into fists; he looked unwell, tired. "I will not bend now," he said. "Not to our neighbours, not to rebellion, not to anyone."

"Arren, you took away people's basic freedoms. Gods' basic freedoms to exist. In Irisia—"

"This isn't Irisia, Elo," said Arren, turning back to face him. "Middren has too many gods, all different, all desperate, and they hurt us. They *killed* us."

They had had this argument so many times. And what more could Elo say to Arren, the last one of his god-twisted family, trying to hold together a kingdom that had come one city away from tearing itself apart?

"We can't run away to Blenraden now. What even for?" said Elo instead. He took a breath. "We go back. To Sakre. I will help you." Perhaps convince him to soften, to welcome people back in.

"No." Arren shook his head, pacing faster, his lips pressed tight together. "Blenraden is our answer. It's important that we go. You're the only one I can trust." He was paler than pale now.

"More important than a coup?"

Arren didn't answer; he flinched, then stumbled, collapsing into the worktop.

"Arren!" Elo leapt up to catch him, but Arren pushed him away. The movement felled him to his knees. There was no assailant, the windows were closed, he had not taken a blow.

"No," Arren growled, clutching his chest, his knuckles white. He looked at Elo desperately. "Not yet."

"What—"

"Wait . . ." Spasms wracked him, through his chest and down to his feet. He crumpled onto his side, curling up in pain. "Please, don't. I didn't want you to . . . see this."

The terror was in Elo again. He could see it. He could see it now, as he saw it then. He would not be pushed away; he lifted Arren's head off the ground, trying to stop him hurting himself.

Blood on the floor. Last breaths rattling out to nothing. Then a spark. A flame.

The shaking slowed. Arren's breath was irregular, wheezing.

Elo waited till his breath was steady, and Arren lifted his hand to grip Elo's arm tight.

"I'm all right," he said, his voice frail. "I'm all right, Elo."

Elo helped him up, and to his seat, then took another stool for himself from by the fire. They sat in silence for a moment, only the crackles of the flames disturbing the air. "My friend," said Elo at last, "what is it you're not telling me?"

Arren looked up, pleading, then away as if ashamed.

"I didn't . . . didn't want to worry you, at least till we were there." Elo passed Arren his cup of wine, which he held unsteadily. "You've done so much for me, I wanted this to be about us, not . . . not this."

Elo reached for the buttons of his shirt. Arren moved to stop him, but when Elo gave him a look the king's hands fell away.

The scar started just beneath Arren's left shoulder. A deep rivet in his flesh where bone and lung had given way. There, his skin was tightly knitted and dark with smoke-script, the language of a god. Elo's breath quickened, his mouth dry. It had been a long time since he had seen where the scar widened, the skin opening around a dark space, an impossible space. A thing that should not be, but a thing that had saved his friend's life: in the darkness, the twigs began. A little nest, rounded with moss, cradling a flame where the king's heart had once been.

And the flame was dwindling.

CHAPTER FOUR

Skediceth

THE GODKILLER SMELLED LIKE OLD LEATHER, WET WOOL, and sweat, and Skedi didn't like it at all.

He also didn't like that he couldn't tell what she was thinking. Mortals were a riot of thoughts, and gods could see the colours they made, twisting the air about them with their more powerful emotions. Each person's colours were different, bright, manipulable. Skedi could tell a liar from a lover, a joker from a fraud. Not the veiga. Her emotions were wrapped tight, hidden. Kissen. A strange name, Skedi thought, for such a hard-bit-looking woman.

He didn't like sharing a horse with her either, a mid-aged gelding that was taking them up the dirt track Inara had just brought him down, finally, for the first time in five years. Most of all, though, he didn't like that he was within reaching distance of the veiga's briddite dagger, no matter where he crawled. He sat now in the crook of Inara's neck and shoulder, protected by her cloak and hair, eyeing its handle warily.

Inara, thankfully, had taken his advice to hold her tongue for now. He needed to think of a way to get them both out of this.

Tell your mother she just found you in the woods, said Skedi straight into Inara's mind.

You think she will believe me? said Inara. *She told me never to leave the manor.*

I will make it stick. She doesn't have to know. We can find another way.

Another way to be free. Inara had protected him, done her best. For that, Skedi was grateful, but he knew he did not belong with her. One day, they would be found and he would be killed. He didn't want to die, he wanted to be what he was. A god. He wanted a home, a shrine.

I can't lie to my mother again, Inara said to him.

She lies to you.

Inara shifted uncomfortably. *She does what's best for me.*

Skedi didn't want to push too hard. Inara admired her mother. Too much. The woman hadn't even noticed she had slipped away; otherwise they would have met a search party on the road. But Lady Craier was the closest thing Inara had to a friend other than Skedi. The snatched moments she had with her mother while Skedi hid in her pocket were her favourite moments in the world.

I don't want to die, Ina, Skedi said instead.

I won't let anyone hurt you, Inara insisted. What power did she have, though, really? It had come as a surprise to both of them that the barkeep hadn't even known Lady Craier had an heir.

Kissen reined in the horse and sat still, sniffing at the breeze.

Skedi sniffed too: a trace of smoke, there, then gone. They were a long way from Ennerton now, and the dark was thick, stirred by the tiny movements of other creatures in the undergrowth, the flit of a bat in the air, just outside the light of Kissen's lantern, which she held over the road. Close at hand there were only Inara's chaotic child-feelings and the muted shades of the godkiller.

Ask the veiga what it is, Ina.

"What is it?" muttered Ina, miserable with chill and the prospect of being in trouble.

"Quiet."

More smoke came, thicker now. A shiver passed through the veiga, and for a moment Skedi saw her emotions flare out red and angry. Skedi tucked closer to Inara's neck, frightened. The colours disappeared as quickly as they'd arrived, but when Kissen spoke, her voice rasped like stones against a saw.

"You said yours was the biggest household around here?" she asked.

Everything's fine, Skedi said to Inara quickly.

"Why?" asked Inara, unnerved. She had seen those colours too. At

Kissen's look, she answered. "Yes. A manor, with outcourt and steadings. It's barely—"

Kissen snuffed out the lantern and kicked her horse into a gallop. They bolted down a road that Skedi could barely see whipping past, trusting the beast's dulled senses. So abrupt, so decisive. Mortals should be more cautious; they did not heal like gods did. Skedi decided that the veiga was too distracted to kill him now. He gathered his nerve and leapt to the top of Inara's head, putting his nose to the air and baring his teeth. Yes, smoke. Too much of it.

"Skedi, what's happening?"

"It will be all right," he said to Inara, out loud this time. "Veiga," he tried, in his biggest voice, "we should turn back." Whatever had made her so suddenly full of terror was not something he wanted to run towards, not with Inara.

The godkiller said nothing. She had one arm around Inara and the other on her horse's bridle, his hooves rattling on the stones of the road. A waft of smoke stung their eyes as they rounded the hill. They reached a break in the trees and saw flames.

The manor was burning. Not just the house. The court, the granaries, the stables, all of them aflame, and more than one of the further steadings. The valley was alight. Kissen reined in her horse. Inara was silenced by the sight, her colours bleaching white with panic.

"What . . . what happened?" Inara asked, as if the fire would answer. Skedi watched as the roof of the manor fell in. The trees in the orchards were starting to blaze as the fire jumped from the building. He trembled. Had someone found out about him? No, this was something else. Something bigger.

"Mama . . ." whispered Inara, and Kissen looked at her. Her mother had been home. For once. Inara should have been too.

We have to help them, Inara said in Skedi's head, then out loud. "We have to help them." Her voice was hoarse.

Who was "them"? They could see no one fighting the fires, no shouting, none of the warning bells were ringing. The road they were on was the only one towards town, the others were miles away, and not one person had passed them looking for help. Skedi could see nothing, only the rush of smoke.

He folded his wings close down to his body. Everyone Inara had ever known. Her mother, her only parent. He had to lie to her; he had to. "It will be all right, Inara," he said. He loved her, almost as much as he loved his own feathers. He had to protect her from the truth.

They were dead.

"We have to help!" said Inara again, trying to spur on the horse. Her colours were in chaos. The horse did not move. Inara wriggled free and leapt down before the godkiller could snatch her and ran, Skedi still clinging to her hair.

"Ina, please," he said, hastening to her shoulder. It was still a long way to the burning buildings. "Stop. It's dangerous! You'll get us killed."

The godkiller had dismounted to follow but was too far behind. It was up to Skedi to stop her. He made himself grow, expanding to the size of a kitten, a hare, a dog, his weight increasing as he did. He clung to her back, hooking his claws into her cloak and dragging her down. He could feel the heat on his face, even from this far. There was no one left. He wanted to live.

"No!" Inara struck him from her and he fell. She did not get far before Skedi felt a wrenching tug on his heart. Inara gave a strangled cry and fell as the invisible chain that bound them together snapped taut. It was excruciating, a pain like this, as if his core were trying to break out of his chest. Hers too. They were both of them crumpled down into the dust, just within the last of the straggle of trees.

A thunder of hooves. Kissen had remounted her horse and raced up behind them. She swung down and lifted Inara bodily from the ground with one arm before pulling into a thicket off the road. Inara, still dazed, couldn't fight her. Skediceth spread out his wings and flapped with them, half-blind with pain. The veiga dismounted, pulling the horse down to lie and keeping tight hold of Inara, hand pressed to her mouth to stop her squeaking.

Kissen had noticed what they hadn't: Skedi heard more horses, coming away from the fire. He hadn't sensed them, he was so focussed on stopping Inara. His heart lightened for the briefest moment, till he heard their riders. Laughing.

The horses walked into the treeline, twenty of them, and the people on their backs were dressed in dark, rough cloth. It was not those colours that frightened Skedi, it was their emotions: violets to reds to gleaming silver, for all humans saw the world differently, but they simmered the same, like a dying fire: those riders were shining with violence.

Quiet, keep quiet, he said to Inara. This time, she listened.

"That old one put up a racket, the one with the braid."

"Lucky you're a good shot, Deegan."

"Didn't stop her yelling though. Not smart enough to prefer the arrows to the fires."

"Aye, Caren won the bet on when they'd give up."

Tethis, the old steward, slept with her hair in a long braid. They had to be describing her, otherwise it might be Inara's mother, but she was young, half into her thirties.

"It was well done. We got them all. House Craier is finished."

A gust of wind dispersed the smoke, and moonlight broke through the trees. Skedi saw chain mail glinting under leather. Soldiers, or knights. They wore no colours of a particular House, but the bridles on their horses were fine and well polished, and their saddles matched. There was blood on their hands, he could smell it. As they came closer, he could see the nuance in their colours, the glimmer of lightness, satisfaction, pride. Faith.

They would see them. Of course they would. The veiga had dragged them barely steps from the road; anyone with half an ear would sense the motion of twigs springing back into place, their breaths. Their fear.

One of them paused, reining in his steed. Skedi saw Kissen put her free hand on her sword, and Skedi had to make a choice: take a chance with the godkiller who hadn't killed him *yet*, or these soldiers who had death written all over their colours. "Got them all?" Not Inara. Inara had escaped. What if they wanted to kill her too? What would happen to him?

Skedi whispered a little white lie.

There is no one here. No one here. There is no one here.

He willed it into the world, allowing it to wrap like gossamer around the colours of the man that had paused, binding his mind with Skedi's will. He felt the brushes of the human's emotions, the sting of violence almost as if it were his own. Skedi flattened his ears as far as they would go.

There is no one here. It is time to go. No one is here. They are all dead.

The soldier turned and rejoined the rest. Kissen did not move until after they had all passed. Inara was crying silently, her tears running over the veiga's fingers.

When they were gone, Skedi watched her release Inara and they both sat back, catching their breath. Skedi remained silent, terrified of drawing attention to himself. For him to survive, Inara had to as well. If she was lost, then whatever bond was keeping him existing without a shrine would break. He was sure of that.

"Who were they?" Inara whispered.

The veiga spat as if to rid her mouth of the taste of smoke, then spoke, first to Skedi.

"What did you do, parasite? He was one breath from seeing us."

Skedi didn't answer, and instead made himself even smaller.

"He saved us," Inara whispered, cupping her hand to him. Skedi felt her fingers shaking, cold. "I told you. He's a god of white lies." Her voice sounded so thin. Skedi grew bigger despite himself, to the size of a hare, and pressed against her cheek. "You would have got us killed, veiga," said Inara, more strongly.

"You're one to talk, running straight into fire," Kissen said. She stood, looking down at the flames below, her face grim. "If I've the salt to guess you've had a lucky escape from a massacre." Those eyes turned back on Inara. "So, just who the fuck are you?"

CHAPTER FIVE

Elogast

ELO SLEPT ON HIS OWN FLOOR, GIVING ARREN HIS BED. FOR the first time in a long while, he did not wake from night terrors, only from the face of the dawn pressing against his shutters.

He sat up, and saw that Arren was also stirring, his shirt wide open where the little flame burned in its clutch of twigs.

Blood on the floor. Arren's breaths, fewer, lighter, further.

It should have been me.

Elo buried his face in his palms. In another life, his friend would have his whole heart, would not bear the responsibilities of kingship in a country whose gods had turned on one another.

"Elogast?" said Arren, sitting up. Elo looked up and clasped his hands together.

"We should have thought of this," he said.

"It wasn't your fault," said Arren.

Elo shivered with shame at the memory, trying to breathe through the pain in his chest, glad his hands were already clasped tight and disguising the tremor. Neither of them ever spoke about it. Guilt buried them in silence. Elo, that he had not been able to save his friend. Arren, that he had chosen to live on a god's will, rather than die.

It should have been me.

"Gods have long memories," said Elo. "If you go to Blenraden they'll want your blood on the stones. Even the god who saved you is killing you now." They would not speak Hestra's name aloud. They didn't know if it might call her through Arren's burning heart. "She wanted something from you, and you haven't given it to her."

Arren didn't deny it. He couldn't. "She didn't ask for anything . . ." he said dismally. A decision made on the chill edge of death could not be undone.

"You said yourself that gods don't give without taking." Elo stood up slowly. "She thought you would preserve her power, and you have not, so she is taking it back." He rubbed his own old wound on his left shoulder, feeling the knotting of scar tissue, and reached a decision. "Arren, you cannot go to Blenraden, not now. I will not let another of your bloodline die in that blasted city."

Arren winced and swung his legs out of bed. "I have no choice," he said. "Only in Blenraden might some shrines to the old or wild gods be left standing where we can find them unguarded."

But it was the old gods that had not liked the new ones multiplying across the Trade Sea, taking prayers and granting wishes. They liked it less that the queen invited these usurpers into her palaces, had their shrines carried up the Godsway road so they could be entertained at the Blenraden court. Gods barely a decade old revered beside those who had lived a thousand lifetimes, and gods of the wild who lived before memory, before Middren. It had only been a matter of time before the queen's favour spilled out in blood. They knew that now.

"Those gods killed your family out of spite," said Elo. He and Arren had been together when they had finally broken into Blenraden after six months of hard fighting, only to find the bodies of the court, his mother, and his brothers: dismembered, mutilated, rotting to the bones. Gods had destroyed the elite and reclaimed the city, running the wild hunt over and through its walls and refusing to let a single soul pass in or out. "What do you think they would do to your life before you opened your mouth to bargain for it? I will go alone."

"Elo, no." But Elo was already moving. Arren followed him into the living space that Elo barely used, adjacent to his bakery. Elo went to his fireplace and reached beneath the mantel. There, his lion-headed pommel; he pulled down his sword. "I won't let you."

"I'll go in secret," Elo continued. "Stop at Lesscia and find some sort of pilgrimage that knows the routes away from the main roads. Through the Bennites, probably."

He looked at the pommel. The new swords for Arren's knights were stamped with a rising sun and a stag's head. Elo couldn't touch those, not the stag. He was fond of the prince's old lion symbol. He would have to wrap it to hide it. If someone recognised him as a knight, they might trace him back to Arren. And no one could know the destroyer of gods needed one to live.

"A pilgrimage?" Arren laughed a little. "You really think people will be so flagrantly breaking my laws?"

"You'd better hope so," said Elo, raising his eyebrow and digging in a box of cloth scraps he used for mending his clothes, looking for the right kind of wrap. "If they are, it means you're right, and powerful gods are still there." He shrugged. "Anyway, people don't change just because you ask them to." He found a long piece of white cotton that he wrapped carefully around the figurine. He was sad to hide it; it was the best gift anyone had got him.

"They should," said Arren, with a haughtiness that reminded Elo briefly and frighteningly of the dead queen. His crooked smile softened the moment. "I didn't think anyone could be as stubborn as you."

"Ha," said Elo.

"Elogast. Please." Arren was pale again, his breathing laboured, though he was trying to hide it.

Elo stopped. Arren had his hand on the mantel. He could not conceal how weak he was this morning. Why had he travelled at all? Soon someone would notice his absence, if they hadn't already.

"How long do you have?" asked Elo. "Answer me honestly."

Arren hesitated. "I don't know," he said after a moment. "At the rate it's fading . . . maybe a month."

A month. Elo cast his eyes up to the rafters, gathering himself, hoping Arren wouldn't see how much that frightened him.

"If you're right," he said, "and the Houses are planning rebellion, your absence will be a chance for them to take power. Worse, if you die, it would leave Middren in chaos. You know that. We know what would happen. Only fear of the gods stopped civil war or invasion while we were fighting in the city."

"Fear and them realising how quickly we could recruit an army between us," said Arren. "Fear and *you*, Elo. You said we should recruit commoners, you took command when no one else would, and you fought by my side even after you wanted to stop. I want you to do this with me, not for me." He put his hand on the pommel of Elo's sword, then hesitated, and took Elo's arm. "We might not have so much time together. I want us to act as brothers, maybe for the last time."

Elo clasped Arren's arm in return. "Your Majesty." He said it pointedly. "We've held the world together once before, and we will do it again. Just this time, you hold it from Sakre." Arren was responsible for a kingdom, not for Elo. "Keep your people's faith in you, and . . . please . . . keep your faith in me. When I took this sword from you, I promised you my life, my blood, my heart. I meant it."

Arren shook his head. "But not your honour. That's what you said to me when you left. Your honour is yours."

"And my honour needs this." Elo moved his hand from Arren's arm, putting it instead over the hole in his chest, feeling the heat of his cooling heart. Arren's expressive face shifted with conflict, hope, pain. "I need this. To go back, to make it right, and to put the past to rest."

Then maybe, just maybe, he could begin to move on.

"I swear to you, my brother," Elo said, "no matter what has changed between us, I will go ask a gift from any powerful gods left in Blenraden and bring you back the life you need."

CHAPTER SIX

Kissen

WHAT THE SWEET SHIT WAS SHE DOING?

Kissen had decided to stay just one night in Ennerton, because fuck the settle. She had wanted a drink after a job done, a little tumble with Rosalie. Was that too much to ask? Usually those who had a problem with her did some spitting and shouting, maybe delivered a dark look or two that they thought were very scary. Easy enough. She'd been a one-legged orphan fished out of the sea and sold at the first opportunity; words couldn't hurt her. She had not planned to be attacked by a rabble of ingrates. Nor to be pestered by a little girl who didn't want her god-parasite to be killed. The last thing she had expected to see was the House of Craier burned to the ground, and to be burdened with its bereft daughter.

Kissen didn't know what to do. Her life had gone to ash when she was a child, and she couldn't just leave Inara Craier, god or no god, abandoned and alone. More than that, this was a problem she couldn't deal with on her own. She needed help.

It was three days' walk to Lesscia, with the help of a sturdy horse. Legs was the name of hers, a little joke she had with herself, seeing as he had more than she did. Inara sat silently on his back, grey and silent with loss.

They'd gone down the valley to get a look at the house, at Inara's insistence, but as the dawn came it was clear there were no survivors. It was too hot to get anywhere near the buildings, but Kissen saw four bodies at least outside the front of the manor, stuck with arrows and charred from heat, having tried to escape from the flames. According to Inara, her mother had been home, and she knew none of the Craier family beyond those walls. Estrangement from family was a noble's luxury, Kissen thought, though this didn't explain why the barkeep hadn't even heard of Inara.

Kissen used her staff to walk beside the girl and horse, and she felt the ache of it in her muscles and bones, with her leg damaged as it was. But when she had Inara walk it was too bloody slow; the kid stumbled along like she was in a dream. The antlered god sometimes peeked out from inside her hood, his hare ears twitching. No one they passed along the roads seemed interested in their little party, which was odd. Kissen often drew looks: a reddish-headed Talician with a longsword, a cutlass, and a broken curse on her face. It was a while before she realised it was that little god of white lies diverting eyes away. If she focussed as she had been taught, she could hear his whispers nipping at the edge of her mind, and everyone else's.

There is a bit of silver on the ground. Your shoe has a stone in it, better check. Look, are those rain clouds? You can't see us. We're nothing interesting.

White lies. Harmless, so he might say. They didn't affect her; Kissen had learned to resist some gods' wills and powers under the guidance of an old godkiller called Pato. Most people couldn't sense the pressure of a god's will, not if they weren't expecting it, and so their attention never landed on the strange little group. If it weren't for the usefulness of his meddling, Kissen would have finished him. Whoever had attacked the manor had wanted the whole household dead, and, if they found out Lady Craier's daughter still lived, they might come after her; they needed to be unseen.

Inara spent most of her time pretending to sleep so Kissen wouldn't ask her questions. Kissen didn't blame her; she suspected that every time the girl closed her eyes she would see the fire burning down the hill. She had to be troubled to drink water or eat a morsel of food. She was too shocked to cry, really. It would come.

Kissen's stomach rumbled as they reached Lesscia at last and she guided Inara through the stalls of the outermarket. Three days of hard travel, but they'd made it. Between the lines of stalls people ferried fish barrels, oils, dried fruits, and the first fresh spring greens, elbowing one another for space. Steam rose from a great vat of rice and vegetables, and a bit too much smoke from green-wood that hadn't dried properly. Lesscia's main trade was knowledge: paper, manuscripts, weavings, prints, inkmaking, art. The city's libraries had been gathered over centuries under the guardianship of the wealthy House Yether, whose yellow flags billowed across the walls every few strides.

At the gates into the city, the keeper wearing a yellow sash gave them a perfunctory glance. Kissen had seen him before, and noted the flash of recognition, then aversion, as he checked Kissen over and waved them all through. Kissen glanced at the gateposts, once carved in the shape of the god of arts and learning who had founded the city and dominated its shrines. Her name had been Scian, and her statues that held up the arch had been hacked away to blurred bits of stone. In her place was a large brass relief of the king holding a stag's head, sun rays spreading out behind him.

"Why are we even here?" Inara muttered. She was looking up at the buildings as they passed under the arch, rising three or four storeys high, with fine painted signs on their fronts.

"Oh, so you still have a tongue to speak with," said Kissen. Legs's hooves were loud on the flat, even stones of the city streets. Lesscia was a pleasant-smelling city as all food trade took place outside. To Kissen it was strange; as a child she had been used to noise, as an adult used to solitude. Lesscia was somewhere in-between.

"It's not an unreasonable question, veiga," said the girl. Kissen smirked. At least the kid still had some bite to her.

"It's home," said Kissen. "I've friends here who can give me advice on what to do about both of you."

"You live *here*?"

Maybe too much bite. Kissen shrugged. The only people they were passing this early were grey-robed archivists or servants paddling or pushing their purchases from the outermarket back to their homes, or to the ones they served. "In a way," said Kissen. Inara scowled. Maybe this was why she hadn't been speaking; she took no pleasure in what Kissen had to say.

They passed over three bridges that covered the canals, which did have a bit of human pungency more natural to such a big city. Over some waterways the houses were made of stone, built on land. On others, wooden-fronted buildings with washing strung between them extended over the current on dozens of stilted legs, like insects hovering on the surface, hoping they would not be swallowed by monsters.

It was deep into the city, not far from one of the cleaner canals, where Kissen brought Legs to a stop. They were in front of a fine, large gate with a sign of a hammer and wheel over it. The house beside it was low to the ground, one storey with a wide front door half covered by ivy.

Home.

Kissen fished her key out of one of her cloak pockets and put it in the lock. It turned, but the door didn't budge. Bolted. She cursed. The morning sun peeked over the roofs, exposing them in the hushed street.

"Yatho," Kissen called, trying to keep her voice low. Her knock on the door shook it on its hinges. "It's the gold hours, Yatho, you dozy wench," she said more loudly, and gave the wood a good kick with her damaged leg, which sent a shooting pain from her foot-that-wasn't-there all the way into her spine. She could feel a tugging at the side of her head, like a sharp plucking at her brain, and as she focussed on it she could hear the god's little voice.

You can't hear us you can't see us you can't hear us.

"Do you really think your hiding chant is helping, parasite?" Kissen snapped, seeing the tips of his antlers propping up the shoulder of Inara's fine cloak.

"Stop calling him that," said Inara.

"I'll call it what I want."

Inara was about to retort, but the door rattled. Skedi shrank to the size of a coin and burrowed against Inara's neck. Yatho, pale, rumpled, and grumpy, opened it, having clearly just shifted herself out of her bed and into her wheelchair, her mind still half in her filigree dreams.

"What the fuck, Kissen?" she said. "Using Maimee's wake-up call? At the door of our own house?"

"You locked me out, Yath." Kissen shrugged. "Reminds me of Maimee."

"It's the gold hours, little ones, time for making money."

That was a voice Kissen liked less than a god's in her head. Maimee the malevolent, who bought unwanted children and set them to be beggars and thieves. Blessed if they succeeded, beaten if they didn't. Bah. She swept the thoughts from her mind as Yatho grinned.

"Silly of us to presume you would turn up at a graceful hour, perhaps even with warning," she said, putting a brake on her wheels and standing to embrace Kissen. Kissen returned her hug, holding her close and long. Yatho's arms were broad and muscled, filling out her shirt to its seams. It had been two months since Kissen had seen her adopted sister and was glad she was looking well, though her eyebrows were half-singed.

"It's high time you were up anyway," said Kissen, her throat tight. "It's past dawn. Furnaces need warming, no?"

"We have a boy for that now," said Yatho, sitting back down and rolling her chair backwards. She caught sight of Inara and raised a charred brow but asked no questions. "He's called Bea. I'll tell him to open the gate so you can let Legs in. We've been bolting since the thefts."

"Someone robbed you?"

"Someone tried."

Inara shrank back as Kissen turned and lifted her straight down from the horse and pushed her into the house. She then took Legs to the gate, which swung open on its tracks only moments later, pulled by a scrawny lad of about sixteen. He touched his head respectfully but avoided her eyes, then went straight back to pump the bellows in the smithy, giving the milk-goat a little pat as he passed.

Though Yatho and Telle didn't keep horses, they were always prepared for Kissen's. She found a fresh trough, hay, and a bag of oats. Legs was relieved when Kissen took the saddle and reins and hung them, then took the time to brush him down, knowing Yatho would settle Inara inside. He nuzzled at her so she would stroke his nose.

"Don't see what you're complaining about," said Kissen, obliging. "The girl's lighter than I am."

They had made it. They were safe. But now, she'd let a god into her own house, Yatho and Telle's house, along with a little noble girl whom apparently no one knew existed and who had no father to speak of.

What now?

When she went inside, Yatho had lit a fire beneath the base of the pot and a bagful of almonds were toasting, smelling delicious. Inara was staring at the flames, dry-eyed and clutching a cup of clean water in her hands.

"Fire is fire still," said Kissen wearily. If she sat down, she was pretty sure she wouldn't get back up, but her own wheelchair was hanging up just by the fireplace. "Just as it was before."

"I know that," Inara muttered, as Kissen lifted her chair down. It folded completely flat when hanging, but after a bit of wrangling and forcing the crossbars in place, it became a serviceable leather seat. She sat down with a great sigh of relief. Her left leg was stabbing with muscle pain in her foot and calf, and her right was biting at the knee from chafing. She could also feel a phantom squeezing in her right shin and ankle. She leaned over to give her booted shins a rub, both legs at the same time. The pain lessened in her right leg, but didn't disappear. Yatho came in with a covered pot of milk and a bag of oats in her lap.

"Here," she said, chucking the bag at Kissen in a burst of dust then handing over the milk. Kissen added them to the pot with a hiss, using her boot to lighten the fire a bit. "Put some water from the kettle in as well," said Yatho, and Kissen did what she was told, cooling the mass to a bubble.

"You know you're the only one who bosses me around?" said Kissen.

"And give me a look at that leg."

Kissen winced.

"Come on, Kissen, I know that limp."

"You don't want to."

Yatho gave her a Look. Kissen sighed and bent over her right leg, untying the cords that bound the bottom of her breeches to her knee and then loosening the buckles around her ankle. They gave her easier access if she needed to repair something, not that she was very good at it. The cloth came away, and Kissen tried not to look at Yatho's face as she revealed the great rent that had been made in the metal during the brawl in the tavern. The leg was finely made, a mixture of briddite and steel wrapped in leather, shifting plates that were light as bone and bound on an internal mechanism that gave her more flexibility than she had ever imagined. Yatho grimaced, not fond of seeing her handiwork ruined.

"What the dreg happened, Kissen?" she said as Kissen fiddled with the straps around the kneecap. She twisted the leg off, boot and all, and studied it herself. She had taken some peeks on the road, but had been under the impression that if she looked at it, it might fall apart. She wasn't far wrong; most of the plates were beyond salvage. It was a miracle it had carried her from the Craier lands to Lesscia. She glanced at Inara, who, despite her misery, was watching with fascinated eyes, and quickly looked away.

"Some kid in a tavern thought I was a piece of grass," she said, handing it over. While she was at it, she unbound the top of her leg and fingered the skin that had been in contact with the prosthesis. It was rough and stinging. When she had first been found, tossed up on a Talician beach, a group of travelling merchants had salvaged her and had to reslice the flesh to dislodge the broken shards of bone, then sew it flat before smuggling her out of Talicia, where burn scars might mark her as a failed sacrifice. They'd done good work, even if only for the purpose of selling her, half-dead and screaming out of her sleep, to Maimee.

"This can't be fixed," said Yatho, peeling back the metal. "This is made to be light, Kissen, not put in the way of axes."

"It was a scythe," said Kissen. "Ah, it's fine. Give it back."

"No." Yatho held it out of her reach. "You'll ruin both your legs; the balance is off. Do you need ointment?"

Kissen grumbled and leaned back. "No," she lied, and pretended she didn't see Inara's hood twitch as her god felt it. She didn't want Yatho worrying about her.

"I've been making the pieces for a new leg anyway," said Yatho. "I knew you'd run into trouble eventually. It won't take long, but I need to weigh you for the final touches."

"Ugh, I weigh just the same."

"A fraction of change can throw off the whole mechanism . . ." Yatho stopped as Kissen started mouthing her words back at her, then laughed. "Stir the damn pot, troublemaker," she said, instead of continuing, and turned her focus to Inara. "So, who's this?"

Inara, who had just finally taken a sip of water, almost choked. She didn't look good. Her fine dark hair was ragged under her kerchief, and her face was pinched with fear and sadness. Her eyes went distant, and Kissen knew she was conversing with her little god, thinking of a lie.

Not in this house.

"She's the daughter of Lady Craier, so she says," said Kissen, before something silver could jump off the girl's tongue, "and she has a pest problem I need Telle's help with."

The girl glared at Kissen with a look that could curdle the milk in the pan.

"*The* Lady Craier?" said Yatho, leaning on one side of her chair. "I didn't know she had any children." She smiled winningly at Inara, who didn't smile back.

Neither did Rosalie, Kissen thought. Still, she believed the girl, even with her little lying god. If she had anywhere else to go, she wouldn't have stayed with Kissen, of that she was certain. Perhaps she was born out of wedlock, though it didn't make a difference in Middren who sired or bore you as long as someone claimed parenthood. Even the king and his luckless siblings were fathered by Queen Aletta's various lovers.

It was a mystery, though. The people of Ennerton were the Craiers' people—why wouldn't they know about their local noble's child?

More of a mystery: how had the little girl acquired a god that didn't have a shrine? Pity aside, if Kissen didn't get rid of the god, no one would take Inara in and break the king's laws, not even her own family. Perhaps Kissen should have killed the little god while the girl was sleeping, but she had seen them both fall when they moved apart; their bond was deep. What if removing him killed her too?

"You do have the look of an heiress," Yatho said, still trying to be nice. "The porters in Blenraden used to tell tales of that mother of yours, quite the adventurer, they said."

Inara looked at her cup. "Yatho," Kissen warned, "the lady is dead."

There was no reason to handle truth like glass. It wouldn't break on arrival. The truth was the truth. That didn't stop the sound of Inara cracking into a sob, or the water spilling from her eyes. Her shoulders heaved and the cup fell from her hands. She pressed them to her face.

"Ah, shit," said Kissen, just as the tiny ball of wings and ears that had been hiding in Inara's cloak leapt out, the size of a cat, not close enough for Kissen to strike but big enough for the beat of his wings to stir the fire.

"How could you?" he cried. "How dare you be so cruel?"

Yatho recoiled. "What the fuck, Kissen?"

The god shrank a little, realising that he was out in the open, exposed.

"And *that*," said Kissen, "is her pest problem."

CHAPTER SEVEN

Inara

IF INARA HAD KNOWN IT WOULD BE THE LAST TIME SHE SAW her, she would not have lied to her mother and slipped away into the night. She would have hugged Tethis, the steward she was sure the soldiers had been joking about, and Erman, her tutor. She would have thanked them for always bringing her pistachio treats and honey. She would have stayed. She would have burned.

Now she was in a strange, short, messy house, full of metal pieces and wires, with a godkiller and her friends, and with nowhere else to go. Yatho's colours were kind enough, muted cornflower blue and lilac, and she had her black hair shaved short enough to show pretty leaf tattoos behind her ears. But Inara had never known anything more than her mother, her home, her title. Those had been life's certainties; like stone walls, they had trapped her inside but also kept her and Skedi safe. And now they were gone.

Then Kissen had thrown the truth at her like a blunt object, and its impact shattered the fragile guard Inara had put around her heart. Gone. Her mother was dead, all of her secrets, the letters she hid, her things burned with her. All of it was gone.

And now Skedi was appalled, exposed. For her. Inara had never seen him so angry; he had never made such a mistake of fury before. But all the truths in the Craier manor had been passed around in soft cloths, made to look pretty. He was always telling her that it was his nature. For him, this was wrong.

"You can't be so . . . hurtful," said Skedi angrily. Inara saw through her tears that he was now the size of a small rabbit under the murderous gaze of Kissen and the horror of Yatho.

The door opened, and after three angry steps, Inara felt a hand on her back, warm and firm. It was another woman, who pulled a handkerchief from her robe and pressed it to Inara's cheeks to soak up her tears. Her hands were dry and rough, but warm, like Tethis's, and she clicked her tongue against her teeth. Her colours were like the steward's too: fresh and bright, calm greens and greys. Inara took the kerchief and held it to her face to soak the tears away. When she gave the cloth back, the new woman gave her a fresh cup of water and then sat beside her. She had soaked the rag and pressed it to the back of Inara's neck. Soothing, cooling.

Inara calmed, taking trembling breaths till at last she plucked up the courage to look up. The woman smiled at her. She was pretty, with dark eyes and fine brows that were scored by three straight scars that cut across her face, one leaving a deep cleft in her upper lip.

This must be Telle. She looked at Kissen pointedly. Kissen, who did not appear at all ashamed, moved her hands in signspeak, to Inara's surprise. She had only seen her mother and one of her servants use sign; Lady Craier had taught it to Inara as a secret language that pirates or people with hearing difficulty used.

How did you know it was me? Kissen signed to Telle, who laughed and replied in sign.

Yatho doesn't make children cry.

"Crying's good for you," Kissen signed and spoke, clearly for Inara's benefit, not knowing that Inara understood every word. Telle must be deaf. "She's from House Craier, and her home burned down three days ago, her mother and servants inside. This one and her pest survived. They were lucky."

Lucky. Inara took a deep, shuddering breath. This didn't feel lucky. She felt kidnapped more than anything else. Stolen by fate.

The pest, Yatho signed. *Is that what I think it is?*

They all looked at Skedi, whose wings had fallen. He crept back towards Inara, antlers tipped forward defensively. Still, Inara was grateful for his outrage on her behalf; it made her feel less alone. She reached out to pick him up and pulled him to her lap, where he sat on his hind legs.

Yatho's mouth narrowed. *This is dangerous,* she said. *Gods are illegal. We're finally respected here, after coming from Blenraden. If we have a god under our roof, we'll be reported.*

Blenraden. That was twice she had mentioned it. These women were from that city?

Kissen unhooked the thickly bubbling pot from the fire using a long-handled tool. She passed it to Telle, who thumped it onto the mess of a working table in the middle of the low-ceilinged room. Yatho went for bowls and Inara kept quiet, watching their conversation. She might have lost everything else, but she had her eyes, her ears, and Skediceth. He would tell her if lies were said between them, helping her interpret the colours of Yatho and Telle.

It's more than that, Kissen said in sign, with a furtive glance at Inara. *The fire was set by soldiers. Maybe from another House. This one's mother was caught up in something, and all her people paid with their lives. I don't know how safe she is.*

You should pay attention to politics, said Telle, signing quickly before she passed Kissen a bowl of porridge and continued: *The Craier family has been split for a generation. The lady was the only one in favour with the king.*

Inara frowned. Favour? No, it was the opposite. And a split . . . Lady Craier had never spoken unkindly of her family; when Inara asked about them, her mother said she would meet them one day.

No one would burn their own land, said Yatho. *Not outside of Talicia.* She grimaced at Kissen, her colours flickering a sad blue, but the godkiller shrugged.

"She can go to court," said Kissen, "claim that king's protection."

"Don't say 'that king' like he's not your king," said Yatho. "He's made you wealthy."

"He's made me look at his damn boy-face everywhere I go," said Kissen, "as if there were one god instead of hundreds." She reached inside her cloak and dumped a clanking bag on the low table by the fire. Telle passed Inara a bowl of hot porridge.

"Kissen, how many times have we told you to keep your money?" said Yatho, staring at the bag.

"I've got nothing to do with it. You two, however, have a business, have a life."

"We're doing perfectly well without. We just put it aside so you can . . ."

"What . . . stop doing my job?" said Kissen with a smirk. Yatho scowled.

"There is safer work you can do. Work that won't get you killed."

Inara suspected this was an old conversation.

The king wouldn't harbour a god, Telle interrupted. Inara looked down at Skedi, whose yellow eyes were worried. Of course King Arren wouldn't take in a god; he would kill him on sight, and the Craier name would be dragged through the mud. That was exactly why Inara had gone to Kissen to start with. It wasn't fair.

I know, said Kissen. *That's where I need your help, Telle. The two of them are bound somehow; he has no shrine of his own. Have you read anything on this?*

Telle shook her head, picking up her own porridge. She took two spoonfuls before pausing on the third, her mouth pursing around the scar that split it. She then gestured with one hand. *Perhaps*, she said. *I'll search today.* She put the bowl down and smoothed her robes, preparing to leave. Inara felt her heart shake. Telle had helped her. She felt familiar, unlike the two rougher women who seemed as like to trade insults as affection.

Eat more, you'll get hungry, said Yatho to Telle. Telle rolled her eyes, took two more bites, then went to kiss her on the mouth with her cheeks full of oats. She pressed her lips then to Kissen's head, gave Inara a reassuring smile, and left without further question, confusion, or rebuke to Kissen for bringing a god and a strange girl into their home.

"I have work too," said Yatho, heading towards the door. "I have three commissions and another letter-set."

"Just don't forget how to forge me a sword," Kissen joked.

"As if you'd let me," she said. "Get some sleep; you look like shit." She nodded at Skedi. "And keep that beast hidden."

Skedi pressed back against Inara's stomach while she lifted her oats with her spoon and let them fall back into the bowl. At home, she would have goat's cheese and dried figs for breakfast, with cold yoghurts from the cellar, drizzled in honey and dusted with rose petals. Sometimes the cook would have made a small pastry filled with almonds and red orange in the shape of a flower. Inara put her tongue to the spoon; the oats were tasteless, with no sweetness to them. The milk had burned in the pot.

Lucky.

"Am I supposed to feel lucky?" she said at last. Her tears had gone, and she felt hot, dried out. Angry.

"Yes." Kissen sighed and leaned back. "You should feel lucky, but you won't for a good while."

"What would you know about it?"

"I know enough."

Another non-answer. Inara twisted her lips. She had been taken command of, manhandled, carried over and away from her home and lands. She wouldn't be spoken to like some kind of imbecile or pet. Her mother had kept her hidden, yes, but she had still raised her.

You are meant for greatness, sweet one, she had told Inara. *They will see that one day. The king himself will see you for who you are.* Inara tried to quell the bitterness in her heart. Her mother had left her alone, with no one else to turn to.

"I won't let you hurt him," said Inara, putting her fingers in Skedi's fur. "I don't know what kind of reward you're expecting to get for helping me, but I've no reason to trust you." Anyone else, she might tell if they were lying like a god could; their colours flickered in an erratic way, contradicting what they said. But with Kissen's colours hidden, Inara had nothing to go on.

Kissen laughed. "I brought your ungrateful hide here," she said. "And as for *that*—" She indicated Skedi. "We'll discuss that later. Right now, you need to eat."

Inara pulled a face at the porridge. Her stomach growled, but she felt sick and lost.

Eat it fast, said Skedi soothingly. *Pretend it's sweet, it will taste all right.* To Kissen he asked: "Why are we in Lesscia? Who are these people?"

It was strange that they had not been scared of Skedi, as if he were not the first nor last god they might see in a day. Kissen chewed her cheek and didn't answer.

"You cannot pretend I don't exist, godkiller," Skedi added boldly. "You don't have the art of lying in you."

Kissen, quite clearly, did not know whether this was an insult or compliment. She grunted. "They're my family," she said. "We were all sold or traded into Blenraden because a woman we called Maimee decided troubled children could turn coin out of sympathetic, god-fearing pockets. Misery made her good silver." A twist of disgust had moved Kissen's mouth as it formed the woman's name, and she looked at the coin she had left on the table, untouched by Yatho or Telle.

Blenraden. So, they were indeed from the dead city the war had destroyed. No wonder her friends were not so swayed by seeing Skedi. He was the only god Inara had seen in her life, but they must have seen thousands.

"So, they have no time for gods," Kissen added, "and less for little white lies, so don't try any ingratiations, pest. Telle is an archivist in the Cloche, and one of the few people who is still allowed to read the old writings on gods. If anyone can figure out how to pull the two of you apart, it's her."

CHAPTER EIGHT

Elogast

IT DID NOT TAKE LONG FOR ELOGAST TO PACK UP HIS LITTLE life. He didn't bring much, only yeast and two small bags of flour for food on the road, and some of his own herb mixes with refined Usican desert salt. For armour he wore only his bracers, with a leather doublet and jerkin over his shirt, but no more than that, and felt naked for it. Still, with the supplies for baking, and having shaved his beard and hair back to the skin, it felt like everything would be just fine.

The first boat down from Estfjor took him through the beginnings of the canal network Arren was constructing, to the struggling town of Sorin, where the canal met the river Roan and veered west, the opposite direction to Lesscia. Sorin had once been a crossroad town that specialised in brass bells, before Talician metalworkers flooded the overseas market; now the best he could do was rent the least rotten mare and take the eastern route to Lesscia.

Lesscia had always been a haven for pilgrims chasing argument, history, and scripture instead of the gaudy promises and pick-pockets of Blenraden. Since Blenraden fell, Lesscia was the second-greatest city in Middren, after the capital Sakre. There were guards stationed throughout the route to keep it safe and the road well-kept so more trade could pass between the towns and cities. Nowadays it took barely a day and a half to reach Lesscia from Sorin, when as a boy it had taken Elo and his mothers four with a pony, tents, and carts.

Elo arrived later than he intended into the outskirts of the city of arts, which were considerably further out than he remembered. Last he had been there was following Arren's victory tour back home. Elo had put himself at the furthest edges of the crowd, no longer one of Arren's retinue. Truly, he should have made his own way home from Blenraden, but with Arren's secret heart burning in his chest, he had wanted to make sure his friend got safely back to Sakre. He never heard the words Arren said, but he had seen the hacking away of the statues of the god that had graced the gates for two hundred years. Around him, the crowds had burst into yells and whooping, furious applause, bellowing Arren's name. If there had been tears or shame, Elo had not seen them.

Now, he couldn't even see the gates from the far edges of the houses, which had tripled in number, a sea of lanterns beneath the winter darkness that was still weighing down the spring evening. Elo dropped the mare off at an inn on the outskirts, but it was another half mile before he found the neat stalls and businesslike jostling of the outermarket where the city's food was traded. Here, Yether guards patrolled in yellow, helping tally up transactions and tax the appropriate cut of the profits.

Elo went swiftly through the official avenues and followed a winding path down to the marshy bridges that extended beyond the city. Here were the more ragged traders, too poor to afford tables in the centre. His mothers had always told him never to go down here, where few guards bothered to come and the stalls were exposed to all the winds of the great river Daes, unprotected by the city's walls rising behind them. Of course, that had only made it more enticing to himself and Arren as youths. This was where they had made illicit bets and, once, traded some cups they had stolen out of the palace for a lot of coin and two bottles of brandy.

A cluster of bloodied and scabby roosters screeched as Elo walked past their tight cages, posted with their odds for the night's cockfight, and eyed instead the stores selling snack foods and services: stuffed dumplings, burnt cakes, couriers, and mended clothes. As the shadows lengthened, he ventured past several different lanes of stalls, looking for a friendly eye or some kind of token of faith.

After a while, he spotted some hot breads served with fresh curries being sold by a man of one of the many peoples of Usic, a neighbour nation to Irisia. His clay oven had a glinting charm hanging beneath it. Only three paces away a trio of pallid men were playing a game of tiles; instead of coin, they used sless seeds—sleeping draughts— which they had bought from a surly-looking trader who was arguing with their dog. Elo's stomach rumbled, and he realised he was famished.

He bought curry packed into the bread and ate it warm before the stall, enjoying a homey taste he found in Estfjor only if cooking for himself. His eyes were drawn to the swinging token beneath the oven. The charm could have just been for luck, or the tag of the oven's maker, but a cutting breeze set it spinning, and Elo saw that it was embossed in the centre with a hand painted blue. The hand of giving, the token of a god of fortune—one that must still be alive.

Elo smiled inwardly; he knew Lesscia was the right choice. Arren could get rid of the gods, ban them from Middren, but it would take more than that to purge the libraries of Lesscia and the people who were drawn to them.

Elo took another bite of curry and caught the stall owner's eye. "Would you tell me a thing, in good faith?"

The owner looked at Elogast's sword and turned to his oven, taking a moment to flip his breads. "Who wants to know?"

"A pilgrim," said Elo, trying a charming smile. Damn, it had been a while since he'd had to charm anyone. "One who has lost his way."

"Pilgrims offer gifts," said the owner flatly. Elo laughed. Gods of wealth rarely attracted the open-handed. He unwrapped a silver half from his thread of coins and ingots, worth a fair deal, and let it peek through his fingers, its weight-imprint and marked hole clear. Back in Estfjor, a silver such as this would have bought half a horse, but here it was worth only a good bribe. It might buy the curry cook a day or two in the top levels of the outermarket.

The Usican pulled out another bread, tucked a little curry into it, and put it on the barrel next to Elo's hand. Elo exchanged the half ingot for it, and the silver disappeared in a glint of light. "The Queen's Way," he said quickly. "In the narrow ginnels to the northwest of the Cloche. A good place for a pilgrim to wet his throat."

Elo stood back. Of course, the Queen's Way. Someone still had a softness for the monarch that had brought them to the brink of ruin.

"The ways lost us, my friend," the owner added. "They will find us again. Very soon."

Elo hesitated. What did he mean by that? He nodded his thanks and turned back to the city gates. It was nothing. Arren knew there was trouble; he had gone back to Sakre, where he would be guarded, be safe.

Elo's bags were searched by the yellow-sashed guard as he entered Lesscia's gates, but his belongings were not enough to constitute trading items that might damage manuscripts. He was let through as the evening bells were ringing.

He took the main avenues towards the Cloche, the great copper dome at the city's heart that housed the most precious of its archives. Lesscia was busy. Cart-pushers were running past with unnecessary urgency, official sigils on their coats and a guard tailing them, surprisingly in Arren's colours of blue and gold rather than the Yether yellow. Workshops were still running into the evening; Elo passed a tile-maker's that had several children running under adults' feet, picking up fallen shards of clay. In the dusk, the dome of the Cloche and the white buildings around it seemed to glow.

The broad avenues narrowed; the ground rose. Canals were fewer and further between in the warren of little streets at the north side of the city. This inland side of Lesscia was almost like Sakre: messy, winding, and filled with lights of inns and resting places, smithies, and cobblers. Elo felt a wave of nostalgia spill through him for his home city, which he and Arren had known as well as each other.

When Elo found the inn, there was no sign hanging, but the imagery painted on the door was enough: three pilgrims following a woman wearing a crown. Elo shook his head. The Queen's Way indeed.

Elogast had met Queen Aletta once, properly, for an inspection of the guard. He had expected a cold woman, aloof, but zeal had burst from her like sunlight, scorching and unrepentant. The last time he had been that close to her was after they had broken into Blenraden. No sunlight then, no power. Elo would never forget Arren's face when they found her and the princes' bodies. Mosen had barely been fifteen. Arren's older sister, Bethine, the queen-that-never-was, had run in in her armour and collapsed to her knees, sobbing with horror and pain. But Arren had been angry.

"*How many died getting here,*" he had said quietly as his sister wept, "*after she let this happen?*"

"*Arren . . .*" Elo had tried. This had only been the first atrocity. In the all-out war for the city afterwards, worshippers and gods took sides, taking up arms against their own neighbours and even against the Middren army. Elo had no count of those citizen deaths, only those of the knights it took to get past the stones, storms, nightmares, and arrows of gods and their faithful.

"*Answer me. Please.*"

"*Twelve hundred,*" Elo said. Arren waited. "*And fifty-six.*"

"*Twelve hundred and fifty-six,*" repeated Arren. "*From every House, every province. Dead. For her foolishness. Save your tears, sister. I ran out of tears for her at one.*"

And those were the better days.

Elo centred himself and went inside the tavern. It was crooked and close, with a smoking coal fire in the stove to ward off the spring chill, but it had made the small room stiflingly hot. The thick glass windows were wrought together with lead, and foul-smelling oil candles floating in scented bowls of water did very little to lighten the air.

Elo made for the bar. The innkeep was pretending to polish a cup while watching him in the array of convex brass mirrors behind the bottles and barrels; an expensive but smart way to keep an eye on patrons. The man wore a sleeveless jerkin, and was lean-shouldered like a brawler. On the back of his bare neck was a tattoo of what looked like a rune or a forked road. His ink extended across his shoulders and down his bare arms; nape to knuckle. That must have hurt.

"I will have one of those spirits, please," Elo said, indicating a woman who was sitting nearby with a glass of clear liquid with syrup pooled at its base. A pleasant scent came from her direction, of citrus or lemon peel.

The keep turned and straightened, putting the cup down with a click. His hair was black, salted with silver, and his pale eyes scanned Elo from his feet up, his eyes resting on his arm bracers, then his sword. Elo wore his blade as if he had no intention of using it, on his back, with his pack. The wrapped pommel made it look stolen, perhaps. He had hoped it would appear just disreputable enough that people wouldn't ask questions.

"We don't see a lot of Irisians around these days," the innkeep said, though the woman who was now hurriedly gathering her papers was clearly at least half-Irisian. Two others began muttering near the fire, and Elo's skin prickled.

He couldn't afford to try every likely stall and tavern in Lesscia. He needed to disappear into the secret ways pilgrims could take over the mountains. He told himself it made sense that the Queen's Way was suspicious of newcomers. It also made sense that there was no image of Arren hanging over the mantel.

"I—" Elo was about to tell him he was born and raised in Middren, but he thought again. Many Irisians had left Middren's shores to practise their faith freely elsewhere. It might make him more trustworthy. "I haven't been to Irisia in a long time," he said with a smile. The keep hesitated, his pale eyes flashing. "I miss its ways."

If he had a god's senses, Elo suspected he would have felt the tavern relax a mote.

"It must be hard, being so far from home," said the keep. Elo recognised his accent, from the forested areas that stretched from the north of Blenraden to the southern foot of Talicia. How many people from those areas, once rich and now half-abandoned, had ended up here? That explained the explosion in size of the outermarket. People from those parts had a pulled-out lift to their vowels, not as clipped and sharp as in Sakre. "What's your name, then?" He glanced behind Elo. The woman had left, her glass half-drunk, but the others remained. "And what do you want?"

He reached for a clear goblet that chimed as he set it down in front of Elo, then pulled a small pickaxe from beneath the bar and chipped some ice from the block hanging above it. This he swept into the cup. Though he wasn't a large man, his muscles were well defined and his nose looked twice broken at least. As the keep turned, Elo could see the tattoos in more detail, repeating the forked-path pattern several times over. A sign of a god, it must be, but cut through with other art, bands and whorls, and, in one place, a silvering of scars over his forearm. He wore his tattoos so openly, freely, that Elo felt the true danger of the rebellion Arren had spoken of. It wasn't just Houses hankering for power, it was normal people. If that was the case, who knew how much further into Middren it stretched?

It wasn't his fight, not this day. He was only here to save his brother. Save the king's life, and then he could deal with the rebellion.

The innkeep pulled a pewter bottle from behind the bar, not even looking at it, poured it over the ice, then added a spoonful of pomegranate molasses from an open jar with a fly in it. It dropped to the bottom of the goblet.

"Of course, the liqueur is authentic Irisian," he said, pushing it forward before Elo had formulated an answer. "Made with dates, isn't it? Got the case sent special last month. You can call me Canovan."

Elo had inadvertently picked an Irisian drink. He frowned at the glass. He had never seen or heard of such a liqueur, but then he was rather behind the fashion. He did not take a sip straight away, but tipped the glass so a single drop fell on the floor, as his mothers did before drinking, thanking the god of change for their bounty. In his boyhood, at their parties, the flagstones and rushes afterwards would be sticky with palm wine. Canovan watched.

"I'm here to seek passage to the lost city," said Elo quietly. "My name is Elo."

Canovan narrowed his eyes. "Elo," he repeated, as if biting a coin to see if it was real all through. "And why would you want to go there?"

Danger hung on the question. "Is that something you need to know?" asked Elo, trying to be mild.

"It depends," said Canovan. He ran his tongue over his teeth before he answered. "Some seek solace; some remember the dead." He folded his arms. The ink, for a moment, seemed to move. "Some seek favours, and power. Those, I tend to have my suspicions of." He looked Elo over again. "That's a knight's sword."

Elo hesitated. "It was," he said.

"Haven't seen a sword like that since the knights broke all the shrines in Blenraden." He thumbed the handle of his pickaxe.

"I was there," said Elo. This threw Canovan; the keep's eyes flashed uncertainly. "I followed the king when his orders made sense to me, but I left the army years ago." He held his hands out, showing them to the keep. "See, the calluses from the sword are faded." He had flour beneath his nails still, and the roughness was on his fingertips and thumbs from folding dough. "I'm no knight. I have no love of the king. I am travelling to seek penance for what I have done."

Canovan looked at Elo's hands, then up at his face, jaw flexing. He didn't believe him. Perhaps he didn't need to.

"Penance," Canovan said. He tilted his head as if listening, casting his eyes over the air around Elo, then put both his hands on the bar and smiled so suddenly, and so coldly, it took Elo aback. "Yes . . . you can make penance. My apologies." Elo got the sense that behind him, the people that remained in the tavern took their hands away from knives or charms. "Take a seat, Master Elo, I'll join you in a moment."

Elo breathed out, and chose the seat the woman had recently vacated. She had spilled something on the table as she rushed out: lemon juice. That explained the scent. Still, he took his sword off his back and rested it by his leg. Showing Canovan his hands had reminded him that he was not as practised as he once had been, with people or with his sword. If he had said the wrong thing, he suspected it would have been the pickaxe he was contending with, and the innkeep looked like he could handle it in a fight. Elo had put himself in danger, and Arren. He tried not to chuckle out loud; if he and Arren had come here together, they would have been three punches deep in a tavern brawl by now.

He took a drink. It was strong enough to bring tears to his eyes, quite different from his usual watered-down wine. When Canovan joined him a short while later, it was with an ale in his hand, and he was now wearing a shirt beneath the jerkin, hiding his tattoos. He sat rather close beside Elo, too close for comfort, and Elo caught the scent of incense on his beard. That, and a dark, foresty smell, like mud or moss.

"It takes some 'gots to take you to Blenraden," he said. "Dangerous, the city of shrines, very dangerous road. I can offer you a map. Good directions, points to stop along the way. I'd even give it to you for the sword, if you'll let me have a look at the blade."

So, this Canovan had decided to go from guard dog to swindler. Did he want to have a look at the blade to check its briddite tang? Elo knew better than to show him; it wasn't hard to tell the gleam of steel from the dull god-killing metal.

"I will travel with a group," said Elogast, taking another sip of his drink. Damn, if the Irisians didn't want to drink themselves joyous with the stinging liquid. "I know the way." This wasn't exactly a lie;

he knew the proper way, the main roads. "It's safety I'm after, safety in numbers." He didn't mention the sword. "And I want to leave tomorrow."

"Why the rush?" said Canovan.

"That is between me and my gods," said Elo.

"I don't like a knight, former or no, wanting routes to Blenraden in a hurry."

"I won't be paying you to like it, will I?" Elo smiled.

Canovan cocked a smile, but he still had tension in his shoulders. "It's seven and one gold," he said, "to leave at week's end." The price was extortionate. Elo bought his whole bakery for six silver and two.

"I'll pay you five," said Elo. "And the sooner the better." One month. No time for lingering. It took eight days to get to Blenraden the main way. It would be ten at least if they went through the mountains.

"Six and a half," said Canovan, scratching a thumb against his nail.

"Five, or I walk." What was he doing? He had barely been invited to sit down, but if he seemed too keen to part with his own silver the man's suspicions would arise again. Anyway, his mothers would have been shamed if he let himself be bandied about by a malcontent. Canovan didn't want a fight, Elo thought, not a real one. If he was a seditionist, and Elo now had no doubt that he was, he wouldn't want attention drawn to his tavern.

Elo stood, banking on his guess, and Canovan stood with him, gripping him by the shoulder, tight. The scent of moss was stronger than before.

"Six and tomorrow," said Canovan through gritted teeth, looking drained. "Agreed, all right? I have pilgrims setting out tomorrow at noon."

Elo's shoulder felt cold where Canovan's hand pressed on it, unpleasant. Elo took the man's wrist and removed it, twisting it into a hunter's shake. He thought he saw a shadow disappear up Canovan's sleeve, but it turned into only a flickering of lamplight on his tattoos.

"Six and tomorrow," Canovan said, looking pale, his earlier fury and bravado gone. He shook Elo's hand briefly, and with distaste. He had been outmanoeuvred, and he didn't like it. "And," he added, "two coppers for the drink."

CHAPTER NINE

Kissen

TELLE'S RETURN SHOOK KISSEN FROM A TROUBLED NAP BY the fire in her wheelchair. She had slept through the bells, and the sky was getting dark. Outside, Yatho's noisy hammering had gone silent. She'd likely turned her hands to her more delicate tasks to keep within the city's evening laws of quiet.

One helpless kid, Telle signed with a smile, *and your defences crack*.

Kissen made an obscene Talician gesture, a curl of her forefinger into the crook of her thumb, and Telle laughed. She poured herself an ale as Kissen rubbed the sleep from her eyes, then passed her some as well. As a kid who'd hated everything, Kissen had hated Telle. Telle had been younger than her, sweet-tempered, Maimee's favourite, favourite of all the other unwanted children. She had made sure they were fed and clothed, even taught them how to read, if they were interested, which Kissen was not, and to sign, which Kissen had grudgingly accepted out of the necessity of knowing a language Maimee didn't. Yatho had moped after pretty Telle in front of Kissen, all the time. How Kissen had loathed her.

But, when Kissen had run away to follow a godkiller called Pato and learn his trade, it was Telle who had helped her. Her obedience had been her shield, her quiet kindnesses her own little rebellions after being given to Maimee. After the God War broke out, when Kissen was halfway across the country, Telle and Yatho had looked after the others until Kissen could return and save them.

Now Yatho's wife, and Kissen's sister, Telle was dearer to her than her own hands. Who'd have thought, one of Maimee's beggar children ending up an archivist alongside second-born nobles and merchant's children?

This life suits you, Kissen signed to Telle. *You look very fine.*

Telle jokingly feigned bashfulness, but she was pleased. She had grown true in confidence since getting out from under Maimee's choking hold. She had forgiven Kissen for her brattish and furious youth as well. Kissen had come back for them, and that had been all that mattered.

How's your leg? Telle asked.

Kissen scoffed. *Fine. Yatho is being foolish.* Sign was not a subtle language. It was direct, to the point. In truth, Kissen's leg still ached, it always ached, but it was better than when they had arrived. The wheelchair was a blessing. She wasn't used to it, and kept wanting to jump up, but it was a relief to be able to rest her hips. *Did you find anything?* Inara was nowhere to be seen. She had sent the girl to her own bed. Perhaps she was still sleeping; perhaps she had run. Kissen did not know what she would do if the lass and her pest ran away.

Some, Telle gestured. *They're all in the smithy. Shall I push your chair?*

Yatho's workshop was open to the yard, lit by lanterns and the hot glow of the furnace. Kissen was surprised to see Inara pumping the bellows, and her little god clinging to them. A straightforward job, but hard work. Skedi clutched the top as the girl determinedly pressed it down. He flapped his wings as he fell and gripped the post as he rose. He was acting like a plaything, as if he didn't know what he was. Kissen's hand itched for a weapon. She had left her waxwool cloak with all her tools inside.

Yatho was working with one of the smallest hammers Kissen had seen, fining down a long, thin bolt of glowing metal, the sing of its striking not loud enough to carry. Behind her, Kissen's new leg was in its several pieces of cooled briddite. A marvel. Yatho had first begun to make things like it when trying to find ways to stop wooden splinters driving into Kissen's knee from the weak pegs Maimee found for her to use. Every spare hour Yatho had spent at the smithies near the war god's shrine in Blenraden, watching anything being made, from washer grids and wringers to armour. She soon branched out to the joiners, the leatherworks, the mechanical artisans and their toys for foreign nobles. Yatho was born to be a maker, to see how things were put together and taken apart.

Yatho plunged the fine piece of metal that Kissen suspected would hold her new shinbone into a bucket of cold water to quench it, then looked up as it steamed. Her face brightened as she caught sight of them, but still she held the metal till the steam lessened, then carefully brought it back up to inspect. With a nod of satisfaction, she plunged it into a different bucket for a few more moments, then set it down on a special frame.

"Rake the coals, Inara," she said. "We're done. Skediceth, use your wings to keep the embers from her face, understand?"

The two of them nodded. Kissen scowled. Though Inara's face was still drawn, Yatho had managed to get more movement from her in an afternoon than Kissen had in three days. It had taken Kissen years to go that close to a blaze again. Even now, the fire was so hot that she reached for a vial she kept on a string at her chest, preferring to hold it when she was near open flame, just in case. Yatho came over, unbuckling the leather apron that she had fashioned just for her chair.

"They're a strange little pair," she said to Kissen as Telle came to give her a greeting kiss. They gathered at the still-lit brazier out in the courtyard, away from Inara and her god.

"You put a noble's girl to work?" Kissen asked and signed so Telle was included.

"She needed to be occupied," replied Yatho in the same way. "Loss is a strange thing. Some people hold it, some attack. She's not unlike you."

"I don't think she'd like to hear you say that."

Telle laughed and sat down on the stool by the brazier. It was a clear evening and the breeze was sharp and cold. The mud by the smithy was beginning to show green shoots that would soon flower as the days warmed, though quite a few had been chewed back by the goat. Kissen looked at Telle expectantly. Knowing her, she was impatient to share what she had learned.

There are no records of gods without shrines, she said, *only the old or powerful gods can travel between several of their shrines, like the god of lost things or the god of safe haven. The more believers, the more shrines, the further they can move. They can sometimes be summoned by their symbol or rune outside a shrine, but only briefly. If a god's centre shrine is destroyed, sometimes they can survive by holding on to one of their others.*

Kissen sighed in exasperation. She knew all this.

The god does not have this? said Telle, and Kissen shook her head. From what little information she had gathered from Inara, she understood that if Skedi could have left the Craier home, he would have. A god would only come to a godkiller if he had no other choice. *His only pull is to her,* said Kissen. *I would not believe it, but I saw them in pain when they moved apart.*

Telle nodded as if that was what she expected.

I thought gods died without their shrine, said Yatho.

Not always, said Kissen. *Not immediately.* Gods began as spirits, drawn to places where people travelled and might need them. One day, they might gather enough willpower to blow dust on the road in the right direction for home or cause a thief's bow to misfire at the perfect moment. Then, someone might give thanks, give offerings, give them shape. *Even when their shrine is gone, their power can linger. A shrine is like the keel of a ship; it holds them together.*

Telle beamed and threw her hands up, *Yes, exactly.* Impressing Telle—that was a first. *The keel keeps them balanced between the things that made them: the water it sails on is people's love, holding them up. The wind is the spirit, the energy that makes them, giving them power. Without the keel, they fall apart, roll over, are destroyed.*

"Spin my wool into gold, why don't you?" said Kissen out loud with a laugh.

Why is the god bound to the girl? asked Yatho.

Telle held up her hands and shook her head to say she didn't know. *But a sudden separation will be like breaking the keel. It will kill him and might kill her too.* That was not what Kissen wanted to hear, and Telle knew it. *This is not a problem that can be solved with a blade or a fist.*

You couldn't do that anyway, Yatho put in. *They're playmates. He's her friend.*

Kissen twisted her nose and was thinking of a smart response when Telle went on.

I did find one text, she said. *It wrote of moving a god and its totem from one shrine to join another, more powerful god in theirs. There may be some truth in it. If a god returns to a place of power they might . . .* She struggled with the word to choose. She spelled it out with her fingers and Yatho nodded.

"What was it?" asked Kissen.

"You still haven't learned your letters?" said Yatho, as if she didn't know that already.

"Shut up, Yatho."

Telle clicked for their attention. *The god might be able to—*

"Entangle, is what she said," added Yatho.

—entangle with another shrine.

A shrine. Illegal in Middren, but Kissen shrugged. *We can find thousands of shrines,* she said. A little carving in someone's kitchen, a token in a drawer to stop the spoons sticking, a pile of stones by a log store to keep the wood dry. Kissen didn't go around stomping into people's houses and scattering their little grottoes of insanity, but she knew they were there.

You're not understanding, said Telle. *Not just any shrine will do. It has to be a shrine to a powerful god, strong enough to let a smaller one live on their "water," the love that gave them purpose.* She hesitated. *There's only one place that still has that power in Middren.*

Yatho flinched, and Kissen's heart fell. *Blenraden,* she gestured. Telle nodded.

I'm not taking a little girl to that god-eaten city, said Kissen. *First, she'll drive me crazy, and then she'll be killed by gods, demons, knights, or all of them.*

The other choice is to take a girl with a god in her heart to the king. Do you know what he would do?

Kissen bit her lip.

We can hide her here, said Yatho.

I'm not asking you to keep a god under your roof, after everything you've built.

You don't need to, said Telle.

Kissen sighed. The money she had left on the table inside was still untouched. She didn't need it, she made enough to live on, but Yatho and Telle were constantly spending their funds on struggling families and children. She had learned that even the boy, Bea, who Yatho had sent home with pay that morning so he didn't see Skedi, was part of their charity, as his brother couldn't look after him. Could they keep Inara for the months it might take her to find somewhere else for Skedi to be?

If you keep her, then I can go ahead to Blenraden.

"Kissen," said Yatho, as Telle shook her head. "We swore we wouldn't go back."

"I broke that promise last time I swore it," said Kissen, "and don't regret it."

Yatho frowned. Though she and Telle had been full grown when the war broke out, they were still Maimee's. She owned them. Perhaps they could have run, but that meant leaving the younger children behind, and they didn't have the heart.

But Kissen had returned just in time. When the armies had spilled into the city and tried to vacate refugees, the gods had gone from bad to worse. The wild gods had wrecked the ships and gone screaming through the streets on the hunt for humans, lighting fires as they went. Kissen, Telle, and Yatho had forced Maimee to release the children, and Kissen had broken them out of the city. Three years later, for the first time, all the little ones had homes, and Yatho and Telle were free. If Inara was safe anywhere, it was with them.

I can find out if I can take her there, Kissen added in sign. *And . . .*

She couldn't forget what Ennerast had said. *When Middren falls to the gods . . .* Kissen had no particular love for Middren as a country, but it was her home, it was where her people lived. She did not want another war, she wanted to do her work. In truth, she wouldn't mind seeing the dead city if only to confirm it was still dead.

Blenraden is where I will find some answers, she said. *Perhaps I can convince a god to appear here, if you keep the girl safe . . .*

"No."

Kissen whirled in the wheelchair. Despite their mostly silent conversation, none of them had noticed Inara slide out of the smithy with Skedi in her arms, his ears twitching. She loosed him and he clambered up to rest on her shoulder, his wings spread out to steady him. Inara dropped her hands.

I will go to Blenraden, she said stiffly.

Kissen was almost as surprised by her signing as by her declaration.

She knew Skedi would understand them—gods had an uncanny understanding of all languages—but Inara? Sign was used more often by commonfolk than by nobles.

"I am not taking you to that cursed city," said Kissen.

"I won't stay here like a stray kitten you picked up," said Inara. "Skedi is my friend, and if I find him a place he's safe then I can go to the king, find out why this happened to my mother and our people." Inara put her hand to his fur. She really did treat him more like a rabbit than a god. "Skediceth is my people too. If we can get his freedom, then . . . then it's the only thing I could . . . save."

She faltered, emotion threatening to break loose, but her eyes were dry and determined.

"You'll be safe here," said and signed Yatho. "Both of you." She cast a warning glance at Kissen, who gave her a warning glance right back. Inara shook her head, vehement.

"I might be my mother's secret, but I'm still her daughter," she said. "I cannot sit here waiting for something else bad to happen."

Blenraden is a bad thing that happens, signed Telle, clearly picking up on those last words.

Skedi sat up in Inara's arms, lifting up his antlers and ears. His whiskers twitched. *We can't stay here forever,* he said, his god-voice piercing through all of their heads. *The longer we're together, the likelier it is that we're discovered. The choice is Blenraden now, or Blenraden later. If Inara says now, then I trust her. She deserves justice for what has happened to her, and I don't want to get in her way.*

Yatho's brows knitted. She was being swayed.

"Yath, no," said Kissen.

I did say she was like you, she said. Kissen frowned.

No, it's too rough a road, said Telle quickly to Yatho. *Let alone for a child who has lost everything.*

My love, signed Yatho, *we know what it's like to lose everything. Has that ever stopped us?*

Kissen looked at Inara, ignoring the fluttering of hands beside her. The girl met her eyes, steady, certain, and angry. Kissen saw her own self staring back. She sighed.

"Don't make me regret this, *liln.*"

CHAPTER TEN

Inara

"THERE'S A PILGRIM TRAIN LEAVING TODAY," SAID YATHO, RUSHING in as they broke their fast in the morning. Inara sipped the sweet black tea Telle had poured for her as Kissen yawned grumpily by the fire. She had slept on the long chair in front of it, stretched out like a great big cat. Inara had been given the godkiller's bed in a small room furnished with a chair, a patchwork quilt, and a broken writing tablet. Inara couldn't imagine not knowing how to write and read.

"How long have you been up for?" said Kissen blearily.

"Long enough." By the gleam in Yatho's eyes and the bags beneath them, Inara wondered if she had slept at all or if she had been working on the leg all night.

Kissen sighed. "What time?" she said. She had been plucking a chicken for dinner, having already eaten her breakfast of dried persimmons dipped in honey and salt, a treat that Telle had brought home the day before.

At high sun, Yatho answered the time question in sign, but the rest she spoke. "From the Fountain of Faces. They were meant to leave at week's end, but that slick-toothed bastard Canovan from the Queen's Way moved up the time."

I wish you wouldn't gamble with that fox, said Telle, reading her lips. *He's trouble.*

He's just . . . angry at the world, said Yatho, and to Kissen and Inara added, *he was married to the smith who made those little metal birds that sang.* Yatho's colours ran with purple sadness, and Inara suspected that the smith no longer made little birds.

"Isn't that the one who hates the king?" said Kissen. "He agreed to send a godkiller to Blenraden?"

Yatho grinned at her sheepishly. "He took some convincing. Actually, it was only when I mentioned that you were a veiga that he agreed. Maybe he wants you to owe him a favour."

"I've got a reputation to keep, Yatho."

"A reputation for being a grumpy git."

Telle flicked her hand in a crooked indication that they were being rude. Inara was trying not to be shocked at how they spoke to each other. Brash and rough, but not hurtful? Her mother hadn't prepared her for this. Her mother hadn't prepared her for anything.

Kissen shrugged and glanced at Inara. The godkiller was careful of her, as if afraid she would prod Inara the wrong way and she would shatter.

"Today's as good a day as any," she said.

Kissen didn't want Skedi near her family. What was she afraid of? That they would like him, or that he would like them? Her god was sitting on the table, the size of a newborn kitten, preening his antlers. Now he had been let out, he was bolder than he'd ever been. He didn't stop his work but spoke directly to Inara.

Let's go now, he said.

It was too soon, surely? Inara still felt gutted and empty from loss. Skedi, however, was keen to be going. He had caught the scent of freedom, and Inara tried to quash the faint stirring of fear that he wanted so badly to leave her. He was afraid of the veiga, did not want to spend too much longer in her company. In fact, if they joined a pilgrim train, at least they would be surrounded by people who loved their gods so much they would risk their own safety.

Why wait? Skedi added gently. *What good will it do?*

Inara gritted her teeth, reminding herself that Skedi wanting to be free was not a bad thing.

"I can leave today," she said, despite the coldness in her chest, and matched her words with her hands so Telle could see. Skedi flicked the edge of his wing excitedly.

Kissen nodded. "Yatho—"

Yatho was already heading for the door. "It's ready to put together," she said, "it's warming in the sun."

Telle stood and brushed her skirts down with a sigh. *I have some clothes that may fit you,* she said to Inara. There was a thread of tension across her forehead, the only thing showing her worry. *But you might need a thicker cloak. The nights will be cold on the pilgrims' trail; they won't stop at inns.*

Kissen levered herself out of her chair and stood, stretching her shortened leg out to the side, then forward, and leaning over to crack her lower back. She sat back down and unlaced her trousers. Inara found herself watching. The flesh of her leg had clearly been burned as well as cut through; the skin was mottled with scarring.

"Why are we joining a pilgrim train?" asked Inara. "Don't we need to stay hidden?"

Kissen pulled a fine cloth from her pocket and picked up the ointment box Yatho had left pointedly on the table. She rubbed the balm carefully into the knotted flesh before binding it with the cotton. "There's safety in numbers," she said. "And I'm not a deft hand at bribing guards. I've heard it takes fair coin to get past them into the city itself, and good relationships. I have neither."

She tucked the soft cotton neatly into itself to fix it in place, and then slid on another, thicker layer of fabric like a glove over the top.

"What happened to your leg?" Inara asked after a while.

"None of your business."

"What if we're attacked on the road by robbers or something? You said it was dangerous."

Kissen laughed. "If we're attacked on the road, you'll hide or run, and you'll do it snap-quick. Don't worry about me."

Inara had to admit, only when the boy had thrown the scythe into Kissen's leg had she realised that it was not made of flesh. The godkiller fought like a fiend. Still, Inara folded her arms. "You can't just give me orders," she said, trying to sound calm and certain, like her mother. "I'm putting my faith in you, Kissen; I need your faith too." That's what she would have said, wasn't it? Something firm, something right.

"Is that what your god says?" Kissen asked.

"He doesn't speak for me."

"Doesn't he." She said it lightly, but it was not a question.

"Like it or not, godkiller," said Skedi, "a pilgrim train is not going to let your kind join them freely. I hope you have a good lie. You two do not look alike enough to be mother and daughter."

Kissen almost choked. "How old do you think I am, god?" she asked, just as Telle came back in. *Telle, how old do I look?*

Telle deposited the clothes in her hands into Inara's arms. They were rough and heavy. *Is that a trick question?* she asked.

I am a god, said Skedi dismissively, *I do not understand human ages.*

Kissen looked at Inara, who had been hoping to avoid eye contact. With her weathered face, tattoos, and injuries, Inara thought Kissen could be about her mother's age. Kissen scowled at the panicked look on her face.

"Bah," said Kissen. "I am six and twenty . . ." *No one would believe that we're related anyway*, she added in sign. *You're clearly highborn, and I . . .* She gestured to herself to finish the sentence. Inara wasn't sure what to say. Yatho came back, wielding something that looked more like a work of art than a leg. Kissen turned to her. "Canovan will take a lie, right, Yatho?"

"Canovan will lie as soon as breathe if you pay him well," said Yatho, then repeated her words to Telle with her hands, who smirked and came over to the leg, delight in her eyes.

"What miracle have you worked now?" Kissen asked, distracted. She hopped out of her chair and used the table to aid her to the stool by Yatho. Yatho turned the limb in her hands, showing its workings. The fine metal beneath the platework sprang and moved, flexed almost, like muscle. Inara came closer. It looked like a bow inside, but when Yatho snapped the shin plate back into place, it had a leglike shape.

"It would be better if you didn't insist on it being twisted into your boot," said Yatho, passing Kissen the prosthesis.

"Better than being made the measure of," said Kissen, drawing up her boot. Out of it she took a tired-looking foot-shaped piece of wood and clipped in the new leg. Then, she detached the cap from the leg with a clunk and slotted the cap onto her knee, binding it there with a thick leather strap around her thigh and two thin strips of cloth that went underneath and around the mechanics. The top of this cap had thinner leather straps that she threaded up her trousers and buckled to the leather girdle she wore above her hips. They fixed at an angle that allowed her to move her leg comfortably, but gave assurance that the cap wouldn't fall off. It was clear that Yatho had also designed the girdle, if not made it.

"You mean by those people who think your legs are grass?"

"Those are the ones."

"You've enough of a reputation now for people to know you have one leg."

"Even more important, then, that they don't know which one."

Kissen reattached the leg to its knee joint, and then put her weight on it. She bent, twisted, testing its balance, and beaming. Inara had thought a person who killed gods would be somewhat monstrous themselves, but Kissen was like a kitten with a new toy.

Do you still get the aches? Telle asked, leaning on the table.

Kissen nodded, performing a couple of jumps.

"What are the aches?" asked Inara, signing a simple *What?* with a frown.

Kissen mimed a sword in her hand and thrust it forward experimentally, then squatted and sprang.

"You're a salt-haired genius, Yatho," said Kissen. She didn't need to sign that. Her joy gave it away. She was youthful for a moment, light-faced and buoyant. "It feels so . . ."

Balanced? said Yatho. *See how fine it is? I've been preparing it for weeks.*

Telle took Inara's attention. *She can still feel her leg hurting,* she said. *Her toes, ankle, shin, pain she can't touch.* She gestured to the scars on her own face. *The body doesn't forget what was once there.* She looked at Kissen, sadness in her face, then added in small gestures. *Nor do hearts.*

Inara looked at the clothes in her hands. She was still wearing the leggings and skirts she had left home in, with her wool jacket and buttoned waistcoat. The pearly buttons, her mother had said, had come from one of her grandmother's robes. They were special. They smelled of forest damp and horse, with just the faintest trace of smoke. But in between bad memories there were soapsuds and apple blossoms, wood polish, and the stone walls after spring rain.

"You could be my bodyguard," said Inara.

Kissen looked at her, affronted. Telle asked her to repeat herself.

Skedi sat up on his hind legs, proud that she had thought of her own lie.

Sometimes our servants would send their children away for a month or so, said Inara. *For training, they said. But I listened. What else had there been to do for a child and a god, but to creep and spy and learn? They sent them away for blessings. We could tell the pilgrims that's why I'm there, for a blessing.*

"I'm not a bodyguard," said Kissen, her hands signing *No,* with more than a speck of petulance.

"Then you may as well tell all the pilgrims that you're there to kill their gods," said Inara, with the haughty voice Tethis hadn't liked. Yatho laughed.

"You have too much knowing to you to be a noble kid," said Kissen suspiciously.

She's smart, said Skedi, flicking one large ear, then added boldly, *smarter than most humans I've met.*

Inara eyed him. It was nice to have him out in the open, but this was not the moment to be needling the godkiller with insults. He was hare-sized now, larger than he had been moments before.

Inara is never going to pass as a commoner, said Yatho, before Kissen had decided she had been slighted. *As soon as she opens her mouth you're had.*

I can convince them of most lies, said Skedi boldly. *If you are too proud to be a bodyguard it will be harder, and I would need help. A piece of hair, perhaps, or . . .*

"If you're suggesting we make you an offering, you are overstepping your bounds," said Yatho before Kissen could. Skedi shrank as the mood in the room changed. *You are in this house because my wife and I offer refuge to lost children. This does not mean we hold sympathy with your kind.* Inara looked at Telle, whose face had closed. She had thought that their fair genial treatment of both of them belied a softness for gods that Kissen did not have.

I need refuge, said Skedi.

You are housed within the body of a little girl, said Telle, her gestures quick and firm. *She has no say in being bound to you.*

I am bound too! said Skedi.

"It isn't his fault," said Inara.

That god could be centuries old, said Telle. *Intentionally or not, remembered or not, he is using you as a shield. We have all of us seen damage done by gods.*

Inara was pained, and surprised. Kissen's family had shown her care and comfort, but for Skedi she knew now it had been no more than tolerance.

Telle flicked her hand to lighten the mood. *But the child is right, many families likely send their children to be blessed by gods still living. Few try Blenraden, but the very pious might. Inara could be a master trader's daughter.*

Kissen sighed and rolled her eyes. "I wonder if the King of Broken Shrines knows about these little rebellions," she said.

"The king probably has bigger things to worry about," said Yatho. "Like manors mysteriously burning down, or how his laws are splitting Middren down into parts: the faithful and the fearful."

You think there's trouble brewing? said Kissen, her movements sharp.

Yatho shrugged. *We keep our heads down,* she said, her colours gloomy. *But the Craiers' home burning does not give much solace . . .*

Telle cleared her throat and gave a pointed glance in Inara's direction. *This is not for children,* she said.

Why were they speaking about trouble? Every one of the Houses had pledged allegiance to King Arren in the days after the war. Inara's mother too. She had joined his grand tour back to Sakre by road, mantled with victory. Inara remembered the shine of her mother's robes, the preparations of the Craier carriage, repainted and garlanded with ivy, jasmine, and meadowsweet.

Kissen rubbed her chin. *I will be a bodyguard,* she said to Inara. *But when you start giving me orders, you make your own way to Blenraden.*

Telle shook her head. *You will not abandon her.*

It was a joke, Kissen signed back.

This isn't like when you rescued us and Maimee's children. You need to keep your temper managed. She sighed and came to Kissen. *I've got to go to work. Kissen, you have to promise.*

They'll be fine, said Yatho.

"Promise," said Telle out loud, framing the words carefully, her voice husky. "Promise me you won't leave her."

Kissen could have taken offence. She did shake her head a little, but then put a hand on Telle's before placing it on her own chest. "I promise," she said clearly, "on the life my father gave me, that I will not leave Inara Craier to the wilds." And then with a smirk, "No matter how much I might want to."

Within an hour Yatho was taking them back outside Lesscia's walls for supplies. She kept Inara entertained, pointing out little things she liked: the printmaker who made beautiful sheets of paper that caught the light, the bookbinder who had interesting tools from Curliu, the shop that sold fine Bridhid ore and anti-god charms. Skedi hid in a satchel that Yatho had given Inara. He hadn't spoken much since they'd left the house, not even to her. His long ears were flat to his back, and he had kept to the size of a mouse, unmoving as a stone. Sulking. Inara put her hand inside the bag and gently stroked his antlers, trying to cheer him.

Outside the city, they stopped at a Talician store that Kissen knew. Its owner, whose fair skin had the tough, worn quality of well-used leather, did not exactly smile to see her, but held out his hand for a wrist-clasp. She spoke to him briefly in rusty Talic, which Inara's tutor, Erman, had taught her to recognise. He turned to look Inara up and down. Kissen's accent was thick, as was his reply. Inara could not discern many words, only *soft*.

He went to his covered cart and rummaged inside, pulling out a thick bundle of cloth that he opened to reveal a buttoned cloak not unlike Kissen's. Laying it on the boards of his stall, he took the measure of Inara with a thumb and hacked a good two spans off the bottom, then lit a little brazier and ran it along the jagged hem. The hem sizzled as the flame singed the stray threads closed. Once he was finished, Inara watched him hand the cut-off pieces and cloak over to Kissen, who passed the bundle to Inara before giving the man a whole silver ingot. He rattled it against the few teeth he had and pocketed it, his colours grey and satisfied.

"*Telic haar*," he said to Kissen. *Well met*. And sat back down on his stool.

Inara eyed the bundle suspiciously. She could have smelled it from six strides away, but up close it made her eyes water: sheep and burning oil.

"I have a travelling cloak," said Inara, thumbing her own as they walked away. She was wearing Telle's cotton trousers, rolled up almost half their length again, over her leggings and under her skirts. Her quilted jacket was in Legs's saddlebags, but she wore her waistcoat with the special buttons. She had considered taking it off, putting it somewhere safe, but found she couldn't.

"That'll soak through in the span of a night," said Kissen. "Whoever told you it was for travelling was pulling your leg. Give it to Yatho."

Her mother had told her it was for travelling, after weeks of Inara pestering to go to Sakre with her. Lady Craier always came back with papers, maps and plans, and never let Inara look at them. She had bought her the cloak, Inara now realised, to appease her. She'd never intended to take her daughter to court.

"I don't want to," said Inara, wishing her mother were there to contradict Kissen. Lady Craier would be able to put the veiga in her place.

"I'll keep it for you," said Yatho, "but she's right. Nothing like Talician waxwool. You'll be happy for it in the cold, wet nights, and you'd regret carrying two cloaks; Legs can only bear so much."

"It stinks."

"You'll get used to it," said Kissen. "You won't be coming if you're not dressed for it."

Inara fingered the cloth of her cloak. Kissen might be right, she was feeling a little chilled already and they hadn't been outside long. She sighed, and took off her cloak, handing it to Yatho, who folded it carefully onto her lap. She wasn't sure she would get used to it. The Talician waxwool was much heavier on her shoulders, and the cloth rough.

They quickly picked up everything they needed from the market: hard sheep cheeses inset with fruits and pistachios, dried pulses, wrinkled chestnuts and fungi, and biscuits for the bag. Kissen added some well-wrapped dried meat and a few choice seasonal vegetables that would stand a bit of bumping around. Legs was calm in the market, allowing his saddlebags to be filled and only occasionally nosing at the stalls. Kissen bought him some apples and honey oats in exchange for the cut-offs from Inara's cloak. Inara supposed it would be enough material for a pair of horrible smelly mittens.

Back inside the city, it was louder in the daytime, particularly as they passed squares and open-fronted stores. People clustered in seemingly random places, argued, rattled words and expensive paper at one another in a multitude of languages. Inara picked out some of the others Erman had taught her: Irisian, Talic, Beltish, and even southeastern Harisi, from where his father had been born.

They followed the paths to the western side of the city, where they entered a huge square, big enough to grow an orchard or run horses. It was a riot of people, their colours, their moods, their arguments. Inara breathed in, trying not to be overwhelmed.

There were two fountains. The larger had a tall stone pillar carved with images of the battles of Blenraden beneath a rising sun, a stag's head in its shadow. The sign of the king.

The Fountain of Faces was smaller, drab in comparison. Perhaps it once had been grand, but it was a faded thing now. Water burst clean and high from a hacked-off pillar barely taller than Inara. The stone was carved with swirls and markings that she distantly recognised, as well as a hundred faces. Some had eyes closed, while others had open gazes of stone. A group of travellers congregated at its edges, as well as a cluster of youths, scarcely older than herself, all in light grey robes being lectured by a harassed archivist in darker robes like those Telle had been wearing.

On the other side of the fountain an ass was taking a long drink from the pool, swishing its tail at imaginary flies. A man sat beside it in a shirt buttoned up to the neck, with a high collar. He spat into the water, but then cupped his hands and drank from it a moment later.

"Ho, Canovan," said Yatho. The man looked up and the ass startled and moved away. Canovan swallowed the water in his mouth and touched his head in greeting. "Your arm is bleeding."

Canovan looked at his arm in surprise. A small line of blood had leaked through the material of his shirt. "Some glass, probably," he said. He had smiled lightly when he saw Yatho, but the expression dropped at Kissen and Inara. He had an intense, angry face, and hard eyes.

"You didn't say there was a kid." His colours were muted, almost as much as Kissen's, but there were so many, running close to the surface like fish in a river. Inara couldn't make them out.

"I said two," said Yatho. "Is that a problem?" Canovan wiped his mouth, looked at the sky, then the ground, then at Kissen. Inara found herself shrinking closer to the godkiller.

"No," he said at last.

"A horse?" Another man joined him, his brown-and-grey beard flapping in the breeze, revealing a collection of shining pewter coins on strings beneath it. He was practically bubbling with irritation, which Inara could see floating around his shoulders in flashes of peach. "No. That is not coming. A gods-cursed *horse?* Two changes to our agreement in less than a day, Canovan. Can I remind you that you owe *me* money? I don't see why I am doing you these favours."

"I didn't realise horses were illegal," said Kissen with a crooked smile.

Inara snorted and the pilgrim drew himself up tall, the way Skedi grew in size when he was feeling prideful.

"Cool your feathers, Jon," said Canovan to the bearded man, clapping him just a touch too hard on the back. "This is Yatho—you must have heard of her worksmithing? I've known her since she was a girl; she used to follow my wife around like a shadow."

Yatho gave Canovan a sympathetic smile and put on her brakes. "This is my client's daughter, Tethis," she said, gesturing to Inara. They had agreed on false names, and Inara had wanted to keep some small thing from home. "My friend Enna here is her bodyguard," Yatho added. Kissen nodded a greeting.

Inara could hear Skedi whispering at the edge of her mind, pressing his will into Yatho's lie; sulking aside, he didn't want to be caught. Jon's annoyance dissipated.

"More people, more cut," he muttered, resigned. "And this time, I expect it in full."

"We'll talk about it when you're back," said Canovan shortly. He nodded at Yatho.

"I owe you that new sign for this," said Yatho. Canovan's mouth twitched and he looked over the other pilgrims. Inara followed his eyes as they paused for a moment on a tall man with a longsword on his back. As if coming to a decision, Canovan straightened up and arranged his face into a more pleasant expression.

"What's done is done," he said. "You owe me no favours, Yatho."

Yatho reached out for Kissen's arm and squeezed. Not as affectionately as she had greeted her, but they had to keep the lie. Friends, not family. "Take care," she said, then lowered her voice. "And spit on Maimee's doorstep for me. Don't tell Telle."

Kissen grinned and patted her hand. "Anything for you."

"Come home soon. We'll take care of your coin for you."

"Don't worry about me, I always come home eventually."

Yatho reached out for Inara, who took her hand. Yatho's palm was wrought with old blisters, her nails either chipped or missing outright. "Good luck," she said. "We're always stronger than people think."

Inara squeezed her hand tight. "Thank you," she said. "You and Telle. I won't forget."

"Don't let 'Enna' prickle you; she is softer than she pretends."

Inara didn't believe her but smiled. Yatho gave one last squeeze, winked at Kissen, then left to rejoin her work and her furnaces.

Inara didn't like seeing her go. She and Kissen would tolerate each other till they separated, she knew that much and it was enough. Then Inara would go to Sakre, find some way to claim her lands and avenge her House and mother. If only Yatho and Telle could come with them. That would be easier, more companionable.

Inara cast her eyes instead over their group, all waiting with varying degrees of patience. They looked kindly enough; three hardy-looking old women had already smiled at her. A young man with red hair and a strangely shaped bag was humming to himself as he gazed at the fountain, and beside him were an anxious fellow and a woman who were holding hands, their nerves a yolky orange shimmer shared between them. The one Canovan had watched was standing apart from the rest. He cast his eyes over Inara, then Kissen. His emotions moved slowly, but there was something wary in the way he studied the others. Occasionally his colours rippled gold, then blue. Inara wasn't sure what they meant.

"Gather," said Jon, gesturing imperiously at them all to come closer as he lowered his voice. Canovan stepped back, watching, his work clearly finished. He turned, and Inara saw lines of ink peeking out from beneath his shirt, thick and dark, in shapes that were faintly familiar. But as the others closed in about her, she lost sight of them.

"Our aim is to reach Haar Hill by sundown," said Jon. "If anyone asks, we are travelling musicians with a couple of old washers for our clothes and food." He glanced at the older women, one of whom tutted with annoyance. "That will keep us safe from knights, at least," he added pointedly.

"You mean House Yether guards?" said the man with the sword. Jon rolled his eyes.

"No, I'm talking about the king's patrols." He thumbed the pewter badges beneath his beard, then tucked them away inside his jacket. "There are many on the roads watching for pilgrims. Least they'd give us is a foot whipping and time in the clink."

Inara winced. Foot whipping didn't sound nice.

"I have rules," Jon added.

"Oh, good," muttered one of the old women, who received an elbow from her companion. "Ow, Svenka," she hissed at her.

"This is important," said the young man who had been humming. He looked as nervous as Inara felt.

"Should we be discussing this in the open?" said another of the old women.

Jon waited, scowling, until they were quiet.

"No praying unless I say so. No chitchat with anyone, and don't buy shit. You don't know who is planted there by the king. Fill your water at every stop I tell you; not all the streams are safe. If you fall sick, we will leave you. If you are caught, we will leave you. If you're mugged and injured, we will leave you. No bad-mouthing." He glared at Kissen, who had clearly already pissed him off. She was good at that, Inara thought. Kissen gave him a bright smile as she scratched Legs's nose, flashing gold from one of her canines. "No crying"—he frowned at Inara—"and no side tracks." He narrowed his eyes at the old woman who had muttered at his rules. "If we lose you, we leave you, so keep pace or go home."

"Yes, my liege," Kissen muttered, and Inara clicked her tongue. Still, her comment attracted a slight chuckle from the man with the sword, who didn't follow as the others broke and moved away from the fountain but stayed and gave Kissen a longer glance. She stared right back, assessing him as he did her. To Inara's surprise, Kissen grinned.

"What are you, pretty-boy?" she said. "Some sort of knight?"

The man blinked, his colours rippling. "I am a baker," he said coldly, finally turning to follow Jon.

"Yeah," said Kissen, "and I'm a grapefruit."

"Can't you be nice, *Enna?*" said Inara, pointedly using her false name. "It was your idea to join these people."

"I am who I am," said Kissen, falling into step behind the train. She watched the back of the man she had called a knight. His shoulders were straight, his stride sure and confident.

Be careful of that one, said Skedi. *He carries lies.*

CHAPTER ELEVEN

Elogast

ELOGAST DID NOT CARE ABOUT THE LAST-MINUTE ADDITIONS to their train, no matter how heavily armed or laden they were, nor the white scar on the woman's face, or what the tattoos on her chest said. He had caught a glimpse of the spiral of ink that spread out above the top of the Talician woman's cuirass, just below her throat, curled and loose. He had spent long enough in the army to know a swear word when he saw one, and this one said *fuck you* in Talic.

Elo did care that the sun was a stride past its peak by the time they had started on their way.

He also cared that the young girl, Tethis, looked wealthy and soft-footed. Under a thick Talician cloak she wore a neatly embroidered waistcoat with matching buttons. If she slowed them down she'd better be going on that horse. This was no journey for a little one.

A strange relationship, too, between a highborn girl and her bodyguard. If noble families were rebelling in small ways, sending their children on dangerous roads for blessings, it was another sign of unrest. Elo felt guilty he had put his head in the sand in Estfjor, in his bakery. The girl could not be more than twelve. It wasn't right that she would be sent on such a journey with a crude guard who, it was clear, had little respect for her, or anyone.

It was not his business. As long as they weren't in his way, he wouldn't stand in theirs.

They followed the inner-city canals to the northern gate, which opened onto the Pilgrims' Road, now renamed the March by Arren. They made it through with little incident, in twos and threes guided by Jon, each telling the story he had given to them, and regrouped on the other side. Then for the first hour, they walked at pace, barely acknowledging one another as they hurried through the outermarket. It seemed a long while before the scraggle of houses that marked the growing boundaries of Lesscia dwindled into farmland.

There were many on the road besides them. Merchants mostly, leading trains of ponies and carts, but Elo spotted some smaller traders, wandering cobblers here and there, and a shepherd or two moving their sheep from pasture to pasture. A couple of surly-looking men carrying heavy sticks followed their group for a while, looking for someone to mug, perhaps, but fell back when they realised how many of them there were, and that two of them had swords.

"What brings you on this journey, friend?" The man from the couple who had a warm, brown face beneath a black beard, fell into step with Elo, clearly keen to create some companionship between them. Likely he had noticed the men with sticks leave when they spotted Elo's blade. "What should I call you?"

"Elo." He didn't answer the first question.

"I'm Berrick," the fellow said. "And this is Batseder, my wife." He said it proudly. Batseder, who had the almond-dark skin of southern Middren where the bloodlines of the Trade Sea had mixed for centuries, nodded and shifted her pack about. They did not look like types that had taken often to road.

"We're here for a fertility blessing," he said, looking around cautiously, but no one paid them a mote of attention. "First time out of Yether lands."

"I'm sure that's very common," said Elogast. He wasn't particularly certain he wanted to be making new friends. He had enough to worry about.

"Oh, we mean to have it removed," said Berrick. "Batseder's parents had her blessed with it as a baby, but now the midwife god is dead."

"Berrick," Batseder warned, "don't give our troubles to the poor man."

Berrick shrugged, looking more than happy to be scolded.

"You know I can't let you take the woman's gamble," he said, adding to Elo, "That's what my mother called it. My cousin died in birth, and Batseder's sister who had the same blessing."

Batseder sighed bitterly. "I wonder if the king ever thought of us women before he turned on the midwife god."

"Arren didn't kill Aia," said Elo quietly, not thinking before he leapt to Arren's defence. Batseder stared at him, but the humming lad who had been gawping at the Fountain of Faces piped up.

"The baker is correct," he said. Mikle was his name, Elo remembered. "The god of war killed Aia as revenge for the king turning on him." He smoothed his hair back proudly. "I am a scholar, you see. We study the songs of Blenraden."

"Huh," said Batseder, not appearing at all interested.

"Well, if you're so knowing of Blenraden's songs," said Berrick, pulling a wrapped cloth packet out of his pocket, "then why are you going? You think you can outsing the hundred bards before you?"

Mikle's ears went red and he hurried ahead. There was a strange shape to his pack that Elo now identified as a harp. He warmed a bit to Berrick, who was more astute than he appeared.

"Would you like one?" asked Berrick, proffering the wrapped cloth, which had a cluster of plump white dumplings in it.

Elo warmed further.

"Please," he said, picking up one of the dumplings, glad to have the feel of bread in his hand. It centred him. He looked at the gift; it was nicely folded and had stuffing inside.

He took a bite, and tried not to wince at the clumpy stickiness of the dough. Disappointing, though the filling, of some kind of sage and mushroom, was delicious.

"Not bad, eh?" said Berrick, giving one to Batseder. "I'm a cobbler, not a baker, but I like to try my hand."

"It's good," Elo said, feigning enthusiasm. It was convincing enough for both Batseder and Berrick to beam at him appreciatively.

A thunder of hooves on the road startled them. Everyone about them shrank down and to the side, making way for two knights wearing blue and gold, not Yether yellow, coming from Lesscia's direction.

"Move! Move!" they yelled, scattering people as they stamped past. A pedlar on the road with a trayful of pewter coins like Jon's shrieked as he saw them, making a break for it. But the knights bore down on him, grabbed him by the collar, and threw him to the ground. One of them dismounted, then kicked him twice for good measure.

"Selling pilgrim badges on the road?" the knight kicking him snarled, while the other held his horse. "You think King Arren would accept this? You think you can shame your king?"

Jon's group clustered into a huddle. Jon tucked his beard over his own badges, symbols of his every pilgrimage. He was too stubborn to take them off, clearly.

The pedlar was sobbing, blood on his teeth. Elo couldn't help it. They were using Arren's name as a bludgeon. That wasn't right. He put a hand on his sword, feeling the lion's head on the pommel in his palm.

"I wouldn't do that if I were you," muttered the red-haired woman with the scar and the horse. "Whatever honourable shit is in your head, spit it out or we're all fucked."

She shouldered past, pulling the horse and the girl on it. Elo got a better look at the scar on her face: the web of white was writing in script shaped like curves and eddies. A curse. A dead curse. He had seen curses up close, and boons, like the writing on Arren's chest: this was the mark of a god.

Elo felt an ache crawl down his back and tighten his stomach. Anyone could be cursed, he told himself. It might be nothing. But there was something in the way she held herself, a certainty that was somehow familiar. She was a fighter, perhaps even an ex-soldier or some kind of mercenary. With a curse like that she might even be a godkiller.

But why would a veiga be going to the lost city of shrines?

Whoever she was, she was right. He took his hand off the pommel and put it in his pocket, hiding the tremor of his fingers as he walked away from the pedlar's cries.

As the farms around them turned to woods, Jon took them off the road. Drizzle blown through the trees by a westerly wind soon dampened them, but it felt safer in the dark of the woods than on the exposed road where any knight might reappear to hunt them. It shamed Elo that such thoughts occurred to him. He followed Jon, who led the way into the forest seemingly by memory alone. The only indications that they were heading right were small cairns topped with little figurines. Some were for the dead god of safe haven, his faithful still trying to bring him back with love. Others were for gods of the ways, of luck, a god of a stream, or even one for a god of cobblers on which Berrick placed the last of his dumplings as he passed. Here on the quiet ways, shrines were still intact.

They reached Haar Hill just before sundown. The hill itself was a flat-topped mound that Jon informed them they were camping beneath. Even from below Elo could still see the last stones of ruins at the top, their shadows lengthening as the light dimmed. By the look of them, they had been burned and abandoned long ago.

A deep stream rushed past them at the hill's foot, likely a tributary to the river Daes. There was a tiny shrine there too, a house made from ivy, tied with ribbons for some little god of the hill.

The three old women, who by now he had learned were Svenka, Haoirse, and Poline, creaked to a halt beneath the hill's shelter, and Berrick broke off to help them. Jon went to pluck up some stones scattered near the beribboned shrine. "We can light a fire," he said. "I've not had a mugging here for a while, and knights are more interested in easy pickings."

"How reassuring," Haoirse muttered under her breath.

"Patrols still might come," continued Jon, ignoring her, "knocking down the shrines, looking for people like us, so no loud noises, no singing. We're far from the wilds yet." He started muttering as he laid the stones down in a circle, marking each one with a different symbol using a stick of charcoal from his pocket. A protection charm. Elo glanced at the bodyguard, but all she did was roll her eyes.

The girl, Tethis, flopped down on the damp ground with a grumble. The sun broke through the clouds near the horizon, casting them in pale gold.

Poline went to the water and peered in. "Fish for supper," she said after a moment. "If we all chip in."

"I'll get wood," said Elo. There wouldn't be much time till they lost the light entirely. Mikle had sat by the stream and extracted the harp from his bag. He was plucking the strings and singing under his breath.

"I'll help," said Enna, stomping back up the bank to Elo from where she had been watering her horse. "Tethis, help the others with the fish."

"But—"

"Or you can scrabble for kindling."

Tethis scowled and waved her away. Now, that was a noble's gesture.

"I'll do it!" Berrick exclaimed cheerily and followed the veiga up the path, tripping on her heels. "What will you need for kindling?"

"Pine roots," said Enna brusquely.

"Is that a tattoo on your face? What does it mean?"

"It means leave me alone," said Enna in an ending tone, turning her stride away from him. Berrick shrugged, but Elo could tell he was a little hurt.

"Two will be enough, Berrick," said Elo. "Why don't you clear a place for it with Mikle?" The boy with the harp looked up sheepishly.

Elo followed Enna, who was digging about the bottom of a pine tree using a knife. Clouds were now closing over the setting sun, and the water on the trees and bushes glittered with the narrowing of the light. Her knife flashed as she pulled out a root, and he saw its dull metal: briddite.

"That's an interesting dagger," he said as she stood up again, stamping the earth back down over the roots. She sheathed her knife and counted the ones she'd pulled, then lifted her eyebrow at him.

"That's an interesting fuck you give about it," she said. He could see he wasn't going to get anywhere with her.

"Why did you stop me, with the patrol?" he said.

"From starting a riot when we're trying not to be noticed?" she said sarcastically. "I wonder."

Elo laughed. "Fair," he said. He, too, had seen a spat between knights turn into an all-out brawl when tensions were high, but this was peacetime.

"Is it always like that these days?" he asked. "Knights attacking people on the road?"

"What cave have you been hiding in?" she said, looking around. Elo winced. "Now are you going to help find some wood or not?"

She took his hand and dumped the roots she had gathered in it. He could smell the pine sap mixed with her sweat, and a thrill of anticipation stirred him. Anticipation of what, he wasn't sure. It was like when the scent of bread changed in the oven, just as it began to crisp.

"What are you looking at?" she said. "Shift yourself."

Elo gestured into the shadows and evening sunlight. "After you."

As they came back to camp with arms of the driest wood they could find, Berrick was already coaxing life out of a twist of moss and dried leaves with Batseder helping guard the tinder from the breeze. Elo added the pine roots, and they crackled as they caught, smelling wonderful. Two of the old women, Poline and Haoirse, were teaching the little girl how to tickle trout in the stream in the last of the light while their companion, Svenka, stood on the bank, gutting one they had already caught. Haoirse was right out in the water, her skirts bound up to her waist. It was nice, companionable. Elo let himself relax, just a little.

A whoop flew up from the bank as Poline tossed a fish out of the water and into Svenka's hands. The young girl was laughing. It was the first time Elo had seen her smile. He didn't know much about children, but he knew they weren't generally as serious as Tethis. She had hung her satchel on the horse's saddle, but Elo noticed she glanced over to it every now and then.

"Could you please keep quiet?" snapped Jon, who was sitting within his circle of stones.

"Do you want fish or don't you?" said Haoirse defensively. Jon tutted as Svenka slit open the second trout and spilled its guts into the stream.

Elo found a flat stone and placed it by the fire, rolling out his preparation mat on it and dusting it with the flour he had brought. No time for rising bread today; he would make quick flatbreads. They had been a staple of his and Arren's. When Arren had been forced to take charge, half of Bethine's command were dead, and most of the rest had run. Elo and Arren had taken to planning everything: the recruitment, the food supplies, the negotiations with gods to try to end the bloody feud Arren had inherited. The evenings, whenever quiet, were spent with bread. They needed those simple pleasures, the moments of calm between the blood and strategising. Even before the final battle, after Elo said he was leaving, they had broken bread together before turning on the god of war. Elo clenched his jaw at the memory.

Berrick and Batseder were now preparing the fish with herbs from their own bags, and Mikle was scribbling something in a leather binder of paper, his eyes alight and fingers twitching as if he were playing his harp. It seemed likely to be a good supper. Elo half wished Arren were there. He would enjoy it.

The sharp shadows on the hill faded into gloom, and the pale light turned spring-silver and dusky. The sun had set.

It took Elo a moment to realise there was something wrong. The lapping of the water was louder, and the twisting of the trees in the evening wind: the birds had fled or fallen silent. Underneath the scent of smoke, Elo caught the traces of something dark and deep. Like blood and moss. A shiver passed over him. He saw the "bodyguard" stand; she was casting around like a hound on a scent. Was Enna even her real name? Elo's hand went to his sword.

He saw it first. A sliding, moving darkness in the deep of the trees. It was too low to be a human— the size of a large dog, or wolf.

"What is it? Knights? Thieves?" Jon asked, crouching with Elo within the circle he had made of stones. They were the only two inside it. Batseder, who had just stepped beyond it, looked up, startled.

"I don't know," said Elo. "Stay calm."

Elo noticed that Enna had shifted towards the stream and her ward, who was still catching fish with Poline and Haoirse. "Tethis, stay still," she said.

The shadow in the trees slid out towards Elo and the ring of stones. Liquid darkness; then Elo saw its teeth. Bright broken bones were twisted into a wide jaw, set back in its head. The thing had tiny marsh-lights for eyes, like embers, but mouthed at the air as if it could taste its quarry.

Mikle yelped, clutching his harp, frozen in place.

"Batseder," hissed Berrick as the creature cast about as if looking for something, "get back in the circle." His wife ignored him, instead shifting to his side and balling her fists. Fists wouldn't help. Elo put his hand on his sword. Only briddite could stop a thing of the gods.

CHAPTER TWELVE

Kissen

IT WASN'T A GOD, BUT IT HAD BEEN SUMMONED BY ONE. JUDGING by the smell, it belonged to something half-wild at least, a god of the woodland or of marshes. An old god, most likely, to have the power to call up a shadow demon. But why here, and who was it after? Inara was behind her, climbing out of the water with the women. Kissen moved to protect her, as she had promised. Shit, and her little godling too. What was it Telle had said? If it died, the girl might follow him.

The beast charged at the ring of stones that Elo and Jon stood within, then rebounded as Jon's rocks bent inwards.

Inara shrieked and ran for her satchel. Kissen was closer; she grabbed it and Inara and yanked them both away from the creature as it rolled upright. The beast regained its feet and launched itself at the nearest thing to it: Mikle, who had frozen in shock.

"Run!" cried Kissen, but it was too late. The summoning had found prey.

Its shadow almost swallowed Mikle as its teeth sank into the boy's neck and shoulder, cutting short his scream and tossing him like a rag. Kissen raged forward, drawing her briddite longsword and slicing clean through the beast's muzzle. The creature shrieked back, leaving its bone-teeth in the lad.

The baker, Elo, drew his own sword as the beast's mouth re-formed and finished it with one strike through its middle. Out spilled white smoke, heavy and hitting the ground. The creature hissed and disintegrated, its teeth peeling off and dropping from its body before crumbling into pale ash.

That sword was briddite. Kissen and the knight eyed each other. He knew what she was, as she did him. A knight and a veiga follow a pilgrim trail and are attacked by gods-made monsters. It sounded like the start of a joke, except no one was laughing.

Luckily, he kept his mouth shut. He sheathed his blade and dropped to his knees by the boy. Mikle was convulsing and gulping, blood pouring from the tear in his throat and shoulder. Elo pressed his hands to it.

"Shit," hissed Kissen, then pointed at Inara. "Stay there." Inara gulped, and Kissen went to kneel beside Elo and hold Mikle still, so he could get a better grasp on his wound. The boy was crying, though he couldn't speak. "Is anyone a healer?"

They both knew it was too late. Elo met her eyes and a spark of acknowledgment passed between them. How many people had he held as the life leached out of them? For Kissen, it was too many.

Most of their group was frozen, horrified. Inara had her hands tight around her satchel with the god in it, her eyes wide with fear.

"I am a healer." Haoirse had finally got up the stream's bank with Svenka's help. She came running over, untucking her green skirts from her belt. She used them to replace Elo's hands, pressing the cloth to Mikle's neck to staunch the blood. The material quickly soaked through, turning dark. Mikle stared at her, struggling to breathe, trying to speak, but sputtering instead. Gods, all any of them could hear were his fading breaths. Haoirse's lips flattened as the blood showed no signs of stopping. Her shoulders fell, and she put a hand to Mikle's hair.

"It's all right, lad," she said as he shook. Her tone was warm, motherly. "Hush now, it's all right to rest."

Mikle whimpered. He was still trembling, his eyes unfocussed.

"My father . . ." he tried. "Tell my father . . ." Inara came closer, looking like she wanted to help.

"Stay back," Kissen said forcefully, her voice tight. She didn't want the girl to see this. Batseder came forward to pull the girl away, but Inara snatched her arm back, stifled a sob, then ran instead to Legs. She pressed her face to the horse's neck and he let her.

Mikle stopped shaking, unable to get his words out. His choking for air faded as Haoirse soothed him. Kissen saw that blood had soaked into the ground, into the knees of Elo's trews, the edges of his shirt. Finally, it stopped.

Batseder and Berrick were clinging to each other. Poline was still in the river, holding Svenka's hand. Jon had pissed himself.

"Does . . . anyone know his father?" asked Batseder, looking to Jon. He shook his head mutely.

Kissen stood and kicked at the ash the creature had left. She watched Elo pick up the boy's harp, his soiled fingers leaving marks on the wood. Two strings had snapped, the wood split.

Bloody gods. As always, they charged into a perfectly decent life and broke it apart. Kissen looked over at Inara, quietly sobbing into her horse's mane, and spotted the twitch of her god's ear as it ducked its head back into the bag. Gods were chaos made into shape. And these pilgrims, that boy, still wanted to piss around and ask them for favours, the knight included. She kicked at the ash a bit more, but the summoning had left nothing behind.

Elo put the harp down on Mikle's chest.

"What was that?" said Haoirse at last, standing up to break the silence. She went to the water to wash the blood from her hands and skirts. Her eyes were dry, but Poline was weeping.

"A thing of gods," said Jon in a whisper. He was clutching his pewter necklace charms, little treasures from a lifetime of pilgrimages, as if they would help him.

"It was a shadow demon," said Kissen. "A beast made by a wild god. Didn't think there were many of those left strong enough to summon something." She glanced at Elo, then looked at Jon. "Pissed anyone off recently, Jon?"

Jon swallowed. "N-no," he said. "I wouldn't still be doing this if my pilgrims did not make it home." His grasp of command had gone. He was staring at Mikle's body. His charge. Dead. His eyes snapped back up to Kissen. "What do you know about it, anyway, *bodyguard?*" His tone rang with suspicion.

Kissen hesitated, but to her surprise, Inara cut in, her voice shaking. "Leave her alone." She had stood back from Legs, her face damp but determined. "*My* bodyguard just helped save us. You think my father would send me for blessing with someone who knew nothing of gods?" Kissen was impressed. Then she focussed: behind Inara's words, she could *feel* her little rabbit using his magic to help them believe her, like cold breath on her skin. She scowled.

"You cut them," Jon persisted. "Your swords." He glared at Kissen and then turned it on the knight. "They're briddite. Made to kill gods."

Fear passed over Elo's face, quickly replaced by a charming smile. "It makes sense to carry a briddite sword these days," he said, clearly trying to placate Jon. "The roads are dangerous."

Kissen threw him a side glance she saw him catch. But she had her own problems that had nothing to do with this "Elo." Beasts like that didn't appear without reason; something had to summon them. Something that would still be alive. Why would it come for their small group? Curses weren't commonplace; the target would have had to be near a god.

Kissen glanced at Inara, who had her hand inside the satchel. A girl and a god of lies. White lies or no. Perhaps there was more to the mystery of the Craier manor fire than even the girl knew. What if destruction was following them?

"Enough," said Poline. "Stop fighting. A poor boy was killed." She was shivering from being in the water too long.

Kissen sighed. "The dead are dead," she said. "We should move on while we still have life left in our feet." The closer they got to splitting the girl and the god, the happier she'd be.

"Speak for yourself," said Svenka.

Jon was staring into the trees, waiting for shadows to move. For a man who had made so many pilgrimages, he did not seem at all comfortable with seeing a god's summoning.

"We should bury him," said Elo. "He deserves that much." He came closer to Kissen. "They're tired and cold. They won't make it travelling through the night."

Kissen scoffed. Where had this noble bastard been unearthed from? Most knights she had the displeasure of meeting were arseholes who liked thuggery or arseholes who worshipped their king beyond all sense and reason. She was about to argue, but then Inara spoke.

"Enna . . . please . . ." she said. "Can we bury him?"

Kissen sighed. The girl was shaken to her core, had lost her mother, and now had seen another death. What would Telle do?

"Fine, please yourselves," she said.

"Jon," said Elo abruptly, "remake the stone circle. It worked well. Poline, find a good space for the boy. Batseder, Berrick, the ground will be too hard to dig; collect the river stones for a cairn. Enna . . ."

It took Kissen a moment to remember her false name. That man was barking commands like he was born to it. "Help me with the body," he said, and held her gaze. "We *pilgrims* should stick together."

Kissen narrowed her eyes at him. They had the measure of each other now. All she had to do was keep his attention on her so he didn't get suspicious of Inara. "Sure. Would be a shame to run into any more monsters out there. Or knights." She flashed him a smile. "Always the worst sources of trouble."

CHAPTER THIRTEEN

Skediceth

SKEDI COULD FEEL THE WETNESS OF THE NEXT MORNING pressing down on his bag as the little group of humans gathered themselves and set off.

The moon had long risen by the time they'd slept the night before, wincing to the ground within Jon's new circle of stones. Inara had fallen into the sleep of exhaustion, clutching Skedi tight within his satchel, after helping bury the boy. All the lad's colours had been gone, and all that was left was a body. Was that what Inara would be one day? Just flesh and no colour?

The knight had taken the first watch, Kissen the second, and they had swapped at intervals, every few hours, having reached some silent agreement. Skedi could feel the wreckage of emotion all around him. The pilgrims had whispered little prayers, muttered into the air in shards of colour, then vanishing to whatever god they prayed to. Skedi had peeked out from his prison, watching them disappear with longing. They weren't for him.

Skedi knew, had always known, he was one of many, even as the king crushed people's love for gods with law. But he had no memories of ever meeting another thing of power before. And the shadow had been powerful, chaotic. He could feel its connection to something bigger, stronger still. He wondered if he should be more afraid. The humans were.

Now, on the road again, Skedi peeked out from his hiding place.

The pilgrims' quiet prayers were still rising from their mouths: their gifts for other gods. Inara, too, was so frightened. He could tell she didn't know what to do except walk and pray. He hadn't made the choice to be attached to Inara, or at least he didn't think he had. He could barely remember anything before her, only flashes, if he thought hard. Churning water and screams, and beasts of hide and blood. And fright, the colours of terror. Then, worse, when all the colours went out. Nothing. Finally, Inara.

All he wanted was to be free to fly where he willed and experience the warmth of other people's longings and spin them the little lies they needed. He wanted to be loved. Gods needed purpose; they needed love and prayers.

They had to make it to Blenraden. He had to be free.

Skedi poked his nose out of the bag. He was the size of a bluebird, and hidden by the satchel's shadows.

He looked at Inara. Her eyes were wet, and she was thumbing the buttons on her waistcoat. Skedi could feel her wishing for her mother.

The creature is gone, he said to her. *We are safe, we can keep moving.*

I know, she thought back to him. *There's nowhere and no one to go back to.* Her face crumpled and she turned it towards the ground so no one would see.

There's nowhere to go back to, he agreed, *but I'm here.* He had promised not to lie to Inara, but that didn't mean he could not agree with her. *Survive this, Ina. We'll get through it together.*

He put a faint pressure of his power, his will, in the words, what little power he did have with no shrine and no offerings. His will wrapped around her colours, altering them, steadying them. It was just enough, only to support her. She let out a very quiet sob, but she was soothed, her colours turning dusky yellow, like the dawn. Skedi was thrilled it worked. Kissen, who was walking beside them, eyed her with concern. Reaching into her cloak for some of the sweet oat clumps she had bought from the market, she gave one to Legs and then touched Inara on the hand.

"Take hold of Legs," she said. "He likes you. Keep him on stable ground and I'll scout ahead." Inara straightened, rubbed her face, then nodded. As she took the horse's reins, her emotions softened further. Skedi found this curious. The veiga hadn't lied to her, told her it would be all right, or tried to make things better. She had just given her something to do.

Skedi turned his attention to the others further up the line. The older women were aching and uncertain, and Batseder and Berrick were whispering nervously to each other. Jon had been skittish, fingering his charms and muttering. Skedi could feel that he trusted in many gods, but clearly not enough to depend on one alone. He had seen a flash of the pilgrim badges last night, had eyed them greedily. Maybe one day someone would wear a coin for him.

"This isn't safe. Should we turn back?" Batseder murmured to Berrick, just within earshot. "Perhaps Aia will yet be reborn? Or perhaps we can avoid pregnancy. There are roots . . ."

"They can be dangerous," said Berrick. "It is your body, my love; it is your choice."

"Are you sure this is what you want?"

Skedi caught the softest dew of sadness that Berrick could not hide from him, at the thought that they would not have children of their own, with her eyes and his chin, mixed in with thoughts that he loved her more than her womb and her blood. Those feelings, combined with fear, could be potent. He wanted them, to feel them, at least.

There, where he toed the line between truth-telling and lies, Skedi slipped in, his will touching Berrick's colours. He could feel Berrick's complex emotions like a toss of the tides, setting his own heart to fluttering.

Do not be sad, he willed towards the man, reducing his voice to the faintest whisper. *You will guilt her with your sadness.*

Berrick's colours changed as the lie took. Firmer, brighter.

"I am sure," he said. "If we risk a life, we risk it here, together, not yours on your own."

Would he know it had been a god who helped him? Would he offer a little prayer to a thing like Skedi, his love giving him strength? Buoyed on by his success, Skedi turned his attention to the older women, who were walking as quickly as they could, their limbs popping and aching. It was rare in this world, to live so long; they were impressive for that alone.

"Ey, Poline, are you all right then?" asked Svenka as Poline picked at a sweetcake they had shared between the three of them. Poline was shaken by sadness down to her core for the boy; it trembled out of her bones and Skedi could feel it like pain. He reached around her colours, his wings aching. She had lost someone, a child. That was why she took his death so hard.

He's not your baby, Poline, Skedi willed at her. *A different boy. A different life.*

"I'm well, Svenka, stop nosing. What about you?"

Tell her it doesn't hurt.

Svenka ached all over; she was tired and cold too, for the dew had settled on her collar and cuffs, pricking her skin.

"Not a thing wrong," Svenka lied brightly. "Glad we had our Haoirse here to take charge." Haoirse dismissed her with a flick of her hand. The three of them brightened.

Skedi crept further out of the bag, feeling the thrill of power. He could change things, little by little. He could change people, all their clamour, all their wild urges, he could move them. Skedi felt his satchel lift, and turned his face to Inara with his triumph, then realised it was the veiga who had him. He retreated, but not before she gave the bag a rough shake.

Watch it, pest. She released her guard to think at him so strongly, her colours so violent, that Skedi found his body shrinking. He hadn't realised he had grown so large, his antlers and haunches had been straining the straps. Kissen thrust the bag at Inara, who caught it with surprise.

"Look after your things," snapped Kissen, and stomped off.

You're welcome, Skedi shot at her, but was blocked by a stone wall of animosity. There was no way into Kissen's mind, no way to change her. She wasn't safe, not for him, and not for Inara. If he managed to find himself a shrine, could he really leave his friend with this careless god-murderer? More than that, if he was no longer attached to Inara Craier, would he still be able to evade the knife of the veiga?

Skedi set his eyes on the man with the sword. Kissen had called him a knight to his face and, though he denied it, his colours had said otherwise. They were mostly steady, but sometimes cracked with emotions like lightning ripping through cloud: great pain, and great regret. Again, potent.

Skedi would not have dared consider a knight like those on the road, but he had seen this one want to stop them. He was going to Blenraden against the king's law. He was kinder too than Kissen. Better suited for a noble girl. Much better suited for a god than a veiga . . .

CHAPTER FOURTEEN

Kissen

THREE DAYS LATER, THEY WERE STILL DEEP IN THE FOREST, but it was clear they were climbing higher, struggling up damp slopes soaked through with the remains of the winter's meltwater. The days and nights were growing colder and the mountains ahead were drawing close. Kissen was surprised yet grateful that their chaotic pilgrim chain was still intact after the mayhem of the first night, but by the little god's meddling or by sheer chance, they hadn't given up. Maybe Kissen had underestimated their dedication to their gods. At least they had not seen another demon.

Kissen believed in coincidences. Sometimes things happened for no reason at all, or because someone somewhere did something really stupid, usually someone with more noble blood and silver coin than brains. But as far as she was concerned, there was no such thing as destiny, and she was quite happy to tear any plans made by gods to pieces. Fate was a fairy story and a bullshit one at that; fate could get fucked and go bother someone else.

But even Kissen had to admit that the coincidences were coming too heavy and fast for her to ignore: a backwater river god whispering of Middren falling, a little girl with an antlered liar turning up at her table, a great House burned to ashes, and now a shadow demon snapping bone-teeth at them. This was more than a coincidence: it was a problem. Something was changing, and she couldn't yet see what. Kissen tapped the sealed vial at her chest.

And now, the worst thing was this knight. She'd suspected it from the first moment she saw him, then the way he had put everyone to rights and drawn that sword. What kind of baker carries a sword? Idiot. How did he think he'd get away with that bullshit? *Trust me, I'm a baker, I'm handsome and can make bread, I boss people around. Everyone should love me.* It stuck in her craw. At least he wasn't completely useless; he knew how to handle a blade. More than she could say of most knights she'd met.

And she knew he was watching her now, because he had guessed she wasn't who she said she was either. Fine. If he ratted her out, she'd do him twice over. But if he spared Inara more than a second glance, she would gather up Legs and the girl and go straight back to Lesscia. She was ready for it, so she had been walking the horse easy, not making him carry too much weight. She had seen too many horses run into the ground as if they were disposable. If they had to run, he would be ready, and well rested.

Unlike Kissen, who was tired and grumpy. Her right leg was aching and felt like it had been clamped in a vice, so she couldn't sleep much at night. It was made worse by the fact she had one eye watching for beasts of shadow, the other on the knight, and whatever senses she had left focussed on their antlered beast of lies, who weaved little threads of influence over the group. The god had been twisting the pilgrims, she had felt it, and she didn't like it at all. He was such a small god, any other time she would have squished him like a rat.

At least he was predictable. The shadow demon didn't make sense. Darkness, blood, and bone, it shouldn't be here. Most of the wild gods were supposed to be dead. This had to be something more than a rogue apparition.

It was gone, though. At the pace they were going, it would take nine more days to get to Blenraden, and she would find a way to separate the god of white lies from the little girl, then leave him or kill him. He would disappear in the dust with the rest of the war.

Their progress had improved at least, as they headed northeast and saw almost no one. Kissen had been worried Inara would struggle on the road, particularly after the grimness of the first night. The lass, however, slept heavy and woke determined. She was more resilient than Kissen had guessed.

She was also damnably curious. Wanting to learn everything about survival out in the green wilds. "What's that?" she asked, pointing to a bundle of yellow flowers by their path.

"Srickwort," said Kissen. "You can eat the leaves, but the flowers ruin your stomach."

"What do you eat the leaves with?"

"Anything," Svenka called back. Kissen was holding the rear of the train as they moved, and the old women were just ahead. She liked Svenka, who had told Kissen she looked just like her first wife and was a good scavenger. Haoirse and Poline, too, were deeply practical. They leaned on each other, with a love that was longer and deeper than romance alone. It was family, when all other family was dead or just gone. She wondered if she, Telle, and Yatho would be like that, one day. The thought was fleeting. Most in her line of work didn't grow old.

"What about those?" said Inara, pointing at a tall shrub with large leaves.

"Don't eat them," said Kissen.

"Why?"

"They taste like shit. But you can use them to bake other things in; the leaves are thick."

Berrick and Batseder had shared the last of their little dumplings, sticky and tacky. Kissen had seen the baker-knight's nose twist as he took a bite. Full of judgment. Kissen had eaten hers with gusto, just to show him.

"And those?"

"They bite your hand off if you ask too many questions."

Inara stuck out her tongue and hitched up her satchel, and Kissen saw a flash of Skedi's cunning eye. He must be bored. It was a close, damp day, and the little breeze they had was refreshing. They had broken from the stream and were walking over the windy ridge of a forested valley, clearly avoiding the village that huddled at the bottom. All the houses had white stones on the roofs to keep the thatch down in high winds from the mountains, and Kissen could see the villagers bobbing about below, clapping birds off the fields they were ploughing and planting. There was evidence that people came up here from time to time: prayer ribbons hanging from trees;

a shrine to a shepherd god with coins and dried sweets on offer, tucked just off the road. Knights didn't come far enough into these quiet places to trash the offerings, and none of the shrines were powerful enough to need a godkiller. Kissen didn't touch them as they passed. It wasn't worth it. She didn't burn the prayers of the poor just for fun.

As they climbed into the hills, trees began to straggle near the rocky ridges and offered no protection from the winds. Up to the east were the high-peaked mountains they were aiming for, some Kissen could name, far above the main city roads; these would allow them to descend again to the coast unnoticed. Inara struggled on the scree-littered paths, but was determined to keep up. Legs hated it, sometimes pushing Kissen off balance so he could get a firmer step. Jon shot him and Kissen an irritated glance every time the horse gave even the slightest whinny, but if the villagers below them saw their passage, they made no attempt to stop them.

That night, they finally settled in a nook of a valley by the river Arrenon, recently renamed in honour of their benevolent king. Pompous git.

They ground to a halt with sighs of relief. Jon immediately began turning stones. He had done so every night. If Kissen had her bearings, they were not too far from the falls of Gefyrton, the famous bridge town, perhaps a day's walk. The evening was still plenty light, and the new green shoots about them shone with fresh life. But as lovely as it looked, spring was the time of the wild gods, and it made Kissen nervous. Wild gods were often older than old, their first shrines buried in earth and stone, long forgotten. They were difficult to kill, and once they were killed, it was even more difficult to make sure they stayed dead.

"The water is too full and fast for fishing without a net," said Poline, sitting heavily down at the bank and gazing at the river, which was strong and thick with the meltwater. Beyond her, Kissen noticed a little boat, hidden under low-hanging bushes. It was oarless and chained to the bank.

"I can make traps," said Batseder, "but that's a chancer's game. We might not catch anything until morning."

"Ach, it would take too long," said Haoirse.

"Canovan said everyone had to be ready to fetch their own game," Jon reminded them, pausing his prayers. The previous nights they had mostly shared food, no one wanting to disappear into the woods for long to hunt, but their fresh supplies would dwindle eventually.

Svenka, Poline, and Haoirse looked at one another, their communication so familiar they didn't need words.

"I can hunt," said Kissen, relieved to have an excuse to put some distance between herself and the group. There was a reason she preferred travelling alone; most people were deeply annoying. "There's rabbits aplenty around here. Come, Tethis, time you learned how to feed yourself."

Inara gulped at her. "I . . . I don't . . ." She looked a little queasy. "I couldn't shoot a rabbit."

"You'd eat one, wouldn't you?"

"Well . . . yes, but—"

"Then live with it. Plant lore is not the only thing for learning."

Svenka hid a laugh, and Kissen was surprised when Inara didn't give further argument. Kissen pulled her bow down from Legs's saddle, then fetched out the pouch she kept its string in to save it from damp. Legs leaned into Inara, nuzzling at her pack as if expecting an apple. To Kissen's surprise, the item appeared, passed up, presumably, by Skedi's antlers. Without startle or complaint, Inara passed it to Legs, who took it. Traitor.

"Have you used a bow before?" Kissen asked, ignoring what she'd just witnessed and hooking the gut to the top of the stave. She didn't like seeing a softer side of Skedi but couldn't, after all, begrudge Legs an apple. "You're probably too small to string this one."

Inara huffed and took the bow off her with an upward turn of her nose. She unhooked the gut from the top, looped it onto the bottom, and drew it up, pulling on the top of the stave to bend it. Kissen watched, folding her arms. Inara put all her weight on the stave, her face turning red as she pulled it down.

"Ow!" It slipped out of her hand and fell onto the damp undergrowth.

"First lesson," said Kissen, picking it up, "don't get too big for your boots."

Batseder laughed but shook her head. "Good on you for trying," said Berrick.

"Not so good on you for being fuller of flap than of wind," said Kissen, stringing the bow, then giving the quiver to Inara to carry. That's what her mother used to say to her and her brothers when their arrogance got in the way of their common sense. Inara was wringing her stung fingers.

"Bit rowdy for a bodyguard, aren't you?" said Jon. "Isn't she your employer?"

Inara and Kissen froze. Elo looked over at them, his dark eyes full of suspicion.

"Her father wants her prepared for the road," said Kissen, the lie coming easily to her lips. Usually, she would not have bothered, but this was for Inara. "So, unless you'd prefer your dried animal carcass over fresh meat, keep your comments to yourself."

Jon shrugged and continued with his rock laying.

Oh, so now you don't mind a little lie? Skedi's voice pierced her mind unbidden, and Inara gave Kissen a flat look, as if tempted to say *See?*

Fuck you, beastie, Kissen threw back.

Kissen took Inara upstream and downwind, eyeing up likely rabbit paths through the prickling gorse.

"I don't know why I have to learn this," said Inara, becoming bolder as the chatter of their fellow travellers faded into the wind and the rush of the river.

Kissen wasn't sure what to say. That she had found herself in the world alone? That she wanted Inara to have the skills Kissen had come to rely on for survival? "We don't know what life will be for you after this," she said shortly. "Here, that's a rabbit path by the burn."

Inara went quiet, following her pointing finger to the trickle of a stream that fed into the river.

"We need to stay downwind of our prey, or they'll smell us," said Kissen. "We follow the natural paths, see. Think at their height and follow where they might move: to water, or to safety. Ground animals love to run, but they love better to hide. They think if they're still we can't see them."

The best grass and bushes for rabbits grew in sunlight, so Kissen wasn't surprised when the path led them to a slight clearing. Inara stepped quietly enough, and Kissen gestured for her to stop and come alongside her.

"See the hare?" said Kissen, keeping her voice soft. Still, the creature sensed them and froze. It was crouched by a bed of grass and green shoots. "They're happier in open spaces. I'm surprised to see one in woodland this dense; it means there are fields nearby. See the curve of its back? Its ears are like leaves, but its back gives it away."

"He looks scared," whispered Inara.

"So he is," said Kissen, taking her bow down from her shoulders, slowly, so as not to startle the animal. "He knows this is a moment in the game of life we play." She nocked an arrow, felt its feathers, drew it back.

She let go. The arrow hissed as it left its gut. The hare moved a moment too late. The arrow caught him in the chest and threw him from his leap. Creatures in the undergrowth that she hadn't seen, including one or two smaller rabbits, scattered. His legs kicked once, and he was done.

Inara swallowed. "I've shot apples," she said. "Targets, but not a breathing thing. Definitely not a breathing thing that looks like Skedi."

Kissen realised the god had climbed to Inara's shoulder, flexing his wings in the afternoon air. She did not like that he no longer thought she would kill him.

"I've never known a creature that didn't feel pain," said Kissen, standing up. "We are no different than them. Even people eat each other to survive." She went over to the dead hare and removed the arrow, wiping it on the grass and then her trews. Inara watched her, the corners of her mouth turned down. Kissen picked up the hare, still warm. He bled a little, and she turned him and strung his feet together before tying him to her belt. "Pain is part of life," she said.

Kissen, for the first time in a long time, saw her father's face in her mind. He had given her his life, and all the pain that went with it.

"All right," said Inara grumpily, "are we done with the lesson in killing?"

Kissen grinned. "No." She dried the bowstring with a cloth and handed it over. "It's your turn."

She took the girl deeper into the trees, following the trails to where the air was thick and quiet. While they went, Kissen picked up fungi and greens, adding them to Skedi's bag while the god flitted about close to Inara's head, the size of a swallow.

At last, they found a still pool under low-hanging branches. Three rabbits scarpered at a slip of the grass, but the rest froze. *Wait*, Kissen signed to Inara. The rabbits began to move again. Like a breath of wind, the time in which they were afraid had passed.

Kissen slowly pulled an arrow and gave it to Inara, who sighed as she nocked it. She drew the bow well, holding it better than Kissen did. Her shoulder and elbow were straight in line, her knuckles at the corner of her mouth.

"The still ones know we're here," Kissen murmured.

"Do I have to?" said Inara, holding the string almost to singing stretch.

"No, you don't have to," said Kissen. "You make your own choices, *liln*, I won't make them for you."

Inara swallowed, stretched the gut further, and released the arrow. It caught a rabbit through the throat, killing it outright. A better shot than Kissen's. The rest fled. Skedi dropped down from a branch by Inara onto her shoulder and glared at Kissen. She ignored him.

"A good death," said Kissen, surprised by how proud she found herself. "Well done, you're a natural hunter."

The fire at the camp was blazing, even though the sun had not yet set. The god was back to hiding and Elo was stretching dough in his hands, preparing to heat it on a flat stone and a preparation mat he had covered in oil. He was really committing to the baking façade. It was quite an effort to carry flour, oils, and yeast on a long walk, just for a pretence. Kissen saw Berrick watching in fascination.

"We take the boat across the river tomorrow," said Jon as they joined. "Its pilot will see the fire and come with the key for the chain at dawn. Then we'll start heading up Mount Tala." He pointed to the snow-capped peak to the east of them.

Haoirse took the rabbits from Inara's hand. "Good shot," she said, turning them over. They had got five in all. Inara flushed with pride and, after dancing from foot to foot, joined the old woman and Kissen by the water to watch. Kissen took out her knife and skinned one of the hares in two strokes: a slit down the back and around the neck, then a strong rip.

"Where did you learn that?" asked Inara, clearly repulsed and fascinated in equal measure.

"From a man called Pato. I apprenticed with him," said Kissen. Ah, Pato. She wondered what that old goat would have made of Skedi. Short work, was the first answer that came to mind. "Keeps the fur intact so you can dry it and use the pelts for warmth. 'Nothing wasted' is a hunter's code."

Haoirse's rabbit was taking a bit more working; she had chosen the neater route of peeling the skin back a bit at a time.

"How long does it take to dry?" asked Inara as Haoirse dallied the skin in the water.

"Two to three days," she said, laying it on the bank, then taking the hare from Kissen's hands. She had swollen knuckles, cracked from the cold winds. "Then some time for tanning. Their brains are good for that, or yolk. Ask Batseder."

"Most travelling tanners carry chickens," agreed Batseder, hearing them as she stirred the pot. "Though my family works mainly with cowhide. Which is how I met Berrick the shoemaker." She smiled at her husband as Inara sat down with her and delivered up the mushrooms they had stripped from an ailing tree. "And why my father likes him," Batseder added.

"No shoes without skins," said Berrick, and she laughed.

They settled down to game stew, mushrooms, and softly risen flatbreads made by Elo. Kissen tore hers apart suspiciously, but when she took a bite, they were the lightest, most delicious breads she had tasted.

"You made this?" she said to Elo, who rolled his eyes in exasperation.

"I told you," he said, "I'm a baker. Of course I made it."

They were definitely better than the sticky dumplings Berrick had insisted on making and boiling in the pot. Jon even awkwardly shared around a stash of Curlish wine which he had been nipping from every evening when he thought no one was looking.

"This is so different than it was when we were girls," said Poline after a while, gnawing meat from one of the bones. "Each town had a little parade for you coming in on pilgrimage, and you were fleeced out of a silver bit for a cup of water."

"Ah, those were good days," said Jon, beaming beneath his beard, which he was absently plaiting.

"I imagine you got some cut of the fleecing," said Haoirse.

He shrugged. "I've walked from the eastern edge of Talicia straight through the mountains of Middren," he said, touching briefly at his pewter pilgrim badges. "Ships I've taken to Irisia, Usic, Restish, Pinet, and Curliu, and walked their ways as well. But nowhere was like Middren. The stories upon stories, the recklessness of the gods, and the things they would give you. The layers and depths of shrines as you came to Blenraden. What a city." He looked around at them. "Did any of you go? Before the war?"

"Never," said Batseder. "My mother was frightened of it."

"Many small minds were," said Jon. "I mean no offence, dear."

Batseder raised her eyebrows. "I hope you allow me to take it, all the same."

"It was full of thieves and mad gods," said Berrick, supporting her.

Jon tutted. "Every corner, a god or a prayer," he said, turning his eyes up to the trees as if he could still see it. "A little shrine full of trinkets. Gods for lost earrings, for broken sandals, for making coin, for pocket thieves and weavers." He smiled at Kissen. "You remember, don't you, Enna? Your charge said you were from there."

"Batseder's right," Kissen said. "It was a town of thieves, mad gods, and worse people. The woman who kept me there depended on it."

"Was that Maimee?" Inara asked innocently, dipping her bread into her stew. Kissen winced.

"Maimee?" said Jon, his eyes sharpening. "You were one of that hedgewitch's wards?"

"Don't speak ill of hedgewitches," said Svenka.

"She still alive?" asked Jon.

Kissen scowled. "I hope not."

Poline stared at her. "What a thing to say!"

"She took in bastards, cripples, and abandons," said Jon, looking Kissen up and down with an eye she didn't like, as if sizing her up for a cell. "Set them harassing my pilgrims for their coin and offerings. Little shits. More than once I had my pocket slit *after* I paid her to leave me alone."

"Seems like you should have better guarded your pockets," said Kissen.

Svenka interrupted before Jon could bristle. "I've been to Blenraden more than once, and the people were madder and pettier than the gods."

"Why are you going back, then?" said Jon. He had been touchy since Mikle died.

Svenka looked at her companions. Haoirse thumbed her bracelets while Poline blushed. "Because we may not get more chances," she said. "There aren't many gods left in Middren who might hear our ask."

Berrick turned their way, his ears pricking for the gossip. Kissen bet that if someone bought a pair of shoes from him they would get a bagful of stories to go with them. "What's your ask?"

"To die," said Haoirse, blunt as ever. "Together. Painlessly. Asleep." Inara choked. "What? Why?"

"Because any children or family we have are long away, or dead," said Poline. She looked sad. "We don't want to be separated, coddled and forgotten. None of us wants to linger while another goes ahead." She sighed. "My only child ran to war in Blenraden. He died alone and far from the people who loved him, like Mikle." Svenka reached over to touch her hand. "Haoirse went to find him, and could only hold the hands of a hundred knights as they perished. Then, the illnesses that spread out from the city as its people fled took Svenka's sisters. We've seen few good deaths. We wish to ask for one."

Kissen looked at Elo. His hands were trembling a little and he was staring resolutely into the fire.

"What would you even offer for a gift like that?" she asked. "Gifts from gods are not free."

"You speak from experience, don't you?" said Haoirse. Kissen shouldn't have opened her mouth. Haoirse touched her cheek to indicate the scar, but it was Osidisen's promise on her chest that Kissen felt. "It's a curse, isn't it? A broken one."

"I've never seen a curse before," said Berrick, leaning forward with interest.

"I've had an interesting life," Kissen said coolly, hoping not to arouse Jon's suspicion again. Or the baker's, for that matter.

The sun, which had been sidling down alongside the river, had barely a tip above the horizon, and each span it dropped had taken more and more warmth with it.

Kissen felt it as the light slipped over the hills. A change in the air like a touch on her skin, setting it crawling. Then the scent came: dirt, moss, and blood. She sprang to her feet and drew her sword.

"What?" Jon scrambled up as well. In the dark of the woods, no longer touched by sun, shadow crept out of the shadow on animal paws. Not one this time: two. "Fuck me and all the gods," hissed Jon. "Not again."

White teeth, glimmering eyes, white claws. Darkness and bone. Kissen breathed in deep as the knight rose carefully to his feet. The blood-stink weighed on her tongue, bringing with it memories of hot flesh and fire.

The beasts charged together, striking Jon's circle and breaking straight through. It was not strong enough to hold against two. Kissen blocked one of the creatures with her sword, wrestling it off its path, and the other slid for Elo. Kissen swiped her blade, forcing the first back, and used the opportunity to pull Inara to her feet.

"Get back to Legs!" she said. "Calm him!"

The horse was panicking, threatening to bolt. Inara grabbed his reins and was almost picked up bodily as he reared. Svenka came to her aid as Berrick scrabbled around for a stone or a branch. He found a log, the worst of both, and brandished it above his head. Haoirse was struggling to get to her feet, and Batseder hurried to her, hauling her upright.

The beast bore Kissen down, dodging her swing of the sword with a lick of shadow and dipping beneath her guard. Its claws caught on her armour, and she dragged it back, reaching inside her cloak for the first thing that came to her hand: the blessed ash from Ennerast's shrine. She smashed the bottle into the creature's mouth. What would have been a gift for a water summoning was like acid for this beast. It shrieked, tearing its claws across her breastplate.

"Get to the water," Kissen called, "all of you! They might not follow you there; they're earthbound things."

"It's too deep!" said Jon. The other beast, which had been grappling with Elo's sword, took after the scent of the blessing. Acid or not, it smelled like power.

"Get on the boat, damn it!" cried Kissen, stepping backwards as the first recovered and the two of them turned on her. "Inara, get to the boat! Leave Legs!"

She had not called her Tethis. She had used the girl's real name. Too late now; she wasn't built for lying. The shadow-flesh of the one she had burned had been stripped, exposing its bone-teeth, the shards gleaming white in a ragged grin. "Baker, get over here."

Elo leapt to Kissen's side. "How has it followed us? Why are there two?"

"Blessed if I know," snapped Kissen.

Jon and Poline were dragging the boat as far as its chain would stretch into the water. Batseder, Berrick, and Haoirse tried to gather their things as they backed away to the bank. Legs was frightened. He snorted loudly, straining away from Svenka, and the noise distracted the shadow beasts. Kissen took that moment to charge. The beasts balked and both separated, quick as air, and one went straight for Inara. Kissen threw one of her knives, catching a creature in its hind leg. It shrieked as it switched its attack towards Haoirse, Batseder and Berrick. Berrick stepped to the fore, holding his log before Haoirse and Batseder, trembling at the knees.

"No, don't!" shouted Batseder, and Haoirse cried out. She pushed Berrick away, and the beast's teeth crunched into her side.

Svenka screamed, releasing Legs and running towards her. Poline left the boat but stumbled in the current and almost fell. Berrick found his feet and swung the log, which did nothing except catch the creature's shadow on the gust as it passed through.

Kissen drew another of her briddite knives and threw it, piercing the neck of the shadow. The creature was like a wild dog, attacking anything that moved. It left Haoirse, meeting Kissen head on. She broke its charge with her sword and bowled it over, cutting it slightly, allowing Berrick and Batseder to pick up Haoirse, who was gasping with pain.

"Together, Haoirse!" cried Poline, trying to drag herself closer to the bank against the current. "It's supposed to be together!"

"Kissen!" shrieked Inara, still clinging on to Legs and also forgetting their false identities in the panic. It didn't matter; what mattered was her safety.

"Leave him now, Inara, get in the boat!"

The beast made a snap for Kissen with its bloody teeth. She caught them on her blade. The knight was swiping the other back, giving the pilgrims time.

"Berrick!" he yelled as he struck. Berrick had made the boat. "It's too hot!"

"What?" Berrick shouted back. "Come to the boat, baker, run!"

"The water is too damn hot for the dumplings!" the baker-knight roared, looking relieved as he got it off his chest. "Makes them sticky! Cool it next time!"

"Is this the time, you flapping fool?" yelled Kissen. "Inara. Now!"

"What about you?" said Inara. "What about Legs?"

"I can hold them, and Legs will look after himself. Get to safety. That's a command."

Jon showed some backbone and dragged himself to help Haoirse and Svenka into the water. Batseder leapt into the boat and helped pull Haoirse in. Her head was lolling back at a frightening angle. Berrick helped Poline over the side, and then Svenka, who was weeping in sympathy.

Inara had not let go. Jon was trying to cast off, picking the lock, the current already tugging them downstream. Without Inara. Kissen growled and put all her strength into the sword, flinging the beast to the side. She ran for Inara, turning her back on the creature against every instinct, as Jon cracked open the lock. She grabbed the girl, intent on throwing her full-force at the boat. Batseder stood and opened her arms, willing to catch her. The chain ran loose.

Inara raised her arms in frail defence. "You promised!" she cried. As she did, Skediceth burst out of her pack, beating his wings at Kissen's face, charged with Inara's emotion. Kissen smacked him aside, but her hand didn't hurt him; he came back on the air, defending Inara.

"Get off, you parasite!" snarled Kissen. The shadow creature she had tossed had found its feet and, unhurt, it ran for them.

Elo sprinted forward, and with an elegant strike thrust his blade straight through its head, then its heart. The creature dissolved. With an inhuman cry the second charged, but Elo was ready, planting his feet. He drove his sword straight through, breaking its claws, teeth, and chest, and ripping the shadow into shreds of air.

Kissen turned back to the water, but the boat was too far now, Batseder staring back at them, agape at the little god that had appeared above Inara's head. Before she could ask a thing, the vessel was sucked into the middle current and swept downriver. They were left alone.

Kissen turned on Inara. "What is wrong with you?"

"What was I supposed to do when we got out of the boat?" snapped Inara. "Find someone else to take me and a god of white lies to a dead city?"

Kissen curled her lip. "You could have died," she said. "Those beasts are following us."

"You promised," said Inara bitterly, her voice hoarse. "You promised not to abandon me."

Kissen was, for a moment, speechless. "I wasn't abandoning you, you ungrateful wretch," she said. "I was trying to save your life. What am I supposed to do if you get killed, eh?"

"You can go back to your stupid life," cried Inara. "But what about me? I have nothing to go back to. What am I supposed to do on my own?"

"You're not on your own," said Skediceth, settling on her shoulder.

"If I find out you convinced her to stay . . ." growled Kissen. Skedi flicked his wings at her.

"You'll what, kill me? That threat is getting a little old."

Kissen heard a polite cough from behind her. They span to face the sound. Not alone. Elo was with them still.

"I take it," he said, "you've not really turned to bodyguarding, Kissen the godkiller."

CHAPTER FIFTEEN

Elogast

HOW HAD HE NOT SEEN IT AS SOON AS HE LOOKED AT HER? The way she moved, slightly favouring one side; her wild reddish hair and smile like a snarl. There were only so many one-legged Talicians living in Middren. Only one of those had made a name as a veiga during the war. He had checked the names of the volunteers himself in their desperate drive for fighters. Kissen.

And she had been there, not just for the attack that took down the wild gods, but after, on the night he tried not to think about. The way she had held herself under his barrage of commands while others trembled and sweated. It was all coming back now, things he had long buried in an effort to keep from falling apart. He had noted at the time the way she barely looked at Arren as the crown prince rallied them for courage, determined to do battle by their sides against their one-time ally: the god of war. Kissen the godkiller had been one of the few with no fear of facing gods and death. Her eyes had been like her tattoo. *Fuck you.*

Now she was looking him up and down with much the same expression.

"I was there at the battle with Mertagh," said Elo. "I gave orders to the veiga. I saw you and the others take down the war god." It pained him to say that, to remember how the godkillers had saved his life, and a god saved Arren, and he had failed at everything.

Kissen's mouth drew up in a shape of disgust. "Oh, fuck. I *knew* you were a knight. What did you do, shit your pants, turn on your friends, or run away?"

The gall of the woman. "None of those," said Elo flatly. Many had, in the blackness and chaos of divine rage; she wasn't wrong. Clearly she didn't remember him. He realised he was a little disappointed. He had been wearing a helmet, maybe that was it.

"Well, the king and half the smart ones turned tail, so it's a fair question," said Kissen, her eyes on his sword. Elo bristled.

"The king was injured—" He caught himself. "Is that why you're so sour on him?"

"No, I thought it was a much smarter idea for him to hide, considering he was the last of his mother's brood left alive. You can't have been a very good knight, if half of them died and now you're a baker."

She was provoking him. She had stepped forward to hide the girl, who was still holding on to the horse, the god, clearly with a will of its own, sitting on her head.

"That girl is not safe with you, veiga."

"What makes you say that?" She smiled, her gold tooth glinting at him in the firelight.

Elo did not drop his blade. He could not predict her movements. She might as easily throw down her sword as stab him in the back.

"We have twice been attacked by smoke demons—"

"Shadow demons."

"I cannot think of a thing that could draw them to us other than a curse like the one on your face."

The veiga laughed. "A white curse is dead, and a dead curse does nothing," she said. "I'd know if I was drawing them, knight."

"Why should I believe you?" said Elo.

"Because I know what I'm talking about. You'd think someone who makes a business out of killing gods might note a thing or two about whether she's been cursed or not. Have you checked your own skin for a curse mark?"

"I have not been near anyone I know in years," said Elo. A curse took a lot of power; someone would really have to hate a person to try and summon one. They'd have to offer at least a finger, their home, or a lifetime of servitude to the god. No one cared for him enough to hate him.

It took Elo a moment to realise the expression on the veiga's face was an amused kind of pity. She was not afraid of him. The little god hopped down into the girl's hand, staring at him. "Well," said Kissen, "that's just sad for you."

Elo growled. He had not meant it that way. The little one covered her mouth to hide a laugh.

"I wouldn't put it past someone to curse Jon," Kissen said, looking at the river. Their companions were long gone. "He hacked me off some. I don't fancy their chances, if so."

"Kissen," the girl scolded. Inara, Kissen had called her.

"I'm in a bad mood," said Kissen, by way of explanation. She eyed Elo. "You can piss off, then."

"Perhaps," said the god out loud, his whiskers twitching as he spoke, "we should set our differences aside for the night and get some rest."

"You've been sitting in a bag all day," said Kissen.

"I'm not talking about me," said the god, the flick of his wing indicating Inara.

Elo stared at him, then at Kissen, who had the decency to look a little sheepish. "That, we can explain."

"You can explain why a godkiller is travelling with a god?"

Her expression turned stony. "Can *you* explain why a knight is travelling to the city he helped destroy?"

Stalemate. Inara broke it. "The god is connected to me," she said. "Kissen is taking us to Blenraden to free us both." She looked at Kissen. "Skedi says Elo means no harm. Maybe we can trust him."

Connected. Elo swallowed. That sounded like Arren and his heart of twigs. Elo looked the girl over. She seemed perfectly whole and well. And the god was outside her, not inside. Either way, he might do well to find out more about them. A godkiller was no companion for a highborn girl, nor the road a good place for her to be. They had already been attacked, their travelling companions murdered, injured, and scattered.

"Didn't I tell you not to trust anyone?" said Kissen to her, barely a drop of civility in her tone.

"Well, you'll have to trust *me*," she said. "Anyway, I am moving no further tonight."

It could have been a young Arren standing there with his sharp tongue and that forthrightness, almost petulance, he used to have. Elo smirked.

"Two swords are better than one," he said, lowering his blade and sheathing it. "And we're headed in the same direction."

"How gallant," said Kissen. The horse had calmed some. Clearly he was well trained to not have bolted and dragged the girl along with him. Kissen went to retie him by his bridle and a rope to a tree, plenty loose so he had free range of movement, and the girl helped by brushing him down again. He accepted a small treat from her hand, not apparently minding the god.

Inara then dusted off her skirts and went to sit by the fire, tucking her thick wool cloak beneath her. After a moment, Kissen joined her with all the willingness of a cat asked to share its dinner. The pot of stew was still bubbling, full and noisy in the absence of their companions. Elo looked about at the wreck of their camp. He had enjoyed it, travelling with people. He had not had nightmares in days with the hard ground and noises of the night about him. He thought of Haoirse and her wounds, Mikle and his harp, Berrick's nosiness and Batseder's pragmatism. Would any that remained make it back on their journey?

Elo came to sit down, feeling more forlorn than he would have liked. Now released from its hiding place, the little god stood by Inara's knees and stretched its dappled wings.

"What is your name, god?" asked Elo. "Whose side did you take in the war?"

The creature gave him a flick of its long ear. A hare's face, but its eyes were yellow as a bird's.

"A name for a name, knight," the god said.

Kissen snorted, then looked annoyed that she did. She unbuckled her cuirass and checked where the shadow demon had torn it. Her shirt fell open, revealing more of her tattoo, and below it a swirl of dark writing flowing and turning like waves in a circle. Water-script.

"Before you ask," she said, noting his gaze, "it is not a curse, it's a boon. One I haven't used, and won't."

Elo sat down carefully, across the fire from her. If she drew one of her knives to throw, the flames would disrupt her aim.

"Elo is my name, that is the truth," he said to the god, who looked pleased to be addressed. "And you?"

"That is not your full name."

Elo hesitated. "Elogast."

The god thought about it. "I am Skediceth, god of white lies. I do not remember the war, and it seems we would all be better forgetting it. Whatever side I took, it was my own."

"Elogast," said the girl quietly to herself. She looked up. "People say the king had a knight commander called Elogast of Sakre. He retired." She eyed him shrewdly. Surnames were not popular in Middren outside the nobility, though in Irisia he would have been traced by his mothers; Elogast of Ellac and Bahba. Arren was Arren Regna, but Elogast was simply called after the city of his birth. "I thought you'd be old."

Elo shifted uncomfortably. He thought what little fame he had had faded with his disappearance from royal duties, but perhaps Estfjor had misled him, with the townspeople's straightforward, unprying nature. Canovan the innkeeper had almost recognised him and half panicked with it. Elo was both proud and appalled.

"People say all sorts of things," said Elo, hoping to deflect the conversation.

"He's lying," said the god. "Half-truthing." Kissen was also staring at him.

God of white lies. Of course. He forgot how gods could discern a lie on sight. Inara pursed her lips.

He relented. "Yes, I was once a knight commander, but I have not been involved with the king for many years. I made a peaceful life."

"'The king's lion' tamed," said Kissen. "How quaint." So she did recognise him. Elo thumbed his sword's lion head beneath the cloth. The young lion had been Arren's symbol, not his; he wasn't a Middren noble, but people called him what they wanted. Now, Arren had taken the war god's stag head and the rising sun as his heraldry. Elo didn't know how he could bear to look at it every day. "Why would the great Ser Elogast of Sakre diminish himself?"

"I did as honour bound me," said Elo, stung. "Why would a beggar of Blenraden pit herself against angry gods?" He touched his cheek to remind her of her curse. "Or choose to do battle with the god of war and then break formation as soon as things changed?"

Kissen curled her lip. "Mertagh was there for revenge," she said.

"Your precious formation had us lined up for him to take it." Elo flinched. She was right. Again.

"You would never have taken on the god without us," said Elo. Kissen scoffed, but didn't deny it.

"Bah," she said. "Look, I couldn't care less about where you're from or why you're here, but I don't trust knights."

Elo chuckled and shrugged. "I don't like you much either."

A heavy silence hung between them as they glared at each other.

"Why do you hate knights?" asked Inara, finally.

"Because," said Kissen, "they belong to kings."

"You work for the king," Inara pointed out.

"I work for myself. All godkillers do; we're mercenaries, not holy soldiers. The king's endorsement just means I make more money for it."

"Why don't you like kings?" asked Elo carefully. Kissen took a piece of bread and broke it apart in her hands.

"Because," she said, taking a bite, "in our world, power turns good people bloody."

"Then shouldn't you be pleased he attacked the god of war, at risk of his own life?"

"Did that fight please *you*, baker?"

Elo frowned. Inara gave a loud sigh and picked up a stick to rescue a burned bit of bread from the flames. "Why don't you tell me about this battle that makes you snap at each other?"

Elo and Kissen both looked away. Inara scowled.

"Fine. Tell me how you got that broken curse on your face so you don't get blamed for demons. Don't you have to be close to a god to be cursed?"

Kissen rubbed her chest over the sea-script as if it pained her. She also wore a leather pendant around her neck, which looked like some sort of vial. Godkillers Elo had seen carried all sorts of equipment: bottles of blessed water, vials of ash or blood, prayers. He had noticed Kissen's cloak clanked sometimes when she moved.

"You have to get pretty close to a god of beauty to kill it," said Kissen, reaching for one of the scattered bowls and passing it to Inara, who dipped her bread in it. Elo took the chance to regard her face more carefully. The god-script that had been broken was the more fractal mark of younger gods that had come to be in towns and cities, unlike the organic, flowing wild-script of gods of the forests and mountains or river-script of gods of water or lakes. Or the boon on Kissen's chest. Elo looked away.

"Why would you kill a god of beauty?" asked Inara, nibbling on her flatbread. Elo was pleased it wasn't wasted. It was hard to bake without a good oven. He opted for a swig of wine from the flask Jon had left behind. "There's nothing wrong with wanting to be pretty."

"Well, this god of beauty was Wyria of Weild," said Kissen.

Elo had not been to Weild, though it wasn't far from Estfjor, under the power of House Crolle. Nobles often turned their ships there if they had small, bright goods: gems and gold. Weild was famous for its jewellers and its prostitutes.

"The townspeople wanted to be beautiful and catch the eyes of lords and ladies," said Kissen. She had decided her armour didn't need mending and began to buckle it back on. She often wore her cuirass at night. A hard, flat surface, it couldn't have been comfortable; she was always ready to run. "She straightened noses, narrowed waists, or softened and thickened them. All she asked for were pieces of sugar, bits of fruit. Pretty treats."

"Doesn't sound so bad," said Skediceth.

"She had so many worshippers that she singled out favourites," Kissen continued. "She asked for more; their breakfasts, their midday meals, their suppers. Children as young as twelve began to fast for days to gain her favour, and sometimes she simply said no, that it wasn't enough, that they had to do more. She became full and beautiful while her worshippers wasted away with the sickness of loving her. Two young girls and a boy died before they posted for a godkiller. My trainer, Pato, picked up the job."

"This is not a children's story," said Elo. Nor did he like it. Inara, however, frowned at him.

"How did she curse you, then?" she asked pointedly.

"She was a smart flap," said Kissen. "Sent her worshippers to guard her gates. They were so frail, we couldn't get past them without hurting them." Elo felt her disgust and anger. She looked at her hands, strong and scarred. "Pato told me to make a plan. It was the first time he let me take on a god alone. So I fasted too, like they did, and brought offerings. Expensive ones. Candied fruits and marzipan. Rich, fresh meat, still dripping. I was a supplicant with bare arms and one leg, and I asked to be made beautiful. Told her how desperately I wanted to be beautiful, more than anything."

"She would have seen your lies," said the little god quietly. His fur was standing up, unnerved.

"I didn't lie," said Kissen. "I was young, scarred, and ugly. The one I loved most loved someone else better, and I had left them behind in an unkind place. That is enough to make a person want what they can't have."

"Yatho," said Inara. Kissen clicked her tongue at her, and Inara blushed. She had hit the mark.

"Wyria couldn't resist a godkiller's apprentice coming for a wish," she added. "Such a great, sweet wish. All the things she thought she could get from me. She had eaten half my candies before she realised there was briddite in them."

Elo choked on the wine. That was underhanded, even for a veiga. Kissen grinned at him, the glitter in her eyes showing she knew exactly what he was thinking.

"Of course, when she realised, she already had a curse of hideousness half out of her mouth. I killed her before it stuck, so now it's just another pretty scar."

"You're not ugly," said Inara. Kissen laughed and looked at Skedi, who shook his wings irritably.

"Of course she's lying," he said, and Inara poked a stick at him.

"He's exaggerating. You look unusual. Right, Elo?"

"I'm not getting involved." He should take that to heart. He wasn't here to pass judgment on the godkiller and her methods. Trickery just felt wrong, like what Arren did in felling the shrines of their allied gods. It was dishonourable. But she certainly wasn't ugly. Not that he was going to tell her that.

"My face is my face, *liln*," said Kissen, picking up a bone from the pot to chew on. "I know it well enough, and I still have most of my teeth and both of my eyes in it. Trust me, of my birth, I am a lucky one."

Inara chewed her lips, her dark eyes taking on depth in the night. The rush of the water that had carried their friends away filled their ears as none of them could think of anything to say. Kissen was not shaken. She looked upstream, picking meat off the bone with her teeth.

"So, you're noble-born?" asked Elo to Inara, picking up on the topic of birth. "Perhaps I know your parents."

Inara flashed him a look of fear and hurt, then glanced at Skedi. He and she communicated in what Elo knew would be the mindspeak of the gods. He wondered how she was so comfortable with it; he had never found the voices of gods in his head to be a pleasant experience. Sharp, jabbing.

"Her father is a merchant," said the god. "He married into the Artemi family and they adopted her. You may not know them."

"Are you trying to usurp my charge, baker?" asked Kissen, spitting a bit of gristle onto the ground. "Am I not highborn enough for you?"

"I am not," said Elo. "But it is good to plan ahead in case something were to happen."

"I assure you I will get Inara to safety and will happily leave you behind to do so," said Kissen. "There's money in the offing, and fewer and fewer gods to go around." Skediceth twitched an ear at her.

"A child's wellbeing is not a bargaining chip," growled Elo.

"Lucky for me it's none of your business," said Kissen. Elo ground his teeth.

"Peace," he said stiffly. He would speak to Inara separately. "I mean no disrespect. You will go on tomorrow?"

Kissen looked at Inara, who nodded. "Yes," said Kissen, and turned back to Elo. "Without the boat, the nearest crossing from here will be Gefyrton."

"We need a plan. Gefyrton's a big trading town; it's sure to have guards looking for pilgrims. There's a reason we've been avoiding places like that."

Kissen laughed. "Lighten up, they see all sorts in Gefyrton. It will take us most of the day to get there, though."

Elo sighed. Another day, another delay. More than half of Arren's month would be gone before Elo set foot in the city of the gods. "Then we'd better sleep and set off early."

He folded himself up in his cloak and lay down facing the fire so he could keep an eye on the veiga and the god. He kept his eyes a little open, resting but not sleeping, as he watched the others. It was not long before Kissen and Inara settled on the uncomfortable ground, but the god stayed awake, his yellow eyes burning into Elo. As Elo felt sleep come on, his consciousness drifted. He found doubts growing in his mind, from a seed of suspicion into rooted fear.

We are not safe with the veiga.

CHAPTER SIXTEEN

Inara

THEY HEARD GEFYRTON BEFORE THEY SAW IT LATE THE NEXT afternoon. The roar of the waterfall built to a thrum in their bones as they scrambled upriver and climbed the overgrown sides of granite cliffs, shaded by trees and cooled by the air from the water. Inara had read about the town: a bridge raised by the god Gefyr on and across the rapids and lip of the great Falls of Salia as part of a pact between warring clans and their local deities. If the town had been renamed since the war to erase the god of bridges, it hadn't stuck. In these parts a *Gefyr* was a good bridge and a *bridge* was a weak one.

The god of the waterfall, Inara remembered, was Sali. Giant monuments to them and Gefyr had been built into the bridge's pillars, rising from a quarry at the foot of the falls to stand within the sheets of water. Vast arms of carved stone stretched above the rapids, holding up the town. However, though their bodies remained, the huge heads of the local gods had been toppled into the white foam and river below.

Inara's small group joined a long line of muddy-calved travellers as they came to the city gates on the western side of the river's rapids. The gates themselves were wrapped in blossoms, coloured ribbons, and new green leaves for some kind of festival. Elogast straightened his garb as they approached, trying to look presentable. Kissen didn't bother.

I can see him as that Commander Elogast, said Skedi to Inara. *A man of honour. He protected the pilgrims.*

Inara could see it too. He was calm and steady, unlike Kissen. Skedi had been pestering her through the morning about his preference for Elogast, but Inara wasn't so sure that they should throw themselves at the first person who wasn't a veiga. *Kissen is bad for us,* Skedi added. *You know that yourself; you won't tell her about the colours you see because you think she'll hate you.*

She has done nothing to hurt us.

Not yet. But we haven't told her everything.

Inara sighed. Skedi was frightened of the veiga, she understood that. But Kissen, despite her rudeness, was strong, trustworthy, kind even, in her rough way. Skedi might be safer with Elo, but Kissen had been a constant in the days since her home burned down. Gruff and cross, but constant. Now their wall of pilgrims had gone, Inara could admit to herself that she was frightened too. Elo had said it right: two swords were better than one.

The damp air about them grew brilliant when the sun came out from behind the clouds, and Inara bounced on her toes, trying to see inside the gates. They celebrated harvest festivals at the Craier steadings. Inara was never allowed to go, but her mother went and danced with her workers after Inara was tucked up tight in bed. They must have had similar throwings in Ennerton, though she only heard the gossip of any such thing. This was not a harvest festival, though; it was still early in spring.

Passage into the town was restricted. Inara could see a bird that flew from the far side of the great bridge where it reached the cliffs, to the near, apparently carrying news of departures; only after it landed was another group allowed in. There was gossiping all about them, and Inara overheard a pair, well-travelled, with an ass and cart in tow, chattering away to their new fellows in the line.

"Did you hear about the Craier manor?"

"What?"

"Burned. Burned down. The whole thing and its people. Thieves, they say. No one has claimed it, the burning or the title. Not yet anyway."

So, the news had spread. Inara felt numb to hear it, like it had happened to someone else.

"What's all this nonsense?" said Kissen loudly to the woman in front, who had sprigs of wild garlic-flowers in her hair. It stank something awful. The veiga put a hand on Inara's shoulder and squeezed. A distraction.

Gods don't like gossips, Inara heard Skedi think at the group. They fell quiet, though they would not have known where the thought had come from; he did not press hard enough for it to hurt.

"Spring festival," said the woman in answer to Kissen's question, as Inara tried to pretend she had heard nothing. "Mutur, we call it in these parts. The seasons changing, days getting longer."

"There's more people than I'd expect."

The woman flapped her hand gleefully, sending gusts of garlic over to them. "House Geralfi declared a mast season coming this summer," she said. "The grazing about these parts will be best in three years, so we're keen to book spaces for their beasts."

"That far in advance?" said Inara, surprised and actually distracted now. Elo looked at the woman sharply, a frown line striking between his brows. Mast seasons were in the late summer or in autumn, not in spring—the tree nuts wouldn't fall till then.

"Fat trees means fat pigs, means fat people," said the woman with a wink. "It will be a good winter, gods bless us. There'll be chestnuts, too, for my goats. They get treats, I bag the rest."

"There's strong competition," said Kissen, looking about them at the crowds. The woman nodded, and looked them over with a shrewd eye, perhaps wondering if they would be trying to beat her for grazing slots. Between the swords, the packs, and the horse, they didn't look like local farmers. She smiled, revealing six yellow teeth. "If you're wanting to come through town you have to stay the night," she said. "Otherwise you'll need to take a boat upriver."

Kissen shrugged, but Elo looked put out. "Why is that?"

"Tax. King says Houses can't charge people for passage in Middren, but they can have you buy food and beds."

"How do they know already it's a mast season?" pressed Inara, more interested in predicting the future than spending the night.

The woman touched her nose, then her head, winked once more, and turned to the front of the queue, where someone was now playing a pocket flute.

Inara gestured for Kissen's attention, then used sign to ask, *What does that mean?*

Gods still living, said Kissen. *Wild gods of the wood.* Inara blinked and looked around. Unlike outside Lesscia, she realised she couldn't see any knights in blue and gold patrolling the road.

You won't cause a fuss?

Kissen laughed. *I pick my battles. I'd get very dead if I just killed any god I crossed paths with.*

Inara scowled. *You tried to kill Skedi.*

Kissen shrugged. *I have an instinct for trouble.*

"Could you pick a language we all understand?" said Elo, eyeing Kissen. She gave him a gesture, curling her forefinger into her thumb. From Elo's raised eyebrow, Inara understood it to be very rude.

"Party season in Gefyr is supposed to be great," said Kissen. "The ale will flow gold tonight."

"And we will leave at sunup," said Elo, looking unamused.

They finally reached the gates, and no one blinked twice as they were signed into the register and asked how long they were staying.

"The Fisher's Stay got berths?" Kissen asked. The harassed-looking gate guard shrugged. He wore the House Geralfi's sign on his chest, a bridge flanked by two ibex, one with a collar of pine, the other with wheat on its horns.

"They'll not take on travellers without good reason," he said. "It's a locals' stay." He looked at the queue behind them. "You're lucky, there aren't many spaces left tonight. We'll be closing the gates soon. Too much weight on the timbers, if you know what I mean." He eyed Legs. "Make sure he gets to the stable."

"Is the bridge safe to stay on?" asked Elo.

"Gefyr sees it so . . ." He blanched, realising he had invoked the name of a god before strangers, which could be enough to be jailed. "The bridge is safe enough, my friend," he covered quickly. "House Geralfi take care of us, and the king keeps watch." He gestured above him to a well-made portrait of King Arren, as always the sun rising behind him and a stag's head beneath his foot. He had a proud-looking face in this etching, and curling light brown hair. Inara glanced at Elo, who was not hiding his frown well. The guard waved them through, happy to see the back of them and clearly hoping he wouldn't be reported.

"The Geralfis still consult the local gods," said Elo, half to himself as they came into town. "I knew there would be lawbreakers but none so . . . obvious."

"It's not our business," said Kissen, shouldering through the crowd that was gathered at the gates.

"It is *your* business."

"Only when someone pays me for it."

The courtyard they entered into was clearly where places were being booked for the mast haul. There were scattered tables all about, with paper ledgers, thick and creamy, being guarded by men in the green and indigo colours of House Geralfi. There was one knight in blue and gold who was leaning against a wall, smoking from a pipe. Did all the House lands now split their guarding with the king's knights? There had been none in Ennerton or the Craier steadings.

She was distracted as a fiddler danced past, chased by two pipers who were winding between the tables, ribbons hanging from their wrists and bells on their ankles. Even here, Inara could smell the tang of mead and apricot brandy over the cold press of the waterfalls. People were drunk.

As they shouldered through, a cry of anger rattled out. An argument had ensued between the garlic woman and another with a cherry blossom in her hair. The holder of the ledger they were arguing over raised it in the air, and a horn blew.

"Lady-Heir Geralfi! Resolution, if you please."

The women ceased their argument and followed the ledger-carrier. Inara watched their trail, but lost them in the crowd, so she put her foot in Legs's stirrup and hoisted herself onto his back. From this angle she could see the throngs parting for them. The ledger was borne before a throne, its armrests formed from curling horns of ibex, its seat and back constructed of young beech, pine, and birch, the branches barely budded. On it sat a girl about Inara's age, in fine green cloth with an indigo-and-silver brocade of what looked like silk. Beside her stood a taller man, clearly her father, from looks and bearing.

The two of them waited for the book to be held before them, and the scribe stated the case. Inara could barely hear it over the other noises, but something about goats and pigs, chestnuts and beeches.

The young lady Geralfi looked to her father for advice, and he leaned down to whisper in her ear. She turned forward and stood.

"The higher reaches will be reserved for goats, where the pigs can't roam. This is declared in the name of Geralfi."

A cheer broke out, and the horn blew again. "Lady-Heir, such grace!"

Inara found herself blushing. The young Geralfi was not hidden away, as she had been. Her father was there beside her. Inara wondered what her own father looked like.

"You, there! No riding in town!"

Inara slid off Legs onto the dust of the bridge. Rosalie, the barkeep from Ennerton, had not even known she was born, yet here was a girl of nobility mingling and leading. Why had Inara's mother hidden her? Was it anything to do with why she had been killed? Was it Inara's fault, somehow?

We will find out, said Skedi, tracing her thoughts. *Perhaps when you go to the Reach at Sakre. Perhaps the knight might know.*

Kissen led them down pathways that took them away from the throng, over the top of the water that thundered below them. Kissen opted to use her staff tucked under her arm to help her walk, so Inara led Legs. She liked that the veiga trusted her with the horse.

Fine spray rose and dampened them as they walked, but that didn't stop the spillover of locals from the bridge gathering on the thick beams below the causeway. Inara could see people through the gaps beneath their feet, a thriving under-bridge market and workers mingled in with the damp from the rapids. One mucky-faced boy was springing from beam to beam, a broom in his hand. He stopped beneath a pipe that jutted over the water and thrust up with the broom to unclog it. After a jab or two, it gushed forth, and up rose the stink of human excrement and vegetable waste. Inara covered her nose. She had drunk from this river's water—far from the falls, true, but she did not want to linger on the thought.

The grand centre of the town rose as they made their way over the bridge. On the upriver side was a place where the riverboats could stop, deliver goods, and be on their way back upstream. There was a small channel in the river where they could cut between the rapids and make it safely in. How busy it must be, and how exciting, ferrying goods from the heart of Middren out to the coast via the great towns of the south. How lonely it was, to be passing it by. Inara's own household wouldn't celebrate another festival; they wouldn't dance in the summer and be caught sleeping in the hay. Her mother wouldn't put her to sleep and tell her stories of life on the seas, of salt winds, of dances in courts and the dizzying smokes of secret leaves. She wouldn't hear the spaces in those stories where her father might be. Where safety might lie. How was she supposed to avenge a House whose people did not know her, and a woman she suddenly realised she barely understood? A woman who hid her letters, silenced her daughter. Who burned and left so little behind.

Inara was not like the little Lady Geralfi. She was something else. All the quiet questions of her life were coming together. Skediceth, her mother, her isolation in the Craier home and lack of family, no known father. The colours. All this death. The fire. The shadow summonings. It had happened when she broke her mother's rules.

Inara gritted her teeth as she felt her world threaten to overwhelm her. She had to rise over it, like a ship on a wave, to get to where she was going. She was brave; she had left her house with Skedi and found the godkiller. She had decided to go to Blenraden, to stay when she could have run.

They passed the centre of the bridge, and the town grew smaller, grimmer, and squat. Inara saw two more knights in the king's colours walking amongst the houses, looking haughty. Elo pulled a hood up before they passed, but if there was any recognition in either direction, Inara didn't see it. Still, Kissen led them away from the centre to the outskirts, where the buildings looked directly over the falls, the path vibrating slightly with the river's power. This area was built like a fort, with slots in the walls for archers, trick-steps in the path that would fell anyone running. She wondered who these defences had been built against. The Craier books of songs and maps told of coastal Talician raiders that had been driven back a century before, but Gefyrton was far inland. Perhaps bickering clans, warrior bands, and thieves descending from the nearby mountains.

The top of the cliff at the eastern side of town was painted copper with bloodstains from the smoking abattoirs, tanneries, and warehouses clustered at its top. Inara traced them down the slopes to the frothing waves below. They must have to track trading goods down the cliffs, probably to the next town downriver, or barrels would smash to smithereens against the boulders within the falls. She was staring into the churning depths before she realised one boulder had shape: a beard, and eyes. The fallen head of one of the gods that had held up the bridge for generations.

She felt Elo come to stand beside her and follow her gaze. His colours flickered, conflicted, when they were usually so steady.

"Why are you sad?" said Inara. Elo blinked, then sighed.

"It seems . . . a pity," he said softly. "They did not fight in Blenraden, but were punished for it."

Inara fiddled with Legs's bridle. "Don't you hate gods too?"

Elo was surprised by the question. "No," he said slowly. "I was raised to believe faith is a choice we make on our own." That seemed strange, for a knight.

Kissen had walked ahead, but stopped now too. Inara doubted she could hear them over the falls.

"Then why did you fight them?"

"I fought to protect my friend, and save our people," said Elo. "Then . . . then King Arren believed the only way to stop another war from happening was to keep fighting." Inara supposed that if there were no gods, then there would be nothing to fight. Or fight for.

"Is that why you left?"

His colours shone gold. Legs was hoofing at the boards, unhappy with the strange surface and the roar of the falls below them. Elo absently reached up to stroke his neck. "Yes," he said at last.

"Oy," said Kissen, irritated, "do you want to sleep here or in a bed?"

Elo looked up and rubbed his hand over his shaved head with a half laugh. His colours softened, the dark purple and golds brightening into a fresh green. "I'm not allowed to make friends now?" he said pointedly.

Kissen scoffed and strode up to them, putting her face close to Elo's and giving him such a glare that Inara didn't know if she might kiss him or kill him. To Inara's surprise, Elo didn't balk or back away, but stared her down, his colours shimmering with amusement rather than anger. "Leave the girl be," said Kissen, and bared her teeth in a dangerous smile, then pulled Legs away. "*And* the horse."

It wasn't much further down the edge of the bridge to a door with a large heron flying in the stained-glass window. The building itself looked small, squeezed between two larger houses which echoed with the sounds of light flirtatious laughter, and the clink of glasses, coming from inside.

"It doesn't look big enough," said Inara.

"They rent hammocks over the water," said Kissen. "Extra coin for a sleep sack. The one year they had mites they burned all the bedding and bought new. That's better than any other place I've had."

"It's the law here," said Elo. "Mites spread to wood."

"People can be a bit choosy about the laws they follow," said Kissen. "The deeper into Middren, the less sway your kingling holds." She was still annoyed with him, clearly.

Elo's jaw flexed. "You know nothing about him," he said, and pushed open the door to the tavern. Inara felt a gust of warm air on her cheeks, but cold on her chin. She looked down, and realised there was a thin gap between the doorstep and the street. Through it, she could see the massive beams of the bridge, and clusters of what looked like caterpillar cocoons strung up beneath them, connected together by wet and bouncy-looking ropes and boardwalks. At least she found none of the same kind of pipe she had smelled unblocking earlier. She hoped she would not need to break her sleep in the night.

"Permit passes," said a boy at a table just inside the door, blocking the way into the inn proper. He looked like he was one argument away from a scream. Inara crept up by Elo, who handed over the folded papers they had been given upon entry.

"We don't keep travellers," the boy said, handing them back. "Not unless they're performers. Geralfi's rules to keep the pilgrims out."

So, the Geralfis consulted the gods, but still had laws to reduce pilgrims. Inara reached into her bag and put her thumb by Skedi, who was the size of a pebble. He licked her for reassurance.

"We are performers," said Inara, and felt him lend some will to the lie.

The fellow blinked and looked them over. "What do you do?"

Read palms. He's your father.

"I'm a palm reader," said Inara. "My father taught me." She held on to Elo's sleeve and he started in surprise. Inara almost felt Kissen roll her eyes behind them. "He had a patronage with House Yeset." She let Skedi's whispers feed straight through her mouth. "But now we're joining our troupe in Arga."

Arga was the farthest northeast point of Craier lands. If they followed the river upstream from the falls, they would come to it at the water's narrowest, iciest points. Inara knew her mother had encouraged artists and players to congregate there.

The boy's eyes clouded a little with doubt as he looked at Elo. "You're her father? No point in two palm readers."

Elo swallowed. "I sing," he said, and managed a quite charming smile.

He sings, he sings, he sings, Skedi echoed, and the doubt cleared. The boy glanced behind them at Kissen, who looked rather like she was suppressing a laugh.

"And you?"

"I'm taking the horse to the stables," she said. "And when I'm back, tell Tip that Kissen the veiga has come."

Inara stared behind her at Kissen, then back at the boy, who had gone quite grey. Inara felt Skedi shiver angrily. She had thwarted his power, dismissed it, ignored it, told the truth.

"Ah, oh," the boy said. "Do you have documents?"

Kissen pulled a leather roll from her heavy cloak and showed him a ragged piece of vellum with a scrawl of ornate writing and a series of stamps on it: three-pointed crosses. Settles' stamps, they looked like, official signings. Inara realised these must be for each god she had killed. There were so many.

"I . . . I don't know if we'll have berths for . . . for—"

"You be asking Tip now," said Kissen with a smile. "We want none of those wet ones by the falls. Out at the edge and dry. I'll be back." She glanced at Elo, then turned to Inara.

"You can come with me while I take Legs."

I'm tired, Ina, Skedi broke in, though Inara was tempted to see more of the town. *You're tired too.*

And she felt it, the weight of her own fatigue wrapping around her. "I'll stay with Father," she said, and added in sign, *I can find out more about him.* Kissen was about to protest, but Elo took Inara's hand with purpose, clearly still smarting from her earlier comment.

"Come, Tethis," he said, ducking into the tavern. The boy didn't stop them. They left Kissen outside with the saddlebags and the horse, glaring at them until the door shut.

CHAPTER SEVENTEEN

Elogast

ELO'S EYES ADJUSTED TO THE LIGHT OF THE INN AS THE BOY bounded off his stool, clearly looking for this Tip fellow. Elo hadn't been sure about Inara's white lie, or Skedi's, he supposed, but Kissen should have told them she would say exactly who she was.

At least the lad had no more urgent interest in them. Behind the table he had vacated were a series of notices, many of them requests for godkillers from nearby towns and villages. This must be how veiga like Kissen found their quarry. Some offered a few coins to dismantle a shrine; others were for gods themselves. Elo saw none he recognised, just a trickster god who curdled milk, a god of wind that had been raging around a village for weeks, and a just-formed tree god that a zealot had reported.

Inside the Fisher's Stay the festival atmosphere was muted; only a few branches and herbs hung along the beams that crisscrossed the ceiling from front to back. The white plaster between them was old enough for smoky streaks to have cut rivers between the fug of the fire and damp. It was hot, close, and sweating, smelling of river fish and pickles. The windows were low and small, and the light through them sharp, cutting across from the west and turning the gusts of bittersweet pipe smoke to monsters and gods twisting the air.

Elo spotted an empty barrel table near a window on the other side of the notice wall, and took Inara to it. It was a good position, defensible, and opposite the trap door that must lead to the berths.

Rough was the common theme of the patrons, unkempt and drinking heavily. Some had visible scars and wore ribbons in blue and gold on their wrists or shirts. Strange. Arren's colours, not House Geralfi's. Elo found his eyes drawn to the mantel, where a stag's head hung, its antlers disfigured with ink: across them was written *Victory*.

Elo's stomach went cold. He couldn't believe her: this was a veterans' tavern. Was she hoping he would get recognised?

No one recognises you, said Skedi, straight into his mind, soothingly. *I won't let them*. Elo was startled; the god's voice hurt as always, but his words were kind. He wondered where the little thing was hiding— probably under Inara's cloak or in her hood, somewhere he could see what was going on. Elo gritted his teeth and pulled up a seat at the table, keeping his head low.

"What's the matter?" asked Inara.

"That veiga has a death wish," he muttered. "This bar is for people who fought in Blenraden."

"What makes you say that?"

Elo looked at the stag's head again and shivered. He didn't want to explain that to her. "I just know."

It wasn't long till they were brought two horn tankards filled with ale by a fellow with a braided beard, yellowed with smoke. "I'm Leir," he said. "I'm the runner here. Food? Soft skink or pie."

"Pie," said Elo, rubbing his temple. "And for my daughter as well."

The man shrugged. "Pay as you leave," and headed back to the bar. Inara looked at him curiously.

"Skink is fish soup; it's terrible with river fish," he said by way of explanation. He glanced about and noted that no one was paying attention, so he relaxed a little.

"Singer?" said Inara, nervously turning her ale mug. "What would you have done if they had asked you to prove it?"

She was a sharp one. Elo shrugged and rubbed his neck. "I would have sung." He took a long, deep drink of his ale, hoping she wouldn't ask again. It was bitter and chill, refreshing. They must have hung the kegs over the falls with the hammocks. "What language is it that you and Kissen do with your hands?" he asked, trying to make conversation. He had to admit, he was curious about the veiga and the girl. Kissen was so protective of her.

"It's called sign in Middren," she said. She also took a sip, then pulled a face. Elo laughed; he suspected she had been raised on sweeter drinks. "It's made by people who are deaf," she added, "but my mother said it's used on the seas by pirates as well; they call it handspeak."

Elo sat back on his stool, surprised. "Your mother must be well travelled then, to have met a pirate."

Inara quickly raised the horn back to her mouth, her eyes widening a little. She shouldn't have let that slip, Elo suspected. He found it curious that Skedi had said her father had married into the Artemi family. They were rich merchants to be sure, but they were from the northwest; Inara's accent was from central Middren.

The pies arrived and interrupted them, complete with bread, butter, and olives on the side. The pastry was dense and baked a golden brown. Elo gave it proper attention and broke into it with the knife on the plate. The pie crunched beautifully, breaking into crisp layers. The innards were fish, pickled cabbage, and capers. Elo took a bite first using the crust as a spoon, then buttered an edge of bread to soak up some of the filling. The butter itself was fresh made and creamy, whipped with orange peel and poppy seeds. He would have to try that when he got back to baking. It soothed the sharp, vinegary taste of the pie and the sourness of the bread.

Inara watched him, not yet eating her own meal. "How did you become the knight commander?" she asked. "You're very young for it. I thought they were usually old knights."

Elo assessed the people nearby, but no one was listening. He swallowed carefully. Clearly she had decided she wanted to direct his attention away from her. He thought about it. Her god, wherever he was hiding, would tell her if he lied. "I feel I should be honest with you," he said, "so you know I mean you no harm. Whatever Kissen might say."

Inara took a bite of her pie, holding its edge with both hands. "Why wouldn't you be honest?" she said innocently, but Elo saw that glint in her eye. Kissen was a bad influence on her, he could tell that after only a few days.

"What do you remember of the beginning of the war?" he asked.

"Not much," said Inara, her mouth full, now trying to detangle her hair with her fingers. "I remember all the Houses took their guards to fight, including ours."

Elo nodded. "It was the king's sister, Bethine, who led us. We didn't know what had happened to the queen and her sons, but Bethine was the queen-to-be without them and Arren the next in line, so I only went as Arren's guard." He sighed. "Even with all the Houses, it took months to besiege Blenraden and break through the hunt the wild gods ran around the city walls. When we finally did, Bethine's first priority was to save the people who had been trapped inside. She made a deal with Restish, and the god of safe haven, Yusef, to get them out."

"Gods fought on your side?"

Did people not know this? "Yes . . . for a time." He didn't want to go deeper into that. Not with the stag's head over the mantel watching them. "We made a path down the Godsway, to the harbour."

Inara's face tightened. So, she knew about this battle.

"Most of the Houses, the commanders, were leading the evacuation," continued Elo, "filling the ships, while Arren and I guarded the palace. The wild gods were over their cliff-shrines, east of the city. Licking their wounds. We thought."

He closed his eyes for a moment, a tremor of memory and pain flooding through him. He put his hands on the table, flat, before they could shake, imagining dough beneath them to calm himself.

"They attacked the ships," Inara whispered.

"Even the great god of safe haven couldn't fight them all," said Elo. "The wild gods swept them all down, hull to mast. And Bethine too."

Inara looked down at her plate. Could she even imagine? Thousands of people, drowning in storm and madness. And all he and Arren could do was watch.

"Most of the command were killed or injured," said Elo. "Many of those who could fight ran. That's how I made knight commander. No special talent, no real experience. We were just part of what was left."

Inara picked at her food. "My mother . . . she was there. She was injured."

They were edging closer to something true. Elo didn't want to press too hard. Maybe he shouldn't. Maybe it really wasn't his business. But he couldn't help being curious.

"How did you win?" asked Inara. She sniffed. "After all that. They were gods."

"We rebuilt the army," said Elo, "with gods and people. Volunteers, common folk." He glanced around them at veterans with the king's colours on their arms. They had called for revenge. Vengeance for the queen, for the dead, for the spilled blood. Vengeance on the gods that had turned on them.

"And then . . . ?"

"Then . . ."

Then, Arren had turned on the gods.

"Arren did what he thought was right, what he thought would protect his people. Your father would do the same for you."

"My mother. I never knew my father."

There.

"Your father who sent you to Blenraden with a veiga?"

Inara's head shot up, her face pale. "I . . ." Her hand flew to her shoulder. "*Skedi*," she hissed.

What? You said it. Elo heard him too. Skedi was including him in the conversation. Elo smiled reassuringly as Inara calmed and tightened her other hand around the buttons on her embroidered waistcoat.

"What is your real name?" Elo asked.

Inara covered her face, red with shame. "Inara Craier."

"Craier?" said Elo. Now *that* was a name. "I thought you might be. You're the right age, and you look like your mother." He laughed. "In honesty, Inara, we have met before."

CHAPTER EIGHTEEN

Inara

BEFORE?

Inara dropped her hands. "You know about me?" she said, forgetting that Skedi had just let her expose their own lie.

"Of course. Your birth was announced at court a few years before the war," said Elo. His colours showed no surprise. He had known she was lying. "We heard stories about Lady Craier. She had a talent for languages and was well travelled. Wild, the Craiers called her." He laughed. "Arren liked that."

He was so calm, so certain.

"No father announced," Elo added. "I do remember that. But that's no matter. When your mother visited court she let Bethine hold you. Of course, she went around showing off little baby Craier like you were a prize."

She had been at court. A queen-to-be had held her, however briefly her regency lasted. Inara was known. Elo knew her.

See? said Skedi. *He can help us. He can help us better than Kissen.*

"Why has she sent you with that woman?" said Elo. "This road is dangerous, and Blenraden too."

Tell the truth to him, Ina; it will do no harm.

"She didn't," said Inara, her voice small. "She's dead."

Elo's face fell. "I am so sorry," he said. "What happened?" He must not have been listening in the queue, wrapped up in his own problems; he hadn't heard what the gossipers said.

Tell him. He will help us.

Inara felt more and more certain that Skedi was right. The thought bore down on all other doubts in her head, crushing them, pushing them aside. Skedi was right. Elo would help them.

"Inara, what is it you're hiding?" asked Elo.

"I . . . our manor, our people. They were attacked. They burned it down."

"Who did?"

"I don't know. That's why we're travelling in secret. Kissen thinks they might be after me too, if they find out I'm alive."

"The godkiller fights gods, not people. She should have brought you to King Arren."

"But what about Skedi?"

"Palm reader!"

The boy from the door threw himself into the empty seat Inara had been holding for Kissen. "Tethis, no? You're with the veiga." He clutched his throat in mock distress. "I almost pissed myself there, but Tip does say he knows her and let me loose." He put his elbows on the table. In his hand was a half-empty tankard the size of his head. "Finally, my shift is over. No more being scoffed at, talked down to, bribed, cajoled, and spat on, Arren be blessed." He delivered Inara a big smile. "I'm Nat. Read my palm, would you? I can pay. Tell me this isn't my life forever."

He thwacked a hand on their barrel. Inara stared at it. She felt dazed and confused, as if she were dreaming. A woman had begun singing by the fire on a slightly raised stage, but she was being completely ignored.

You don't work for free, said Skedi, and Inara found herself speaking.

"I'm not cheap," she said. The boy blinked at her, reached into a pocket, and flipped out a tiny silver coin with the king's head stamped on one side and the Geralfi arms on the other. A new thing; Inara had never seen one before. It was about the size of her fourth nail. Kissen had mostly paid in heavy ingots, silver bits—illegal currency—and brass. This was more than enough for the night's lodging. Skedi grew, she felt it. An offering.

"Look here, lad," said Elo, but Inara held up a hand.

"*Fair coin for a reading*," Skedi spoke through Inara, and she found she had lost control over her own voice. Still, she preferred it. She could sit back, watch. Skedi was in command. She reached out, took Nat's hands, and turned them over. He beamed. Inara felt Skedi slide down her hood and back into the satchel, so he could peek up at the boy's face without being seen as she looked at his hands.

Hungry, said Skedi. Inara could see it. The colours were there, shivering, intense, pink and vermilion. He was perhaps two years older than she, with a shock of wavy black hair that stuck out, and piercings in his ears which he had threaded through with a brass wire. His colours turned and moved, like sunlight through glass. Violet now. For Inara, purple was a serious colour; her mother wore it for special occasions. But for the boy . . . *Fanciful*, said Skedi. *Not so bright.*

"*You have a strong life line,*" the god said out loud, through Inara's voice. She pointed to a random place on his left palm. "*You will live to an old age.*" A flutter of turquoise at his brow. This confirmed a suspicion. His family had a history of long life.

All wishes have warnings, Inara felt Skedi think.

"*Be careful,*" she found her tongue forming, Skedi's sweet lies tripping over it. Nat leaned in as Inara pointed to a line that deviated but did not break. "*This suggests a fall, or accident, that could make you lame, dependent on others. You will be a proud man, and a fall will go hard.*"

Nat frowned and sighed. "Well, that happens to half the people on this rickety bridge." Elo was carefully guarding his expression, but Inara could see his colours too. Silver sparkles of astonishment, and a coral cloud of suspicion.

"*It is not here you are most at risk,*" said Skedi. Inara pointed at a line around his third finger. "*You may choose to stay, or you may leave.*"

"Will I be a knight?" he asked, grinning. Almost imperceptibly, Elo sucked his teeth.

"No," said Skedi. "*You do not believe that yourself.*" He was right; as Nat had asked the question, he had glimmered with grey doubt. "*Instead, there will be wealth. Focus on opportunity closer to home.*" Inara pointed to where the lines on his palm intersected, forming a triangle. "*With a sharp eye and care, you will be able to build the life you want.*"

Nat sat back, a rich blue of satisfaction paling to something more forlorn. He blinked at his palms. Skedi's bag stretched at the seams as he grew.

"Then . . . I should keep working here?" Nat said.

Inara took her hands away. Skedi had never spoken through her before. At first it had felt fine, but as he took over further, she felt strange. Unlike herself, as if she were half-asleep.

"Palm reading is not for specific questions," said Elo. "You've had your reading; be on your way."

"But how many children will I have?" he asked. "What's this opportunity I should look for? Can you give me a hint?"

Inara shut her teeth before Skedi could speak. She felt words crowd her tongue, dropping from Skedi's excited, singsong voice in her head into her mouth.

Tell him he will have three children. To look for the golden hare with antlers and wings, and it will show him the opportunity. Tell him to leave his work, there are better jobs. Tell him to pray to the god of white lies. I could get him what he wanted.

"That's enough reading," said Inara, to Nat and to Skediceth. She put her hand on the bag and squeezed his fur, sending a thought to him. *You promised you would never use your powers on me,* she said.

I didn't use them on you, he thought back.

If Kissen had been here . . .

She's not, and we are glad she's not.

Inara found that she was glad. She wasn't sure why, but at least they hadn't got caught telling such lies.

"Wait," said Nat, interrupting. "You can't just stop when you choose. I gave you a whole silver."

"She said no, child," said Elo, his voice deep and cold. "She said it politely. I suggest you leave or I will say it less politely."

"I was just asking," he said. "I paid." His pout lasted only a moment, then he squared his shoulders at Elo, wanting to get some power back. "What kind of performer threatens a paying customer?" he said. He took the coin he had offered to Inara back off the table and pocketed it. "And what kind of singer carries a sword?" He narrowed his eyes. "I'd suggest demonstrating your own skills, or I'll have the keep call Geralfi's guard."

Elo's colours twisted with a fire of worry, haste, and anger that turned into a glint in his eye, not unlike the one Kissen got when she felt a fight brewing. What was worse, being arrested or being potentially recognised? He smiled, coming to a decision.

"I have never heard of a guard arresting a singer enjoying a good meal," he said. "But fair enough to you, little ratchet. You might have to tell the musician that you're rejecting her services, and Tip and Leir."

He purposefully chose the name Kissen had dropped, and the older runner who had introduced himself. The bard on the stage was indeed still singing valiantly, though another musical group with a whistle was chirruping up notes in the corner and nibbling away any attention she had held. The singer was going yellow with annoyance.

Nat, however, was at war with himself as he chewed his tongue, eyes narrowing at Elo. The boy's aggression, Inara could see, was blue-grey and stormy. He wanted to humiliate Elo because he was embarrassed himself. Elo had risen to the challenge, and that only made Nat want to upset him all the more. His sense of self-preservation was fading quickly.

Skedi, what were you doing? said Ina, turning her thoughts to the god while Elo and Nat engaged in their battle of wills, Nat's colours filtering through with prodding pinks, and Elo's indigo at his edges.

I wouldn't do anything to hurt you, Ina, he said, reassuring. He turned very small, and, while Nat was distracted, crept across the bag and into her palm, curling in it. Safe, comforting. She relaxed a little. He was her Skedi, her friend; he wouldn't hurt her.

Nat realised Elo wasn't going to back down. He threw his seat aside and marched over to the bard. He had to stand on tiptoe to whisper in her ear. She stilled the little lute she was playing, rolled her eyes, then stalked to the bar, leaving a marigold crackle of ire in her wake. Nat folded his arms, in too deep now, and flicked his chin at Elo.

"He can't make you," said Ina, pressing Elo's arm. Through the fog of good feeling and weariness, she realised they were in danger here. She didn't want Elo to obey the boy. She wanted Kissen to come back and throw a table over. She wanted the runner, or the musician, to scold Nat for being so rude. Where was this Tip that Kissen had spoken of? She wanted her mother.

"Do not worry," said Elo, standing and massaging his throat. He took off his sword and put it down. "This is a veterans' bar. But please, close your ears."

He picked his way over to the stage, which was against the wall. No one paid him the least bit of attention over the roar of the water, the clatter of bone and pewter, and the incessant quibbling of the whistle from the other musical group. Still, Elo bowed anyway to Nat, a little mocking gesture.

Ina, of course, did not close her ears.

"*For I was a soldier at the walls of the city,*" Elo began,
"*And all of my lovers at home were far gone*
"*And the gods of our loving were all gone so wrong*
"*So I did not know what to do with myself*
"*While marching the walls of the city.*"

His voice rang out a rich and surprising tenor, and loud, like the singers that came at the winter solstice. He sang slow, catching the crowd's attention. A couple of tired-looking drinkers blinked in his direction. The pipe stopped, and the man playing it, who had only one arm, grinned with his remaining three teeth. Elo entered into the second verse, picking up the pace now that they recognised what he was singing. The tune held the same, like a nursery rhyme.

"*For I was a soldier at the walls of the city*
"*And all of my lovers at home were far gone*
"*And the gods of our loving were all gone so wrong*
"*So I did not know what to do with myself*
"*Should I kiss all the toadies*
"*While marching the walls of the city?*"

The chatter of the bar had ceased. Several heads had turned, and at least three people had hummed the last line with Elo. With the next verse, three women with bows on their backs burst into singing where they sat, nearer the edge of the falls, one who had bright white scars like Kissen's, like lightning had gone down her neck. It seemed they were more interested in the song than in who was singing it.

"*For I was a soldier at the walls of the city*
"*And all of my lovers at home were far gone*
"*And the gods of our loving were all gone so wrong*
"*So I did not know what to do with myself*
"*Should I kiss all the toadies,*
"*Make love to the roadies,*
"*While marching the walls of the city?*"

Inara blushed. She remembered, distinctly, hearing the old guards of her mother's estate making jokes about the war after they had escorted Lady Craier back with her injury from the battle in the harbour. The few who returned spoke of the "toadies," the hangers-on at the edge of the war train, often wastrels or malcontents, looking for scraps of food or things to steal. Not what one would desire to kiss. Make love? The roadies were the merchants that followed the train, setting up camp and stall beside the captive audiences of a siege.

Elo was singing a *naughty* song.

Leir at the bar started clapping his hands to the rhythm. The whistle-blower joined in the tune, and some small groups of the mast season renters who had been mingling with old compatriots started stamping their feet. *Should I kiss all the toadies? Make love to the roadies? Tug on the sword blade? See how much whoring pays? While marching the walls of the city.*

The tavern was shaking as the whole lot of them began stomping and singing, each verse adding a line, each ruder than the last. Nat was now looking at the door to the back room of the inn, where an old man had entered, hair sticking out of his ears and a scowl on his face. With him was Kissen, whose jaw dropped when she saw who was singing on the stage.

"Stop!" cried the man. "No stamping! No shaking! Gefyr is at limit in the festival."

The boards were creaking, and Elo himself could barely be heard over the riotous singing. The singer from before, who was now drinking a brandy, looked quite smug.

"No!" The man by Kissen took to the stage, his hair flying like white flags. "No stamping, no dancing! No licence for it. Keep your ribald nonsense to your hammocks, holy war heroes or no."

The crowd waved their hands and laughed, settling back to their drinks, some still singing the ditty to themselves and giggling.

"Who asked for this?" demanded the keep, glaring at Elo. Inara suspected this was Tip by the red of authority beaming off his crown. Elo kept silent. Nat was nervously creeping away. The thwarted musician raised her glass.

"It was wee Nat!" she said.

Nat looked like he was about to faint. He took a rather large step away from Tip, but not fast enough to avoid the grab made for his shirt so Tip could yank him off his feet. "I'll be telling your pa about this, Nattino Barkson."

They disappeared out the door and onto the bridge outside. The inn fell back into its separate groups, the song itself mostly forgotten.

Elo came down from the stage and back to Ina. Eyes followed. He was a tall man, tall enough that if his hair were growing it would brush the ceiling; he stood out in the tavern like a flame in the dark.

"You didn't close your ears," he said.

"Who was supposed to know you'd sing a sex song?" said Kissen, joining them. She clapped her hand onto his back. "Took me by surprise and a half. Blood and salt, baker, I didn't think you had that in you."

A woman from one of the other tables strode over, clapping her hands delightedly. "You! You're . . . eh, what was his name? Commander Elogast?"

Kissen's hand tightened on Elo's shoulder, perhaps regretting the position she had put him in.

"Oh, for fuck's sake, not again," she said loudly. "He's a baker, not a damn knight. If he could actually use his sword, or if he had the guts to go to Blenraden, I'd know about it, wouldn't I?"

Not a knight, not a knight, not a knight, said Skedi, and his lie took. He spread it further; Inara could feel his will stretching through her, amplified, over the tavern. A few flickerings of recognition died, and any lingering curiosity about Elo dissipated. Still, he fixed Kissen with a hard stare.

The other woman raised her hands. Her cheeks were quite pink with alcohol. "Sorry, sorry," she said, "didn't know he was taken." She walked away.

Elo shrugged off Kissen's hand and nodded towards Inara and Skedi. "Thank you, both," he said, and to Kissen, "Why did you choose this place?"

"You don't need to get defensive, unless you're looking for romancing, in which case"—she gestured around the room—"you can take your pick. You're a rare looker for us common folks."

Elo flushed. "Veiga, you brought us here knowing that someone might recognise me. Why?"

Kissen shrugged and sat in Nat's seat. Inara wished she could see the veiga's colours, understand what she was thinking.

Does a trustworthy person hide from you? said Skedi.

"To find out more about you," Kissen said, picking up Elo's beer and taking a long draught, "and why you're going in secret to an illegal city you besieged." She then added pointedly, "And to spend one night sleeping in a hammock rather than keeping watch on hard ground. All the beds in town are taken and *my* friend Tip kicked out some loafers so we'll have some warmth. You're lucky I didn't have you booted too." She paused. "I considered it before I heard your dirty singing."

"Keep your voice down, damn it," said Elo, leaning in. "What if the demons come here? Are you going to be responsible for other people dying?"

Kissen's lip curled.

"Gods have limits," she said. "Demons showed up on the first and fifth nights. If I know gods, that means it took four days to build up the strength after a summoning to create more beasts. It won't be tonight."

"So . . . they'll be back in three days?" said Inara. If the pattern held, that also meant there would be more of them: three or four. Elo did not look amused.

"I don't trust your judgment," he said coolly, "about Inara, or about the demons. We're already losing time on our journey. The sooner we get to Blenraden, the better."

He picked up his sword and left Kissen still smirking. Inara wasn't sure there was much to smirk about. She had placed her faith in Kissen because the godkiller had been her only choice. Was that still true?

Tip returned and put his hand on the veiga's shoulder. "Trust you to bring foul-mouthed bards along with you," he said. He looked at Inara. "Ah, hello, little palm reader. Welcome to the Fisher's Stay. Lucky you to be travelling with a veiga." He grinned. "Kissen here has free berth every day of her life, in return for saving mine. Your food and drinks too; have your fill."

Inara wanted to ask for water, she felt so wadded and disoriented, but she had seen the excrement going into the river. Ale seemed safer. She smiled her thanks and Tip turned back to Kissen.

"The bard?" he asked. Inara stared at her. She wouldn't betray Elo, would she?

"Another face from the war," said Kissen. "I didn't know him very well. Tight as a purse string."

Tip nodded. "Ah, sleep well, and next time stay another night so we can drink to the death of Mertagh." He glanced at the stag's head and spat at the god's name, hitting his floor and treading the spittle into the dust. "No wars no more." He whistled and went back to the bar.

"Elo didn't like you bringing us here," said Inara to Kissen. She had something else important to say to Kissen, she was sure, but it kept slipping her mind. Her weariness was weighing her down, and Skedi, too, was heavy in her hand, though he was still small.

"Elo doesn't like me anyway." A little burst of irritation from Kissen. Did she want to be liked? She didn't show it.

"He might have if you hadn't tested him," said Ina. "He was warming to you."

"What makes you say that?" asked Kissen, curious.

His colours, that flurry of fresh green. She didn't say it. Not to Kissen.

Don't trust her. Don't trust her not to turn her hatred of gods on you as well as me.

I am not a god, Skedi.

"I told him," Inara said out loud, finding the thought at last, like catching a tickled trout. Slippery. Why? "He knows who I am."

Kissen groaned and pressed her head to the table.

"You're going to be the death of me, girl."

"I think he's safe," said Ina. "Skedi thinks so too."

"Oh, then by all means . . ." Her tone dripped with sarcasm.

It's all right, Inara, Skedi spoke to her directly. *Walk away from the godkiller. Go to Elo. Elo can help.*

"I think he can help me," said Inara. "He knew my name, my mother. Better than you. We can trust him."

"People you trust can turn on you if it pleases them."

Inara was frustrated. She didn't know what to say, how to make Kissen *listen*. Understand. Care at all about what she wanted. Skedi was angry too. He didn't like Kissen, didn't want her. His will was stronger than Inara's.

"*How would you know?*" Skedi spoke through her. Inara tried to calm him, but realised she could not speak. Her tongue was not her own, her mind twisting with confusion, fatigue, doubt, suspicion. Lies. But Skedi had used her voice. Kissen must think she had asked.

Kissen's colours shimmered just over her skin for a moment, taking Inara by surprise. They were flat and dark, grey, like sea and storm clouds, edged with orange fire. Anger radiated from her. "Because they did," she said. "End of discussion."

"*Maybe if you weren't such an untrusting, blunt-edged cow they wouldn't have,*" Skedi-as-Inara snapped.

Kissen's face hardened. The colours disappeared back inside her as she closed herself off, pulling them in, sealing all vulnerabilities. Inara didn't like this. It wasn't right. It wasn't what she felt.

What are you doing, Skedi? Let me go.

Skedi didn't respond.

"*I will not travel with you any more,*" lied Skedi through Inara. "*I don't feel safe with you.*"

"I made a promise, Inara," said Kissen. "I don't make promises lightly, and I don't break them."

"*I am going with Elo, and I want you to leave us alone. Go back to Lesscia, and godkilling, and keep your knives away from Skediceth.*"

Inara's will was overrun by Skedi's. Her only friend had taken control, from within her own mind. She tried again to call him, to move, but he did not stir, and he did not answer.

CHAPTER NINETEEN

Skediceth

WHAT HAD HE DONE? HE HAD ALREADY BEEN PRESSING HIS will at Ina, just slightly, sowing his assurances into her colours as he had done with the pilgrims. Kissen was wrong for them.

He had to. He didn't want to be near her, no matter what Inara wanted. Kissen had no respect for him, his life, his desires. He could not bear this any longer. He was a god.

Then that boy had given an offering, had loved his lies. Inara had let him in, allowed him to move his will through her. He'd had his moment and couldn't let it go. All it took was to burrow further into Inara, weaving his will into her mind. Now he was there to stay, just for a while, just till they were both safe.

You will understand, Inara.

He made her sleep. He could do that, he found, by pressing restful white lies into her mind: that she did not hear the roar of the waters, that this was just a dream, that she was home in her feather bed. The bed was in fact a covered hammock, like a peapod, lined with furs and rough wool. The skins on top kept the water out, but not the smell of damp and old sleepers' sweat. Skedi curled on Inara's chest and willed her to smell jasmine, old wood, and blossoms. Did he feel guilt? Some. He owed a lot to Ina; he loved her. He tried not to delve into her emotions, to see her fright and betrayal. He was a god of white lies, and he had to use his power to protect them.

He woke her before dawn. A morning caller was on her rounds, poking awake those who had asked to be roused early. Skedi could hear the creak of the ropes as people moved or a hammock released a shower of water onto someone below. The waterfall had no manners. It changed and twisted and sprayed. Sometimes they had a steady hammer of drops and fine spray, with a solid drip, drip from the hammock above them. Then, something would change, a gust of wind, pressure released, and they would be hammered.

Time to go. For me, Ina.

She moved as he willed her, gathering her things. She hesitated at the waxwool cloak, but still pulled it over her shoulders. Her mind was a havoc of noise, but he reined it in.

Skedi rode within her hood as Inara buckled her cloak and descended the slippery ladderway from the sodden bunk to the damp boards. He was hidden by her curls, safe and warm.

This way.

He had noted where Elo was sleeping. He carried her up the ropes and ways, her winglessness slowing them both down. No, not sleeping—Elo was awake, stirring, the prickle of grey wariness clustering about his hands. He could hear them coming, feel the sway of the weight changing in the boards as they drew closer. Perhaps he had a knife. Perhaps Skedi was bringing Inara to harm.

Skedi flew on little wings to the opening of Elo's awning, the extent of the distance he could go from Ina. The knight muffled a cry.

"Do not strike, knight, it's us!"

Elo blinked at Skedi, then looked down at Ina.

"What is it, Inara? What did Kissen do?"

"*Nothing*," Skedi spoke through her mouth, in her voice. "*We want to go with you, now, before she wakes up. It's her drawing the demons, I am sure of it. I don't want to die.*"

Inara was crying, Skedi realised. Water leaked from her face and onto her chin.

Stop it, he said. *This is for us. I promise, I'll let you go when we're out.*

"I—" Elo hesitated, his emotions swirling about him. Doubt, a strong one. Doubting himself. And with it, loyalty. A quenching, consuming azure loyalty that could overwhelm all other things. "Inara, I am on an important quest . . . I cannot—"

He was vulnerable. He did not have his will enclosed as Kissen did. He could be turned.

She will be safer with you, said Skedi, pressing his will against the man's mind. *She is like King Arren, is she not? Arren would want her protected, Bethine too. Keep her safe.*

"*Please*," he said out loud. Intentionally or not, Inara's tears swayed Elo too. Skedi's will wrapped around Elo's colours, feeling his uncertainty and soothing it, choking it. He could do it, he could hold them both, because these were little lies they almost wanted to believe. A sense of honour rose in Elo's colours, the shade of a peach dawn, and he nodded.

"Very well," he said. It was almost sweet; he really did believe in helping people. He grabbed his pack and swung out of the hammock. Skedi flew back to Inara and turned her around, his fur rising with his own power; he could almost feel his antlers growing larger. Humans were so gullible! Like fish in a net, once he had them. He had taken control of his fate and Inara's, for the first time since they had found each other and had been forced to live in fear. He would ask them for offerings in return for rescuing them from the veiga and the demons. He would be a true god.

They climbed the stairs to the tavern, coming up through the floor as Skedi dove back inside Inara's hood. Someone was clattering in the kitchen, and the smells of a fresh coal fire were rising from the grate. A couple were sitting by the flames, eating sour plum stew and steaming their clothes that had soaked in the waterfall spray.

Elo gestured at Inara to follow him out the door. Unlike the girl, he was like a toy on a spring; he had been wound up with a good lie and now off he went. Skedi let his wings feel the thrill of his excitement. The further they got from Kissen, the happier Skedi felt.

They stepped out onto the stone of the central avenue of the bridge. Hawkers had already hauled up a fresh morning catch from the river and were spilling the fish into crates for sale that day. Two children were setting to work gutting, and the narrow street was stinking with scales and blood. Inara and Elo had to splash straight through the offal to the east side of town.

The gates on this side were low and squat compared to the ones on the west bank but similarly pinned with garlands. Skedi peeked through Inara's hair. Those who could not afford a bed were clustered there, packing up their sleeping things and queuing to leave. A few were stirring little vats of nettle soup or eating biscuits crushed with salt and dried berries.

The gates were half-open, a tired-looking scribe crossing off names from a ledger and adding some entrants from the east. Beyond it, Skedi could see cut-back trees and the open road. There were many travellers on foot, some with horses.

Amongst them stood the godkiller.

Her wild hair was pinned back beneath a band of plaits, and she was well dressed, not out of breath, her pack on her shoulder and Legs nudging at her hand, looking better rested than the lot of them. She smiled. Skedi shrank back despite himself. Women like that made him question his immortality.

Inara's emotions ran wild. Skedi stamped them down, keeping his will on Elo, trapping his belief in the white lies. Skedi was at the edge of the little power he had. But what could he do? They could not turn back. They could not cause a scene, and be discovered, arrested, questioned. Skedi couldn't put Inara in danger, nor himself. That was not what he intended.

He moved Inara forward and they signed out of the city, their false names checked off the list, and met Kissen on the road.

"You're moving slow this morning," she said. Elo put a hand on Inara's shoulder.

"She is coming with me," he said. "It was her request, and I will grant it. You're free of your duty, so go on your way."

"It is no duty," said Kissen. Her sea-grey eyes landed on Inara. "It was a promise." She did not know it was Skedi. She could not. He hid behind Inara's neck. "Now, baker, let's not fight here."

Elo moved his hand carefully to his sword, but didn't draw it. A rainbow of conflict shivered over his colours, the fresh green of his initial warmth for Kissen, that loyal blue and peach-shaded honour, then grey caution and spikes of gold—vicious, violent—grew stronger as he glanced at the travellers around them. Too many people. "No," he said. "Not here."

They followed the crowd of people leaving Gefyrton. Skedi didn't have to see Kissen's colours to know the two of them were simmering, ready to burst. Colours changed the air to grey and gold about Elo, turning Skedi's fur all on end. Thrilling. He had done this. Elo would win in a fight; he was trained, poised. He had a god on his side.

The flagstones of the town road led to a beaten dirt trail edged by felled trees and growing vineyards. Horses and cattle dominated the way, and it was difficult to lose the other travellers. Most took the first road coastwards, but there was a good number going deeper into the mountains, heading north between greening meadows and slopes of winter-blackened bracken. Some slopes still had snow tucked into shaded crannies beneath the first buds of birches. Inara had stopped struggling against Skedi, while Elo put himself between her and Kissen and the horse. Kissen eyed him sideways, taking it as an insult that he thought she might grab the girl and run. Perhaps it was. Perhaps she would.

They kept quiet, though. It wasn't long before they met two knights in the king's colours on the road where it narrowed between rocky outcrops. They were more alert than the pipe-smoking guard they had seen at the gates the day before. These had set up a sigil on the ground: a piece of wood carved with a shape like the branch of a tree, or a trident. They rounded up travellers, forcing them to step on the wood as they passed, causing congestion. It must be the sign of a god, and they were making them stamp on it to prove they had no loyalty. Kissen, Elo, and Inara were ordered to walk over it as they passed, and they did without hesitation, the conflict between them greater than the curiosities of the road.

They were only steps away when they heard a scuffle. Skedi peeked over the top of Inara's hood and saw the knights seize an old woman by her arms. She had refused to step on the symbol.

"Please!" she said. "It's the symbol of Lethen. She guides lost travellers home."

"The king is your guidance," one of the knights growled.

"I'm a travelling merchant. You cannot ask me to stamp on her and invite calamity!"

The knight who had spoken struck her hard with their gloved hand, then grabbed her by the neck and pressed her down onto the symbol, crushing her face into it. Skedi felt Elo waver, his will clashing with anger. He stopped in his tracks, his own desires threatening to break Skedi's.

You cannot help her. What about your pilgrimage? What can you do here to change what is done?

Elo's thoughts were clear as day. Arren would not want this. Arren would not do this. The thoughts faded, leaving him with: Arren; Brother; Friend; Help him.

Help Inara, whispered Skedi. *Help me.*

Help.

For the second time on this journey Elo turned away from the knights he might once have called his comrades, simmering with anger, shame, and regret.

It was barely a league on that they came across a stone sign patched with yellow lichen. Its arrows pointed to significant towns to the north, east, and south. At the top, a long fissure had been hacked over the writing, rough pieces hewn away and the stone lighter beneath than it was on the surface. The only letters left were the first, half a *B*, and the belly of the *d*. Blenraden.

They took the route in silence, facing towards the sun. It passed its zenith before they could deviate from the road and slip onto a footpath that led upwards. The forest grew dense again around them, and young fawns and their mothers scattered through the wood as they passed. Slowly, the afternoon eked out its light between the trees and they ascended higher into the foothills of the Bennite Mountains, finding themselves on rockier ground. They came to a clearing, damp with melting snow and spring rains. The colours about Elo were changing. Stilling.

It was there that they found themselves completely alone.

Elo stopped first. He drew his sword, its briddite blade murky, his emotions dark.

"Wait, Elo—" Inara's voice broke through. Skedi dug his claws into her shoulder, cramming his will again on top of hers. She was just a human, a little girl; she couldn't resist the intense pressure of a god.

Quiet, quiet is better, said Skedi. *I promise this is for the best. I promise.*

"Veiga," said Elo, as Kissen led Legs to a patch of grass and directed him to graze. She unbuckled her cloak, and dropped it on his saddle, then gave him a last pat and stroke of his soft ears. Her eyes scanned

Inara and Skedi, then she looked at Elo. Could she see? The way Skedi's will tangled him up, baffled his mind with lies? Were they white lies any more, if they brought her to harm? They were not said with that intent. Skedi washed himself of guilt.

"Knight," Kissen said, with a mock salute. Without her cloak, she looked bigger somehow; her shoulders were broad and thick with muscle. But she stood a head and a half shorter than Elo; there was no way she could win in a fight.

"Let's not play this game any more," said Elo. "The girl does not want to travel with you. Leave us be."

"Honestly," said Kissen as she rolled up the sleeves of her shirt casually, "part of me would like nothing more than to let a troublesome little trollen and her sly beast skip off my hands, but I promised I wouldn't leave her, and I keep my promises."

Quiet is best, Skedi pressed into Inara, spreading his wings, exerting his power. Her mouth shut. He could work her better, perhaps, make her speak, make Kissen leave, but he would rather there were no chance the veiga would come back. He should have done this days ago, years even. After that stupid promise not to use his power on Ina. She hadn't given him anything for it, it wasn't binding, it wasn't a boon. They could be anywhere now. He could have enticed her to Sakre, convinced her mother to take her, and woven in with the liars and politicians, soldiers and merchants, found out what sweet secrets Lessa Craier must have been writing in the letters she wouldn't let Inara see. He could have come to Blenraden years ago, to find out what had happened to his shrine, why he was like this, jailed and impotent. He would not be on this small path between smaller places.

"Inara Craier will be safest with me," said Elo. "I grew up in Sakre's court; I am a knight of the realm."

Kissen laughed. "I thought you were a baker," she said. Elo narrowed his eyes, his fingers tightening on the cloth that wrapped his pommel, and Kissen made her favourite gesture, curling her forefinger and thumb into a spiral like the one tattooed on her chest. *Fuck you.*

"You are a danger to her," said Elo, "and to yourself, veiga. Let her go with me and face your demons alone."

"I don't think I will," said Kissen.

"Kissen, please!" Inara managed through her teeth.

Quiet. Let the grown-ups talk.

"I will not ask again," said Elo. "I do not want to hurt you."

"Then that will make this easier," said Kissen.

She started forward, drawing her blade as she did. Not her long-sword, which Skedi realised was strapped to Legs, but a shorter one-handed weapon: a cutlass. It rang on Elo's sword as it moved to block her then he stepped in for a quick strike. The shine of Kissen's blade caught the gold afternoon light, and she moved quickly, batting aside Elo's heavier longsword and twisting in. Her shoulder connected with his chest and threw him back.

Elo found his feet easily, his stance firm and strong. He parried her next strikes, which darted for his arms and legs. Elo's movement was refined, poised. He met Kissen's attack with strength, not wasting energy. He was unnerved by her competence in a way that only a god could see, but he did not show it in his expression, which was taut with concentration. Neither of them was aiming to kill, Skedi noted—just maim, disable.

Elo pressed into his front foot and knocked Kissen's to the side, uprooting her shorter stance. Their blades met again, and pressed, bringing them close together, close enough to kiss. Elo blinked, then hooked his foot against her false leg. She shifted away, but wasn't fast enough to avoid his heavy strike against the guard of her blade as she struggled to keep her stance. Her grip broke, and Elo tore the sword from her hands. It clattered to the rocks.

Yes.

Skedi's web of lies was tightening. It had pulled them together, to this. He watched, his antlers growing, his wings stretching. He half felt Inara's distress, the cry he kept from her mouth. She was clutching her waistcoat, her fingers pressing into the buttons.

She is taking the child, Skedi whispered to Elo. *She is taking her away. She wants to bring her to harm. Inara needs you. Your king needs you.*

Kissen stepped back, drawing a long knife from a sheath on her thigh, her gold tooth glinting as she smiled. Skedi didn't like that. She had lost her sword; she should not be smiling.

Elo made a strike for her good leg, hoping to nick it and end their scrap. Clearly, he had noticed which one she favoured. She moved more swiftly this time, letting his blade fly past her flesh, and stepped around it. With her leather armguard, she blocked his sword and moved in close, striking for the base of his hip. Elo avoided, just, cracking his elbow into her jaw. This she returned with a palm to his face which snapped his neck back. His guard opened and she followed him, stepping within the reach of his blade. Swords were for hacking, keeping distance, not for a brawl.

No, you're well, knight. You must win.

Elo recovered and made a quick grab for her knife wrist, trying to throw her to the ground, but she twisted out of it and knocked him back, switching hands with her knife, forcing him to parry with his hilt.

Stop. Inara's voice, breaking through Skedi's barriers. This was not supposed to happen.

Kissen had slipped her hand through Elo's guard and grabbed his lapel, pulling him down and slamming her capped knee into his chest, then nutted him in the head. She had the advantage now. She was winning.

Stop it, Skedi.

He will recover.

No. Inara's will was growing stronger. Skedi could feel it pushing him out. *Stop.* She was desperate; she didn't want anyone else to be hurt, she didn't want to be alone. Elo was backing away, trying to regain his advantage.

Let it be, Inara.

Inara's eyes turned on him, and Skedi quailed. His control was slipping. Why? He was a god; she was a little girl. But her eyes were furious . . . powerful. She turned to Elo and Kissen.

"Stop it!" she cried. It was more than a cry. It was an unravelling. A colour burst from her that Skedi had never seen in a human, a colour like the depths of the ocean, or the farthest reaches of the sky, edged with light. Her will. It broke through Skedi's power, shattering its hold on her. He felt himself diminished, as if pressed by a great heat. The power swept across Kissen and Elogast, stripping them of animosity and anger, and dissolving the white lies that had tangled Elo's soul.

The light faded, and whatever strength Inara had released was swept into nothing. She swayed on her feet, and Skedi trembled, terrified of looking at her.

"Stop fighting," she said. "Please."

Elo lowered his sword, confused. Kissen was still poised to strike, her lip and nose bleeding, but didn't finish the blow. "You're lucky, knight," she said at last, "that I don't kill people."

"I didn't mean it," said Inara, her voice choking. "I didn't . . . Kissen . . ."

Kissen turned her stare on Inara, wary at first, but on seeing the girl's expression she softened. "If I were so easy to get rid of, I wouldn't be good at my job," she said, sheathing her knife, then wiping her nose on her sleeve. "You people are so easily tangled up by a tiny god."

Skedi folded his wings and tried to be inconspicuous, but Inara turned and swept him from her shoulder to the ground. Skedi tumbled, surprised, to her feet, his wings flapping wildly.

"Inara . . ." he said. He tried her mind: *Inara.*

No. It was closed to him. Skedi pressed his ears flat.

"How could you?" Inara said out loud to him, backing away. "How could you do that?"

"Manipulated." Elogast said it with astonishment, and anger. He put his sword back in his scabbard and let out a breath. Gold pounded through his colours, now in turmoil. He was bleeding from the mouth, and from a cut on his hand where Kissen's blade had nicked it.

"Lied to," said Kissen.

Skedi felt their eyes on him. He shrank as small as he could, wings pressed down, chin to the ground. He reached out to Inara again. *Inara, I was just . . .* The way was cold. She had pulled her colours inside, like Kissen did.

"I can try killing him now, if you like," said Kissen.

Inara hesitated, and that was what frightened Skedi the most. More than fire, more than the veiga: the loss of Inara's faith, the only thing he had needed. The only thing that had kept him alive.

"Ina . . ." he tried again out loud, but she shook her head.

"No," she said, and looked at Kissen. "Please." She stepped forward, away from Skedi. "Please, can we just stop?"

Kissen met eyes with Elo. What would she do? She was angry, it showed in how starkly white the scar stood out on her pale face, and doubt creased her brow, but she was also somewhat . . . amused? After a moment's pause, she held out her hand. "Pact?" she said. A Middrenite saying between *peace* and *promise*.

Elo slowly uncurled his fingers from his sword and took her hand gently, his face troubled. "I . . ." He tightened his grip. "You are good with a blade," he said.

"You're better than I expected for a baker," said Kissen. She turned to Inara and held out her hand again. "Ina?"

Inara clenched her fists and swallowed, then flung her arms around Kissen's waist.

"I'm sorry. I'm so, so sorry."

This was not the way Skedi wanted their bond weakened: through losing her love. He had done it for her, for both of them. Would that be what tore them apart? He would disappear, he knew it, and Inara would be just a little girl again, one who no longer wanted him. A little girl who, only moments before, had broken the power of a god.

CHAPTER TWENTY

Elogast

THESE CUNNING GODS AND THEIR CUNNING GAMES. IT HAD been years since Elo had faced off with the power of a god, so long that he hadn't even noticed Skedi bending him to his will. He was weak, just as he had been then. If he'd missed that, what else had he missed? He could fight a veiga, but he had not prepared himself to deal with gods. He could fail Arren again.

"I need you for one last fight, Elo. Just one. Please. My life, my blood, my heart, I need you tonight."

That last, terrible night in Blenraden. Elo had already told Arren he was hanging up his sword. He could no longer tear down shrines of innocent people's gods. Killing the wild ones was enough.

Then Arren came pleading, and Elo decided to do this one last thing for him, his brother: destroy the bloody god of war. The god with the stag's head.

"Knight."

Elo jumped, ripped back to the present as Kissen called him. His shoulder stabbed with pain like it was barely healed, his chest tight and aching too. He felt sick; his hands were shaking, his breath refusing to come. Every time he closed his eyes, he saw the gold of Mertagh's armour, the swing of his hammer, the death and the blood, and the fire burning where his friend's heart had been. A heart that was now dying. Elo had been helpless against the gods, he had been weak, he had failed.

And today he had almost failed again. He had let a god play with his mind, pull him from his path. His path was Arren, to fix the mistake he had made those years before. He had to find a way to save him, to locate the powerful gods who could somehow fix his fading heart. Perhaps, then, he could find reasons to go on past the pain, the memories. He could find the strength to come back and fight for a country that seemed to be falling apart.

"Are you all right?" Kissen asked. Elo forced himself to take a breath, and another. It was a memory, it shouldn't hurt him, he should be stronger than that. He was crouched over the roots of a birch tree which he had been stripping for kindling. It was not quite dark, and their little party had stopped in a sheltered clearing after a very awkward few hours of walking. Almost killing each other had that effect.

Elo stood abruptly to face Kissen, putting his hands behind his back and pretending he couldn't feel the imaginary pain that wouldn't leave him. She regarded him closely. Inara and Skedi were nowhere to be seen.

"I'm well," Elogast lied. "Yourself?"

Kissen's nose looked sore, but she laughed. "I've had worse, petal," she said.

Elo found himself smiling, feeling more anchored in the present by the twinge of his own aching jaw. The bull-headed woman was better with a blade than he had expected. One to one, sword to sword, he likely would have overpowered her. She had predicted that, adapted her skills to undermine his own. He liked it, being outwitted.

She had known she would have to fight him, and that Skedi had wheedled his way in, changing him. She had seen how it would play out. If he had injured her and left her on the wild roads, as he'd very much intended to do, she likely would have died. And he would still be in the clutches of a god.

"I am sorry," he said, meaning it. "And thank you."

"I've no use for thanks or sorries," said the veiga, shrugging. "I sent the girl away to hunt."

"Alone? Is that wise?" The god would have to go with her, and he had so recently tried to take her over. Kissen raised an eyebrow at him and folded her arms. Perhaps it was not his best play to question the veiga's wisdom so soon after trying to stab her.

"I'm not worried about those two," she said. "Betrayal snaps sense into a person faster than a whip. And it's best for us to talk. Honest-like. Sit down with me."

He was impressed by how she made an offer seem like a threat. He took a breath and wiped his brow. He had been sweating, though his skin felt cold, but the memories of the battle with Mertagh faded into the back of his mind again, ready to spring on him at the worst moment. The veiga sat down on a fallen log, tapping at the vial around her neck.

"I will leave tomorrow," said Elo. "I have my own work to do."

"I'm not telling you to leave," she said, and breathed in. "We're still headed in the same direction. Despite it all, I think we should still stick together." The gloom of the coming night had settled on her face, softening her features. It was an interesting face, full of movement.

Elo blinked. "What for?" He smiled. "Do you actually . . . like me, veiga?"

"Ha. Wind your sails in, knight. I want you to stay because there are a few things making strange sense to me. This quest of yours, for starters . . ."

Elo shook his head. "I cannot—"

"I'm not asking you to tell me your pretty little secrets," she interrupted. "I'm asking for your help. Whatever your bloody quest is, there's danger on the road and danger in that city. I'd rather have four eyes watching the little godling and his girl. Whatever demons you're fighting . . ." She looked him up and down, and Elo reddened. She saw through him ". . . the ones following us have sharper teeth."

Elo sighed. "You're certain they'll come?"

Kissen looked into the trees and lowered her voice. "Pretty certain. Three days waiting, then strike the next evening. And there'll be more of them. If they're not following you, or me, then I'm starting to think someone *really* wants young Craier dead. You were willing to kill to help her . . ."

"I was tricked."

"That's by the by; it's the killing I want, not the excuses."

Elo surprised himself by laughing. He liked her. It had been a while since he spoke to someone so willing to meet him where he was, as he was. Ex-knight, full of secrets, full of terror. "What makes you think it's the girl?"

Kissen had her hand to her breastplate, absently tapping at her chest beneath her throat. Elo noticed that she had freckles on her hands between the burns. "Did you not feel it earlier?" she said. "She broke a god's power. I've never seen something like that before."

Elo couldn't deny it; he'd felt it like a change in the air before lightning struck.

"You care for her, don't you?" he said.

Kissen shifted and rubbed her chin, clearly uncomfortable with being noted for vulnerabilities. "I was a lost little girl once," she said after a moment, touching her chest. "No one deserves to be alone in this world."

Elo resisted the temptation to reach out and touch her arm, to tell her that he was also lost, also alone. So alone it hurt.

"I want to help her," Kissen said and shrugged. "I'm scared for her." Then she smiled crookedly. "Now, I'm a little scared *of* her."

Elo laughed. They heard movement in the trees and saw Inara, a hare and a fowl in her hand. Skediceth was flying from tree to tree behind her, and she was steadfastly ignoring him. She hesitated when she saw them together, then steeled herself and came forward, laying her kills down on the ground. She had a harder look than Elo had seen in her before. She reminded him of Arren during the war, after Bethine had died, knowing that the only way was forward.

"My quest comes first," said Elo to both of them. He had to make it right for Arren; he had to save him like Kissen wanted to save Inara. But he was tired from lack of sleep, and he wouldn't mind someone that good with a cutlass and a knife watching his back. "But if we keep pact till Blenraden, when we get there I'll need to speak to a god, a powerful one." He glanced sideways at Kissen. "You know, don't you, whose advice to seek? You're a godkiller from Blenraden who joined a pilgrim train. You must have some information."

Kissen sighed. "I have one in mind," she said. "An old god, a quiet but powerful one."

"Hestra?" Elo asked, his heart skipping three beats as he thought of the god that had put those flames in Arren's chest. She looked at him strangely.

"No, a river god." She began bundling twigs together, taking Elo's kindling off him, then set a flint to lighting it. "If it's advice you seek, she'll know what you need."

Elo watched Kissen make the nest that would become the heart of the fire, the same type of bundle that now sat in Arren's chest. The moss caught the sparks, smouldering, and Kissen leaned down to blow on it, her hand still gripping the vial at her neck.

"Very well, then," said Elo, quietly relieved. He smiled at Inara, who tried a little smile back. The godkiller was right; there was something strange about her. How had she broken Skediceth's will? Why had her House been razed to the ground, and why were demons after her? She looked like just a normal little girl in a difficult situation, and Elo pitied that. "I'll come with you."

CHAPTER TWENTY-ONE

Inara

THEY MOVED QUICKLY THE NEXT TWO DAYS, FOLLOWING THE quiet foot-roads higher into the Bennites, still taking the path that Jon would have taken them on, away from the coastal road.

"I've walked this way once before," Kissen said, directing them east up winding slopes. "After the god of safe haven was killed, the roads from Blenraden were filled with highway bandits trying their chances on people carrying their lives on their backs. It was better to take the higher, quiet roads. Poor Yatho had to ride Legs the whole time."

Inara watched as Kissen patted her horse, who was taking the climb well, carrying most of the weight of their bags. He did not enjoy the rocky slopes, but he did like munching the fresh buds on the birches which Inara had pulled down for him. Clouds moved slowly across the horizon, trailing purple veils of snow over the peaks. This path must have been frustrating for Yatho. Kissen herself seemed to be finding some of the rougher slopes difficult, and had picked up her staff from Legs's back to help her balance.

"I spoke with him once. Yusef," said Elo quietly. He had become less taciturn since Gefyrton. Inara suspected that he liked having a plan, much like her mother. "Before the battle for the harbour. He had a man's face, friendly, as if he were just anyone from Restish . . ." He cleared his throat and glanced at Inara.

"I didn't say before, but your mother fought bravely in that battle. She did everything she could to try to save Yusef. And when she left to treat her wounds, she asked her guard to stay behind and fight for the king. We were grateful for that. She was a brave woman."

Elo was just trying to be kind, and it made Inara feel worse. She had allowed Skedi to trick her, trick him, and she could have got him or Kissen killed. Her god was riding on Legs, still small and quiet. She hadn't spoken to him in two days. She didn't want him near her, touching her, and she hated that it made her heart heavy.

Did he regret what he had done? Was he sorry? He had tried to say so, but she didn't know if she could believe him any more. He had stolen her voice, stolen her will. Skedi had always been there for her, through everything, and he had turned against her.

She'd never felt more alone.

"There's a lake at the plateau here," said Kissen, rubbing her capped knee and pointing upwards to the next summit. "It's the highest point we need to get to. We should make it a span before sundown. Plenty of time to set up camp and prepare for the shadow demons."

"Do you have a plan?" asked Elo.

"Sharp edges of briddite," said Kissen. "That's my plan."

"I thought veiga had more tricks of the trade than sharp edges and a blunt manner," said Elo. Kissen grinned.

Mount Tala, her sides half in shadow, rose above them as they reached the plateau, and the lake Kissen remembered was gleaming silver in the early evening. There were still a few shrines that Skedi nosed around when they got close enough, to water gods, gods of ways, gods of luck, fishing, a hunt. Even a ribboned tree for the god Yusef that Kissen and Elo had mentioned. He would be reborn soon, Inara thought. Begin again, as something new, but he wouldn't remember her mother; he couldn't tell her about the woman who had survived fighting by his side only to be killed by flame.

Kissen ignored the little shrines, forcing Skedi to follow by leading them to a large outcrop that looked like a leaning troll, its shoulders hunched and protective.

"Not long till sundown," said Kissen. She had pulled a small pair of pliers from her cloak and was adjusting the tiniest screw between her kneecap and her calf. "Inara, go find somewhere to hide. Take Legs with you, he deserves a break."

Inara took a breath and pulled Kissen's bow down from Legs's saddle instead of answering. The arrows too.

"What are you doing?" said Kissen.

"I'm not hiding," she said, glad her voice didn't shake. "These arrows are briddite-tipped, and I'm a better shot than you, anyway."

Elo snorted, then tried to hide it as he surveyed the area. Kissen tongued her gold tooth and sighed. "Summonings are pieces of gods," she said. "They have the same weaknesses, and they're easily distracted. They aren't picky about what they kill. You saw what they did to that boy."

Inara swallowed. No. She wouldn't be afraid. She would take care of herself.

"I'm staying," she said. Kissen threw her hands up. Her quiet colours shimmered with worry, then disappeared.

"Fine," she said, with a meaningful glance at Elo, who raised his shoulders helplessly. "Tie Legs over there so he doesn't bolt, and brush him down a bit."

Inara tied the horse to a sturdy branch, and he pressed his nose to her hair and nickered affectionately.

"This is a bad idea, Inara," said Skedi from his back. Inara ignored him, sweeping the rough brush over Legs's flanks to dislodge the mud from the road, then put the bow and arrows on her shoulder. "Inara . . ." Skedi tried again. "It's dangerous."

Inara returned to Kissen and Elo. Kissen had pulled a string of beads out of her cloak, which glowed faintly, to Inara's eyes, with colours. Prayers. An offering Kissen must have taken from a shrine she had broken. Skedi took half a step towards the veiga before his wings flicked in distress and he retreated to Inara's ankles. The temptation of the prayers had instinctively drawn him to them.

"We should take the high ground," said Elo, pointing up to the outcrop. Kissen gave him a withering glance, disliking taking orders, but took the bow from Inara, strung it, and passed it back, then went for the boulder anyway. Inara's breath rose above her as she followed both of them to the top, clutching the jutting edges of the stones with already cold fingers. Skedi scrambled and flew up to join them, sitting on his hind legs, his ears twitching in all directions.

From the top they could see across the flat of the lake, to a tiny fire on the other side that marked another camp. Inara shivered and pulled her cloak about her. She thought about the other pilgrims and wondered if they were now sitting about a fire, not thinking about shadow, blood, and bone.

Elo sat with his sword across his knees, breathing deep, steadying breaths. Kissen was crouched, ready to move into fighting stance. The knight looked towards the waters, and Kissen looked towards the wood.

The gloom of the evening stretched across the plateau and up the slopes, like cloth slipping over skin. The wind rose, biting their necks and hands, exposed as they were on the top of the rock. Inara forgot to flex her fingers and they grew brittle-stiff with the cold. Skedi, crouching by her boot, grew larger, to his doggish size, perhaps to keep the wind from her legs.

"Maybe they're not coming," Inara said, not finding the will to move away from the god. She was too cold for it. The arrow she had nocked was slipping down the stave.

"Hm," said Kissen. Her nose was a bit red from the frosty air.

"Focus," said Elo.

Finally, the light slipped away.

There. A shift of shadow. Moving, forming, waking. Bursting to life from the dark. One, two, three. Four.

"Shit," said Kissen, fingering her beads. "I hate being right."

That was when Skedi would have said *liar*.

The creatures slid through the night below them, flowing clouds of dark come together on an ill wind. Inara drew the arrow with her numbing hands and shot at one. It scraped the creature's shoulder but did no damage. Kissen flung out her hand, and a bead shot from her fingers. It fell into the midst of the summonings and they snapped around, twisting into a knot, searching for the prayer. Inara was half afraid Skedi would leap after it as well, but he stayed by her.

Elo leapt down from the outcrop as Inara nocked another arrow, her hands shaking and her mouth dry. Kissen swung down too, using her arms. Inara let the arrow fly, and the briddite arrowhead pierced the limb of one of the beasts. It snarled, biting for its unseen assailant, and Elo took the moment to strike it through its head. The demon collapsed into nothing.

"Stay up there!" said Kissen to Inara. A summoning charged her, drawn by her voice over the lure. Kissen met it with a strike that threw it to the side. It landed like liquid in water, baring its broken teeth.

"Come on, ugly fucker," said Kissen.

The beast charged her again. Inara fumbled for another arrow as its teeth grew longer, sharper, its bone cracking to extend its jaw, the tiny lights of its eyes glowing. Kissen leapt to the side. Her right leg slipped against the loose stones of the bank, and she barely caught herself. She swept back with her blade, its tip searing the beast along its torso. The summoning shrieked, inky shadow breaking from its side.

Inara kept the bowstring taut. What if she hit Kissen? Or Elo? The knight was facing two of the creatures. He used his blade more like a staff, catching its flat with one hand to send it whipping around into the demons at thrice the speed. Inara fired as one moved back, but it was too fast for her arrow to strike.

The creature ripped away from Elo and made for the outcrop. Inara drew another arrow and nocked it hurriedly. It misfired, skittering along the rocks. The creature scrabbled higher.

"Ina!" Kissen cried, reaching for her throwing knives. Inara fumbled for another arrow. The creature's claws struck sparks from the stone as it reached the top. She didn't have her arrow; she wasn't ready.

Inara.

Skediceth leapt forward, growing from a dog's size to a wolf's, the largest she had ever seen him. He propelled himself into the beast, antlers first. They locked into the creature's neck as Skedi battered it with his wings, the creature snarling and scrabbling. Feathers went flying as Skedi roared and shoved, using all his might to throw the beast back down onto the stones below.

Skedi . . .

I'm not hurt. A white lie; his wing was torn but healing. She hadn't realised gods could fight other gods without briddite. *Are you all right?*

Yes.

Kissen had been ready when the creature fell. She gave it chase as it recovered, thumbing another bead and throwing it to the ground. As the beast dove for it, she leapt, bringing her knife around to slice it open through the belly. The summoning screamed, disintegrating.

Kissen rolled to her knees as the first creature she had injured came back for her. It flew blindly at her, bone-teeth bared. Kissen moved her sword to defend. Too slow.

Elo stepped between Kissen and the beast. Its jaws closed on his arm instead of Kissen's throat. He bellowed his pain as he drove his sword into the creature's neck. The summoning he had abandoned to save her tried its moment, but Inara had hers. She released her arrow, and it silvered the air a moment before striking through the creature's head. The arrow hit the earth, trailing blackness on its feathers, and the beast fell apart.

Elo was hurt. Inara scrabbled down from the outcrop, then cried out as her heart bit with pain, pulled by an unseen anchor. Skedi. He had fallen behind, back to a hare's size, limping a little as he healed.

"Come," said Ina, wincing and holding out her arm. Skedi jumped to her shoulder. She felt the familiar weight of him, the way he softened his landing so he wouldn't hurt her, and swallowed.

Legs's whinny distracted them, for it was quickly followed by his squeal. Inara whipped around. A man had untied him and was trying to pull him into the undergrowth, and Legs was not pleased about it. He reared onto his hind legs, tugging back at his reins and twisting away. He landed on his forelegs and kicked out with his hinds, catching the would-be thief a blow to his chest, sending him flying. Legs stamped and turned, marking his territory as if daring anyone to try and ride him without his permission. Inara was surprised; he was normally so docile around Kissen.

There were sounds in the undergrowth. Kissen turned her knife in her hand and threw. It cut into the bark of a tree, sending splinters into the face of another grease-haired ruffian who was leaping out. He fell back, yowling as two others made themselves seen, their blades already drawn.

"Oh, look," said Kissen, smiling sweetly. "I missed."

The chancers stared at her. The one Legs had taken down was still on the ground by the lake, whimpering. Elo raised his sword with his good arm, staring down his blade, and Inara drew another arrow, pointing it at the intruders.

"The fuck do you want?" said Kissen.

"We thought . . ." one said, a red-haired, rake-thin man from Talicia. His colours were sly and green, with a shimmer of yellow aggression. "We thought you'd killed each other."

Inara almost laughed. She suspected Skedi was thinking that anyone with half a brain would have lied and said they were coming to help.

"Do we look dead to you, fire-top?" snarled Kissen. Elo's arm was bleeding badly; it was all Inara could do not to run to stop it as quick as she could. He kept his blade straight and still. "If you thought we'd killed each other, why are your daggers drawn?"

She was right. All of them had blades shining from their hands apart from the one Legs had felled who was trying to crawl upright.

"We meant no harm," said fire-top. "Just wanted to help, you know." There it was. They didn't seem minded to leave.

"We need none of yours," said Kissen. "Piss off."

It was bravado. Inara could see their thinking. Here were a little girl, an injured man, and a woman. Even with one of their own flopped against a tree, these bandits thought they had a chance, that it was worth the risk for a horse, some swords, some silver.

Inara felt Skedi shift, paw by paw, then, gathering his courage again, he leapt down to the ground, growing once more. He landed the size of a small deer.

Forgive me, Inara, he said, just to her.

His wings were bright as he spread them, the wound now healed; his antlers, too, to Inara's eyes, had a condensed glow of power, a god's power. He did not have colours like humans did; Skedi *was* colour. His eyes flashed golden.

"Ask a god's business and become a god's business," he said in his loudest voice, at the same time piercing those words into their minds. He put himself before them all, defending them. If blades were thrown, they would hit him first. "Tell me, where were you when Blenraden fell?"

Fire-top ran before he'd finished speaking. The other two whimpered and clattered into the trees, pausing only briefly to drag the groaning horse thief away with them. Their colours turned milky white as one, all showing the same shine of fear and surrender.

Skedi's fur rippled as he shrank again, back to the size of a hare, exhausted. His nose was lowered, but Inara caught the smug twitch of his whiskers as he folded his wings. He had protected them, her, a second time, striking terror into the hearts of the thieves. Even as he diminished, Inara couldn't unsee the colour of fear. To her, Skedi had been her companion, her friend. Others saw him as a god. Something to be frightened of. But Skedi didn't want people to be frightened of him, he wanted to be loved. He wanted to survive, more than anything, and he had just put himself at risk for her. Because . . . he loved her, and despite it all, she loved him too.

I will try to forgive you, she said to him.

CHAPTER TWENTY-TWO

Kissen

ONLY KISSEN COULD SEE THE TREMBLE OF ELO'S BLADE AS he held it up. He let it drop as soon as the would-be robbers were gone, and Inara ran towards them.

"It will be well," said Elo, lifting his arm out of the way. Was he trying not to frighten Inara? The kid had just injured a shadow beast, almost been mauled herself, killed another, then turned the point of her arrow towards a man.

"Let me be the judge of that, knight," said Kissen, grabbing his arm and taking a look. The vambrace had done something to stop the creature's teeth, but there were broken shards of bone still buried in his skin. He wasn't bleeding enough for her to fear for his arm. "What possessed you to use your flesh as a shield?" Kissen said. "Don't they teach you not to do shit like that in knight school? Ina, Skediceth, get a fire lit beneath the outcrop."

Skedi hesitated, staring at her. She realised she had addressed him directly.

"Just get on with it," said Kissen, sheathing her sword. She hadn't got to Inara in time. The god had saved her and been injured for it. She had never seen a god act . . . selflessly. Just like Elo had. She was not used to being surprised. "And bring me the saddlebags."

Legs, at least, had settled down. He came trotting over, looking for a treat. He had a mean kick; the unlucky thief would have a few cracked ribs to help him remember for next time. Kissen patted him on the nose and he nickered affectionately. He was a loyal one.

Elo had already been tugging at his jacket and hood, and she helped him, yanking them roughly over his arms.

"Ow," he said pointedly as she unbuckled his vambrace. She rolled her eyes as she pressed the wound to find the bone-teeth still lodged in it. It was difficult to see in the gloom, so she dragged him over to the fire, which Inara was lighting. Luckily, she had loaded up Legs with dry wood at the last forest they passed.

"It's fine, veiga," he said to her. Kissen drew her shorter blade and put it in near the heart of the flames as Skedi nudged more wood in with his antlers. It would take a while to get hot, and her scarred hands weren't dexterous enough to extract the bone. She bent down and used her teeth, finding the smaller fragment with her mouth to his skin, then spitting it onto the ground with a good wad of blood. The larger piece she was more careful with, slowly extracting it before dropping it into her hand.

"You recognise this?" she said, poking at it and looking up. Elo was staring at her, his jaw flexing, clearly flustered. She remembered he had said no one he knew had been close enough to him to lay a curse in some time, and smirked a little. It was fun to fluster a pretty knight. He shook himself slightly and looked down at the gleaming shard.

"I don't spend a lot of time looking at teeth."

"Ina, do you recognise this?" The god was sitting a respectable distance away, but she needed all of their eyes. "Skediceth?"

The god twitched at her calling him by name, standing on his hind legs in mild surprise, then came to look at the piece of bone. "Looks like a mess," he said.

Inara had brought the saddlebags. She peered at it closely, but as she did, it crumbled into nothing, just dirt and white dust. Kissen sighed and wiped her mouth.

"Fucking gods," she said, pressing down on Elo's wound to stop it bleeding further. Inara didn't meet her eyes; Skedi hopped back on her shoulder and Kissen clicked her tongue.

When the knife was glowing, she pulled it out of the flames.

"Gut and needles work better," said Elo, eyeing the hot blade.

"Not being a healer or a musician," she said, "I'm fresh out of clean catgut. Want some hipgin?"

She pulled a small leather gourd out of her saddlebags. She had been saving it for a really bad day, and this seemed like a good reason to use it. She held it out to him, and he considered it a moment, then sighed and took a long drink. As soon as the gin left his lips, Kissen took hold of his wrist and pressed the hot blade into the wound, searing off the blood and closing it. Elo gritted his teeth and hissed through them as she pulled the knife out and focussed on another place where his flesh had torn. Inara watched, fascinated, as the skin burned.

It was sealed. The bleeding stopped.

"Idiot," muttered Kissen, putting the hot blade down against a log to cool. Elo let out a shaking breath. That shit hurt, Kissen knew personally. She took a swig of gin herself.

"Aren't you going to thank me for saving your neck?" Elo said, his smile wry. He had a little crease by his mouth that deepened when he grinned.

"I won't thank you for doing something so stupid," Kissen said, disliking being drawn in by a handsome face.

"Hm." He took the gin back and splashed some of it on the wound. Kissen rummaged in her bag with one hand for a pot of Irisian poultice she had bought from a market in Sakre a year before, after seeing off a god of fortune who had started robbing people blind in the slums. Elo took it.

"One of my mothers made poultices like this," he said. "It's expensive now. You bought this and not gut?"

"I get scrapes more than bites," said Kissen.

"It's an old wives' ointment."

"Do you want it or don't you?"

Elo popped open the lid with his finger and lifted it to his nose, then laughed. "Sorry, veiga, it's rancid."

Kissen leaned over and sniffed it. It smelled just as it always had. "What do you mean, rancid?"

"The poultice has to be used within six months," he said. "Three, preferably."

Kissen scoffed, realised she was still holding his wrist, and let go. "Ungrateful," she said. "Well then, cold water will have to do you."

The lake looked fresh and inviting, still catching the gloam of the sky though the mountains were around them were dark. The light from the fire touched the crests of the ripples in the water. She hadn't washed in almost two weeks, and it was past due. Elo flexed his fingers and followed her eyes, looking exactly how she felt.

Kissen took Elo's other arm, removing the vambrace for him so he wouldn't have to do it himself, then wrestled off her breastplate. She had made her leather armour so it would hold her breasts flat without restricting the movement of her arms too much, but, salt, it was sweet to take it off and breathe free. She dropped it by the fire and pulled out her staff from where it was threaded through the saddlebags. Then, she set to her leg, unbuckling her knee first beneath her trews then twisting it out, her staff hooked under her armpit.

"What if those men come back?" said Inara, clearly preferring two-legged Kissen to one-legged Kissen.

"And mess with a god?" said Kissen, laying down the leg under her cloak. It was pleasant, removing it. The cold tickled at her uncovered knee, and she could feel the ghost of her shin aching down her ankle and calf, pinching particularly above her ankle. "At a half-holy place like this? I don't think it likely."

She met eyes with Skedi and stopped. He didn't know where he stood, and she didn't either. It was smart thinking, to scare the piss out of the bandits. They both broke the gaze.

"Join us, Ina," said Kissen, undoing her girdle and taking off that and her trews. She didn't like the cramped feeling the girdle gave her hips, but it was the best way to keep her straps secure. "You smell pretty bad for a noble."

Inara reddened and tried to smell beneath her clothes. Elo was walking into the waters in his bloodied shirt, but not quick enough for Kissen not to glimpse his muscled thighs. Well, looking did no harm. She had to take some pleasures travelling with a baker-knight.

Kissen went in her shirt too, using her staff hooked firmly under her arm to hop to the shore and then taking a leap in amongst the stones. She kept her vial on her neck; it was sealed with wax, water wouldn't hurt it, and it rested against Osidisen's promise. The cold lashed at her ribs, thrilling from her neck through her breasts to the sole of her foot. Her skin tingled with life, both of her legs prickling with the sharp cold. Nobles could have their hot baths and scented oils; Kissen would take a cold lake under Mount Tala over almost any other pleasure. The stars were glimmering awake above them, and the moon, waning, had peeked over the shadows of the mountains. Elo was washing his burned and bloodied arm.

Inara looked at them both like they were mad and exchanged a glance with Skedi, who was fanning the fire with his wings.

"I will stay here; it's close enough to the water," he said. "Gods don't bathe."

"Maybe they should."

She was teasing him, and he ruffled his wings happily, still keeping his head low.

Inara dallied a bit further, then finally shuffled out of her clothes and into her slip, tiptoeing into the water and squealing as it lapped at her calves. Kissen watched her dance as it reached her knees and soaked her dress. This would be a good opportunity to check her for curses, perhaps when they were out of the lake. She would try and broach the subject later. She didn't want to frighten Inara more than she already was. A god had to be close to lay a curse that drew demons to a person; how could that have happened without Skedi noticing? It's not like the god of white lies had that kind of power, even if he wanted to put himself and Inara in danger. And he didn't, he had put himself in harm's way to save Inara so quickly after betraying her. He had taken the extreme decision to kidnap Inara and influence Elo because he didn't like Kissen. That was fine; she didn't like him either.

"I can't swim," said Inara, on her tiptoes in the water.

"You don't need to," said Kissen, trying not to laugh. "Just get your belly in, be still and float."

"It's cold."

"It is better when you're in it," said Elo, up to his waist washing his chest and head. He had missed a couple of days shaving and his hair was growing thick and springy. Inara shivered, then pushed out into the water, shrieking as it reached her neck. She moved her limbs quickly, breathing little breaths. Kissen stayed close, in case she panicked. The moon rose as the dark gathered, cutting dapples in the lake around them.

"Piss, it's cold," said Ina, and Kissen almost choked on her tongue. Elo laughed, to Kissen's surprise. She thought he'd tell her she was a bad influence. "Oh, Kissen," said Inara. She had looked up at the slopes around them, for a moment forgetting the chill. "The mountains glow!" Kissen followed her gaze up the mountainsides, gleaming in greens, silvers, and white. It was enough to lighten all of them in the water. Kissen smiled. When she had first travelled with Pato, after he had accepted her apprenticeship, he had complained every day that she was slowing him down, too expensive to feed, too annoying to train. After a few weeks, he stopped, and Kissen now understood why. After so many years working alone, sharing the road with fellows made the world brighter.

She followed the mountains and brought her gaze back to Elo, who had removed his shirt and was shaking it in the water to dislodge the grime of the road. His arm looked like it had mainly stopped bleeding. He had a vicious scar across his shoulder, almost splitting his back open, the scar tissue a knotted rope through his flesh.

Kissen blinked, her eyes catching on something darker within the scar, on his shoulder. A tattoo, or an etching. No. God-script, like hers, but tangled, edged: wild-script, spreading out from a smaller, darker mark, about the size of a thumbnail. It looked like a fork in a road, the one that had been on the wooden board those knights outside Gefyr had made them walk across. The sign of Lethen of the ways.

"What the fuck is that?" she said.

Elo started and looked back at her, unsure whether she was feeling colourful or angry. She swam towards him, then used his shoulder to hoist herself to her foot, taking a closer look.

A curse. The script radiating out from the symbol was a span down his back, and even under her eye it was spreading. Like poison.

"There you were blaming me for demons, knight."

He almost ripped away from her, but paused, not wanting her to lose her balance. "That's not funny," he said.

"What's going on?" said Inara, wading closer. Her chin was shaking with shivers, her wet curls plastered about her ears. She winced, and in the same moment Skedi let out a little chirrup of pain; she had moved too far away. The little god leapt up from the bank, his wings flashing in the moonlight, and he landed on Inara's head, slightly off balance. Kissen was more focussed on Elo's shoulder and its curse.

"It was you," said Skedi, genuinely surprised.

"No," said Elo. He turned, stretching to see the mark, and finally caught sight of it. Kissen could not read his expression in the darkness, but he went very still. After a moment he moved away from her and waded for the shore. Kissen dove after him, swimming back to her staff, and Inara followed, splashing in her hurry. Elo was already halfway up the bank, stark naked, carrying his shirt, blood dripping again from his arm. By the light of the flames, he looked again; the script was clear.

"I don't understand," he said, quiet. Then angry. "It makes no sense."

He pulled his leggings over his still-damp legs, then cursed as his arm bit with pain.

"Fuck, right. Here," said Kissen. She threw her cloak over her shoulders and sat on it by the fire. "Sit."

"I don't—"

"I said sit. I thought knights took orders."

Elo stared at her, then sat down as Kissen pulled bandages out of her saddlebag, tearing them with her hands.

"What are we going to do?" asked Inara, skipping from foot to foot with the cold.

"You're going to get your togs on and build up that fire," said Kissen.

"But—"

"Ina."

Inara obeyed, going to stoke up the flames. Elo was in shock, staring into the middle distance. Being cursed wasn't a fault. Failing to recognise it, however, was idiocy. Arsehole should have bathed earlier.

Kissen recleaned his wound with her flask, inwardly cursing at the waste of gin, and bandaged his arm. It wasn't Ina. That was good. But what now?

"You'll get cold," said Elo, but she ignored him. She was already cold. She needed to think. She needed to put her leg back on. She preferred feeling ready to run.

"Veiga . . ." he said. He put his hand on hers to stop their business. "I did not lie to you."

Kissen batted him away. She had let her guard down and had let danger near them. She had believed a god, and a knight. People were fools.

"Ask the god if you don't believe me," said Elo.

"I don't need to ask the liar if you think you're telling the truth," said Kissen as she finished tying the bandages. The blood soaked through. "Now let me look at it."

She pushed him around and stared at his back. She hadn't seen a curse like this before. It was simple, brutal, deeply ingrained. A curse like the one on her face was intended to disfigure, but when broken it had merely stained her skin white. Other curses were promises, like if such a fellow set foot on this land again, he'd be turned into a deer. That type of thing. This was a death curse: slow or fast, death would come in shadow on the road. "It's just going to keep growing," she said.

"You can read it?"

"I can't read nothing, but the lines go from dark to light. In four days they'll be longer, and they'll call more beasts to you. To us."

She let go. Elo pressed his hands to his crown. "I've put you all in danger," he said.

"No shit."

"It's not your fault, Elo," said Inara.

"Now who's a liar?" muttered Skedi, shaking droplets of water from his wings.

"He didn't know," snapped Inara. She was trying to hang their pot over the fire, jumping on her feet to warm herself up and coming to look at the curse again. "I've seen this before," she said.

"We walked over it days ago," said Kissen.

"No . . . before that."

"Shit," said Elo, looking up, distracting Kissen from Inara. "Canovan."

"What?" said Kissen.

"The one who sent us off on the pilgrimage with Jon." He shook his head. "He recognised me, I think, and he had this symbol tattooed on his arm. Tattooed everywhere." He put his hand on his shoulder, as if trying to remember the feeling of being cursed. "I thought he was just a malcontent who suspected me of trying to infiltrate the pilgrimages. But I wonder now. The Queen's Way, his inn was called, and there was a woman there . . . writing in lemon juice ink."

"The fuck have lemons to do with—"

"Writing in lemon juice hides the writing till the paper is held over a flame. It's used for secret messages, dissidents. We used it during the siege, and Arren said that rebellion is brewing in Middren, that some of the Houses are behind it." He laughed, half disbelieving. "Perhaps the Queen's Way is a dissidents' meeting place. No wonder they all panicked when I walked in."

Inara started, stepping back. Skedi flew to her shoulder.

"What makes you think they had anything to do with a rebellion?" said Inara.

"Then Canovan put his hand on my shoulder," Elo said obliviously, pressing his shoulder as if he could feel it, the mistake he had made. "I smelled moss and blood, like the beasts. He only *thought* I was a knight."

Kissen shook her head. "Screw rebels. How could Canovan place a curse?" She had seen humans carry curses for their gods, but it was usually painful, and obvious. Elo didn't strike her as an idiot.

"I-I'm not sure." He frowned. "There were no other signs."

Kissen remembered another. "My friend Yatho," she said, "she saw that Canovan was bleeding from his arm." She frowned. "Could have been a blood sacrifice. But you still would have seen a god powerful enough to place a curse like this. And, he could have killed us all. Why?"

"*You didn't say there was a kid.*" That's what he had said to Yatho when she and Inara had turned up. He had guilt in his face, and the turn of his mouth; Kissen had thought it was fear of being caught, but she had been wrong. "He must have thought . . . I was a bonus," she said, and looked at Inara. "A veiga joining one of his pilgrimages, and a curse already planted. The others were just a sacrifice."

A boy had died, maybe an old woman too, just to kill a knight he didn't like? Lethen was no sweetheart; she took animal sacrifices on the moss of elm trees ringed in beads. An old god, yes and half-wild, who guided travellers home or led them astray, but she had not fought in Blenraden that Kissen remembered. Still, her world had changed. No sacrifices, no worshippers, the faithful punished on the road.

But why would she and Canovan go so far as to set a curse on Elogast?

"Skedi, do you recognise it?" said Inara.

Skedi blinked; his fur shook. Inara frowned, swallowed, sat down.

He must have said something to her, straight into her head. "No," he said, avoiding their eyes. Liar, Kissen thought.

"I will leave," said Elo, not noticing. "Just give me a day or so to get ahead and we will be parted."

Kissen wasn't going to let him stupid that easily. There were threads here, connections she couldn't see, she didn't know. "What did the king lose in Blenraden? What are you travelling for that might set a stranger's curse on you?"

Elo stared down at his hands, considering his words as he flexed his fingers. His hands were shaking again, and he grasped his shoulder as if in pain. He had a haunting in his eyes, and went distant, as he sometimes did. He was remembering something, old traumas. He thought he hid it well; perhaps he did, but Kissen knew pain.

"I cannot tell you," he said. "And I can assure you I did not tell this Canovan either."

"If you lied to him, though," said Skedi. "If he has a strong connection with a god, perhaps she was with him. Perhaps she told him you were lying." He sat back, his wings half-unfurled.

"I would have seen her," said Elo uncertainly.

"You didn't see me," said Skedi.

"Oh, for fuck's sake," said Kissen. "Then tell me this. Why now?"

Elo looked at the sky, then down at his sword before his eyes met hers, dark and serious. Focussed again. "Arren is not well," he said. "And he is running out of time. Between that, rebellion, and Restish biting at our shores, he is afraid that Middren is about to fall."

CHAPTER TWENTY-THREE

Inara

THAT SYMBOL. INARA HAD SEEN IT BEFORE THE BOARD ON the road. That day was imprinted on her memory: the day she left her mother. She had gone into her study, and Lady Craier had a candle lit and a letter. A letter marked with Lethen's symbol, while the scent of lemons had hung in the air. A wild god's sign in a land that had banned gods. She had hidden it from her daughter.

"If I go now," Elo was saying, straightening his shoulders and grabbing his shirt with his good hand, "I'll draw them off."

"What, and die?" said Kissen. This seemed to distress her more than it might have days before. "You can't fight those demons alone."

"I thought I had little time, but now I have less. And if those rebels set demons on a pilgrim train for one knight, I can't imagine what they're capable of."

The demons were doubling in number. After the next four days, there would be eight of them. Eight against just Elo, and he was already injured.

"You can't," said Inara as Kissen folded her arms and sat down. She frowned at the fire, then turned her back on Elo, pulling on her leg. "Kissen, we can't let him."

Kissen was tying on her straps. Inara and Elo were at least dressed, but she still only had a cloak around her. She sighed and stopped. "This isn't your fight," she said to Inara, then looked regretfully at Elo. "I promised I would keep her safe."

"What if it is my fight?" said Inara.

Inara, Skedi warned, *we don't know whose side she was on.*

Her mother had told her nothing. Her mother was gone, Elo was still alive, and she had to stop him getting himself killed.

"My mother was involved." She clutched the buttons on her waistcoat. "Lady Craier. In rebellion. I'm sure of it."

Kissen and Elo stared.

"She wrote letters like that," Inara said. How much had Lessa Craier hidden from her daughter? She had got them all killed, left Inara alone, for what? Tears were scratching at her throat. "Letters with that symbol. Her study smelled like lemons. All the time when she was writing. She was always going to Sakre too; the servants said she was trying to regain the king's favour."

Elo shared a glance with Kissen. "Inara," said Kissen, "you think she was working for this . . . rebellion . . . or against them?"

"I—I don't know. The symbol was on a letter, I know that, but I don't know what else."

"You said . . . they burned the Craier manor," said Elo. Inara nodded numbly. "Arren would never do such a thing. Never. She must have been working for him, finding out what was going on, and the rebels hunted her." He looked into the distance, thinking. "Your House is a powerful one, Inara. Without a leader it leaves Arren exposed."

Elo's colours remained steadfast, no hint of a lie. She believed him. Her heart flooded with relief. Her mother was not a rebel. She had been fighting for her king, like Elo.

"Then . . ." said Inara, "it's my duty to help you."

"Inara . . ." Kissen and Skedi warned at once, then both recoiled, annoyed.

"Kissen," said Inara pointedly, stronger now. "You said you knew a powerful god. Can they break Elo's curse?"

Kissen hesitated. "Curse-breakers are rare," she said, shaking her head and pulling on her trews. "Powerful. Most old gods, even, couldn't break the curse of another unless they are given an offering of equal power." Inara's heart fell, and Kissen grumbled under her breath. Her hand went to the vial at her neck. "But," she said wearily, "a water god knows everything that water knows. She could help." She tongued her gold tooth, considering Elo, then looked at Inara.

"We shouldn't get involved in this," she said. "You wanted to be safe. Like it or not, those demons will come back, and we might not be able to fight them all."

She's right, Inara, said Skedi. *We were lucky last time. I am not a god built for war.*

It's lucky, then, said Inara, pointedly, *that we will separate in the city.* Skedi shrank a little, his ears flattening. *You want to be safe, Skedi, you want a home. You know the path you want. It's time I chose mine.*

But, Ina . . .

Inara shut him out. She was giving him what he wanted, what he had betrayed her to get. But she was the daughter of House Craier, and she had broken Skedi's power. She wanted to *do* something, take command of her own fate. "I know it's dangerous," she said. She held Kissen's gaze, and whatever the godkiller saw in her, she understood.

Kissen looked up at Elo, who was hesitating, then held out her hand.

"She's a little girl," warned Elo.

"Little girls grow up fast," said Kissen.

Elo reached for her, and she took his hand, and she almost pulled him over by yanking herself to her feet. In the firelight, Inara saw Elo's colours ripple with a faint blush. Kissen smiled. Neither of them stepped back. "I have a mind to stick by you as well," she said. "I have no love of people who burn for their gods. If I can, I will help the young Lady Craier stop it from happening again."

Inara flushed. Lady Craier. Kissen was right, that was who she was now. Her mother's legacy.

CHAPTER TWENTY-FOUR

Elogast

HE SHOULD HAVE LEFT. HE SHOULD HAVE STAYED ALONE, AS he was used to. It was a bleak, cold night under the rock beneath Mount Tala, and even as Elo sat keeping watch over the fire he could feel the terrible weight of the curse on his shoulder. Now he knew it was there, he swore he could feel it growing, each moment a grain of sand counting towards the end of his life. He surprised himself by feeling almost . . . relieved, then guilty for it. No, he had to live. For Arren.

But they couldn't keep going in the dark. The moon gave them a clear path when it shone, but when it drifted into cloud the night turned black and perilous. Kissen said the narrow routes down the mountain would see them dead before dawn if they attempted them cold and tired as they were.

How had he been so stupid? Canovan's hand on his shoulder, the wrongness of it. He had attributed it to his old war wound that ached when his memories were hurting him, but no. He had let this happen, a boy had died, and now he had only days to save his friend. He had failed to save him last time; he had left his side and lived a small life as rebellion festered. He must not fail again.

A sound disturbed him from his thoughts. A huff of breath, and a chattering. It was Kissen, he could tell. He knew the sound of her sleeping from their nights together. She was wrapped tight in her waxwool cloak, her wild hair sticking out from under her hood.

And she was shivering. She had spent too long after the lake tending his arm and checking his curse, too long without enough clothes to warm her.

Naked Kissen. No, he should not be thinking of that. This was not the time.

Elo stoked up the fire, hoping to warm her, but the crackle of it startled her from her sleep. She leapt upright, drawing a knife from inside her cloak, staring wildly around with her teeth bared.

"It's all right," said Elo gently. Inara was sleeping, her god back in her arms, his wings neatly folded and his eyes closed. Even out here, the girl could sleep so easily. Elo couldn't remember the last time he'd slept that well. Before the war, probably, when the world was simpler.

Kissen focussed on him and relaxed, putting away her knife, then shivering again. "Shit," she said, rubbing her hands against her chest. The wind over the lake was cutting like a blade, stroking at Elo's cheeks and neck.

"Cold?" he asked.

"No," she said quickly. Then added, "It's your fault."

"I know," said Elo. He poked the fire again, and she eyed it suspiciously, her hands going to her vial. "What is that?" he asked.

"A precaution," she said. "And a last resort. Pato made a bargain for it with a god, and when he died it became mine." She shuffled closer to the fire, wrapping her cloak more tightly around her.

"Pato trained you, no?" She had mentioned him before.

"He didn't have much of a choice. I ran away from Blenraden and followed him till he did."

"Did he die in the war?"

Kissen was rubbing her hands together to warm them. "Sort of. We were halfway across Middren hunting a god of sleep, but three wild gods came looking for veiga to kill. Mara, god of wolves, was one of them." Elo knew that name. "Pato was old, and even between the two of us we couldn't fight three. I survived; he didn't." She shrugged. "He said it was the way of things."

Elo frowned. "Mara. We hunted her in the city."

"I know," said Kissen. "I was there." She smiled lightly, coldly. "After I got my family over this very same mountain, I went back to sign up with the other godkillers who had a death wish or a bone to pick."

"You went for revenge."

Kissen wrapped her arms around her legs and put her chin on her knee. Her lips were slightly blue, and her eyes flickered as she stared into the flames. "Revenge takes a lifetime," she said quietly. "Sometimes . . . you've got to take what you can get of it." Elo felt there was more to her story than just Pato's death, but was distracted by her shivering again.

"I can help," he said, glad to be able to do something.

"With what?"

"The cold."

She looked at him suspiciously, then her eyes widened slightly as she understood what he was suggesting.

"Don't knights swear to some holy vow of chastity or something?"

Elo laughed quietly. "No," he said, "but even if they did, I'm not a knight, and I'm only offering you some warmth." That was not quite true. He would have liked to offer her more.

No. He had a mission, a quest.

Kissen rubbed her chest now, looking from Elo to the fire. "Fine," she said.

She picked herself up and sat down with an irritated harrumph in front of Elo, so both of them were facing the fire. He opened his arms and wrapped them around her chest and shoulders beneath her cloak. She let him, stiffly at first. She was chilled to the bone, he could tell by how tight her muscles were and the way she sat. He held her carefully, and after a while she settled back into him, leaning against his chest. She still shivered from time to time, but softer. As her skin warmed, so did his, sharing their heat together. He could see the burn scars on her neck, glimmering in the firelight, and the white stain of the broken curse. She was a resilient woman. A powerful one.

"Thank you," he said quietly.

"What for?" Her voice was slightly muffled, her chin buried into her cloak. The wind whistled, whipping up the flame.

"You could have let me go," he said. "Inara would have listened to you."

Kissen was quiet. "That girl doesn't like listening to anyone," she said.

"Reminds me of someone," said Elo pointedly, and Kissen laughed. Elo tightened his arms.

"Well," said Kissen, "you're not bad for a knight, and you're pretty good for a baker."

Elo grinned, and decided to be bold and rest his chin on her head. She let him, to his surprise.

This was a side to Kissen he wasn't sure he had met yet, perhaps more vulnerable than she would like to admit. The people with the sharpest edges sometimes hid the deepest wounds. If these were his last days, Elo decided to be grateful for them.

"I understand why Inara wants to help me," said Elo. "She wants her own piece of vengeance, to part from the god, and to take her place in her House. But what about you, Kissen? You said you work alone, that you don't like teams, you don't like kings. I almost killed you, brought demons on you. Why would you stay?"

"I take my own side, knight, I always have," said Kissen carefully. "If no one fights in your corner, then you learn to fight for yourself." She spoke as bluntly as he had come to expect from her. She made no compromises, had her own kind of honour.

Elo waited, and she didn't continue. "But . . . ?" he prompted.

"But"—she sighed—"I was born in Talicia." He felt a flicker of tension pass over her shoulders, then fade. Elo warmed with a wave of sympathy for her. Talicia had become a cruel land beneath a cruel god. It had been the only country that refused to offer Middren aid during the war. Even Restish, who would benefit from Middren's weakened dominance of the Trade Sea, had offered ships and food. "And now Middren is my home. It's where the people I love live." He felt her hands shift up to her chest again, pressing flat against where the god's promise was imprinted in her skin. Elo wondered what the promise was, and what had been sacrificed for it. "And we have all seen enough of death for gods. So, I'll help you. And the girl. If I can. If it stops a war."

Elo smiled, then added quietly, "Is that the only reason you keep me around?"

Kissen stayed silent, not drawing her eyes from the flames. Moment by moment, she was leaning more heavily into him, sleepy, perhaps, or cosy. Beyond the firelight was complete darkness, as if the whole world had folded away, leaving just the two of them. Her breath slowly fell into a deep, steady rhythm, and he knew she had fallen asleep.

He kept his arms around her, feeling deeply alone. He did not have long, if the curse could not be lifted, and had only Arren to fight for. But at least, at the very least, he now had someone to fight alongside, though he would not in a thousand years have suspected it would be a god, a godkiller, and a child.

CHAPTER TWENTY-FIVE

Inara

THEY DESCENDED THE BENNITES OVER THE NEXT THREE days, and the eastern slopes grew warmer as they did. The trees thinned and the landscape of snow fell away into damp black bracken and stone. The air was sharp and clear, and the wind strong. It had blown the haze of the mountains away to show, with brilliant clarity, the sea in the far distance. They saw glimpses of it between treetops and winding paths, shining blue.

As they descended the paths grew wide, and then the trees were gone altogether. The mountainsides near them were gutted and pock-marked, torn open for stone, the quarries now brown, scrubby, and abandoned. New saplings were growing in straggles on the slopes that had long ago been stripped of trees for the famous Blenraden timber and shipping yards. Below them flatlands spread from the sea cliffs inwards. Farms and fields, now marked only by the strangely rippled lines of unchecked growth.

It was on the third day that Inara saw it in the distance, perched on the cliffs beneath the mountains over a great azure harbour: Blenraden. The city of a thousand shrines, its limestone walls gleaming in noonday sun and towers scraping the clouds. Upright and proud after devastation. Kissen and Elo both paused, quiet as they saw a place that held so much memory, so much death, and so many gods. Inara was finally there, a veiga, a knight, and her god of white lies at her side, and a bow in her hand.

She found thoughts of her mother crowding into her mind. It was Lessa who'd taught her how to shoot a bow before the war, before Skedi. Almost as soon as she could walk.

"*You never know, my little love,*" she had said, "*when a fight might come to you.*"

Maybe she should have listened to her own words.

Kissen's bow was not like her bow at home; her mother had got her a new one every year as she grew. Those had been soft, carved wood, beautifully polished and designed for Inara. The arrows had been shafted with wild-turkey feathers, only the best for the House's daughter. Kissen's arrows had goose feathers, the bow was polished from the use of her hands and oiled with something that didn't smell like beeswax. Inara wondered what her mother would have thought, seeing her now. No longer stuffed away in a grand house of many rooms, none of them filled, while her mother worked in secret. Now Inara was out in the wilds, forging her own fate. Would her mother be proud? Afraid? Inara would never know.

Skedi swooped down and landed on the horse Inara was leading. Legs huffed but kept moving, happier now that the paths were flatter and they were below the snowline again. They were coming to sea level, and Inara could see the main road they would have taken when the city was still living, rolling along the coast, where it must stop in every town built into Middren's natural harbours.

"I can feel you thinking, Ina," said Skedi out loud. He was still tentative with her. Good. "What's wrong?"

They had not spoken much of what had happened between them. Inara couldn't shake the fright of having lost power over her own tongue, her own body. Nor could she forget the feeling of breaking his will. A snapping, as her colours burst out, tearing through his control. Then, he had defended her, protected her. Did love fix betrayal?

"How do you like your new home?" said Inara, looking at the city. Skedi was quiet for a moment, stung perhaps.

"You're thinking about your mother, aren't you?" he said.

She chewed the inside of her cheek, thumbing the buttons of her waistcoat with her other hand. "I'm angry with her," she said at last. "She kept me in the house, hid her letters from me, told me nothing about what was going on before she died. Why?"

Skedi was quiet for a minute. His whiskers twitched as he thought, catching the light of the sun. Behind them, Kissen and Elo were walking, both lost in their own thoughts.

"Maybe," Skedi said at last, "the same reason you hid me. To keep you safe. That's why people need white lies, isn't it? To protect them from a truth that causes pain."

"Then why did *you* lie to me?" she said. He was so familiar to her, as familiar as her own hand. He was a part of her. Did her power come from their connection? Like how she could see the colours? What would it be like without them? "You caused me pain, Skedi. You took my will from me."

"You broke mine," he pointed out.

"It is not the same."

"No." He shook his head, his voice quiet. "I am sorry, Inara Craier. We are chained, against both of our wills, and I took yours away." He flattened his ears. "I was scared of dying. I am scared. But I was wrong. I will never do it again."

"No," said Inara. She went down a step and pulled Legs after her. Kissen had come to trust her completely with the horse. "Because you'll be here, and I'll be gone."

And she would have to face the world alone, without the colours, without her god. She didn't say it; she tried not to think it. Skedi said nothing, but he did grow slightly smaller.

"I suppose so," he said. He rallied himself, and took off from Legs's back, peeling away into the sky. He caught each gust in his wings and strained as high as he could. Was it further than he had gone before? Inara wasn't sure; he looked distant in the sky. There was no one in the half-wild lands about them, the green of spring just beginning to poke through the rotten vegetation of the previous year. Inara felt the little painful tug on her heart as the wind blew him too far, and he came back to float above her.

"Watch your step," said Elo as they entered the first abandoned fields on the lower slopes. "When the people ran, a lot was left behind. Ploughs, weapons, traps."

The fields they hiked through were thick with bracken and tangled briars, devastated by only a few years of abandonment. The young trees that once would have been carefully tended now grew wild branches up their spindly trunks, weighed down with spring oranges that would break their branches, eager for light but not willing to wait. No one to tell them to grow slow and strong. The steadings and grand houses they passed were gutted, glass windows removed or broken. One house Inara glimpsed had a cluster of white at the bottom of its steps. She looked closer, and saw they were bones, bleached in the salt air.

"Funerals are for the living," said Kissen as she noticed Inara looking. "The dead don't mind what the world does to them."

Inara looked away, trying not to think about the bones of House Craier resting beneath an open sky.

It was at one of these steadings that they stopped to eat. They could now see the city again. Closer, its ruin was more apparent. The towers that at a distance had seemed whole were clearly half-fallen and ruined. The walls in some places were broken into rubble. Blue banners still hung from them, flapping and ragged in the wind, plastered with the king's symbol of the sun and the dark antlers of the stag.

"I never thought I'd have to look on these walls again," said Elo. Kissen nodded. She was cleaning out Legs's hooves while he put up with it.

"There's a watch," she said. Inara followed her gaze up. A flicker of movement amongst the rubble, more than just the shaking of the banners in the southern wind. "Poor sods, being positioned out here. Ah, patience, lad." Legs had tried to put his hoof down, starting to get annoyed at the scraping. "We don't have Jon's planned route in, or the protection of a pilgrim train." She looked at Elo. "So . . . what about you? You know a secret way in? We don't have the time to worry about a night in a cell."

Elo broke a crust apart. "Yes," he said. He had taken the news of his impending death by demon in stride. He was now focussed, determined. "I know a way."

"I knew it."

"But . . ." said Elo. "It's no good for horses."

Inara looked at Legs. She couldn't imagine walking without his quiet companionship. By the look on Kissen's face, she felt the same. "Are you sure?" Inara asked.

Elo lifted his shoulders, and Kissen pressed her lips together, releasing Legs's hoof. He turned and nudged at her, expecting a reward, but when she reached up to scratch his nose he backed away, huffing that it wasn't what he'd asked for. She sighed. "All right. Shit. This had better be worth it."

They left Legs in one of the abandoned steadings, to his confusion, filling a trough with plenty of fresh water from a nearby mill to keep him for a couple of days, and another with his oats and feed. Kissen refused to lock him in, only partly closed the door, and took off his bridle and saddle, hiding them in the bushes.

"What if he runs away?" asked Inara as Kissen gave him a last brushing-down.

Kissen shrugged. "I owe him more than a slow death in a cage. If he runs, he runs, and good luck to him. Anyway, you've seen what he does to people who try to ride him without asking politely." Legs nickered, and Kissen brushed his neck. "Good lad," she added. "I'll come back for you. I promise."

They left their heavier things too, Kissen's staff and cooking supplies, the larger bags; she shoved them all in with the saddle.

After Legs was settled, whinnying at them as they left, they crept closer and closer to the city across the barren lands, till it loomed above them, trusting Elo's subtle leadership. He took them up through thick undergrowth towards the wall closest to the palace, which sat far back from the harbour and at the top of a long slope. Once, Inara knew, the towers of Blenraden's high palace had reached far over the walls. Now only a sparse few watchtowers remained, half-shored-up with reclaimed wood.

Skedi had been flying as small as a yellow spring bird. He swept down to Inara's shoulder. "Two knights on the wall," he said. "Sitting, drinking."

"Idiots," muttered Elo.

"Incompetence plays in our favour," said Kissen.

"They're still knights."

Skedi was as tiny as he could be on Inara's shoulder, whispering *You cannot see us, you cannot see us, you cannot see us* at the world about them and throwing his will out like a cloak.

Elo skirted further around the wall and towards a drainage crevice that ran beneath it. Water pooled there, long stagnant; Inara could see the channel it used to cut from the divot running down the hill. Whatever had filled it had either stopped or been diverted elsewhere. Elo slid into the pool, then helped Inara down behind him. The murky water soaked her to her waist. It was not like the cold, still lake beneath Tala, crisp and fresh as frost. It stank.

Kissen muttered under her breath as she gathered her heavy cloak with its godkilling tools above her shoulders and followed them into the drain beneath the wall. Inara wondered what she couldn't get wet. She looked back as the light shone on Kissen's red hair, sliding over her crown, then faded to black.

Inside the drain, the darkness grew absolute. The air smelled worse, fetid. Inara stretched her hands out to keep her balance, trying not to retch as her fingers brushed up against the wall and felt the sucking kiss of slime. She followed the sounds of Elo's sloshing walk for what seemed like forever, then . . . silence. She stopped, and heard the sound of palms on metal.

Inara found Elo's cloak, then felt her way around to the metal grid he was holding. They were trapped.

"This is your big plan?" Kissen muttered.

"Follow me," he said. He took hold of the grid and began to climb, his breath catching as his wound bit with pain. Even in the dark, Inara could see his colours. Pain flashed as gold as his panic. She wondered what must have happened, for gold to be such a frightening colour for a knight.

Inara felt Kissen reach for her elbow to help her up. The grid crackled beneath her hands, the lifting flakes of iron and rust crunching under the pressure.

She climbed after the sounds of Elo's feet, aware that he was just ahead of her, then he was gone. She hit a stone ceiling, almost as slimy as the walls, and panicked.

"Elo?" She did not like the sound of her voice in the dark. She sounded small. Below her, Kissen stopped.

Behind, said Skedi, who was light as he could be, the size of a mouse, as she climbed, sitting in her hood.

"It's all right," Elo said. She felt his hand on her arm. "Let me help."

He lifted her backwards and onto a ledge she couldn't see. The ceiling was low, too low to stand. "Keep forward," he said. They both jumped at a thud and a suppressed curse from Kissen. "I'll help the veiga."

"The veiga doesn't need your help," said Kissen through gritted teeth.

She hit her head, said Skedi, amused. Inara chewed back a smile and groped forward. She found a lip carved into the rock, and another above it. A ladder cut into the stone, leading upwards. She followed it, feeling for each rough-hewn ledge. Then her hands touched wood.

Elo climbed up behind her, reaching for the same door. They could both just fit in the narrow passageway. He put his shoulder to it and lifted, grunting. It moved only a little way. Inara swallowed. What would they do if the hatch was barred? But then he slid it across.

Light. Not much of it. A dim glow of a closed room with a high, small window, reflected into a polished piece of bronze. Just enough to see by.

Skedi climbed up Inara's hand to the surface, his nose twitching. Inara and Elo followed.

The cellar they had emerged into was full of empty and broken casks. The air smelled of alcohol, and the walls were black and furred with thick mould. Good mould for a brandy cellar; the Craiers' own had the same coating, the distillers were thrilled about it. Here, whatever the cellar had been keeping was long gone.

"How the salted piss did you know about this place?" Kissen muttered, lifting herself out of the passageway. The panel and the floor were wood. When shut, the door slotted finely into the planks. Kissen slid it to, and it all but disappeared.

"These are the palace cellars," said Elo. "That sewer runs right beneath the stables and kitchens to here. It was built as an escape route. When we besieged the city, it took months to get close enough to the walls to reach it. When we did, we attacked from inside and out, and were able to let our battalions through the gate." He paused. "And Arren and I used it once to go out drinking before the war."

"Once?" asked Kissen, sounding highly suspicious.

"Maybe a few times. We didn't spend much time in Blenraden; the queen usually only took her favourites."

"Humph, how many of these tunnels are there?"

"That would be telling."

Kissen chuckled. "I thought I knew everything there was to know about this blasted city," she said. "I should have suspected nobles were as sneaky as beggars."

Inara found herself baffled by the thought of these two in the same city. Elogast with the prince, sneaking out to drink and be merry, and Kissen begging and cutting pockets.

The door up to the next cellar was half-open, and they followed stairs into greater, wider vaults. There were no windows in this area, but Inara could feel the space about them, hear it in the echoes of their feet. The smell of brandy grew stronger, but through it ran the stink of rot.

"Only covered lanterns could be brought in here," said Elogast, the dregs of sunlight showing the shape of his face. "It might be too dangerous still to expose an open flame."

"Speaking for myself," said Kissen, "I'd rather not risk death by fire. It's particularly unpleasant." Inara shivered in the dark. "Do you remember enough of your rebellious jaunts and besieging to find our way to the door, knight?"

"Perhaps," said Elo thoughtfully. They had just enough light from the room below to see each other's shapes in the gloom, but beyond that all was black. It made Inara think of the shadow demons, as if she could sense them padding around in the dark. There would be eight of them tomorrow, after Elo, to kill him. Inara groped for and took hold of Kissen's hand. The veiga jumped, surprised, then squeezed her fingers and took a step forward.

Her foot came into contact with something. She lurched, cursed, stumbled, and Inara had to hold on to her to stop her falling back down the stairs.

"Hush," said Elo.

"I can't feel my way as easy as you two-legs," she said pointedly, "and someone made me leave my staff."

"Ah . . ." He came back towards them and held out his hand, his fingers just visible in the slip of sun from below. "I'll lead," he said.

Kissen looked at his hand, then sighed and put her own into it. Elo led them into the dark, moving at a steady pace on a slight upward slope and nudging aside any debris that lay across their path before Inara and Kissen reached it. It didn't take long for him to find something he was looking for.

"They used these runners to ferry the carts out of the castle," he said. Inara felt with her booted feet, finding a metal ridge in the stone floor. "It will lead us to the door."

The door was up another set of steps, and it swung open into a vast, bright corridor with an arched ceiling, marking out cubbies to the right and left of them. The high windows let in the early-evening sun and highlighted the carvings over many doorways into more vaults. Little clusters of berries hung like living vines growing from the stone. Between them were craters of exploded rock.

"Never seen carvings acting as shrines," said Kissen, following her line of sight. "I imagine these were for Tet."

Elo nodded. "The god of wine was carved all through these corridors. Any that didn't split when he was killed with the rest of the wild gods, the knights cut out."

Kissen realised she was still holding Elo's hand, and released it quickly, then Inara's. Elo's and Kissen's eyes met, and he grinned. Was Kissen *blushing*?

They continued down the corridor, past six doors till they found the one Elo was looking for. Inara had been expecting another corridor, but instead found stairs that they climbed, coming out beneath open sky.

A vast chamber, its roof shattered, beams blasted and broken as the ribs of a dead body. These curved down what once would have been great pointed arches around shrines set at regular intervals in the walls, their symbols destroyed, their cups still holding the remains of ash.

The wind had made the room its home. It whirled along the corners, stirring leaves out and along a shattered table which still held gold and shining plates, cups of absent wine, the rain-washed bones of a deer and a lamb, picked clean. Some of the foods had sprouted new life, growing small plants and trees that must have sprung from seeds dropped by passing birds. No one had looted this place.

Inara breathed in. Something stirred in the air: power. Tremendous will and crackling energy still sounded from the walls and sat at the table, wrestling with the wind. Terror lingered too, like washed-out ink. As she looked closer, Inara saw between the leaves old bloodstains on the floor. Wind and rain had not been able to soothe them away.

"This was where it started, wasn't it?" she asked. Elo was looking stone-faced at the broken scene.

"This was where the queen held her banquets," he said. "The fight between the wild gods and the new gods began here. We cleared the bodies, gave them a burial, but everything else . . . felt wrong to touch."

"I don't understand what led the gods to fight so cruelly," said Inara, looking around at the destruction.

"Love and power," said Kissen, her lip curling. "Fights between gods were common in Blenraden, scrapping for the most attention. Old gods, new gods, merchant gods, wild gods. More than once I walked into a spat that had people losing limbs. It's only when it reached the high lords and ladies that people paid attention."

"Why did they turn violent?" asked Skedi, his fur rippling in the breeze.

"Because," said Kissen, "trade and riches in cities like this drew people to new gods of fortune, like golden Agni, and away from wild gods like Tet, the god of wine who began this. People don't need wild gods any more when they're fat and rich and comfortable. Gods don't take kindly to being forgotten."

Tet had made Agni's own followers tear him apart, and then each other. The queen amongst them. Inara wondered which bloodstains were hers. "But gods need humans," said Skedi. "This is . . . cruel."

"Well, the new gods of the city didn't like it either," said Kissen, looking around the room with her lip curled. "The younger, more powerful ones went for Tet's shrines, then the old gods retaliated. The whole fucking place went mad, and took the people with it."

"All for this stupid vanity," said Elo. He rubbed his shoulder, the cursed and scarred one. "We should go."

Inara didn't like it here. It was a bad place. All her senses told her so. Full of lost souls and all that fright. Skedi wasn't too bothered; he flapped his wings and took off to nose about the dead shrines with interest, perhaps looking for one that was familiar.

"Can we please get out of here?" said Ina. It was like the colours of terror were seeping up from the ground. So many people had thought this place was safe. *Skediceth*, she called. He turned about and flew into her arms.

What is it?

Doesn't this place frighten you?

Skedi looked at her curiously. *The power here can't hurt you,* he said. *But the stones remember it, and the wind tries to calm them.*

It feels wrong.

I'm a god of white lies, said Skedi gently. *I am not the god of fright and terror. What remains here does not belong to me.*

Elo led them past the long table and into another room, less damaged than the first, but also stripped of whatever had been there. His colours turned cobalt and lilac with faith and affection. Arren, he was thinking of Arren. "This was where guards and . . . less preferred heirs . . . ate during banquets. Slept in here too."

They left through a grand door into a fountain courtyard, cornered in five points by towers, broken and burned. The fountain itself was clogged with weeds, and beyond it was a great gate, its stonework riddled with scorch marks. Its doors were cracked and hanging loose. Through it, they could see the gleam of the sun, bright and sparkling on the sea, so close.

Movement. Colour.

A person.

Skedi dwindled in Inara's arms, and Kissen put her hand to her blade. Inara realised that she already had Kissen's bow in her hand, ready for a fight.

I saw their blazon, said Skedi. *It's a knight.*

CHAPTER TWENTY-SIX

Elogast

ELO WISHED HE STILL PRAYED.

A knight. He hadn't needed Skedi to tell him that; he too had seen Arren's sun-and-stag blazon on their back. He hadn't expected the palace to be guarded. There was nothing there any more. Luckily the knight was not looking inside.

Elo gestured to Kissen, who was soft-stepping forward, her hand on her sword. *Stop.* He pointed to himself. He had got them here, so he would get them out. They couldn't afford to be caught, not now. But it was a miracle they had not been seen already. If the knight turned around now, they might be spotted.

Elo flexed his injured arm and slipped closer to the open gate on his damp shoes. Below it unrolled the Godsway, the sweeping road that ran from the palace to the city proper. It was as beautiful as Elo remembered; even cracked and dismantled, it wound like a pale river down the hill. Once, the palace had been a fortress against raiders from Talicia, then it had been the hub of the trade sea. Now, it was nothing but old beauty, destroyed by war.

Elo's heart was pounding, not only because of the guard, but at being back in this city, on this path, at having walked through that place where he remembered the ghosts of the dead. His shoulder ached and sweat stood out on his head. He took a deep, shaking breath, then another. The knight was barely steps away.

Elo breathed out, focussed. The guard was bored, judging by the angle of their shoulders, but was still standing upright, unlike those Elo had seen on the wall. The uniform was not as neat as Elo would have liked, the cloak tossed back and crumpled. And they wore no helmet, only a loose hat, showing tightly braided hair and dark skin like Elo's. Smart, perhaps, for the cool weather, but it would be easy enough for Elo to knock them down.

Elo ghosted through the gate and slid behind the sighing knight. The man turned to the side, following the line of the sun west, his profile clear and clipped with light. Elo stopped.

"Benjen?"

Benjen startled, twisting into a fighting stance and reaching for his sword. Elo panicked and threw himself at him before he could draw, bowling both of them to the ground.

Benjen's armour weighed him down. As he struggled to rise, Elo twisted around and took hold of the knight's sword, grunting as the gashes in his arm flexed, and pulled it from his sheath as he rolled up to standing. He held the blade low, low enough to strike, and Benjen knew it. An old trick.

"Yield," said Elo, hoping his sore arm wouldn't shake.

"Ser Elogast," the knight gasped, struggling to his feet. He had no weapon, and was at a loss for words, staring at Elo like he had seen a ghost. Finally, he settled on a baffled smile, his eyes on his sword in Elo's hand. "You have not changed."

Elo loosened his stance, half wanting to go and embrace Benjen, half wishing he had knocked him on the head from behind so they could all be on their way. "Squire Benjen," he said, then eased them both with a laugh. Hopefully Kissen would hear that, know that everything was in hand. "You lost your sword."

"It's Ser Benjen now," the knight said with a flush of pride. Elo inclined his head.

"Ser Benjen. You deserve the title."

Elo did not drop the blade. There was a quickness to Benjen's eye that he didn't like, and he had after all taught the boy himself. Benjen hadn't found Elo a soft touch when under his command, and he wouldn't find him to be one now.

"What are you doing here, Ser Elogast?" Benjen asked. More accusation than question.

Elo didn't know how to answer. "You know I am not a ser any more."

Benjen had recovered from his surprise, and now moved slightly, putting the sun behind him so it shone on his armour. Elo didn't know whether to be proud or irritated. "I also know that no one can set foot in Blenraden without the king's permission."

"So, all those pilgrims that bribe their way through the gates have permission, do they?" said Elo defensively. Benjen's mouth twitched. He had hit a mark.

"Let me pass, Benjen. I'll do no more harm than them."

Benjen glanced to the side, shifting his feet. At last he shook his head, a shadow of resentment, anger, passing over his brow. "You left us," he said. "After you taught us common folk to swear ourselves to the king; our lives, our blood, our hearts. We gave our all to fight by his side, by *your* side. Down in that square." He pointed across the city. From here, they couldn't see it, but Elo knew the place. Every day, it burst into his memories like a festering wound. Benjen had been one of the recruits after the massacre of the harbour, called to fight in desperation. "You left us. Why?"

"I don't owe you an explanation."

"I fought for you. I was prepared to die for you. But you turned your back on us, and closed your eyes, and did nothing."

That cut deep, deeper than Benjen could know.

"You fought neither for Arren nor for the gods. You stopped fighting altogether."

Elo flinched. The guilt and loneliness that filled his heart felt as heavy as a tomb. The pain of it was physical, the tightening of his lungs, the aching of his shoulder; the shame at leaving his army, Arren, his soldiers and knights, the land now teetering on the edge of another war. Because of him. Because of his negligence.

"I cannot let you of all people break the king's laws, Ser Elogast." Benjen pulled a dagger from his waist. "You should do what you do best and lay down your sword."

Elo cursed inwardly. What should he do? What would Kissen do? He was running out of time; if he wasn't careful Kissen would come out and cause a scene, then all of Blenraden would bear down on them. He spent much of Arren's final month just getting to the city, and had only one more day before the summonings attacked. He didn't have time for this.

"Careful, Ser Benjen," said Elo, and held Benjen's blade aloft. "It's your sword you need to worry about."

Benjen couldn't win, he knew it. He paled, but did not stand down. "My life, my blood, my heart, is the king's," he said. "That's what you taught me."

He leapt forward with his knife, striking hard, striking to kill. Elo countered, keeping Benjen at arm's length. This was not Kissen; the lad could not fight one sword with a knife, let alone two, but Elo didn't want to hurt him. He batted another strike away, then whirled around for Benjen's leg, tripping him. The lad stumbled but didn't fall. He caught himself and ran forward again.

Kissen appeared behind him and caught his cloak in her hand, yanking him back. Benjen yelped as he lost balance. She wrapped him in a neck-lock, catching his yell in his lungs. With her other hand she had his knife wrist and twisted it, hard. He dropped the blade, focussing instead on grappling with her strong forearm around his throat, scrabbling for a foothold. Benjen choked, spluttered.

"Don't kill him," said Elo. "Please."

"Godsblood, what have I told you?" she said. She released his wrist and struck him, hard, in the head, then tightened her grip. Benjen paled, the veins standing out at his temples. His eyes rolled back, and he went limp. She held him a few more moments, just to be sure, then dropped him. He didn't move, but he breathed.

"I don't kill people," she said. She stared down at Benjen. "We'd better tie him up, though."

CHAPTER TWENTY-SEVEN

Kissen

THE STEPS OF THE GODSWAY WERE TOO EXPOSED. ELO'S "friend" the knight would wriggle free of the ropes they'd used to bind him eventually, or someone would come looking for him. That meant they had only a couple of hours at most before the rest of the shiny-armoured dogs started sniffing around. From every possible angle, they were out of time.

Instead, Kissen led them down a side track that the servants once used. It went through the sporting ground made for hunts and fishing, and had a small road for carts and carriages. Everyone else who could walk used the steps. Even the nobles.

It took them an age to get through the hunting grounds and into the city proper, slipping through the grand plazas that marked the inner ring of the city. Kissen avoided Victory Square, the place where the war god Mertagh's greatest Blenraden shrine had been. She was pretty certain that whatever Elo was here for, it was connected to that battle, and she didn't want him to get that look of pain on his face and the shaking in his hands that she suspected came from the memory of the war. King Arren had been injured then; she knew that. She hadn't seen much in the battle after the torches went out, only the gold of the god's armour, the flash of the chain in her hands, and the closeness of other veiga.

They moved deeper into the dead city, and the wind and the birds were the only things that moved. No bells rang the change in hours, no windows lit with lanterns as the shadows grew. The smells of the day's chamber pots were not seeping down the walls and into the drains. Still, Kissen knew where they were going; she could walk these streets with her eyes closed.

"What's that?" asked Inara. Kissen looked ahead. There. A shadow. It passed over the street, slow and drifting, but there was nothing in the sky to cast it. For a terrible moment she thought it was one of the demons come a night early, but the sun had not fully set, and the shadow seemed unaware of them. The being had no substance, but she could hear its voice like a nail in her head.

Thread the warp and lift the loom, press the weft with teeth of comb . . .

Kissen stopped then, holding Inara by her shoulder. Skedi's fur was on end, his wings rising. She had heard of these things, gods who had lost their main shrine but still had some little ones stashed away. Its faithful must be gone too. Still, it clung to life, half-remembering itself.

Bring the colours, string them through, down the paths of weaver's wool . . .

Its faded will, directionless, twitched at Kissen's fingers, make them long for cloth and thread. A weaver god. Or it had been, once. It stopped, blocking their path, perhaps sensing people nearby.

"Don't get close," Kissen warned, putting her hand on her sword. What would happen if they got too near its unchecked will? It might drag them into its reverie, fill them with its thoughts until they forgot everything but the god.

Perhaps she should kill it, put it out of its misery. She turned to Inara to ask for her bow, and her eyes found Skediceth. His wings had fallen, his ears too, and he had shrunk down small, gazing at the god in terror. The weaver god had been alive once, like Skedi.

"Come," said Kissen, surprising herself by taking them down a side street instead, away from the passage of the faded god. It was not worth the risk. She led them instead through the inkers' district, the canal that ran through clean as she'd ever seen it, and into the spice streets, full of lost colours. Had she just felt sympathy for a god? A god of white lies? She was getting soft. Her feelings about her companions had become tangled, complicated. He had shown his weaknesses, and his love for Inara. She hated gods, all gods, but this was the first time she had got to know one.

In what had once been Sundial Square at the centre of the spicers' roads, a huge incense ball remained where it had been overturned, its fist-deep ashes spilled. Kissen thought she could still catch the lingering scent of a hundred thousand offerings. Scattered about were the little wooden shrines of the market, cracked and broken, shadows skittering between them. At one point, several burst out like rats, and Elo picked Inara up as they leapt over them.

It wasn't long before they passed another god, a shadow standing against the wall of an alley. Small, the height of Inara's knee. Kissen's hand went to her blade again, but the being didn't move, simply stood. She went to move on, but Inara stopped her.

"Wait," she said.

"Ina, we don't have much time," said Elo.

"Just a moment," said Inara. She turned to the shadow. Skedi was still on her shoulder, flattened to it. The little god had been so excited to reach the gates of the palace, but now he was afraid.

"Hello?" Inara said. They had given her Benjen's briddite-edged shortsword, but she didn't draw it. It was too heavy for her anyway.

"Don't—" said Kissen, but it was too late. The shadow, thin enough to be a stain on the wall, took form as it turned towards the attention. It shrank too, becoming smaller and darker, and showing its true form. Its face was carved out of a fine, smooth wood in the shape of a mouse, and it had a furred body and long tail, with a bird's claws for feet. It looked at Inara for a baleful moment, then turned into the alley. Kissen peered through the shadows and saw it. A tiny shrine, this one intact, complete with a little shoe totem, a mouse carved into the heel. A god of broken sandals.

The tiny god turned back to them, cocking its head. It didn't speak. Perhaps it couldn't any more, but Kissen knew what it wanted; they all did. An offering. It took a step towards Inara's feet, and Kissen went to pull her back, but she held up her hand.

"Don't you feel sorry for them?" she said. The little creature reached her feet and plucked at her shoes. Boots, not sandals. Its power was small.

Kissen did feel sorry for it. She pitied the creature as she would pity a kitten that needed its mother's milk, even if it might grow to a tiger.

Inara was holding on to the mother-of-pearl buttons of her waist-coat. She did that for comfort, Kissen had noticed. Her fingers closed on one that had loosened some, and she pulled it off, passing it down to the little god.

"What's your name?" she said.

It didn't answer, but it stood on its hind feet and took the button, then scurried back to its shrine. It looked a touch more solid, as if light had rippled across it and given it shape. It put the button down by its carving, touching it and arranging its tiny homage.

"The sun is sinking," said Elo.

Inara turned away. The god could not quite remember how to be a god. Kissen led them on, but as she did, they all heard a tiny whisper.

Kelt.

Kissen worried at her gold tooth. She knew Blenraden was dangerous. A god of broken sandals was one thing, but what of a god of thieves? Murderers? One who had been powerful enough, had blood offerings rather than little trinkets?

"Didn't do a very thorough job, did you?" said Kissen to Elo, half hoping her remark would knock him out of brooding.

"No," he said quietly.

Whoareyouwheredoyougo? Which waydoyou go? Whichway?

Kissen flinched as a strange god's voice burrowed into her head. They had come to another shadowed crossroads. The remaining windows in the buildings above were shining with reflected evening light, but the lamp in the centre of the crossroads was dark. Kissen had to blink twice to see the god at its base, its darkness blending with the rest.

Come you here?

The being turned, and its eyes flickered with dwindling flames. Kissen understood. His shrine beneath the lamp had been destroyed, but his totem had not: the lamp itself. The lights that had once brightened the dark nights now only shone from the god's eyes. It saw them, for they were in its domain.

Rest, rest here, rest with me . . . restyourfeetrest yoursoul and . . . stay.

There were rat bones around the bottom of the lamp, the mould-ering corpse of a fox. The wraith stepped closer, its shapeless feet leaving some mark like ash on the ground.

Do not go on, only terror awaits.

At his feet was a larger set of bones, a human skull.

Kissen and Elo drew their swords. A child, perhaps one that had been lost in the city, running through battles, and caught, stopped, kept by a shrineless god. This god was dangerous, a trap springing shut. Its eyes glowed brighter, as if more oil had been added to the flame. Kissen raised her blade.

"Don't touch him," Inara warned.

She was right. He wanted Kissen to come close so he could bind her, swallow her. Her attention gave him power, gave him will.

Only terror ahead. Stay here awhile, just a little. This is a place of talking talk. Laughter and . . . exchanges. So sweet to stay.

His shape collapsed. He twisted outwards around the crossroads, trying to surround them.

"We will pass through," said Elo, taking on a fighting stance. But he understood what Kissen had: fighting something so shapeless that surrounded them would be like fighting the sea; it would only swallow them.

You will not go.

Kissen cursed. She would have to try. She reached inside her cloak, but Inara stepped in front of her.

"Stop," she said. No, she commanded, fierce and firm. What had been a god was arrested in his tracks. He stared at Ina, lamp eyes burning. Kissen breathed in, shallow. The thing, neither spirit nor god, wound up again, condensing and becoming smaller. These lost gods of Blenraden were something she was not used to. Nothing to lose and everything to gain, they had no need for reason, for exchange; they were bundles of shapeless desire. What difference to them between a button and a life? Unstoppable. Except by Inara.

"Quickly," said Ina, hurrying past. Kissen found herself following, exchanging a look with Elo. He had not sheathed his blade, only gave Kissen a worried glance.

Beyond the crossroads, the wraith's will fell away. Inara paused, her hand on her chest as she breathed. Skedi flew up, around her head, seeming unsure where to land. He eventually decided on Kissen's shoulder, to her irritation, but she couldn't very well bat him off. He wanted to look at Inara. She looked just the same, leaning back against a wall.

"How did you do that, Ina?" asked Skedi from Kissen's shoulder, voicing her question aloud.

"I don't know," she said, looking at Kissen, then Skedi. She blushed. "I just wanted it to stop."

"It could have killed you."

"We couldn't kill it, or all the gods here would feel it. They need purpose. If we killed it their purpose would be to find us."

"How do you know?" said Elo.

Inara looked at Skedi, who shifted. "I—" She looked down. "It was just a guess."

A lie? Kissen wasn't sure. She felt nothing from Skedi, but then he was pretty close to her sword and wouldn't have risked it. This, after seeing her unravelling Skedi's will, worried Kissen. Was it the god's effect on her? Surely not; he would not have given her power over him, and a god of white lies couldn't command another as Inara had just done to the god of the crossroads.

"I think the polite thing to say," said Elo, sheathing his sword, "is thank you." He looked at the sky. It glowed, like the last light of the sun was compressed, intensified, by its closeness to the earth. Time was slipping by, and Kissen cursed under her breath. How had she ended up with three idiots, all of them neck-deep in trouble? Maybe *she* was the idiot.

"Fine," said Kissen, "let's go."

She took the paths she knew, shortcutting through her own district, where she had been sold after being picked up in Talicia, mended enough to be worth a little something in Blenraden. Many of the buildings were gutted and ruined, burned by fires or burst by gods. So many little gods in the poorer district, so many hopes and promises, so many faithful to turn.

They passed her street, the bottom of the pisspile. She stopped. Yatho had asked her for something.

The front wall of her old home was fallen, and the roof was a carcass of rafters. The remaining windows still had their bars, and over the door was the half-charred frontwork of a sign: *Marmee's Orphans*.

"Maimee" had suited her better.

"This is where you lived?" Inara asked, sharp as ever. Elo looked at her with surprise.

"This is where I was worked," said Kissen. "Maimee bought her kids, fixed us up just enough, or broke us a little more, and set us to do her money grabbing." She went over to the door, hawked, and spat on the doorstep, just as Yatho had asked. "Scarred my sister Telle's face so she would get more coin and less attention. Took Yatho from her parents as collateral for their debt. Nothing comes free here. Keep that in mind where we're going next." She was relieved when Elo didn't ask what had brought her here the first time. "Follow me."

They smelled the hot springs before they saw them. One of the few scents that remained of the Blenraden she had known. The baths were set back from the river, in a square lined with trees with thick flowerbuds just about ready to bloom. There was a lamp lit within the carved stone archway of the bathing complex, and the ivy that had been encroaching on the walls had been trimmed back. Bold. It seemed that whatever pilgrims paid to get into the city, they had an agreement not to be bothered by the knights while there. It was strangely relieving, to see at least one part of the city still living. The cypress trees at the main entrance stood a little wilder than before, but the pathway to the arch was recently swept.

"Go to your person, little god," said Kissen as they stepped inside. Skediceth darted down from her shoulder and back to Inara, creeping beneath her thick dark hair. It hung almost as wildly as Kissen's now, bunched into a rough plait, and her brown cheeks were fresh-nipped by the sun and cold wind. She had an edge of sureness to her now that suited her. Like she was coming home to herself, and had found strength there.

Kissen decided to be more proud than afraid.

Inside the door was an atrium before the halls that led into the baths proper. Here was a large basin and a running stream of water that came from up the wall, and an array of well-travelled shoes beside it. Above them hung cotton robes. Whoever was still maintaining the baths cared about even the smallest details.

They all washed away the stink from the fetid waters beneath the palace, and Inara and Elo dressed in the robes available, leaving their own hanging at the doorway to dry. Kissen deliberated some before doing the same, but still strapped her breastplate over the top and brought her cloak with her. None of them left their weapons. Not even this quiet space was safe, considering the trials they had been through to get there.

"This way," said Kissen when they were ready. There were two tunnels into the baths. The free public ones were off to the left, leading to open pools. The private, older ones were the other way, for those who did not like to mingle naked with half the commoners of the world. They used to cost good coin, but there was no one to collect it now.

Kissen took them down the private route, taking no small pleasure in walking the way that was always shut to her, but this was also where the pool she wanted to access was housed. The path was lit by a ceiling of glass and stonework, the evening sky setting the tiny holes alight in greens, purples, blues, and oranges, barely enough to light their way.

The long hall opened into a broad, wide room, sectioned by panels of carved limestone that sequestered steaming pools. The vapour in the air tightened Kissen's lungs, heavy with the taste of deep earth and stone.

The springs here were old, older than the city, and little gods and faithful pilgrims had always gathered at their sanctuary. There were several of both in the baths as they entered. Kissen caught the shine of one godling running along the stones in the shape of a tiny dragon. Another drifted through the steam in a cloak of grass and little coins. Healing gods. They had many shrines, and a number of them gathered at baths like this one, where doctors worked and people came to soothe their ailments. Kissen rarely had a bone to pick with a healing god.

The cloisters that guarded private pools echoed with singsong sloshes and patters as someone slid into a pool, followed by a sigh or a little laugh of pleasure. As they passed through, someone came out of one cloister and walked naked into another, paying them no heed. They were all equal in this holy place.

Kissen led them to the back, past a god shaped like a red bear with pointed white ears, deep in conversation with three pilgrims. Nearby, a formless spirit flitted over the water near a new shrine where pilgrims had been leaving trinkets. It would take shape soon, perhaps like the little hummingbird figurine that was in the shrine's centre.

Near the end of the baths, the cold waters were cut into a circle around a deep, hot pool. The cold waters were fed by the river Aan from deep in the Bennites at the border between Talicia and Middren, interlacing over and under stone to the coast. The hot came from deep beneath the city like the other springs. This pool was shaded by a thick inside wall, but its outer wall had fallen inwards, revealing an overgrown garden behind it. The sea breeze came through, clean and honest.

Kissen lifted the top of her longsword and used it to cut the edge of her hand, then held her closed fist over the pool. A drop of blood fell into the water.

"Aan," she called, simply. It wouldn't take long. Aan was everywhere her river was.

You seek me once more, godkiller?

Water rose over the edges of the cold streams and flooded into the pool, manifesting in the shape of a god. Aan of the river was a god full of flesh and life, her arms round and supple, like fruits in autumn. Her belly too, soft and yielding. She had the most kissable body, from the folds of her beautiful neck to the hair on her arms and the black curling line that traced from her belly to her sex.

"You've met a god without killing them?" said Skediceth from within Inara's collar. Aan laughed, her chuckle bubbling from the pool and bouncing off the walls.

"You think she could, little droplet?" said Aan.

Kissen scowled. No amount of shrine-tipping could trouble Aan, and the lures of godkillers were not enough to tempt her. She rarely troubled herself with the squabbles of young gods and short-lived humans, and seemed to enter bargains only for the entertainment of it.

"Aan," said Kissen again, this time in greeting, putting her hand on her heart and bowing her head. Aan was right; she hoped this god would never be her prey. She was likely as deadly as she was beautiful.

"You still carry that gift you stole," Aan said, letting her hand drift through the water, twisting her long, dark hair in her fingers. Kissen's mouth twitched, feeling the weight of the vial at her neck. It wasn't stolen; it was Pato's.

"Inherited," Kissen corrected. "What was I supposed to do, bury it with him?"

"And now you are back," Aan continued, ignoring her interruption, "with the same sword that killed my foolish young cousin." She looked at Kissen directly, her eyes dark fathoms deep. "Ennerast's anger came screaming all the way to the sea."

Kissen paused. Old gods were unpredictable in their anger. "It is sheathed and will stay sheathed," she said. "I do not regret my kill. Anyway, I have come asking, not taking."

Aan laughed again, and Kissen breathed out, glancing sideways at Elogast. He looked just as fascinated as she was. "I have seen so many come and go," the god said. "What's done is done. Kneel."

It was a command, not a question. Kneeling was neither comfortable nor defensible for Kissen, and Aan knew it. The god put her elbows on the edge of the pool and her chin in her hands, smiling at Kissen all sweet, knowing what she had asked.

Elo went graciously to his knees and Inara followed. Kissen clenched her jaw and got to her knees as easily as she could. Aan grinned.

"If you have come asking, I hope you have brought something worth an answer," she said, turning her attention on Elo. "What about this young man? Is he yours? Better than the scraggly old goat you were with last time." In fairness, Pato had been quite scraggly. Elo blushed.

"He needs a curse-breaker, Aan," she said, "and fast."

Aan raised her eyebrows at Elo, who shifted. Kissen got the distinct impression that, given a choice, he would have saved his own life second; whatever he wanted for Arren would have been first. Still, Elo unbuttoned his shirt to reveal the black from the curse mark, beginning to creep over his shoulder in its dark script. Aan touched her fingers to it, tracing the markings with a pout.

Her eyes flicked to Kissen, then slid to Inara. She tipped her head.

"And what thing are you, little unraveller?" she asked, drifting closer to Inara, staring as if the girl were a fascinating insect that had crawled out of a mire. "What do you come asking?"

Inara was shy of her attention, and looked at Kissen, her hand rising to Skedi. "We want you to set Skediceth free," she said, keeping her voice steady. Impressive, to hold her nerve under the gaze of an old god.

"We want to unbind the curse that ties us," said Skediceth, his whiskers trembling. "Tell us why it was set, what happened to my shrine, and how to live without one."

Aan blinked, then turned to Kissen. "And you?"

Kissen shrugged. "I'm here for them."

The cold water in the streams around Aan's pool frothed and span. "Do you mock me, girl?" she asked. Though her voice was gentle, Kissen's skin prickled. "Come bringing me other gods' bindings, expecting me to break them? You know breaking the power of others is not within my gifts."

Kissen scowled. "You broke the curse on Pato."

That was how she had met Aan the first time, up at the river's source. Pato had been stung by a god of old age who made his ankles swell.

"A little, trifling creature," she said. "That was healing, not breaking. But these are powerful promises, just like yours."

Kissen tutted. "Then what *can* you do?"

"We have little in the way of time," Elo put in.

"I can see that," said Aan, waving a hand dismissively. "For you, I can limit the power of the curse, but I cannot stop it. You need a more powerful god than I, or a powerful sacrifice." Kissen bristled. "Which, *of course*, I would never ask for."

She addressed Inara and Skedi. "For you, it is no simple promise or curse that binds you. All I can give is advice." She sat back, pouting. "All for a price."

"What do you want?" asked Elo.

"Nothing from you yet," said Aan, and looked at Kissen. Kissen put her hand to the vial. She had carried it for years. The gift Pato had bought from Aan, and she had taken from him. She wondered, sometimes, if he had always meant it for her, though at the time she would have been too proud to take a gift from a god. She unhooked it from her neck.

"You advise the girl, and you can have it back," she said. "The knight can pay his own fare."

"Wait, no," said Inara, to Kissen's surprise. "The advice is not for you."

"What can I give?" said Skedi. He flew down from Inara's shoulder and grew to the size of a hare. "It is my life," he continued. "Let me pay for it."

A nice try, but Aan scoffed with the derision Kissen expected.

"You are a god. What can you give me that I do not have already? You can owe me a favour, little liar."

Skedi's ears twitched, but he nodded, and Aan turned to Inara.

"I have little," said Inara. "And I've learned too much to offer you an open favour." Kissen tried not to smile. Aan cocked her head.

"For advice," she said, "I would not milk you dry. All I want is a hair."

"A hair?" said Inara. "From my head?"

"From anywhere you like, my dear," said Aan.

"Ina," warned Kissen, but Inara put her hand in hers and squeezed. Kissen swallowed. Inara's hand felt small and cold. She had only known the kid half a month, but if anything happened to her, Kissen might happily commit a murder.

"What do you want it for?" Inara asked the god. "And Skediceth will tell me if you lie."

"Such affection for one who hates our kind," said Aan, nodding at where their hands knitted and drifting back in the pool. She smiled with her teeth this time, showing black gums. "I want your hair so I can see you if I want, find you if I need." When Kissen glowered at her, she added, "I swear I mean no ill will to you and yours. In fact, I will give you something of mine, to seal that promise."

She reached up and plucked a hair from her head. It fell in a long, waving strand. If she had a god's eyes, Kissen thought, she would be able to see it shining with an inner light. Aan held it out to Inara. "Do we have a deal?"

Inara looked at Kissen. As deals went, it was a good one. Aan did not need Inara's hair to spy on her if she wished; she could follow wherever water was. "I won't stop you," she said. "Aan is wise, and it's a good deal."

"Flatterer," said Aan as Inara took the strand of her hair. Kissen took a spare vial from her cloak and held it out to Inara, who put Aan's hair in, and Kissen stoppered it. Such a thing would be worth a lot of money; it would let her speak with the god from anywhere, even without a shrine. Kissen would tell her that later. Inara touched her hair, then pulled out a strand. The light caught it as she passed it to Aan, who twisted it around her fingers. Her flesh glimmered with water, and the thread disappeared.

Kissen wrapped Inara's vial with a piece of string. She would seal it with wax too, and it would be a mirror to her own. She returned it to Inara, who put it around her neck. Aan was pleased; the water in the cool streams rippled happily.

"Your shrine is broken," she said, focussing on the small god, "or you would have been able to leave her. This, you survived, and a youngling became your keeper. Such a bond can only be made through a covenant of great strength. If it didn't come from you, then it was made with another god. A powerful god. You must remember your past, god of white lies, to be free of it."

"But I do not remember anything before I came to Inara," said Skedi.

"I tell you what I know, not what you do not," said Aan. "But I can tell you what the water says."

She ran her hand over the pool, and the water rushed higher, curling up in waves. "You are not made of water, god, but it knows you." The pool formed the shape of a ship, cracking foam over high seas, above it a droplet flying, a little winged thing.

Skediceth.

He dove for the deck of the ship, which tumbled again into the waves. The pool became still. "Our memories as gods are stored in our shrines," said Aan. "They root us in this world. When they are broken, so are we. Our memories, our will. Gone." She did not say it bitterly, more as fact. "If your shrine was broken, and you came to the girl, then I suspect the covenant was made with someone of her blood, so her heart became your home."

"People can't be shrines," said Kissen, more out of hope than certainty.

"Not people like you," said Aan. She reached out of the water and took Inara's other hand. "But it is rare I see a thing such as this." She smiled. "Perhaps go ask your mother who bore you what mysteries were in your making."

Kissen felt her heart go cold. She was just a little girl, a little girl with a god problem. Inara took her hand away from Aan first, then from Kissen.

"My mother is no longer living," said Ina.

"Perhaps then, if you are lucky, you are your father's daughter."

Skedi flicked his wings in confusion as he and Inara looked at each other. Kissen felt like Telle must feel when she knew people were communicating rapidly in speech and she couldn't read their lips. Aan waited. She had all the time in the world. Elo did not; he had his hand on his shoulder, trying to be patient.

"We were told he could find another shrine," said Inara.

Aan shrugged. "To move shrines, the little god of white lies must find a god willing to make the same promise," she said, "to share their shrine, their offerings, their love, as you have done. There is little enough love for gods to go around, even here. None will give you what you need."

Kissen could almost feel Skedi thinking of Kelt, all but faded even with his shrine intact. The baths were full of gods, but what would pilgrims need from a god of white lies? Pilgrims were wish seekers, truth seekers.

"You've got to give them more than that," said Kissen. "This is the only place in Middren that still has gods powerful enough to take him." She had dragged Inara through danger and demons to find Skedi a place here, but even Kissen was no longer sure they'd made the right journey. Would Skedi stay, knowing that he would fade to nothing in a matter of years? Or turn into a shadow that lied to anyone that passed? Could Inara do that to him? He had betrayed her, yes, but saved her too.

What was worse was that Kissen no longer thought she could do that to him either.

"I give what I give," said Aan, her eyes losing their gleam. "I speak the truth, no matter how much you like it."

"Is there no other way?" said Skedi quietly. Aan tipped her chin with something like pity.

"There are ways," she said. "To become known enough to live like a wild god of old, so close to people's memories, in such constant calling that you are less bound to a shrine."

"I am no ancient deity."

"All you need is to be wanted. Go where others need you, and your ties to Inara Craier will loosen. That is all I can tell you." She cocked her head at Kissen. "Advice given. Promise fulfilled. But I could tell some more tales if you wanted, godkiller. I can feel your curiosity about the girl. I can tell you what she is, and you can decide whether she is worth your care, and you hers."

Kissen clicked her tongue. Another god trying to give her what she didn't need from them. "I need know nothing about Inara that she doesn't want to tell me," she said, mostly meaning it. She moved to stand. "We are done here."

"You don't want to know about the coming war?"

She had her by the gut. Aan wanted her vial; she wanted her gift back.

"She said they were done," broke in Elo, noticing her waver. "And I have more questions to ask you. Questions to ask alone."

"Ooh, so direct," said Aan. "Are you going to ask me to slow your curse? Or give you a quick death?"

"Elogast . . ." said Inara.

Elogast's face was troubled, but he remained still and calm. His hand was on the wrapped pommel of his sword. "You have your answers, Inara," said Elo. "I came here for mine. Go find your god his new shrine."

Elo did not look at Kissen, just focussed on Aan, and Kissen did the unthinkable. She decided to trust him.

"Well then," she said, getting to her feet. "Come, Skedi, Inara."

"But, Kissen—" said Ina.

"But nothing." She looked back at the water and tucked the vial beneath her breastplate, where it sat against Osidisen's promise; her two gifts from gods. She had not asked for them, but she had them all the same.

As they came out of the baths, most of the other booths were now silent, the secret pilgrims gone to seek whatever beds they had bribed for in the ruins of the city. The gods retreated to their shrines, or went elsewhere if they could, thrilling with their little doses of adoration.

"We can't just leave him," said Inara.

"You think he'd let his guard down while we're standing there?" said Kissen as they entered the atrium with the shoes, pulling off the breastplate and cotton robe so she could change back into her familiar things. She looked pointedly at Skedi. The god blinked. Kissen swallowed her pride. It took some swallowing. "How far *can* you go from each other?"

CHAPTER TWENTY-EIGHT

Skediceth

SKEDI CREPT BACK INTO THE BATHS, THROUGH THE SHRINES of gods that still had people who loved them. He did not like the steam of the waters, nor the damp in his feathers. Too hot, too warm. He wanted fresh cold air. But would a god have some space for him here? Enough love to live on? He kept to the ground, ducking his head in doorways, peeking through the gaps in the stone. Ten paces, twenty, twenty-one. They could move further apart now than they had before; was it because Inara loved him less? Or because Kissen and Elo cared for him more?

He was glanced at briefly by a woman still bathing in dark silence with a god shaped like a pure white fox, her colours silver with isolation, a desire not to be interrupted. He moved on. Another god, toad-shaped, was sitting in the wall like a stone. Smaller than Skedi, but older. Skedi could tell, it was like a solidity, a radiance that came from a god that had lived long, like Aan. It regarded him in silence.

"You are not the first to come begging at the springs," the god said. "There is not enough for sharing."

Skedi did not argue. The promise of a shrine in Blenraden had lost its appeal. More so now that he had hurt the trust that Inara had in him. He had a little life, but a good one, with someone who loved him. He had risked it all . . . for what? For this?

He crept onwards, feeling the bond that kept him and Inara together stretching, but not hurting. Kissen had asked something of him, without threat of murder. Perhaps just days ago he would have said no, but he too wanted to know what Elo was asking for, and if the knight would get a better answer than Skedi and Inara had.

A promise, Aan had said. What promise could have tied him to a child? Even a child like Ina. He tried to think back before her, pressing for memories that had drifted to nothing. He had flown above ships. The water had known it. That felt right, though he disliked being wet. So why would he have done it? What need had ships for white lies? He tried to imagine the air, the waves, and he grasped a distant drop of memory, of titans clashing in the sky, the taste of salt.

Fly, he remembered a command. *Fly, little Skediceth.*

A god's voice. A friend. Who needed him.

"He lives?" Skedi flicked his ears, shrinking down to a birdlike size. Thirty-three paces, and he was back at Aan's shrine, the bond with Inara tugging with only slight pain. He could not go much further. Elogast was speaking, around him his steady colours, his deep waters. They were burning cobalt and lilac; he was asking about Arren. Aan had her hand to his shoulder, her water swirling about the curse mark.

"So it seems," she said.

"Then there is still hope."

"A god's binding to a person is not easily undone. Not without the will of both, like the little girl and the liar. It could kill him outright." Elo nodded, his colours shifting in fear, slicing through with bloodied gold. He had his sword across his lap, its pommel unwrapped, and Skedi could see that its hilt was topped not with a sun or stag, but with a lion's head. The colours about Elo's fingers were so bright they were hard to look at. This blade, this pommel, meant the world to him. Skedi would give anything for such a token. It seemed Elo had taken Aan's offer to hinder the curse, but what he held was surely worth more than that.

Skedi crept closer.

"He needs time," said Elo. "Healing. That's what I'm here for."

"Such a wound cannot be healed," said Aan, coming closer. "It surprises me that any god chose to save him and was able. If you wish him to live, you must replace whoever's gift it was with one that will last, with a god's heart that is not so bound to changing faiths in Middren."

Skedi pressed his wings flat to his back, his ears too. A heart? This was what the king had lost? That could not be possible. What god would have saved the king? Elo fell silent for a long, painful moment. Then, "Could you make him such a thing?"

"I would not," she said. "No matter the offer. I will not be bound to a mortal."

"It could stop a civil war."

"It might not." Aan had her chin on the edge of the pool, her arms folded beneath it. Her black hair floated behind her, and her calves steamed where they breached the surface, like soft islands beneath a cloud. "Gods are not always the enemy; even your godkiller knows that. People make gods, and, for better or worse, gods make people. We show each other for what we truly are. Yearning beings, desperate for love, power, safety." She paused. "Besides, your brother-king has lived on this heart for three years. The god who gave it warms his blood, gives him life from theirs, and it is not a heart of water. I would know. Water speaks to itself, from drop to pool to river to sea. I cannot help you. Instead, you must think carefully about the kind of heart he needs."

Elo frowned, and Aan tipped her head to one side. "More than that. Only the old gods remaining still have such power, and such recklessness. If they are part wild, from before your little cities, all the better." Skedi shrank down to the size of a small ingot. Aan reached out to touch Elo's face. "So loyal," she said. "Loyal enough to break your own heart. Ask your next question."

"What will a god need in return?" Elo said.

"I think you know the answer to that, Ser Elogast," said Aan quietly. "Life for life. A life you care for. Gods love martyrs."

Skedi stepped back. Sacrifice. She was speaking of sacrifice. Elo bowed his head, tightening his hands around his offering.

"So," said Aan, "you must decide, Elogast, knight, baker, man of honour and divided loves. Whose heart is worth your king's?"

Skedi had heard enough. He darted away and back to the door. He could not let Elo catch him there. In a moment he had flown back through the corridor, into Inara's waiting arms where she had been sitting, dallying her feet in the pool with her travel clothes back on.

"We must go," he said. He flexed his wings, looked at Kissen, who had been leaning in the open door looking out at the evening, also dressed and ready. "Please."

Inara stood up straight, feeling his fear, though she could not understand it.

For Ina, he spoke to Kissen's mind, pressing so hard with his will that it broke through. She started and stared at him, hesitating for a moment. Skedi stretched his wings and flew to the ground in the doorway to the garden, growing to the size of a large cat. Sacrifice, Elo needed a sacrifice. And they were the only people near him.

A clatter from the garden outside the baths. They turned to see three knights hurrying up the way on horseback, their swords already drawn. Kissen put her hand on her blade. Skedi was out in the open, completely visible. He froze.

"You," said the foremost knight. It was Benjen, looking ruffled. His suspicion hooked on Kissen and Skedi. Inara hesitated inside, just out of sight. Benjen hadn't seen any of them at the palace, but Inara was still wearing his sword. If they saw her, they would take them all. "Have you seen a tall, dark-skinned man?"

"What's it to you?" said Kissen.

They had not blinked at Skedi. Of course not. He was in the city of gods. Benjen scowled.

"It means I will resist sending you on a fast run to Sakre's gaols. Whipped feet will be the least of your troubles."

Kissen smiled dangerously, and Skedi sat up on his hind legs. "An Irisian man stopped here," he said. "He took a track towards the embankments and the harbour."

He applied his will to the lie, pushing it towards the group. It took easily. They blinked, their attention falling away from Kissen, and turned off down the hill towards the sea. Skedi looked up at Inara, who breathed a sigh of relief. His shrine, his friend.

He had to save her, and Kissen too. He had seen she and Elo getting closer; what if Elo chose her to sacrifice? And Skedi realised he no longer wanted to think of a world without Kissen to protect them.

"Veiga?"

Too late. Elo had stepped out of the corridor into the atrium. He still had his sword. Strange, for Aan to let him keep it, but Skedi noticed the lion's head from the pommel was gone. The sword itself was not the source of affection; it was the symbol of the young lion. The king's old symbol. Skedi bristled, but Elo's hand wasn't on the hilt; he wasn't there to fight. Around him were clouds of deception and sadness. He sighed and looked down towards the sea. "It is too late for anything more tonight," he said.

"I thought you were in a hurry?" said Kissen suspiciously.

Elo contemplated the horizon, his colours an odd, regretful grey. His shirt was open, and Skedi could see script not unlike the markings on Kissen's chest, tiny dots that threaded through the black ink, binding it. Water-script, from Aan, to stifle the power of the curse. Did this give Elo more time, or reduce the number of demons that would come for him? Kissen saw it too. Skedi still couldn't see her colours, but he was starting to understand her facial expressions. These drifted from annoyed to relieved. People were complicated.

"What could I find in a pitch-dark city amidst wraiths and wreckage?" said Elo with a shrug. "I might prefer a last evening with friends."

So, he wouldn't fight them now. Why? To wait till they were asleep? The urgency in his step before had been lost, but the determination in him was still there, it had not changed. He would save the king. Skedi didn't want to sleep with a man looking for a sacrifice. But what could he say without drawing back the knights? Frightening Ina?

"Sure," said Kissen, with a sideways glance at Skedi. "I know a place that might still be standing. Or at least it was in the last days of the war. Did you find out what you wanted?"

Elo thought about it for a moment. "Yes," he said.

What did you hear? said Inara. Skedi wanted to lie to her.

Nothing good, he said.

Kissen led them onwards to a grand-looking house six streets up from Maimee's orphanage. It even had a tall belltower. The door was off its hinges, possibly from looting, but the insides had kept much of their grandeur. They passed up the stairs and through several rooms filled with long tables, desks, and loungers till they found one that looked promising.

"I could see this schoolhouse from Maimee's," said Kissen. "Always looked so shiny and warm. I stayed here after the fight with Mertagh."

She looked at Elo, who did not react. Any mention of that battle usually sent a wave of terror, anger, fear, and guilt through his colours that set his hands to shaking. But this time, nothing.

"Check that no one is outside, Skedi," said Elo. "Let's make a fire."

Skedi reluctantly flew to the window. From there, he could indeed see Maimee's house below with his good night vision. Further than that, he could see the sea, stretched, grey and fading under the dark sky.

He climbed higher, wondering if there would be any more knights clattering about looking for Elo, or if he would see places in the city that might be promising for him to make a home. He found he could glimpse the harbour through a gap in the buildings. The high seawalls of Blenraden's port were crushed, the towers that had once guided ships in and out now simply nubs of stone. Between them, Skedi could see the shattered remains of several ships, so broken and rotten that they all had become one graveyard to the dead.

Those poor people in the ships must have been so frightened as the wild gods descended on them for daring to leave the city. He could still feel the echoes of their fear. Such power, and devastation, to kill a god and a thousand souls.

Then the god of safe haven had risen to defend them. One great new god against the gathered strength of the wild.

Memory tugged at Skedi's whiskers like a dream-wind.

Salt and storm. The rage and howling of winds, gods and nightmares, and a thousand people screaming. On the shore, the Middren army fighting like mice might fight a tidal wave. Within it all, lies, little lies, telling them that they would be safe, that they would get out, that it would be all right. Lies that stayed lies forever.

"Skediceth."

Skedi jumped, and realised it was not Inara calling him but Kissen. He had been hanging on to the window panes. Kissen gestured him down, and he flew to the table by her as she drew the curtains shut.

Skedi found himself alone with the godkiller, and once again at a crossroads. Just days before, he had been willing to betray Inara, allow Kissen to be killed, so he could join with the knight. Now Inara was moving furniture with a cursed man who wanted a sacrifice. A heart. Elo's colours had not much changed, still sorrowful, full of danger, but it disturbed Skedi that he seemed lighter than he ever had before, laughing at Inara's frustration as she struggled with a heavy chair.

"You would never hurt Inara, would you?" said Skedi to Kissen, quietly. Of that, he was certain. "You want her to be safe, to protect her like the other children you saved from Maimee's." He lifted his antlers, looking up at her. "So do I. Do you believe me?"

Kissen thought about it. "I believe you care for her," said Kissen. "I believe some of that is out of self-interest."

"And what about you?" said Skedi. "What do you get out of all this?"

Kissen held out her hand to him. Skedi stared at her fingers: hard, worn, calloused.

"I don't have it in me to leave a child to face the world alone," she said. "So, tell me what you heard, and I will think about believing you."

Skedi stepped into her hand, and she lifted him to her shoulder, where he settled. He could see the leather thread of the vial that Aan wanted. If he desired, perhaps he could snatch it, flee, exchange whatever it was she desired for a sharing of her shrine. Perhaps he could bite the godkiller's throat, and be free of her, break Inara's heart entirely, and disappear in one last terrible act. No, that was not him. That was not what he did. White lies were lies to soften, lies to help, lies to change and connive. The godkiller had reached out to him, and now it was his turn.

Skedi regarded Elo. He had sat down with Inara and was teaching her how to strike flint.

"He needs a sacrifice," he said. "A heart for a heart, to save his king's. That's what Aan told him."

Kissen's colours burst out from under her guard, white with anger. She believed him.

"Ina, get back from him," she said. Inara blinked at her. "Now."

Inara stood but didn't move far. "Why?" she said. Elo, too, was staring at her, then he noticed Skedi.

"You sent the god to spy on me?" he asked.

"I owe you no loyalty," said Kissen.

"You have nothing to fear from me," he said.

"Desperation is always something to fear."

Elo got to his feet, and Skedi rose on Kissen's shoulder.

"I heard you," he said, pitching his wings high. "You gave the head of your sword to her. She told you that you needed a god's heart to replace Arren's."

"You know nothing about this."

"Skedi," said Inara, "I don't think Elo would hurt us."

"What makes you so certain?" said Kissen. Inara bit her tongue, meeting eyes with Skedi. The colours. She couldn't say what she saw, not to Kissen, not even now. It was true, Elo's colours showed no violence. But what if he was hiding them, like Kissen?

"Have I not earned your trust by now, godkiller?" said Elo.

"Trust?" Kissen laughed, then gestured to herself. "You think a woman like me has lived a life of trust? If you want to talk about trust, why don't you tell me what really happened in that last battle against Mertagh? Why does your king break his own laws now and send his so-called friend on a quest to the gods to offer up a sacrifice? In return for what? More power?"

Elo pressed his lips together, torn. "Veiga, he is our king; we shouldn't question him."

"He's *your* king. I told you, I was born in Talicia. I know what people do for gods, kings, power, all of it. And it's never anything good."

"This isn't the same."

"They put all their hopes in a saviour; they raise his pictures on all their walls."

"Don't you dare—" Elo was getting angry now.

"They gather followers like your knights to beat people into line, and then are so surprised when folk don't like it. No wonder he's brought Middren back to the edge of war."

"It is not happening here," said Elo. "I won't let it."

"A god's heart, knight? That's what your king needs?" Kissen strode forward, Skedi clinging to her shoulder. "Don't you hear what that sounds like?"

Elo squared up to her. "No," he said, and shook his head vehemently, drawing his hand in a firm line. "Arren is a good man. You must believe me."

"Why should we?" said Kissen. "Why do you believe yourself? What if you're wrong?"

Elo raised his chin. He was furious, but he breathed deeply, calmly, and looked at Kissen.

"I know Arren better than you ever could."

"People change, knight."

"Not this person. Whoever hurt you in your past—"

"*I was a sacrifice.*"

Elo stopped, freezing. Inara's fingers flew to her mouth. Kissen's colours were bursting through her guard, storm greys, blues, and the yellow of flame. She stood her ground. "My *own people* burned me and my family, all of us, because they thought it would serve them well. People we'd grown up with, eaten with, starved with."

Skedi decided her shoulder was not a place to be any more; he took wing to Inara and she caught him. Could she see Kissen's pain too? It was so vast, so shattering. Her anger took up the whole room, dwarfed them all. Was this what she kept hidden? All of the time? Buried in her heart only to rise up as hatred for the gods?

"They drugged us, bound us, burned us." She rubbed her wrists, then put her hand to her chest. "My father saved me. Cut my leg free, sacrificed his own life so Osidisen would rescue me. Just to keep me alive." She tugged down her breastplate to show the boon beneath the tattoo. "This is the last thing my father ever gave me, this promise. It's the last thing I have of him before Osidisen dragged me bleeding to the shore and left me to die. All that love, all that pain, and we were nothing. So forgive me if I don't trust a knight I've barely known a few days and a king who beats the prayerful with one hand then begs gifts from gods with the other."

"How could the sea god not fulfil a promise?" said Skedi, aghast. Gods' promises were the matter that made them, the force that kept them bound to humans, to life. A promise was like his bond with Ina, constantly tugging on his heart. He swallowed. *Fly, little Skediceth.*

"Because I told him to get fucked," said Kissen. "Because I couldn't let him take back the last thing I have of my father, my family. My anger. I will not let it go."

Skedi shivered. Now that he could see her colours, he didn't want to any more. If he tried to reach into them, to soften her with white lies, he would drown. Elo, too, both of them raging on two sides of a battle neither of them had chosen. It was too much, all this feeling. He cowered.

"I promise you, veiga," said Elo, his voice tight, "I would never hurt you."

"I have heard such things before."

"Not from me." He stepped closer to Kissen, taking her hand. "What was done to you was wrong," he said. "It should never have happened. It should never happen again."

Kissen chuckled, pulling her hand back. "Don't tell me white lies," she said. "A heart for a heart. Whose heart is worth your king's? Because if you want one of ours, you'll find they don't come so easily."

Elo was silent. The fire crackled as it caught. Skedi almost felt the snap of Kissen's breath as she squared her shoulders.

"Absolutely the fuck not," she said.

"I don't remember asking your opinion."

"I won't let you."

Elo laughed a strange, sad laughter. "A god won't give a heart without taking one," he said. "What am I supposed to do? Let Middren break out in civil war? Let him die?"

"Yes, exactly," said Kissen. "Let him die. I'm sure he lets other people die for him all the time. Let him have a try."

"He did," snapped Elo. "He died for me."

Kissen swallowed. She and Elo stared at each other.

"The battle with the god of war. Against Mertagh," said Kissen, more calmly. "You said he was injured."

"It was my fault," said Elo, his voice hoarse, straining under the emotion. His hands shook; his colours flashed gold. "He was dying. He did die . . . and I let him. The last of his line. One final fight, I told him. Just this one, because he needed me, and I let him die."

CHAPTER TWENTY-NINE

Elogast

HE HAD SAID IT. HE OWED ARREN. EVERYTHING. IF ANYTHING, it made Kissen angrier.

"Right," said Kissen. "Inara, stay here. You." She pointed at Elo. "You're coming with me."

"Wait," said Inara, but she fell silent at Kissen's expression. Kissen signed something to her. Elo couldn't understand it, but he suspected it was violent. He found himself being grabbed by the shirt and dragged from the room.

"Kissen . . ." he tried.

"You don't get to call me by my name," she said. She was furious, and her hair seemed to have a rageful life of its own, slipping from her braids.

"I make my own choices."

"No one who loves you would ask you to throw your life away."

She dragged him into the next room, then the next, putting enough distance between them and Inara so she wouldn't hear them.

"He has not asked me to."

Kissen's nose flared and she shoved him against a wall, pressing her face up and close to his, her eyes bright and fierce in the dark. "Well, I'm *telling* you not to."

"Why?"

"Oh, fuck it with why, people don't always need a reason." She released him and turned away in disgust. They had reached some sort of study, its shelves ransacked and items shattered on the floor, but its desk still standing. Waning moonlight was gleaming in the windows.

"I owe him my life, veiga," he said. So she didn't want him calling her by her name. Fine.

"If he died, then how come he's still up there ruling?"

Elo could not tell her, but something fell into place behind her eyes. "You've got to be joking," she said. "The breaker of gods made a pact with one, didn't he?"

"No," said Elo quickly. "No. She asked for nothing. She offered to save him."

"Who?"

What use were secrets now? "Hestra, the god of hearths."

Kissen was nonplussed. "That half-wild thing asked for nothing?" She shook her head. "That means she hasn't extracted her price yet. You said yourself, a god won't give a heart without taking one."

"She's extracting it now," said Elo. "She's killing him."

She was not as disturbed by this as he expected. "And what, that means it's your turn to die?"

"If he dies, then this rebellion that killed Inara's mother will have nothing to stop them."

"You fucking martyr." She laughed derisively. "And once you're all sacrificed and gone and your friend lives with a heart you died for, does that stop gods and people trying to claim each other?"

That was harsh. "Veiga—" he tried.

"You think he should have to live with that?" She grabbed both his arms, trying to shake him into seeing her point of view. "That weight of loss you would give to him?"

Elo shook his head. "This isn't about me," he said tightly. Her father's promise. "Your father did what he chose to. I get my own choice."

"I didn't ask him to!" shouted Kissen. "He could have run. He could have lived. Gone into the sea and come back to the village, wreaked havoc on the lot of them. But he didn't. Instead, he gave me a stupid, shattered life that I didn't want."

"This isn't the same!"

"Isn't it? Why do you get to give up? Why do you get to decide what your life is worth?

"I am not giving up!" growled Elo. "I did once. I left the war, my people, my king, because I couldn't support him. For what? For shame and failure. Now I have a chance, to repay him what I owe him, to give back the life he gave to me."

"I won't let you."

"Then what would you have me do?"

"Other than tell Inara that a life is just to be given away to whoever asked for it first?"

"Kissen . . . please."

"Were you in love with him? Did you used to fuck? Is that it? Because this would make a lot more sense if you did."

"No," said Elo, sighing. "Not everything is about sex."

"Well, colour me surprised," she said.

"Is that it? You want to fuck, Kissen? Because you know I would be glad to."

"You . . ." Elo was faintly amused at her being lost for words. "If you're trying to martyr-fuck me, I'll tear both your legs off." She barely sounded the words through her clenched teeth.

"I wouldn't dare," said Elo. He pressed his palms to his eyes, a calming technique one of his mothers had taught him.

"Veiga, I am alive because of Arren," he said. Kissen released him and grumpily kicked aside a bit of debris, before coming to slump beside him. "And what have I done with that life these last few years? All I have are memories of a war and endless regrets. This isn't a life worth a king's."

He had never said anything like that before. He had never voiced those thoughts aloud.

"Elogast," said Kissen softly, like a sigh, and Elo felt his heart shift. He turned to look at her. She was staring out the window, and in the light her skin shone, her white scar, her freckles, and her expressive face. She had not called him Elogast before, only "baker", only "knight." Elogast. "You are worth more than you think. You are still alive; make something of it. Of life, not death."

Elo shook his head mutely. Why did she care so much? She had protected Inara, had stayed with him despite his curse, his mistakes. How, with all her rage, did she have such capacity for love? Elo dared himself to brush one of her curls away from her face, where dust from the road had stuck it. "I'm glad you're alive too, Kissen," he said. She caught his hand and held it, closing her eyes for a moment, then she took a breath and looked at him.

"We'll find another way," she said. "I promise. But a good friend would never forgive you for dying for him, just as you cannot forgive yourself."

"Why does it matter what happens to me?" said Elo.

"Because we could be the same, you and I," she said after a moment. "What happened to us does not define us, what we do next is what matters."

They were not the same. Kissen was magnificent, fierce and foolish. She allowed herself to make mistakes and own them. And, unlike Arren, she reached out a hand to him, met him where he was.

Elo leaned in, intending to kiss her cheek, but she turned and caught it on her mouth. She breathed sharply with surprise, retreating, then cast her eyes over him carefully. The moods in her face shifted, wary. Elo didn't move, regretting nothing, and then he saw her eyes crease in a wicked smile. She stepped towards him, pressing her mouth to his, and Elo welcomed it, the warmth of her lips, cracked and rough. He faltered a moment, torn between decency and desire, then reached to pull her closer. He kissed her harder, and her mouth parted for his tongue. She turned and pressed him back to the wall again, this time chest to chest, her metal and leather knee tapping against its wood panels.

Elo shivered from his spine down to his feet, and he hardened. Should he push her away? Gods, he didn't want to. He traced the strength of her back with his hands, following her leather cuirass to its edge, then pressing his fingers beneath it. Her mouth tasted of the sage leaves she had chewed, plucking them absently as they'd walked away from the baths.

He moved her towards the grand wooden desk that dominated the room, too heavy to steal, and she grinned, unbuckling her breastplate as they went. He helped her, a strap at a time, till he could slide his hand beneath it to find her breast. Her breath quickened with pleasure, and she ran her own hands up his back, onto his neck, and pulled him to her so he would kiss her harder. He obliged for a long thrill of a moment, then shifted and pressed his mouth to her ear, tracing down her neck to her breastbone, to her tattoo, where it showed above the block of her armour.

It had to come off. Kissen helped him with her cloak first, then the cuirass, lifting it over her head and throwing it to the floor. He had only his jerkin, and she unbound it easily, sliding off his shirt and pulling him towards her as he felt her thighs. She kissed him as ferociously as he might have imagined. She unhooked her own shirt buttons as he kissed down her breasts and with a hand worked upwards to her trews where the girdle was belted through them. He was dizzy with desire; it had been too long since he had felt it.

He undid her buckles, slightly hindered by his wounded arm, then he pulled her trousers free of her boots, and she was almost naked. He rubbed his hands over her scars and her thigh, beneath the straps that held on her leg. It was beautiful, gleaming in the light from the window.

"Off or on?" she asked about her leg.

"Whatever's best for you," he said, kissing up her legs till his mouth found the hot, wet nub between them. She gasped in surprise and wrapped her legs behind his back, one hot, one cold, half laughing, half moaning with pleasure as she undid her prosthesis. She bit her lip to keep quieter.

Her straps came free, her leg released, and she lifted him to her as she helped him now with his belt, then put her mouth to his. "Now it's my turn, knight," she whispered. "Let me remind you what living can be."

CHAPTER THIRTY

Kissen

WHEN KISSEN WOKE IN THE MORNING BY THE REMNANTS of the fire, her first feeling was satisfaction. Her second was a slight panic as she tried to find the powder she used to cut off any chance the night's fun could produce an unwanted side effect nine months later, seeing as neither of them had had a sheath; one of the reasons that sex with men wasn't her go-to. Still, gods, it had been good. Baker-knights—who knew?

She looked around for Elo, allowing herself a slight smile, but his space was empty.

Her stomach dropped. Kissen whirled around, hoping she was wrong.

That bastard. He had taken the last watch, presumably after Inara, who had been annoyed but not suspicious when the two of them had returned, rumpled and flushed. The girl was still sleeping soundly with Skedi curled in her arms. Kissen groaned and Skedi opened his eyes and looked at her.

"You're awake?" she said, pulling on her cloak.

"I'm a god, I don't need sleep."

"Then why have we been taking all these watches?"

"Because you didn't trust me," he said pertly. "Where are you going?"

"To stop that lying bastard giving free candies to a greedy fucking king and a greedy fucking god." She paused. "Did you see him leave?"

Skedi fluttered to his feet. Inara stirred, rubbing her eyes, then her head. She looked at Kissen, standing, glowering in her cloak, and for a moment fear troubled her face. "What is it?" she asked.

"Elo's gone," said Skedi. Inara sat fully upright. "Yes, I saw him leave, and he gave me a coin to give him a lie."

"He did what?" said Kissen.

"Just to cover his steps and let him go quietly," Skedi huffed. "I'm a god without a shrine, how was I supposed to refuse a boon? I thought you had worked out your differences."

Inara groaned. "Skedi . . ."

"Bah," snapped Kissen. "Inara, will you be all right here?"

Inara scrambled to her feet. "I'm coming with you," she said, casting around for her bow and shortsword. Kissen felt a smile pluck at her lips.

"No," she said, buckling on her cutlass first. Her right leg stabbed with pain as she strapped her prosthesis back on. She had relaxed too much last night. Shit. "He's gone to the shrines of the wild gods," said Kissen. "That's the only place he could be. I would not take you there if someone held a knife to my throat."

"You took me to Aan."

"Compared to them, Aan is a soft touch of rain. You're staying here."

"I can help!"

"No," said Kissen firmly, hoping that Inara would actually listen to her. Inara looked from Kissen to Skedi. Some communication passed between them, and Inara screwed up her face unhappily, but relented.

"You're strong, Ina," said Kissen. She took her hand as Inara had hers the evening before. "You know what you and Skedi need to do, and it's your choice now. If I don't come back, take what you can carry and find Legs. You're a good hunter, and he'll get you back to Lesscia."

Inara looked panicked. "You're coming back, right? You promised."

Kissen didn't let go of her hand. "I don't tell lies, Ina. It's a dangerous place the knight has gone to. But if you ask me to stay, I will." She meant it. War or no war, knight or no knight, the squabbles of gods and kings could get fucked. A king having a wild god's heart was the worst she could imagine in the aftermath of Blenraden, who knows what he would do with it. But the world wasn't hers to save. If Inara asked it, she would stay with her.

"No," said Inara. She squeezed her fingers. "Please stop him. Help him."

Kissen nodded. She adjusted the straps of her leg to her knee and removed one of the metal plates from the calf for lightness. Yatho had always included the ability to change the equilibrium for a fight, and Kissen knew she was in for a good one. With Elo, with the knights, or with whatever god he tried to summon. Perhaps she should just let him follow his compulsion for self-sacrifice to his doom, but she couldn't. He was a good man, even if he was an idiot.

Inara helped her belt on her longsword and find her knives, then pull on her cloak with its god-hunting tools. She usually used the lures, but this time she fingered the weapons. Briddite bombs made in gourds with blackfire, carefully corked and waxed. Warding salts too, and chains.

"Stay smart, *liln*," said Kissen. "You're too good to get killed for nothing. I believe that for certain." She paused. "And don't tell Telle that I abandoned you." Inara laughed, sniffed, and, to Kissen's surprise, threw her arms around her waist, squeezing her as tight as she could. Kissen returned the embrace, holding her as she wished she had been held when the world tipped her over.

"Look after her, Skediceth," she said gruffly. The god met her eyes and stood on his hind legs.

"Come back, veiga," he replied.

Kissen moved swiftly through the streets, down to the cliff edges and what was called the Long Walk, the harbour path which rounded all the sea-facing houses up to the heights. Hundreds of stones lay on its wall now, each marked with the name of one of the knights that fell there in the battle for the harbour. The wind from the south cut across them, finally bringing the warm song of spring over the parapets. How could he? How *dare* he? She had let him get close to her, had let him know her. She wasn't going to let him get away with this, no matter how pissing noble he thought he was being.

If she didn't run into trouble.

She turned a corner and almost tumbled over two knights who were patrolling the walk, presumably still looking for Elo. She turned on her good heel and changed direction, away from the shoreline and into the warren of alleys. But it had been easier to disappear when she was young and short and there were thousands in the city. Now she was just one lone walker on barren stone.

"Hey," they said. "Halt! Stop!"

She did not stop. If she told them she was a veiga they might leave her alone, or they might lock her up for daring to be in the city where they made their extra pilgrim coin. She didn't have the time or desire to find out which.

One caught her, their hand dropping onto her shoulder. She used it, twisting back on her boot, already missing the weight she had discarded, and leaned under his reach to roll him over her back. He landed flat on his spine, winded. The other could have wrestled her but instead decided to draw their sword. Fool. Kissen grabbed the knight's wrist and threw the blade back into its sheath, bringing her other hand around in a vicious jab to their throat. The knight choked, stumbling back, and Kissen finished with a backhand to their ear. Stunned, the knight fell.

The one she had winded was just trying to get to his knees, wheezing. Kissen slammed her metal heel into his back and he went down again, face flat to the ground.

Time to run.

CHAPTER THIRTY-ONE

Elogast

ELO'S QUEST HAD NOT CHANGED. HE WOULD SAVE ARREN, give him back the life he had sacrificed. Give him back the future, and let his own sad life fade. He should not have slept with Kissen, he should not have let himself feel even for a moment that there was an alternative, that he could let Arren die. There was only one path for him, one option. If he stayed with Kissen, Inara, and Skedi, the demons would keep coming, they would keep fighting, and they would die. For him.

He wouldn't let them. They would understand. He was doing the right thing.

Elo took the paths he knew into the city, crossing back towards the palace, to the many great plazas at the foot of the hill. To the one he was looking for: Victory Square. It had once been dedicated to Mertagh, the god of war.

It was here that they made their stand. Mertagh had fought with the humans. An old god, but a god made from forged weapons and waged wars, he had wanted Middren to win against the wild. But, to his chagrin, he had not been excluded from Arren's decision to eliminate the gods from Middren. When his shrines had begun to fall, Mertagh had taken his vengeance against Aia, the midwife god, tearing her apart above the Middren host, calling Arren out to defeat him in battle. And Arren had answered.

One last fight.

The eight entrances to Mertagh's square were now blasted to nothing as Elo tried to recognise the place that had caused so much heartache. It was all reduced to windswept rubble, even the great shrine to Mertagh was just a bundle of stones, crushed into shards. Unlike the other shrines in the city, nothing remained here. They had dismantled the shrine as their first act of battle, taking down the braziers, the offerings, the incense, the gilded statue and its horns.

Then, Mertagh had come in his golden armour, and he had come for death—ten times the size of a man, his head a stag's like his statue's, his bloody antlers scraping the sky.

His power had been unimaginable. Even now Elo could recall the battering ram of the god of war's will: terror and violence. Torches gone, moonlight gone. Blackness took them, then screaming. Chaos.

Elo had tried. He had run for his friend, calling orders that no one listened to, fighting through swords swung wildly at him by his own soldiers. "Relight the fires! Protect the king! Your life, your blood, your heart!"

There. The shape of Arren's helmet, his mail glinting in the light of a flame that his brave guard was kindling.

He'd made it to Arren as Mertagh appeared in a flash of red and gold, swinging his hammer. Elo dragged his friend to the side and the hammer missed, instead hitting the guard whose head was swept into the dark.

"*Arren, run,*" he had said, wrenching him between the bodies that bloodied the stones. "*We can't win. Not this time. Not without the gods.*"

"*No! I won't leave you.*"

"*You must!*"

Mertagh's hammer was swift. Elo used both his sword and his buckler to stop the blow from splitting Arren in two. The strike had buried deep into his shoulder, sending him to his knees and tearing his sword from his grasp.

Mertagh drew the hammer back and brought it around again on its chain. There was a halberd at the god's feet, too far to reach. Elo had no weapon. He stood, ready then for death. The pointed end of the hammer sang through the night.

Then Arren threw himself between Elo and the spike.

Elo closed his eyes. The memory alone hurt him to his marrow.

He would never forget the crunch of bone and armour. The choking sound Arren made as the blade pierced his heart. Couldn't Kissen understand? She must, surely, know what he would give to take that moment back, to change it all. Luck was the only reason Mertagh hadn't taken him too. He had leapt for the halberd as Mertagh howled out his victory and thrust it into the god's face, the point of it crushing his eye and the axe tearing into his mouth.

Then the godkillers had come. Chains whipping out of the night, snapping around Mertagh's neck, burning him. Torches had been lit, the madness fading. It had not been Arren who killed the god of war, despite his portraits. It was the veiga. Mertagh screamed, his stag's head rearing back, as Elo dragged Arren away over the bodies of the dead and dying. The king's armour gaped, his life pouring out of his chest. Too late.

"*Hold on, Arren, please hold on.*" Elo had found an open door at the edge of the square. He couldn't even tell which one now. He had laid him down by a hearth.

"*It's all right, Elo.*"

"*It should have been me.*" He didn't know what to do. He didn't know how to save him.

"*You're the only one who ever loved me, Elo. The only one who ever . . . believed in me.*" He gripped him tightly, struggling for his voice. "*I could have done it.*" His breaths were fewer, lighter, further. "*We could have changed the world, you and I.*"

A flicker, a glimmer of light, it ran across the blood on the floor. It had come from the hearth. It sparked again, bigger and brighter. The empty fireplace blazed, and out of the fire stepped a small god, a bundle of twigs and bones in the shape of a human. At her centre, a lick of flame.

I am Hestra, god of hearths. How had she known where to come? Elo still didn't understand. *I can save this life.*

Why would a god save Arren after he had sworn to destroy them? But Arren had turned, reaching for Hestra. "*I could have changed it . . .*" he whispered. "*Let me change it.*"

Hestra had put her hand to Arren's. Her form of twigs and sparks collapsed, and branches burst out in Arren's chest in a crackle and blaze. He screamed as his flesh knitted together, knotted with moss and roots. He stopped bleeding as his ribs re-formed around a nest of branches. A wood god, would that work?

But no, within it: flame. It was flame that warmed him, flame that kept him alive, the flame that was dying.

Fire. Arren needed a heart of fire.

Elo breathed out. A fire god, a powerful one. That would right his wrongs, lighten his shame.

He knew where he had to go.

The last time he had ascended the stairs of the Long Walk to the upper cliffs had been when he had fought with Mertagh, not against him, to vanquish the gods of the wilds. Elo kept himself moving, not allowing time to question or to hesitate. Perhaps things could have been different. Perhaps if he had met Kissen sooner. But there was nothing left for him, not even her, only death. What else could he do but the last thing that Arren needed, repaying the debt he owed?

He made it to the top of the stairs and the ring of shattered shrines. Weather-beaten. Empty. Elo's heart fell as he looked at the ruins they had left behind. The altars had been hacked to pieces. The gods that were killed would not come back here: hunt, storm, dreams, terror. Those that survived . . . there was little left even if they were living. Some cracked urns, some snapped columns, some broken-open coin boxes. Even the god of death, who had taken no part in the war, had only the faintest etchings of a chessboard worn into the stone, its pieces all missing.

The ringing of a little bell turned him. There: a shrine made of sheets of black stone. Coal. He couldn't see the bell until he moved and caught the glint of it in the light of the rising sun.

He went over to the shrine, hardly daring to hope. The bronze bell was of Talician make, carvings marking it from waist to crown, an artist's impression of coils of smoke. He tipped it and saw beneath that there were flames engraved on the clapper, hanging on a beautifully moulded yoke.

Behind it was a small oil lamp, a flame inside it, burning.

Elo stepped back.

This was the bell of Hseth. A fire god, more powerful than Hestra. An old, wild god who demanded sacrifice but provided riches. Loved enough that someone had made the perilous road to Blenraden to re-erect her shrine. The god of fire that he needed. She had not even fought in Blenraden, had no apparent interest in Middren. It was perfect, meant to be.

They drugged us, bound us, burned us.

Elo took a shaking breath. Kissen would kill him. If that was the god that she had been burned for, she would murder him, and he would deserve it. Well, that didn't matter now. It might not have been Hseth; there were any number of gods that took burned offerings. Kissen was just one person, Inara made two. Arren was king.

He drew his sword and placed the edge of the blade against the back of his wrist, feeling the absence of Arren's pommel. The sign of their friendship, Elo's good luck charm. Aan had laughed as she had taken it into her waters, delighted by such a totem. No matter now. Elo clenched his jaw and cut, then put his hand on the altar, letting blood run over his fingers and onto the stone. Then, he rang the bell.

"Hseth," he whispered, pressing his desperation into his call, his will, his purpose.

The music of it echoed around the empty shrines, weaving with the wind and the pinks of the dawn sky. Louder it reverberated, growing rather than fading. The air smelled hot with it. Elo found himself sweating, his breath drying in his mouth. His lungs ached as heat built in waves with the sound of the ringing bell, an endless expansion of scalding and sound. Louder still, so loud Elo wondered if Kissen and Inara would hear it from across the city and realise he had betrayed them both.

The heat grew unbearable. Elo didn't dare step back. His eyes dried, and he felt his growing hair crisping at the ends. His palm burned, his fingernails seared his skin, his lips cracked open.

A spark drifted up from the lantern's flame, a shining ember, then burst out like a star, spinning in all directions, licking up the shrine walls as if the ringing of the bell had become eddies to dance in. The flames span wider, twisting into the shape of skirts, arms, skin. Candle-pale and scattered with freckles like embers.

Hseth opened her eyes. Blue, vivid, and glowing beneath a riot of red and white hair.

She looked like Kissen. Kissen older, if Kissen were a deity. He would not tell her this. He would not get a chance.

"What desire brings me hence?" she said, bending down to look at him. Elo took his palm away and tried not to raise his sword. "Ah," she said. "It's you. At last."

CHAPTER THIRTY-TWO

Inara

INARA WOULD NOT STAY PUT, KISSEN BE DAMNED. AFTER all that adventuring, to be patted on the head, given a bow, and told to take herself home. All the while Elo might be dying, dead, and Kissen gone to save him as if she could just save everyone. Inara liked Elo; she couldn't help it. He was warm, determined, kind. Kissen, too, with her gruff affection, her shrewd care. Inara would not be left alone.

Not quite alone.

"This is a bad idea," said Skedi, as they watched Kissen stride away from the groaning mess she had made of the two knights. Inara had followed her, choosing to sneak after the godkiller's steps rather than engage in an argument. She had abandoned her skirts and was wearing only her leggings, trousers, shirt, waistcoat, and waxwool cloak. She had strung the bow with Skedi's help, him growing to weigh it down, and bound the shortsword at her waist as Elo had shown her. She felt strange, powerful.

"These have all been bad ideas," whispered Ina. "Going to Kissen was a bad idea, remember? But it saved us both. If we have any power at all I want to help them."

Skedi was quiet for a moment. He wasn't riding her shoulder, and instead flew beside her. "Me too," he said at last.

Inara followed Kissen at a quiet distance, tracing her twisting footsteps through the streets of the dead city. The veiga had a cadence to her walk that Inara recognised, and she followed the sound. Kissen was taking a shadowed, winding route, hoping not to attract attention, and Inara was struggling to keep up.

"Take the cliff stairs," said Skedi. "She's not looking back."

"It's too exposed," whispered Ina, trying to catch her breath.

"I can hide us, remember? Anyway, no one's looking for you, it's Elo they'll be after."

Inara took to the steps that went up the harbourside, Skedi soaring by her. *We are not seen, we are not dangerous, we mean no harm.*

They almost kept pace with Kissen, the clip of her cloak, the shock of her auburn hair. Inara kept low to the inner wall where ivy crept up between the stones. Moss had grown through the edges, like blood seeping through a wound, overtaking the stone and cracking it through. The next wild winter would crumble the stairs right away where they edged over the water, and it was a long, straight fall from the cliffs into the sea. The higher she climbed, the more precarious the stone.

She was almost at the precipice when she heard the faint ring of a bell. Then she felt the heat, rising like a great wave from the shrines at the summit. Even from this distance, the fine hairs of her face stung with it. Skedi darted down as it hit, folding his wings tight. She clutched him to her belly as he squirmed in panic, eyes wide and chest fluttering.

Inara stumbled, remembering the smoke, the smell of flaming orchards, of home and bodies. Burning. Her breath stopped, her throat hot as if she herself were breathing in flames. She gasped for air. Dead, dead, everyone gone.

She was on her knees, barely able to breathe as panic gripped her. Her vision swam and all she could see was the fire in the windows, the barns, the walls. There was terror in fire, a savage joy and wild life in burning. Inara closed her eyes. Too bright, too horrible. She curled around Skedi, stifling her sobs as they shook her to her bones.

After a long moment, Skedi stirred, putting his nose to her chin.

"It's all right," he said, unable to hide the tremor in his voice. "It's just fear, it's all right."

"I can't . . ." said Ina, her voice rasping, her throat tight. Tears had wet her face. She could barely bring her shaking hands to wipe them.

"It is all right, Inara Craier. Memories can hurt you. It's all right to be hurt. You're safe."

She focussed on breathing, her lungs relaxing. She could breathe. There was no smoke, only power. She could feel it. More power than she had ever felt before. She looked up. Skedi was gazing at her, his yellow eyes full of worry.

"Skedi, I'm sorry," she said. "All you wanted was to be free, and I couldn't give you that."

Skedi's fur rippled. "All I wanted was a shrine, to be loved." He shook his head. "I should have seen that what I had was enough. You are enough, if you'll have my love." He pressed his antlers to her head. "I choose you."

Inara stifled a sob, holding him to her. Not alone. Not quite. Never. "You have my love too," she whispered into his wings. "We have each other." Inara took deep breaths. One, to fill her. Two, to steady her. Three, to get her to her feet. Beyond the summit, there was light. Not the soft pink light of dawn, but the burning of a great flame.

Elo had called on a god of fire. And the whole city could see it.

CHAPTER THIRTY-THREE

Kissen

KISSEN HEARD THE BELL FIRST. THAT CHIME, THE SONG SHE had heard first when a child, not caring what it could mean. The promise of money, of power, of a god. It rang in her bones.

Then she could smell burning flesh; could hear her brothers' cries, her mother's prayers; could feel the pain. Her mouth, her hands, her leg. It shot with agony, all the way through to her heel, as if her father had broken through it once more.

Kissen was long used to her memories. She barely checked her stride.

"Fucking. Bastard," she snarled. Her heart stood in her throat, bile rising with it. Of all the gods in the world, he had better have been very bloody desperate to summon this one. A wild god who had tamed a country. She felt for the vial at her chest, more a lucky charm than something she ever thought she would use. She was glad now she had refused to return it to Aan.

A column of fire rose above her as she reached the pinnacle where the circle of the wild gods' shrines were open to the sea and wind and storm. She saw the wild, flowing skirts, the burning arms of Hseth, the ringing of her bell, all she had last seen tearing down her home, crushing her family in flame. The god towered higher than the city towers had ever stood, and before her was Elo. Kissen was too far to save him, a small figure, shadowed by an inferno.

CHAPTER THIRTY-FOUR

Elogast

THE FOLDS OF HSETH'S FLAMING SKIRTS SPILLED ONTO THE flagstones, leaving ashen trails where they touched. She could burn him in an instant if she desired. Elo drew his breath, feeling the heat pressing on his lungs. This was going to hurt.

"I am here to ask for a boon, Hseth the fire god," he said.

"Oh?" she said, the word rolling out like flame from a furnace, her eyes alight. "You want a new heart, I suppose? Nice and fresh and hot."

Elo swallowed. She could not know that. Aan? Had Kissen's connection betrayed him? Hseth threw back her head and laughed, her hair flowing back with her, rippling over her shoulders. Elogast winced from the heat, feeling his cheekbones blister with it.

"And what would you offer, for a heart for your king?" she said. Elo steeled himself.

"Anything that is mine to give," he said.

"It would take your life."

"Then . . ." Elo breathed in, then out. "My life is Arren's."

The air changed, thickened with power. "An offering is made!" Hseth grinned, her teeth white and sparking. Elo held his nerve, though his gut told him something was terribly wrong. "How *delicious*. Darling knight, I had my doubts, but he knew it would work."

Hseth put her hands to the ground and lifted them slowly. A nest of twigs grew beneath them, a fire starter, burning, under the arch of her shrine. A shrine that was shaped like a hearth. Elo stepped back as the nest cracked open, holding out his sword. The twigs grew into the shape of Hestra. Her moment was brief. In a lick of flame her shoulders broke open, changing shape, lengthening, becoming one Elo recognised.

Arren, in a body of twigs and flame.

"Elogast," said Arren, his eyes glowing like embers.

"Is this a trick?" Elo said, almost dropping his sword. His hands were once again shaking. Arren. Why was Arren here?

Arren's chin tipped up. In his chest burned the flames that Hestra had put there in their nest of twigs. Not fading. Bright and vivid. Alive.

"Your life, your blood, your heart, Elo." He quirked a smile, a smile that was only Arren's. "You did promise."

Elo found his blood could run cold in the face of fire. Arren was his friend. His brother. He had chosen to sacrifice everything for him. His king. Not the frail and hurting man he had seen in his home. This Arren stood tall and bold, and smiling. Water spoke to water, Aan had said. Fire, it seemed, spoke to fire. Aan had not betrayed him.

It was Arren.

"What have you done?" Elo whispered.

Visiting his house, begging for his help, telling him he was going to die so Elo would go back to Blenraden. Go back here, where shrines still stood, where Hseth could be found.

"His offer is made, the sacrifice stands," the god said, and turned her eyes back to Elo. "A broken heart can be more powerful than one that's whole. Lucky you were able to coax him to my only shrine in Middren to do it."

"Arren," said Elo, his voice hoarse with the heat. "What are you doing?"

Arren turned back to him, his face lit by the void where his heart should have been. "Our people need gods," he said. "They are desperate for them, to save them from their everyday lives." He opened his branching arms. "So, I am becoming what they desire. I'm becoming the king my people *need*."

Elo couldn't believe what he was hearing, seeing. He stepped back. "No, Arren, this isn't you. It can't be." Arren smiled. "This is Hestra," said Elo desperately, "plotting with Hseth. Remember

Mertagh, what he did when you didn't rule as he wanted? Undo this. Let me help."

"Help? I haven't needed your help in a long time, Elo," said Arren. His smile faded. He strode forward, proud, assured, and came face to face with his one-time knight. "My people move against me. It takes too long to gain a foothold in their hearts, their wills, their faith, as Hseth did in Talicia. I want to make Middren great, for them to unite under me, my banner, as when we turned the tide of the war. I need power, Elo."

"You have power," said Elo. His skin was so hot, anything metal he wore was heating just from standing near Hseth's flames, near Arren's. He could only hold his sword because of the cloth that still covered its empty pommel.

"Not enough. Not enough! Don't you understand? You knew me as Arren, but now I am king. My face hangs in every inn, they say blessings in *my* name. Sunbringer, my court has named me. I never understood power before. I was pathetic, unloved, unknown. Except by you." He laughed bitterly. "Only you remember that child that I was, but now I am something else entirely. I can be something new! Hseth and Hestra see that; they took their moments. I need to seize mine." Embers cracked from his shoulders. "The bastards who want me dead will burn."

"It was you." Pain. Elo had felt pain, pain in his chest, his shoulder, and his bones, every day. Pain of almost losing Arren, pain of thousands of lives lost, of his mothers fleeing the country they had raised him in. But Arren had been his constant, his certainty. This agony struck him through his core, through his feet. "You burned the Craier manor, didn't you?"

Arren blinked, his flames faltering with his surprise. "I did," he said. "Lessa Craier could have broken everything."

"A whole House, Arren, its people, its children." Inara was innocent; she knew nothing. He would have burned her too.

Arren frowned. His flames flickered, dimmed, and he looked up at Hseth. He was Arren and not-Arren. This was a man he didn't know.

"We do what we must," said Hseth.

Arren turned back to Elo. "We do what we must," he repeated.

Elo couldn't bear it any longer. He lifted his sword and lunged to attack, but was thrown back by a wave of heat from Hseth. Arren, for a moment, looked pained, but he stepped forward again.

"I did not want it to be this way, Elo," said Arren. "But your heart is my sacrifice for Hseth's power, her strength. I will be the first man to become a god, immortal, strong, bound to no shrine. I will crush this rebellion before it takes flight, and show them what power will do for us in Middren." His heart flared brightly and he advanced. "Together, my friend, you with me. Always."

Gods love martyrs.

Elo could feel his will seeping out of him, draining his determination, leaving him only with pain. "You wanted to put an end to the gods," he said quietly.

"An end to chaos!" said Arren, his voice mingled with Hestra's, like smokes merging in a fire. Above him, Hseth's flames ran blue down her body, rippling with her pride. "Hseth brought all the crushed lands in Talicia together. One god, one purpose. Faith can do wonderful things, you said so yourself to me. You believed it so strongly that you left everything behind."

"I said people should be free to choose."

"They will choose me, or they are fools," snapped Arren. "Fools like my mother, my brothers and sister. Fools who saw nothing in me. All dead. All gone." He stood tall, no longer looking at Elo but beyond him, over him. "You have offered your heart to me, Elogast. We accept your sacrifice. A human heart for a god's heart. For Hseth's to merge with mine and Hestra's."

Elo blinked, and in that moment Hseth moved, her hand landing on his chest. Her will caught him there, pinning him. Excruciating.

"It will be worth it, knight," said Hseth, digging her fingers in. Arren watched as Elo screamed, his twig-face impassive. "To move our might into the world. They will make stories of us, greater than all the gods. They will wish for glory, riches, and empire, for fresh furnaces and iron smithies, for fire, blood, and fury, for sacrifice and gods as kings, forever bound." She pressed her face close to his, as if about to kiss him. "With this offering, I can give him power beyond imagining. You are the last thing that Arren loves, and he has chosen to lose you."

The hand seared. Elo could smell his own flesh as her palm sank in, overwhelming.

"Stop!"

Hseth was thrown back by an invisible force. She stumbled and froze, a wild god held at bay. Elogast felt a brush of wind, the cool air of wings above him.

You are all right, you aren't hurt, you can move, you can run.

Elo wrenched himself backwards from the frozen, flaming hand, but he did not run. He struck out with his sword, the briddite edge slicing it away. Hseth screamed, and as she did a barrel of red hair, flesh, and rage launched itself at the god.

"Kissen!" he cried.

Two swipes of Kissen's longsword pushed Hseth back. The god's hair stood on end with fury, her fire-flesh re-forming where Elo and Kissen had hurt her.

"Go, Arren, Hestra!" Hseth cried. "I will deal with this!"

Arren's body of twigs and flame shattered and fell. The king disappeared in a rush of blood-smelling smoke. Kissen whirled around, catching Elo as he dropped to one knee. The pain was blinding, consuming. He could still feel Hseth's fingers in his chest, her grip reaching for his heart.

Kissen plucked out the vial she kept beneath her breastplate and broke it open. Silver water rushed into her palms. Aan's water. Holy. A blessing in a vial. She pressed her hand against his seared flesh. The heat cooled from excruciating to bearable, and she touched her fingers to his lips so he would swallow some of the water down. Whatever Hseth's heat had done to his insides, the water soothed it, cleared it, healed it. He came to himself, and relief washed over Kissen's face. She splashed some on her own neck and face. She had been wearing one leather mitt, and she dragged on another. Briddite plates were sewn into the hands.

"You heartful fool," she said, pulling him to his feet. Despite the water, he could barely breathe for pain. Hseth's attention was on the top of the steps, on Inara, who was coming towards them, nocking an arrow to her bow.

"What manner of being are you?" said the god, but Inara didn't balk. She pulled her bow tight and released the arrow. Hseth flicked her hand and the shaft burned in midair. The god drew her arm back, building flame to strike her down. Elo raised his sword, grunting as his chest seared, and drove a wild strike at her skirts. It worked. She shrieked and stepped back, distracted from Inara. Her flame skirts were just like her flesh, part of her body, like the ring of the bell. The briddite edge could cut them.

Hseth snapped her arm towards Elo and Kissen, and he met it with his blade. His clothes singed, burst into flame, but his chest was protected by Kissen's water. Hseth snarled with the pain but pressed harder against the edge of the blade, cutting herself so she could reach him.

Kissen let a dagger fly, another, a third: hand, shoulder, face. Hseth pulled back to defend her eyes and Kissen grabbed Elo.

"Run, Elogast!" she said, and pulled a small gourd from inside her cloak, lobbing it over her shoulder, straight into Hseth's fire.

The gourd struck, and exploded in a shower of briddite shards, tearing up Hseth's skirts. Kissen threw her cloak up and around herself and Elo. She had covered it with a second layer; thin, crinkled skin that deterred much of the flame but couldn't guard against the briddite shrapnel. Two shards cut through the cloth, one catching Elo a slight graze on the ankle, and the other striking Kissen across the shoulder.

Hseth howled. The attack had angered her more than harmed her. Her fire spread like nets of flame, running along the flagstones. Inara rushed in closer, and as she ran the inferno roiled back from her feet, as if she repelled it. Skedi flew above.

"Knights are coming!" he called. As he said so, an arrow skittered over his wings from two knights that had scaled the summit just behind Ina. They didn't know what they were firing at: the god flying, the god of flame, or Elogast.

Elogast or Kissen.

She hadn't seen the arrows; her focus was on Hseth. Elo pulled her out of the exposed area as arrows struck where they had crouched. The knights blew their horns of warning, mingling with the sounds of the bell as Hseth gathered her powers. She tried to strike again, but Inara drew another arrow and fired it towards Hseth's eye, distracting her. It scathed her cheek and gave Elo time to grab Inara too as Hseth retaliated with a burst of flame. It roared out, but they ran at its edge, just escaping its tongues.

Elo, Kissen, and Inara skidded to a halt against the god of death's shrine as the blaze reached them, bursting against the columns. It quickly stopped as Hseth was distracted by a volley of arrows from the knights on the crest, seeing something big and hot, knowing they should be hitting something. They were less prepared for Hseth's wrath. She swept her arms towards them and sent furious wildfire through the sky, ripping out like the sound of the bell. The horn cut short as the two knights ducked for cover. A third and fourth behind them were swallowed in a scream of flame. Elo turned away. He had done this.

"Elo, your chest," said Ina. Her eyes were wide with horror as she stared at the boiled mark of the god's hand. As Lethen's curse spread over Elo's shoulder, despite Aan's prevention, it would meet it, finger to finger. Skedi flitted down to crouch with them, breathing hard.

"Kissen balmed it, don't worry," said Elo, not looking at Skedi as he lied. Every breath felt like Hseth's grip, his burned skin stretching. Kissen wasn't listening; she was staring out of the shrine, her eyes on Hseth. She flinched back as fire pounded the shrine again, and then the shriek of another knight echoed over the sounds of the wind and waves and the bell. There was no way to escape without facing Hseth. It had taken a battalion of knights and veiga to kill the god of war, and Hseth was something else entirely. Something uncontrollable. If she'd wanted to run, she would have. Instead, she would wait forever for her prey.

"Get Inara out of here," said Kissen. "Get her somewhere safe."

"Kissen . . ." The pain of his chest was almost blinding.

"You can't fight like that," said Kissen, her tone matter-of-fact. "Aan's water will only do so much." It unnerved him that she wasn't swearing at him. "She's after you, Elo, and for good reason. You know what this fool king has become, and you can do something about it. You're a threat. I'm just a godkiller." Her eyes lit with Hseth's flame. "And I kill gods."

She couldn't win. Not against Hseth. Inara shook her head, holding on to Kissen's arm. "You already tried to make me leave," said Inara. "Skedi and I can help."

Kissen grabbed her hand. "I know you can," she said. "But even if we could defeat Hseth, this place will be swarming with knights. If you leave now, you have a chance while they're distracted. Get to Lesscia, find this rebellion, and fix this, before another city falls."

She looked at Elo. She had a gaze that he knew: of someone who had already decided her fate.

"You told me not to give my life away," said Elo, grabbing her hand. What had he done? His voice was tight, his breath croaking with pain. "You want me to watch you do the same?"

"This isn't sacrifice," said Kissen, pouring the last of Aan's water on her arms and crown. It silvered through her hair, her brow, her eyes. She smiled at Ina. "This is vengeance." Kissen looked back at Hseth, so bright she outburned the dawn. "This is an opportunity I thought I'd never have." Elo had been right. It was Hseth who had burned her family, and he had brought the two of them together.

"You promised," said Inara, desperately reaching for reasons for Kissen to stay.

"This is bigger than both of us, *liln*," said Kissen, unhooking her inner cloak, heavy with the tools of her trade. "This is what my father did. I hated it, and I'm sorry. You can hate me if you want, but if I don't save you now, then what kind of bodyguard am I?" The waxwool cloak dropped, clanking with her items, and she handed it to Ina, keeping the thin outer layer on. "You'll need this to defeat the demons," she said, and looked at the god of white lies. He stood on his hind legs, and they regarded each other. Kissen sighed.

"Just don't get into any trouble, Skediceth. And you, Elo, let anything happen to her and I swear on all the gods I've killed that I'll haunt you to your dying day."

"I can think of worse things," he said. She smiled, her gold tooth glinting, then leaned in. She kissed him once, quickly, and stood.

"For luck," she said.

"Kissen!" cried Inara, trying to grab her back, but Kissen stepped aside and strode out into the arena of shrines, her sleeves rolled up to show the burn scars on her arms. Elo didn't stop her. Everything he knew had changed. Kissen had unfinished business with the gods.

And so did he.

CHAPTER THIRTY-FIVE

Kissen

KISSEN WENT TO MEET HER MAKER.

When Middren falls to the gods . . . That's what Ennerast had said. Was this what she meant? The rebellion, this god-king, and the fire god of Talicia? Between them they would tear the lands to pieces. Kissen wouldn't let that happen.

The first time she had tried to summon Hseth, it had been in the Talician shrines down by the harbour. Maimee sent her on her first begging, her skin still tender with her scars. She had received a beating for ringing the bell, the shrine's master being one of those who saw burns as unlucky.

The second time, she had been on the Talician border with Pato just before he had asked for Aan's vial. In the snows where Middren ended and Talicia began, she had rung and rung at one of the many shrines for Hseth raised in the mountains, risking avalanche. Pato had come to find her and told her why no gods had come: she had only murder in her heart.

Now she didn't need to summon the god. She could go straight to her.

As she moved out from the cover of the shrine, she raised her hide cloak, cajoled and bartered from one of the hedgewitches who made them for Talician fire-guards. Hseth blasted her with flame and it rolled over the skin like boiling air from a lava flow. Aan's gift protected her arms, throat, and face from the heat. It would not last forever, but perhaps just long enough for Kissen to take a chunk out of the god that had killed her family.

"Run!" she yelled.

Elo obeyed. He dragged Inara up and sprinted, his sword drawn, making for the steps and pelting through the remaining knights, disregarding his wounds entirely. He pulled Inara along, ducking under the wild sword of one knight and batting it aside. Another made a grab for Inara and he kicked them away. Skedi flew with them, using his antlers and wings to distract, protect, guide them through.

"Sneaks!" Hseth snarled, turning her flames again to overwhelm them. "Come back here, knight; make good on your offering!"

Elo ran just ahead of the blaze, but two of the knights that followed him were not as lucky, skewered on its edges. Kissen took advantage of Hseth's distraction, moving in towards her and striking with her sword, but she was only able to reach as high as Hseth's thigh. It was just enough. Hseth stumbled, and Kissen took hold of her leg with her briddite gloves, putting her full weight into dragging the god down. Hseth's aim broke, she howled with the feel of briddite searing her calf, and the fire shot up into the air. Now she knew what burning felt like. She swiped, but Kissen had already rolled away, slashing her cutlass through one of the god's fingers and taking it with her.

She had Hseth's attention now. The god screeched in anger, unused to pain. Blood wept from her wound, thick and stinking hot. The blood of her victims. Her expression was terrifying, different from the face Kissen remembered through the flames of her childhood. More human, more fleshy. More like her mother's.

Yes, she looked every bit a woman of Talicia, with her wild hair and twists of braids, her broad shoulders, strong legs, and haughty nose. She looked like a queen. Talicia had had no queens, no kings, no ruler. Not till Hseth.

You dare challenge the will of a god? Hseth said, her mindspeak searing into Kissen's head, melting her defences as easily as hoarfrost. Kissen tried not to let it scare her. She had to stay calm, keep distracting her, keep her from Inara, Skedi, and Elo. *You who have been blessed by flame? If you let me swat him now, I will grant you a quick death.*

"Begging for relief already?" said Kissen, stepping sideways slowly, away from the steps, keeping Hseth's eyes fixed on her. Her shoulder stung where the shard of briddite had hit it.

"A slow death it is," said the god. "I'll get the knight and the halfling, and I'll be back for you."

She turned for the steps. Kissen saw it coming. With all the strength she had, she launched one of her remaining gourds of blackfire and briddite straight into Hseth's path. It exploded as Hseth touched it, closer to the god this time and shooting her through with pellets of briddite. She shrieked, clutching at her wounds, sizzling hot and smoking, then whirled on Kissen, slapping her sideways with a back-hand faster than fire on oil, sending her sprawling.

Kissen's head span from the force of her fall, but before Hseth's second swipe could crush the light from her she stabbed up with her sword, biting Hseth through the palm. The god hissed, wringing her hand as if a cat just scratched her.

"You mean to stop me, little mortal? I have eaten children bigger than you before the sun rose on their birthing morning."

Kissen pushed herself to her feet, trying not to show how difficult it was to breathe. She felt at her belt. One more bomb. If Hseth came too close it might rip through her own flesh more painfully than it did Hseth's fire, and hers took longer to grow back. It would be over, and she would have bought Elo and Inara barely enough time to die a bit later.

"I escaped you once, you saltless fucker; I'll do it again." Skedi wasn't here to tell her she was lying.

Hseth leaned in closer, twisting her mouth like a pretty girl with a small problem, clearly unafraid. "Do I know you?" she said. "I have burned so many people. Left you with such nice scars too. Shame you had to ruin them with another god's curses."

Hseth moved. Kissen retreated, but too slow. Hseth grabbed her by the false leg and picked her bodily up into the air, dangling her high so they were face to face. Her other hand she put to Kissen's cheek where the god of beauty's curse had died.

"Sweet little curse," she said, "it doesn't look right on you." She smiled and sent her fire to her hand. She wanted to burn the scar away. The air swam with heat. Aan's water protected Kissen's face, but not her legs. Hseth tried harder when she did not scream, and Yatho's metal plates heated, burning the flesh of her right leg.

"Maybe you need one to match," said Kissen through gritted teeth. She lashed out with her sword, striking Hseth across the nose. Hseth threw her and Kissen landed heavily on her shoulder near the cliff edge, rolling to reduce the pain. She had dropped her longsword but kept her cutlass, trying not to cut herself as she grabbed at the stones on the ground before she fell over the edge. There were no balustrades to stop her tumbling from the heights into the sea.

Hseth touched the cut Kissen had made, her eyes wide with surprise. "Did I hurt you, little girl?" The scar wouldn't take long to disappear; the other wounds Kissen had made were already gone. She took her hand away and advanced.

Kissen's leg had blistered against her metal limb; her false shin bar was bent and warped. She crawled to her feet, using her blade to lift her up.

"Did I kill someone you liked, is that it?" Hseth shrank down to almost human size, her tongue a lick of flame. "A lover or something? Poor you."

Kissen knew gods; she knew they did not remember, nor care, once the first body turned into hundreds. She tempered her anger, honed it. She had the one gourd of blackfire and briddite left, three knives, and her cutlass.

"Did you cry, little one?" said Hseth. "Did you beg?"

Kissen ran. She countered the off-kilter balances of her broken leg, the wrenching of her shoulder. She threw her knives, one, two. Hseth laughed and circled her, dancing away from the blades, taunting. Kissen let herself be cornered, corralled. Then she countered: her last knife flying to Hseth's left, then the gourd to her right. Hseth dodged the knife right into the path of the gourd, which caught her full in the chest. It exploded into her body, turning her laughter to a howl of smoke and steel. Blood fell from her, sizzling on the stones.

It was not enough. Kissen stepped back, trying not to retch as she remembered the smell of her own hot blood on boiling metal, the sizzling of her father's flesh. She had aimed true, catching Hseth in the centre, but the briddite had only wounded her, biting like salt into her chest. Not nearly enough. The bomb was more than Kissen could do with a sword, and its damage wouldn't last. She was out of tricks.

And Hseth knew it.

"Which pathetic, keening village was it?" she whispered; her eyes alight with rage. Kissen had made it back to her longsword; she picked it up and sheathed her cutlass. She had hoped, truly hoped, to do more harm. But she still had the god's attention. That was a feat at least, for an old god, a wild god not of green, but of flame. She decided to be proud of it. The longer she held Hseth's anger, the longer Inara and Elo were safe. "Did it even have a name?"

Kissen readied herself. She wasn't afraid of death, but she didn't like pain. She knew pain. It was not pleasant. "The village was Senkørsa," she said.

Hseth cocked her head to the side, making a show of thinking. She waved her hand dismissively. "That old wreck," she said, laughing. "That's what you're mewling for? It fell into the sea long ago. It wasn't worth anything. Nothing at all."

This time, she caught Kissen off guard. In a breath, Hseth drew a spear of flame from her palms and flashed forward. She whirled the spear towards Kissen's throat, and Kissen fended it off, once, twice, with all the strength left in her. She kept her blade close, using two hands to protect her body from the attack. It hurt Hseth, to strike briddite with her flame, but not enough to bother her. Her front was bloody, her skirts and hair flaming and wild. Kissen gave ground. Hseth's spear arm was straight, strong, her flames bright and true. Kissen took her blows, back, back.

"Didn't they give me a family?" Hseth pondered. "Oh, of course. Osidisen's little pets. That old fool." She smiled and span so fast with her spear that she was a blur of light. She lashed out, struck through Kissen's guard and tore her leather cuirass straight through to her shoulder, biting into her flesh, the fire as sharp as any blade. Kissen saw the flash of flame before she felt it burn. She yelled through her gritted teeth and grabbed on to the spear with her gloved hand.

"I forget their names, the ones that burn," said Hseth. "I barely remember the sea god when he beats at my borders, wears down the cliffs. It took him years to tip your little village's houses into the sea, as if that would turn the world away from the power I offer them."

The village, gone. They murdered her family for wealth and success and gained none of it. All of it wasted.

Kissen tightened her hand on the spear and dragged it from her shoulder, then used her sword to snap it in two.

"Their names were Tidean, Lunsen, and Mellsenro," she said as the fire of the spear disappeared. She broke forward with her sword, and Hseth regrew her weapon to parry her. "Kilean was my mother, and Bern, my father. They were simple people and hurt no one."

"They were fools and they died fools," said Hseth, batting aside her blows. She whirled and struck hard, but this time Kissen was ready for the trick, stepping side-on to miss it and slicing her sword up the god's arm. Hseth bared her sparking teeth and went to pierce her belly, but Kissen swerved on her broken leg and darted inside the god's guard. She was there. She was close. She pressed in with her blade, towards the heart.

Hseth had been waiting for this. All the flames of her body darted inwards, leaving her skin white and ashen. They streamed to where the sword touched, heating it beyond sense, beyond feeling, melting the blade even as it hurt her.

"This world is my world," said Hseth. "Who needs a god of war when you have a god of fire? A god of riches when you can make your own? It does not matter what is burned in the furnace for the flame. You are a small, damaged, wasted human. You do not matter at all."

The heat was too much, even with Aan's water. Kissen felt tears rise to her eyes and evaporate. The bell rang in her ears, round and round, the rippling pressure of the air pushing on the sound. Hseth was too powerful. There was no way Kissen would be able to cut through to her heart, not in a thousand years.

Yet Kissen didn't need to cut. She needed to be clever.

"Even big gods are not so bright." Kissen grinned, released the blade, and grabbed hold of Hseth by the ashen arms. The metal stitched on her fingers caught in the god's flesh, searing it, sealing it. Even the fire god could not escape briddite. Hseth cried out as Kissen bound her in a lover's embrace, even as the flames fought back at her unprotected skin. "Even small lives are worth something."

They had reached the edge of the shrines, where Kissen had been leading her. Kissen leapt, and pulled the god with her off the ledge, holding on to her with her warrior's hands and dragging her down by her own weight through the air, the wind tearing at her fire, her skirt, her hair, scattering them. Hseth screamed as they hit the sea in a choke of water and flame.

CHAPTER THIRTY-SIX

Inara

INARA SAW HER FALL. THEY HAD MADE IT FAR ALONG THE
city streets, keeping to the straight roads along the cliffs. Elo didn't
know the city as well as Kissen did; he took the fastest way. He had
no qualms now about hurting knights that tried to stop them. Most
of the ones they saw were so baffled by the lights in the sky that they
paid them no heed. Pilgrims, too, were gathered in the morning sun
on the coast, staring up in fear towards the shrines of the wild gods.

"Look!" one said, pointing.

Inara turned. She saw the bright light spinning down the cliff face,
weighed down by a small figure amidst the flame.

"Kissen," she whispered. The light hit the sea and blinked out. "We
have to go back." She held on to Elo. "We have to go find her," she
pleaded. Tears rose to her eyes. First her mother, now Kissen. Elo
was breathing badly, his face a sheet of stone. He looked at the cliff,
torn, then down at Inara.

"No one could survive that fall," said Skedi, holding on tight to
Inara's shoulder. "Not in the arms of a fire god. Not even Kissen."

Elo nodded. His shirt fell open around his terrible burn from
Hseth. Inara had seen it, the colours of his offering as she tried to
take his heart. The great power of his love for Arren, shining out of
him in Hseth's hand, sapphire and silver with heartbreak. Shattered,
exploding. The memory of the colours was worse than the scar of the
wound. "She asked this of us," Elo said, his voice hoarse. His colours

whirled now, the sapphire flecked with gold fear and red-brown pain. The pain was growing. "To save us, Ina. She knew what she was doing."

Was, he said. She was gone. Kissen was gone.

"Stay strong," he said, pulling her forward. His voice was steady, but his colours were not, shattering and crashing, turning and wild with loss. But still, he moved. She found she couldn't resist. First a step, then another. Run, Kissen had asked them to run.

Inara dashed her tears away, biting them down. Tears later: when they were safe. That's what Kissen would have told her.

Elo was leading them to the outer city stables, further down the cliffs. They rounded corners at breakneck speed, trying to find the gateway, but when they did, it was guarded. Elo wrenched them all back, pressing them against the wall. Inara caught her breath, trying to quiet her movements.

"Elogast!"

Inara held his hand tightly. That was a man's voice. He had heard them. Skedi prepared a lie, but Elo held up his hand.

"Ser Elogast, I know you're there."

It was Benjen. If he knew they were there, a white lie might not hold enough power. He must have guessed Elo's plan of escape, not knowing that his mentor had come to die. Elo straightened despite his wound and let go of Inara's hand.

"Let us find another way," Inara whispered. "Please, Elo, I can't lose you too."

Despite his pain, Elo smiled. "I am not lost yet. Is he alone?"

Skedi flew up to the rooftops, and back down. His bond with Inara was still there but looser, more relaxed now they understood each other.

He is alone.

Elo's colours changed. Certainty was a cool rose hue for him. He strode out, drawing his sword fully, and Inara let him.

"I don't have time to parry with you, Benjen," he said. "Let us through."

Inara peeked around the corner. Benjen was also prepared, his new sword drawn.

"I never thought you to be an underhanded trickster, Elogast," said Benjen. "Letting someone get behind me. Nor a traitor. Where are your companions?"

Kissen. The thought of her hurt Inara to her soul.

"Where are yours?" said Elo.

Benjen scowled. "Dealing with a god problem. Judging by the burn on your chest, it's a problem that you started. Give up, Elo, for your king."

Elo huffed out a laugh. "My king," he said. "A king who betrays his own people is no king of mine." He sounded more certain than he ever had before. "Is a king who hurts innocents a king of yours?"

"Elogast . . ." Benjen hesitated. "King Arren does what he must."

"What he must . . ." repeated Elo. "Well then, so will I." He raised his blade. "Ser Benjen, I have picked up my sword, and now you should all be afraid."

Benjen sprang forward, twisting his sword from left to right and bending with a strike that would go straight though Elo. Inara stuffed her hand in her mouth to keep from crying out. Elo stepped away, his stance light, conserving his energy. He pushed the sword aside, moved his weight, and threaded his blade into the gap it exposed. The blade shone as it sliced Benjen straight across his legs where there was a break in his armour.

Benjen fell. He hit the ground in a clatter, tried to stand and found he couldn't. He tried again, using his sword to lift him, but Elo kicked it from his hands, sending it skittering to the other side of the street. Elo sheathed his sword. His stony expression had cracked, and anger drove him. "Come," he said to Inara, turning his back on the knight. She hurried over to join him, astonished by the simplicity, the brutality, with which he felled his friend. This was not Elo the baker; this was Elogast the warrior.

"You said you would die before betraying your king," yelled Benjen. "You told me . . . you told me!"

"What about him?" she said.

"He will live or die as he pleases," said Elo grimly. "I am not Kissen. I do kill people."

"Elo, come back!" said Benjen. "Your life, your blood, your heart. You swore!"

Elo did not turn; his colours did not falter.

"There!" cried Skedi as they moved through the stables, ducking into the sheds. They followed where he flew and found three mares and a gelding feeding. None were saddled or reined.

"I can fashion a bit," said Elo, wincing as he removed his jacket. "I've not ridden bareback for a while."

"Wait." Inara fished inside Kissen's cloak, feeling around vials and beads and other items before she found what she was looking for, the last of Legs's honey oats, carefully rationed over their journey. She held them up, and a mare was the first to come, not too bothered by Elo's open wound and haggard appearance. He looked around for something to work as reins. How long would it take? Would the horse let them steal her, or would she buck and rear like Legs? A kick to Elo's chest would finish him.

"Tethis?"

Inara whirled around. Skedi, who was sitting beside her, staring down the horse as if he could stop it bolting, shrank, but not swiftly enough to hide. Inara knew that voice; she had heard no end of it in the first days of their pilgrimage: Berrick. And beside him was Batseder.

They looked road-worn but unhurt, and led a horse with them, well shod and calm, still saddled. Batseder looked from her, to Elogast, to Skedi, who was trying to pretend he didn't exist. They had seen him; he couldn't lie that away.

"That's a god, isn't it?" said Batseder, her colours wrapping her in a shine of fear, but not surprise; Inara remembered, Batseder had seen Skedi as they escaped in the boat.

"Please," said Ina, before they could speak again. "Please keep quiet." Batseder blinked. The shine softened.

"Baker," said Berrick to Elo, then smiled. "My dumplings, you fixed them, you—" He stopped, his face falling as he saw the burn on Elo's chest.

"We have to go," said Elo. He had found some rope on the gate and was fashioning a bit from a wooden bolt. "We're in trouble."

"What happened to Enna, Tethis?" Batseder asked. She looked suspicious.

Inara swallowed past the stone in her throat. Skedi cast about for something to say. *I do not think my lies will take*, he said.

The truth will take, said Ina. She took hold of Batseder's hands. "My name isn't Tethis," she said. "It's Inara Craier."

"Craier?"

"I'm the heir to House Craier, and the king wants us dead. Enna is . . . was a godkiller called Kissen. She died protecting us." Batseder started back. "Elogast is a knight who is helping me and Skediceth get home."

"Was a knight," corrected Elo. The mare was tired. She held up her head as Elo tried to bridle her, whinnying her irritation. He was quickly losing energy.

"We need to get out of Blenraden," said Inara, squeezing Batseder's fingers. "As fast as we can. Please. Help us."

Batseder pressed her lips together. She shared a glance with Berrick. "We made it here thanks to . . . Kissen and Ser Elogast. Of course we will help." She stood back and tugged their horse forward. She came easily. "Take Peony. She can carry two; we bought her after the others turned back."

Inara hesitated. Could they? She fished around in Kissen's cloak for coin, but the first thing her fingers found was the small pair of pliers that Kissen used to adjust her leg. She froze, her will threatening to break and overwhelm her.

Berrick patted her on the shoulder. "We will take nothing for it," he said. "You think a tanner and a shoemaker can't make coin on the road?" Batseder handed the horse's reins to Inara. "She has food in the saddlebags." Berrick lifted her onto the horse's back. "Are you all right?" he asked.

"I'll be fine," said Inara, her throat tight. Skedi flew to her shoulder. "We'll be fine."

Elo left the mare alone. He was limping from a cut on his ankle. He steeled himself, putting a hand on Berrick's shoulder. "Will you help me?" he asked. Berrick nodded and knelt, putting his hands under Elo's boot to help lift him onto the horse. He made it to the saddle behind Inara, the colours of his pain gushing around him.

"We won't forget your kindness," he said, rasping from the effort needed to keep from crying out.

"Nor we yours."

Elo hesitated, then added, "There is a wounded man back there," he said. "Help him. Please. If you can."

The couple nodded. Elo spurred the horse on. They ran through the stable yards, and Peony was thrilled to be galloping, clattering over the stones and passing two or three other pilgrims just arriving with the morning. They stood back as the horse thundered past, as did the guards at the outer gate who were mid-barter with an elderly woman, somehow unaware of any of the chaos that had gone on in the city behind them.

They rode past farmsteads and ruins as the sun rose higher in the sky, keeping up pace though there was no evidence of anyone following. It was evening when they found the empty house where they had left Legs, and the patient horse himself was grazing on the grass in front of the stable, content to wait for his master. His master who wouldn't come.

Elo slid down from Peony and almost dropped to his knees as he hit the ground, only holding himself up by the saddle. His chest wound was weeping plasma, his shirt sticking to it. Whatever had been in the water Kissen had used on him, it was wearing off.

Skedi leapt to the ground and grew to the size of a wolf beside Elo so the knight could lean on him. Elo grasped the fur between Skedi's feathers and straightened up.

Inara hopped off the horse and led her to Legs. Kissen's horse nickered towards Inara, then looked past her and nickered again, seeking the veiga.

"She's not coming," said Inara, and tied Peony beside him. He didn't understand her. He went back to grazing. Inara held her breath and returned to Elo.

"Sit down," she said, going inside the bushes to fetch out Kissen's saddlebags, her cooking things, her hipgin.

"We have to keep moving," said Elo.

"Moving till when? You collapse or the demons get us? Aan said she could slow the curse, not stop it. Will they come back tonight?"

"Yes," Elo managed. "She could only limit the number that could be summoned."

"We stay, then."

Elo fell as if her words had brought him down, still holding on to Skedi. Inara ran to him, helping him to his feet, and together she and Skedi walked him to the shelter of the shed. The sun was sinking. They didn't have much time.

"Find the bandages," she said to Skedi, uncorking the hipgin. She had seen what Kissen did. She splashed it over Elo's burn. He took shallow, swift breaths, but with every movement his chest stretched, the hand's mark pulsing over his heart. He took the gin off her and managed a long, deep gulp as Inara tugged at his shirt, pulling it away from the wound. It bled where the cloth had stuck.

"You need a healer," she said as Skedi brought the bandages. She unwound the gauze and tried not to gag as she pressed it to his chest, rolling it around him as the night shadows drew in. They had not the time of summer days, spring evenings came too fast, and Lethen's curse would not pause for injury. She could see the black ink stretching over Elo's skin.

"I need you to take Skedi, Legs, and Peony to a safe distance," he said, holding the bandage on so she could wrap it better. She went around his back, then passed the roll between her hands at his front to build up the layers.

"You won't last an hour without me," said Inara.

"You mustn't go to Sakre," Elo went on. "Find Canovan. Your mother … she was one of the rebels; they might have been working together."

"You're speaking as if you've already died," said Inara, angry. Enough, enough death. Elo gritted his teeth.

"I cannot die," he said, and looked at Kissen's cloak. "I need to live."

He rummaged in the veiga's things, trying to find some tools he could use. He pulled out a vial or two with paper inside, a roll of beads. It was clear he did not really know how to use them. A thin, weighted briddite chain he looked happier with. "We'll survive this," he said, seemingly to himself as much as her. "We have to."

Inara passed the ends of the bandages to tear and tie in place. She was distracted by the curse symbol. A man and a god had put it there to stop Elo on his quest, to prevent a human king gaining the power of a god.

Like her. She could see colours like gods could, could break the will of other gods. She had stopped Hseth in her tracks.

She focussed on the curse. She could feel it like she could see Elo's colours, a tangle of will. Canovan's will, and Lethen's: dark bloody reds, greys and green, yellow fear in little glimmers like lantern-light. Within it, Aan's will shone like droplets of water amongst thorns, clear and bright.

Skedi looked up. As did Elo. The sun was falling past the mountains. Elo took breaths as deep as he could, drew his sword from the sheath, and rested it across his legs, ready to move.

"It's like a promise knot," said Inara. "Like Kissen's promise from Osidisen. Tied there. The colours are like threads."

"Ina," said Elo, "draw your sword." Both horses shied from the growing shadows, sensing the change in the air as the last of the light went out.

Little unraveller, Aan had called her. She had broken Skedi's will, stopped the movement of the crossroads god. Held back the great god of fire. This was such a little curse. A tiny, secret knot. Drawing the beasts to them.

A growl disturbed her thoughts, the smell of blood, moss, and bone. Inara glanced up; five beasts, not eight, were crawling out of the undergrowth a good ten strides away. Inara did not whisper thanks to Aan; this was still more than they could fight without Kissen.

"Stay still," said Inara to Elo. He swallowed.

"Ina . . ."

"Trust me and stay still."

Elo took a breath and nodded. Inara pressed her hands into his shoulder. He winced, but she felt it there. The tangle, the curse. A will. She used her own, her will to be safe, to save him, to save them both. A will of love, for Kissen, for Skedi, for her mother. A will that stopped the god of fire. Emerald was her love colour, cerulean and violet her strength. She wrapped her colours around the curse, and *pulled*.

The curse began to give, pulling from his skin like a scab. Elo grunted with pain, but held it in. The beasts were advancing. She pulled harder. The writing ran with it, roots tugging from his shoulder, tangling about her fingers like poison and black ink. Aan's drops came with it, clinging and shaking.

The curse came into her hand as a ball of shadow as the creatures charged. Elo stood and dashed one straight in the face with his sword, slicing it entire. Another crept in its wake, leaping over the disintegrating corpse. Elo moved to protect Inara, catching the beast on his blade and throwing it aside.

"Skedi!" cried Inara. He knew what she wanted. She wanted a lie. Skedi grabbed the curse from her hand with his paws and took wing.

"He's here!" *He's here!* he cried, soaring into the evening with the curse writhing in his grasp. The creatures whimpered, confused, then turned, followed.

Skedi threw the thing down into the far field and fled back as the creatures dove upon it and each other, tearing their shadow-flesh from their own limbs, rending one another with their teeth now that there was nothing to find. Elo watched them, holding his shoulder. His wounded arm was bloody, his chest, too, but his back and shoulder were clean. The curse was gone.

He turned and looked at Inara with surprise. She regarded her own hands as the light faded, then gazed back at Elo.

"I am not safe," she said. "I am dangerous. And I am going with you to avenge my mother, to avenge Kissen. This is the last time I will be left behind."

CHAPTER THIRTY-SEVEN

Kissen

KISSEN DID NOT REMEMBER HITTING THE WATER. ONLY THE FIRE. The agony of it. Hseth raged and boiled, pummelling her, but she did not let go, she would not. It would take more than water to kill the god.

But they were in the sea, and there was more than water for the fire god to contend with.

Osidisen! Kissen called.

This was not his sea, but still he came from the north in a rush, in a moment, all the oceans giving him passage. He knew an opportunity when he heard one.

The water changed. Kissen still had enough instincts from her youth to know it was time to let go. She released Hseth and kicked back. Before Hseth could move, the sea churned around her and contracted, slamming into her on both sides with Osidisen's will, force enough to quench her in an instant.

Hseth was gone, only a trace of burned blood seeping through the current. In Middren, in Talicia, all of her shrines would have cracked, shattered, their bells breaking, their flames put out.

The sea god was with Kissen, a turning darkness in the water that she could see even as her sight darkened. A man with grey eyes, and a beard of foam. Osidisen.

"It's you," he said, drifting alongside her. His face changed, and for a moment it was her father's face, clear as he had been all those years ago. He remembered.

Osidisen watched her sink, the last bubbles of air floating to the surface where the sun danced. She was dying, Kissen knew. At least she wasn't burning.

You have become a strange thing, little girl, Osidisen said, taking her into his arms. *Named for me and hating me. Kis-sen-na. Born on the love of the sea. Will you die, still, for bitterness?*

Kissen closed her eyes. She was too weak and dazed to move, her right leg weighing her down. She could not save herself, but she would not call on him. Not Osidisen. She would not use the last remnant of her father's life. The promise would die with her. The god would not like it, a boon unfulfilled, but he would drift on. That was all she could do. Hold on to her father's wish and annoy him.

You promised.

It was not Osidisen's but Inara's voice that sounded in her head. Inara, a strange girl alone in a dangerous world on the edge of ruin, without family, full of fear and anger.

No, Kissen would not leave Inara to the life she had. Not for bitterness. Her father wouldn't have wanted that.

Osidisen, she called, opening her eyes. The promise on her chest blossomed with sea-light, green and dim and deep. Osidisen waited.

Save me.

Acknowledgments

THANK YOU TO MY FAMILY, ALL OF THEM. TO MY FIERCE, intelligent, and steadfast parents who work so hard. You raised me with such love and enabled me the space to challenge myself, and helped me pick up the pieces when I hit my limits. I'll try not to hit them so hard all the time.

To my sister, who is my strength, and my brothers who raise me up and keep me grounded. Thank you for all those weeks you let me spend devouring or spilling out stories in the corners of the house till the moon had set and the sun was rising, all those pages I begged you over and over to read. Thank you for helping me believe I could be just as I am. Thank you also to my nana who accepted and loved me for all my strangeness, and to Jane and Kath for your art and encouragement. Thank you also to the people who won't be able to read this, but would be so proud.

To Loulou Brown; you told me I was a writer at fourteen and that everything else was details. Girls learn young that it's hard to be taken seriously, but you showed me that the first step is for yourself. The time you spent made me feel real, and I would not have got so far without your support. Thank you.

Juliet Mushens; patient, passionate, and determined. Thank you for not giving up on me. Your advice and guidance has been essential. Thank you also for creating such a lovely community of writers who reach out to and support each other; from the very beginning it's been a privilege.

Thanks, of course, to Natasha Bardon, for your insight and your dedication, and the work you do to add colour, structure, vibrancy, and pace, and to bring this book to life. I'm so proud to be able to work with you.

My thanks to my UK team at Harper Voyager who brought this book to life. To Tom Roberts, for the most beautiful covers I've ever seen, and my authenticity editors: Annie Katz, Jennifer Owens, and Helen Gould.

My endless gratitude and love to the team in the US who have transported *Godkiller* over the Atlantic, and Ginger Clark for navigating it to shore. To Julia Elliott, for your fierce leadership. To Jes Lyons and Deanna Bailey, for your brilliant advocacy and insight, and so many others: Danielle, Kaitlin, Alexander, Michelle, Jennifer, and Liate. You make dreams real.

Thank you to my friends, my marras, Alice, Laura, Lauren, Abhaya, Aileen, Kate, Xin, Josh, the Alexes, Greg, and so many more—you've always supported me without doubt or hesitation, and I can't thank you enough. You all inspire me, all of the time. Yemi—thank you as well for the focaccia; it was the last piece my knight and I needed.

Thank you also to the writers who have changed my life through their work and their friendship; you've brought me wisdom, hilarity, and fierce love. I've learned so much from all of you amazing people: El Lam, Elizabeth May, my Scots from California, Saara El-Arifi, Katalina Watt, Kate Dylan, and Tasha Suri, and honorary writer Carly Suri. Meeting some of you years ago, and some of you over this last year, has been nothing short of enlightening.

Thank you to Ali for your kindness, humour, and love. It's been my privilege to share this strange time with you between long-distance messages and rambling voice notes. If you think I'm mad now, just you wait.

Thank you to me, I hope you don't mind me saying so. Thank you for your bloody-minded, hell-for-leather stubbornness. You will need it again. This is only the beginning.

About the Author

HANNAH KANER IS THE #1 INTERNATIONALLY BESTSELLING author of *Godkiller*. A Northumbrian writer living in Scotland, she is inspired by world mythologies, angry women, speculative fiction, and the stories we tell ourselves about being human.